Books by Stanley Elkin

Boswell
Criers and Kibitzers, Kibitzers and Criers
A Bad Man
The Dick Gibson Show
Searches and Seizures

Searches and Seizures

STANLEY ELKIN

Searches and Seizures

RANDOM HOUSE *NEW YORK*

All rights reserved under International and Pan-American Copyright Con-
ventions. Published in the United States by Random House, Inc., New
York, and simultaneously in Canada by Random House of Canada Limited,
Toronto.

Portions of this book originally appeared in *Tri-Quarterly* and *Works in
Progress*.

Library of Congress Cataloging in Publication Data
Elkin, Stanley, 1930–
Searches and seizures.
CONTENTS: The bailbondsman.—The making of Ashenden.—
The condominium.
I. Title.
PZ4.E44Se [PS3555.L47] 813'.5'4 73-3989
ISBN 0-394-48329-4 (hardbound)
ISBN 0-394-70998-5 (paperbound)

Manufactured in the United States of America

First Edition

I want to thank the National Endowment for the Arts and Humanities for its generous assistance during the preparation of this work.

One for Phil and one for Bernie and one for Molly

Contents

The Bailbondsman

THIS BUCK NIGGER comes running up calling my name. "Mist' Main, Mist' Main," he's yelling. He looks familiar but I can't place him, so right there's my clue. Because I know everybody I have had dealings with, their names and faces, their heights and weights, each identifying characteristic, every wart and all pimples, perfect pitch for human shape and their voices in my head like catchy tunes. What a witness I would make, a police artist's dream with my eye for detail, the crease of their gloves and the shine on their shoes like so many square inches of masterpiece in an art historian's noggin. Not "male Caucasian, mid-twenties, sandy hair and slightly built, five foot ten inches and between 130 and 135 pounds." That's given, that's understood; I do that like the guess-your-age-and-weight man at the fair. But the weave of his trousers and the pinch of his hat, which hole he buckles his belt and the wave in his hair like the force number on the Beaufort scale. A marksman's eye for his pupils and its length to a fraction of the cuff rolled back on his sweater. I have by heart the wrinkles on his trousers and know the condition of his heels like a butcher his fillets. Everything. The roller coaster of his flies when he sits, where his hands get dirty, which teeth need attention, the sunsets on his fingernails. Everything.

"Mist' Main, Mist' Main."

But I forget. When it's finished I forget, chuck it in the mind's wastebasket as you'd throw away a phone number in your wallet when it no longer has meaning. Well, what am I? The rogues' gallery? A computer bank? Must I walk around with sin like a stuffed nose? Of course I forget. But *something* familiar, tip-of-your-tongue, like at least you recognize the number is your own handwriting.

"Mist' Main?"

So what does it cost me to be polite? "Dat you, Rastus? Dat you, boy, sho 'nuff?"

"Mist' Main, it's Billy. Billy Basket."

Or go along with him for a while? "Billy Basket, you old field hand, you fuckin' cotton chopper, you. How you doin', muthah? Gimme skin, gimme five, put 'er there, my man." He sticks out his paw but I don't take it. I don't shake hands. I will handcuff myself to anyone regardless of race, creed or color because that's business, but I won't shake hands. I dislike holding men.

"I seen you cross the hall and I wanted to tell you hello and thank you."

Court is about to be convened. "Sure thing," I say, "see you later, alligator."

"Don't you remember me? You went my bail last year. You believed in me when they said I done that rape."

"Yeah, sure. I try to see the good side in everybody. Now I remember." I do. "Couldn't place you there for a minute. Now I see the size of the cock on you it all comes back. You guys are really hung, you know that? Like pictures, like drapes in palaces. See you, kid. Next time you get into trouble. Now you know the way."

I take off. Basket calls after me. "I wanted you to know in case you missed it in the papers," he says as I slip into the courtroom, "they found the guy who done it. They cleared my name. I was innocent all along, just like you believed."

Innocent? Guilty? What difference does it make? Six of one, half dozen of the other. As a matter of fact, innocence is bad for business, a pain in the ass. Stuff the jails I say, crowd them. Shove in the innocent with the guilty. I don't want to see educational programs in the pens, I don't want to know from rehabilitation. That shit knocks down recidivism. Shorter sentences, that's something else, a different story entirely. Shorter sentences are *good* for business. That gets 'em back on the streets again, the villains and stickup guys. That's what we call turnover, and

I'm all for it. Billy Basket is making me late for the hearings. I might not get a good seat. Adams or Klein or Fetterman will be over the prospects I've spotted like the muggers.

"Go, go," I tell him. "The sun's shining, the parks are full of white girls with their heads on the grass and their skirts hiked. Near bushes they lie, tanning their titties. What the hell you doing here, you dark fool? Go. Run, Spot! Run in the park!"

I'm Alexander Main the Bailbondsman. I go surety. Generous as a godfather or an uncle in films, each day paying out pledge like a rope in the sea, flying my streamers of confidence. Like the bunting of anniversary my cracking pennants of assurance. Dealing in signature, notary's round Braille, in triplicates engaged, fair copy, dotted line where my penciled x's (never omitted: there, levitating like a phenomenon, a chipper fragment of askew alphabet above those two and a half inches of devastating dots at the bottom of the contract, drawing the attention, rubbing their noses in it, even the hard guys and two-time losers, even the saboteurs, and people finally out of aliases who haven't used their real names in years—who can barely remember them but who use them now, you can bet) pull their names like trumps. Signed, sealed and deliverance.

I love a contract like the devil, admire the tall paper and the small print—I mean the *print*, the lawful shapes and stately content. Forget word games, secret clause, forget hidden meaning and ambiguity, all those dense thickets of type where the fast ones lie like lost balls. Your forest-for-the-trees crap is myth, the sucker's special pleading. I'll fuck you in letters nine feet high if I've a mind. I beat no one with loophole. Everything spelled out, all clear, aboveboard as chessmen: truth in advertising and a language even the dishonest understand. No, I'm talking the *look* of the instrument, texture, watermark, the silk flourish of the bright ribbon, the legend perfected centuries (I'll tell you in a moment about the Phoenicians), the beautiful formulas simple as pie, old-fashioned quid pro quo like a recipe in the family generations. My conditions classic and my terms terminal. Listen, I haven't much law—though what I have is on my side, binding as clay, advantage to the house—but am as at home in replevin, debenture and gage as someone on his own toilet seat with the door closed and the house empty. I have mainpernor, bottomry, caution and hypothecation the way others might have a second language. I have always lived by *casus foederis*; do the same and we'll never tangle assholes.

Well, it's the blood. I had a cousin a usurer, an uncle in storm windows. An aunt bought up second mortgages, bad paper. Crap artists the lot, dealing in misunderstanding, leading folks on like bad daddies walking backwards in water with their hands out to kids wading inches beyond their reach. Not me, but we've something in common: that we take people's word, I suppose, so long as it's in triplicate. But not my style finally the cancerously compounding interest with repossession at the end of the rainbow. Hit them up front, I say, and be done with it. Not for me the jumped car and crossed wire, the hot shot at dawn or midnight. I eschew schlock, fingerprints on the screen of the burned-out TV, the old man's greasy veronica where he's dozed in the wing chair, all that wall-to-wall with its thinned nap where the weight's come down like the lawn mowers of time. To hell with *merchandise*, houses surrendered after they've been lived in seventeen years. Junk, jetsam. Maybe it has to do with the fact that I have no sense of smell, except for the stinks I imagine in my head.

The Phoenicians. Lebanon and Syria now, Phoenicia that was. My people—I am Phoenician—wrote the first bailbond. (It's "Ba'al" incidentally, from the Hebrew, not "bail.") The notion that the system began in medieval England is false. What happened was that the Crusaders brought the practice back with them from the desert. Phoenician justice was swift: a trial immediately followed arrest; the suspect was taken before the judge or Lord (the Ba'al), evidence was heard and the man was punished or went free. But once a foreigner was arrested, a Canaanite. The charge was he'd fired a crop. The man denied it and said he had witnesses, relatives who had returned to Canaan and could prove that he'd had nothing to do with it. They would swear, he said, that he'd been with them miles from the scene at the time. Well, it would take time to get word back to Canaan that we were holding one of their lads. A messenger would have to be sent. A three-day camel trek, another few days to find the relatives and convince them to return, another three-day camel trek ("trek" is a Phoenician word; "track" comes from it, "race track," "railroad track") to get back, ten or eleven days in all. Now, there were no jails in Phoenicia. The concept of captivity didn't come in until much later, a Hellenic idea. Where do you keep a guy like that, a guy accused of setting fire to an entire crop? Do you take him to your tent, an alleged incendiary? A man who might have burned fields, what could he do with can-vas? There was no jail, only justice. If your eye offended they plucked it out, if your kick they tore your leg off. So where do you put a fellow up who claims he's innocent?

Like all great ideas the answer is simple. You don't. This was a nomadic people, this was a people lived in a sandbox like somebody else would live in Pennsylvania—gill-less they were, tough, with a horned, spiky skin that took the sunburn and converted it to energy, maybe even into water itself, adaptive, resourceful, shag-ging the evolutionary moment like a fly ball—whose very beasts, you'll remember, went without water thirty and forty days, a people who *invented* oasis. You think not? You think maybe God spread a little golf course in the desert like a prayer rug? You think? *Invented* oasis. The process is lost, all gone now the old techniques, but probably using the sand itself, working in the medium of sand. Sand and lenses. Taking a camel's eye, say, and the desert's own hot sun and igniting the sands, focusing, burning them molten, turning them liquid, making them water, seasoning them with their own piss and the camel's blood. Plant-ing seeds, maybe shooting off into the mess, stirring it at night when it cooled. More piss, more blood. Resourceful, resource-ful, sand and water alchemists, collecting whatever rain there was, oiling it with their sweat, conservationists of the bleak, minding the broth, getting it going, one green shoot by one green shoot, nursing each, growing a world. Maybe I exaggerate —I'm proud of my people—but something like that.

So let the kid go, this Canaanite, resourceful and Semitic as themselves. Just because he *could* be guilty, the elders reasoned, it wasn't a good idea to have him around. He might, out of spite, put out their oasis. But make sure he comes back. Take something of value. His rings, say, or his animals. Turn this bad apple and good scout back out into the desert with fair warning, fixing him with that stare which had fired the sands. "All right. Ten days. Come back or we fetch you."

"Hey, Phoenician," a lawyer calls, "over here." It's Farb. He's standing with a white male, aged thirty-three or -four, well dressed and very nervous. It can't amount to much, but in my business you don't cut a lawyer. I pat Farb's shoulder.

"Shoplifting, right?"

"How about that Phoenician?" Farb says. "Does he know a thing or two?"

"She never did anything like this," the guy says. "We even have a charge account at the store."

"Who's up? Cooper?"

"Cooper," Farb says, "Cooper, I think."

"He'll fix your wife's bond at five hundred," I tell the man. He's biting his nails. "You can make that. What do you need me?"

"He doesn't want it on his record that he put up collateral with a court," Farb says.

"You got kids?"

"A son."

"Seven years old, eight?"

"He's nine."

"Your wife's people, they're alive?"

"Yes, but . . ."

"They live in Cincinnati?"

"They're divorced. I don't understand what . . ."

"He's determining the risk," Farb explains.

"What risk? I'm good for the money. What do I look like?"

"Everybody's got a good suit, sonny. They come to court like they're sitting for portraits in banks."

"Don't get excited," Farb counsels his client, "answer his questions. There's nothing personal."

"There's everything personal," I say. "She got siblings, your wife? A brother she's close to?"

"There's a sister in California, but I don't . . ."

"They write letters, they call long distance? Presents, does your sister-in-law send the kid presents? Does she remember his birthday?"

"Usually. I think so. Yes, usually."

"I'll ride the river with you, a bridge over troubled waters. My fee is ten percent of the bond. Like show business, like your wife was a movie star instead of a shoplifter. I take the fifty up front. You got fifty bucks? Yes? Done. I'll see you when Cooper sets the bail. Take this form meanwhile. Fill in the blanks as if you were your wife, and have her sign where I've penciled the x."

"Thanks, Phoenician," Farb says.

"Rudy, you used to be a big shot, Rudy. The syndicate you had, ax murderers."

"I'm slowing down, Phoenician. Doctor's orders."

It's true. He looks shitty. I recall talk. He's been to the hospital for tests. "Rudy, I appreciate your business, but you've got to specialize. The way you're going with this nickel-and-dime we'll both starve. I'll give you a tip. In the next year the big thing in crime will be ripping off the guys who collect for insurance companies in the bad neighborhoods. That's the new action, Rudy, that's the wave of the future. It's going to be bigger than cab drivers. If you like I'll put the word out that Rudy Farb is the best defender of debit-man murderers in the city. The kids will come running, they'll pay your retainer in loose change they took from the body. Think it over, Rudy, think it over, kid. See you in court."

So I'm Alexander Main, the Phoenician Bailbondsman, other men's difficulties my heritage. Alexander Main the Ba'albondsman, doing his duty by the generations and loving it, thriving on the idea of freedom which is my money in the bank, which is my element as the sand was my ancestors'.

So give the Phoenician your murderer, your rapist, your petty thief yearning to breathe free. Give him your stickup guy and embezzler, your juvenile delinquent and car robber. Give him your subversives and menslaughterers. I *like* dealing with the public.

Yes, and the private too. Tell me. If a man climbs his bath-room scale in the morning and the dial spins, settling finally on his weight, and then suddenly he shivers, say, or barks his morn-ing hack and jiggles the scale and the dial goes spinning again though his feet have never left the scale, jerking a few pounds more or a few less, I ask you this: does that man in those few seconds weigh more? Less? Has he become momentarily weight-less? This is philosophy. Do saints have more rights than ordi-nary men? Which is more important, Arcturus or Jupiter? Do people living in Nome, Alaska, get less out of life than Parisians? The Phoenician loves his philosophy, is charmed by the sharp propositions that precede the thick texts and weighty arguments. As for the rest, the proofs that win, the arduous, numbing con-nections—I have no patience, or perhaps the equipment is want-ing. But the examples, ah! I've a weakness for example, a sweet tooth for instance and all the gossip inherent in idea. A joke better than a story, an hypothesis richer than a case. I'm queer for conditions, I say, a scientist distracted by personality. Farmer Brown has an apple, Farmer Jones a pear. If a pear has a sixth more market value than an apple, how much apple must Farmer Brown give to eat a quarter of Farmer Jones' pear? The Phoe-nician loves such problems. Make it figs and he'll hug you.

But I am merely a bailbondsman. I spring you, something neu-tral in the freedom I sell. At least you won't be cornholed, or beaten by the guards, or have to eat the civic slime. For the time being and the duration of due process you're your own man still, and may it serve you better than it did before. *For the time being.* Yes, I am chained to the calendar. I live by it. What your watch is to you my calendar is to me. As it happens, I got cal-endars all over the place, tools of the trade. I get them from garages (French maids in satin uniforms, their bloomers like white carnations), funeral directors (Audubon prints, Niagara Falls), banks (kids with fishing poles, covered bridges in New England), the Hong Kong tailors (panoramas of the harbor),

insurance companies (views of downtown Hartford); from truck-
ing firms and liquor stores and laundries. I hang them all in my
shop, a storefront across from Cincinnati police headquarters.
What views I have! Not a window in the place—the Venetian
blinds, always drawn, across the width of the shop—but everywhere I look nature in its green abundance and staggering forma-
tions. You've come a long way from Phoenicia. But I *don't* look.
All I see are the numbers like seven columns of sums, the red Sundays like a bankrupt's homework and the glowing, feverish
holidays, New Year's, Washington's birthday, clean March,
April, June and August. May's flush Memorial Day and July's
gaudy Fourth and all the burning rest. I note who's to appear
where, circle when they show and the case is closed, and make
a thick arrow where I'm disappointed. My calendars are like
maps and I am secretary to the year itself, up on all its appointments.

The shop looks as if it had once been something else—the
source of its own calendars, perhaps, like a liquor store or a
real-estate office. It never was. It was always what it is now.
Like the sixteen other bondsmen's offices in the three blocks
around police headquarters and the municipal and federal courts.
Your bailbond architecture is storefront gypsy, nigger church.
The city has a referendum coming up next year, a proposal for
a bond issue that would provide a new civic courts complex on
some cleared land near the stadium. If it passes I'll have to move
—a nomad still—and if I can't buy out the small one-man grocery
I got my eye on, what I put up will look just like this place, a
replica like a little tourist attraction. I wouldn't feel comfortable
writing a bond in one of those chrome and naugahyde bank
manager places with their big notched-leaf plants and their clear
aquariums with cruising iridescent fish. I need wooden desk
from the high school teacher's office, a broken set of unmatched
folding card-table chairs, squat black telephones, a pencil sharp-
ener on the lintel of the window, green metal wastebaskets, dirty
linoleum, walls that will take the nails to hold my calendars and
a bare floor that can stand up to my small, heavy safe. I need a
toilet and washstand in something that used to be a closet, the

scaly ceiling and the cheap glass ashtrays, plugs for space heaters and a transom over the front door like the place where they
put the old air-conditioning unit in a barbershop. And a place
for my arsenal. (I'm armed. I have what the cops have: pistols,
mace, a helmet, handcuffs, a rifle, a cosh, even a bulletproof
vest.) And shelves, of course, for my library of statutes from
those three quarters of the fifty states where bailbonding is still
legal. Like a clinic for the poor, something crummy and vaguely
volunteer in the air. And tough.

And this is what *I* seem to look like. Mid-fifties, a hairline like
a tattered flag, and something in my mug placid and vicious,
some kinky catered lust perhaps, used two times a month, say
on fourteen-year-old black chicks, my cock moon-pulled, tidal-
torn, and you think here's a guy that turns the tables on those
girls, who produces not the fifty he's promised but the fiver that
will not even cover their expenses, and a boot in the blackbird's
ass if she whines, power and cynicism planted there on my
municipal kisser and in my eyes that puts me beyond law or
retribution or redress, the mien of the mean, the phiz of the
respectably ferocious, like a hunter who drinks sour mash. I look
professional, you see, a cross between a railroad conductor and
a deputy sheriff. You'd expect to see yourself fun-housed in my
sunglasses. This is the look of me, the reputation I propagate
with my cliché of a face, my death's pan, the features actually
trained into the face. Because the truth is your hood looks up to
the impassive: he loves the anesthetized look of the deputy, the
sober cosmetics of the hanging judge. Give the public what it
wants; the customer is always right. Yes, and business never better. No complaints. Let them scream law and order, yell crime
in the streets like the tocsin of a leper. Our times—here's to
'em. Here's to the complicated trade routes of the drug traffic,
to micro-dot tabs of LSD, to folks' vengeant itchiness as the
discrepancies bloom apace and injustices shake the earth like underground faults. Here's to moonshots and the confusion of priorities. To TV in the ghetto and ads in the glossies and whatever
engines that raise expectations like the hard-on, and drive men
up one wall and down the other. To hard times and our golden
age of blood!

I'm in the corridor of municipal court by 8:30 each morning, a half-hour before the judge begins to process everybody who was arrested the day before. The old hallway smells of disinfectant, though I can no longer smell it, haven't smelled it for years, or tasted anything for years either—the twin senses reamed out long ago by ammonia, C-N, all the dirt poisons (I do not taste the liquor I stand the lawyers to, or feel its warmth, though I go *ah*, smack my lips, applaud on my belly my pantomimed thirst) steaming in pails, the heavy, old-fashioned wringers colorless as the pails themselves, as the bleached gray mops and handles.

I see my colleagues, the other bondsmen. They confer with lawyers, approach relatives, those sad-ass poor who huddle there each morning, the faces changed daily but somehow the same, the questions the same, the complaints, the whiny tales of wages docked, not appreciating their small holiday, their kids wild in the hallway and the guards tolerant. (Can they chip marble or leave marks on such tough city property?) There's no smoking but the Phoenician smokes, not tasting it though his cough seems to betray its effects—I seem marked for lung cancer—like some novice at the beach who does not feel the sun which that night will sear him, turning him red as those useless days on my calendars.

Though I'm here at 8:30, by detaching myself from any single lawyer or group of relatives, by drifting around the hallway from clutch to clutch, I manage somehow to seem to have arrived later than the rest, to make a series of entrances, the spurious authority of the regular on me, the old-timer. It's only here that I smoke, where no one else may. (I fixed the guard. Years ago I started to give him a hundred bucks a year for the dispensation. I take it off my taxes, a business expense, the cigarettes too.) I move about the crowded corridor, size up the still invisible prisoners by the impression their families make on me, kibitzing one and all, determining in advance whose business to seek out, whose to renounce. I like to see family there because that means roots, strong community ties, and cuts down the risk that a guy will skip, though *too* much depth on the bench is no good. A good mix is what I like best—a brother or brother-in-law there with the wife, maybe a first cousin. A solitary parent is good, even a girl friend if she's attractive, one or two kids if they're well behaved. I also take in the lawyer, culling the shyster from the bespoke, the man who's already on the case—or even better, the guy on retainer, who doesn't come downtown often. He's the fellow I nod at, making my bid like a dealer at auctions, though I'm more amiable with the others. I come on strongest with my fellow bondsmen, distracting them, though from time to time there's real business to discuss, something so big we have to split the bond. But standing in no one place very long, getting a feel for what I want by floating around like a guy at a party casing possibility.

Dan Tucker's in the corridor, a gray and handsome man, taller than the half-dozen bondsmen who circle him, chatting him up, trying to find out what an important corporation counsel like himself is doing in the halls. He sees me and waves.

Dan and I go way back. During the thirties Dan was an ambulance chaser, a divorce man, a writer of wills, a house closer. It was in this very building that it happened, that I took fire. In the thirties they stole bread, they took sweaters in winter and galoshes in the rainy season, pails of fuel. The shoplifters were men—hunters, practically. A gentle age, the Depression. So it was, I forget exactly, but a day in winter, some cold day following some colder one, and there they were: the bread and sweater thieves out in force, or at least their relatives, the bread thieves and sweater swipers and fuel filchers, all that lot of conditional takers, nickers of necessities without a mean bone in their body—if anything the opposite, tender-hearted as raw liver, or their relatives I mean, that sad boatload of the dependent. Old Dan Tucker was there, well dressed as now, dapper in his graduation suit but coming in as much to get warm, you understand, as to round up a client. Who could pay? There wasn't a retainer between the sorry lot of them, let alone a fee, so Dan was in off the street to chat up a pal probably, though there weren't even any other lawyers around (that's how bad times were, so bad that trouble drew no troubleshooters, rotten luck no retinue) and, dapper as he was, a little sad himself, as though if times didn't change soon he might be busted for grab-

bing a loaf or an overcoat himself one day, and not many bailbondsmen there to speak of either, for it's a trade which follows
the ego. Freedom and fraud go hand in hand, I think, liberty
and larceny, hope and heists, spirit and spoils. So no bailbondsmen there to speak of, maybe one or two old-timers from the
roaring twenties, bewildered now that Prohibition was off and
gangland killings were down at par value. And the Phoenician's
angry, plenty mad, and the madder he is the more he needs to
make himself an oasis. He'll have an oasis. Let there be an oasis
in this desert of mood, this sandy blandness of meager evil.

"Oyez, oyez," he shouts, erupts. "Make a circle, oyez. The
pregnant here and the orphaned there, small orphans closer to
the radiators, hold those smaller orphans' hands, you taller orphans, be gloves to them, that's it, that's right. Now the feverish
on that side and the coughers on this. Let's get some order here.
Where are my old people, my widowed mothers and my gassed
dads? All right, all right, perfect the circle. Now the rest of you
form according to your mood, despair to anger like the do re
mi. The innocent next, the falsely accused, all those cases of mistaken identity and people whose alibis will stand up in court.
Oyez, oyez. Are you an orphan, boy?"

"Sir, I'm not."

"Who's inside for you then?"

"It's my brother, sir."

"Stand next to that tall orphan. Oyez, are you formed? Are
you arranged, oyez?" They shuffle a bit. "Is your tenuous connection to guilt orchestrated proper? I'll find you out later but
I'll take your word. Can I have your word? Can I?"

They nod, excited.

"Good. Oyez. In a few minutes the hearings begin. They'll let
your people in, but they won't let them go. It's jail for the poor
man, crust and water for the down-and-outer. I'm Alexander
Main the Bailbondsman and you need me, oyez. See that man?
The tall bloke in the stripy suit? Recognize him? Know who
he is? Tip of your tongue, right? You know him. A big shot, the
biggest. You read his name in the papers before you stuff them
inside your clothes to keep the draft off. He goes to the night

clubs. His photo's in the columns. He's had his picture taken more times than you've had hot dinners. His brother's inside now, the cops have him. They keep him apart from your people, the brave men who steal to feed and clothe you. He's with them now but he won't be with them long. The judge will set his bail and I'll pay it. A guy lucky enough to have work and see how he takes advantage? And *what* work! You know what he does? What this man's brother does? He's high up in the Cincinnati Reds and he defrauds the railroads and the club too. Worked out some deal on the fares with certain railroads and pockets the dough for the tickets. It's very complicated, very tricky. I don't know, I think the infield and bullpen travel on a child's ticket. A buck for the line and two for the lining of his pocket. You know what that adds up to in a season? Thousands, oyez, thousands. So what's *he* doing here, then? Stripy suit? He's asked me to go his brother's bond. Fifteen thousand and he could pay it himself, so what does he need me with my Jew's hard terms and my tricksy vigorish? Because the rich man's money is tied up is why. Because the rich man's money is tied up and earns more than the lousy ten percent it would cost him to undo the knots. So his brother—if they *are* brothers; they live together, they *say* they're brothers—comes to me.

"Do what the rich do, you suckers. Do what the rich men do, my brothers. You, lady, you got a ring there, your wedding band. Should your husband rot in jail while Stripy Suit's pal goes free? Give me the ring, my brother. I'll go his bond too. The band for the bond. What have you got? I'll take real estate, furniture, canned goods. Who's still got a car? Anybody got a car? Raise your hands you got a car."

"I have a car. It's up on blocks. Its tires are flat. There's no money for gas."

"I'll take it. This day your husband will be with you in paradise. I'll take it. Done, oyez. Who else? Anybody else? Pianos then, a fiddle. An heirloom, maybe, from the good old days. A pile carpet, stamp collections, a rare song your grandmother taught you. Suckers, *brothers*, his lordship here comes because his principal's tied up. These are your husbands and sons and fathers who are tied up. If this rich bastard won't touch what is only his principal—they *are* brothers, they must be, in this light suddenly I see the resemblance—surely you won't touch yours which is flesh and blood. Here's pen, here's paper. Write down what you have, make a list of what's left, what you'll trade for your sweethearts."

And they did. These good family people did and I took their possessions. And old Dan Tucker just stood by lookin'. And never raised a protest against a single thing I said. Dan and I go back.

The court is convened and we file in.

Slim pickings today. Basket and Farb have wasted my time and Dan Tucker is there only to have a word with the clerk. I salvage what I can, sign up Farb's shoplifter and a few punks—maybe two hundred fifty, two hundred seventy-five bucks' worth of business—then go to my office, call the main switchboard at the University of Cincinnati and give the operator the extension.

"Yes, please?" A secretary.

I wink at my own. "Your opposite number, Mr. Crainpool," I tell him, my hand over the mouthpiece. "Put the chancellor on, Miss."

"Who's calling, please?"

"It's his bailbondsman, Miss."

"Who?"

"Miss, it's the chancellor of the University of Cincinnati's bailbondsman here, Miss."

"The chancellor is in conference," she tells me nervously.

"Suits me."

"Just a minute, please. Is this important?"

"Life and death," I say, shrugging.

"May I have your name, please?"

"The Phoenician. You tell that schoolteacher the Phoenician bondsman wants a word with him."

In seconds he's on the phone. Conference dismissed.

"Yes?"

"Doctor?"

"Yes?"

"I read about the troubles, Doctor, and I'm calling to see if there's anything I can do."

"The troubles?"

"I take the campus paper. I have it delivered special in a taxi-cab. There's going to be sit-ins, break-ins, rumbles you could read on the Richter scale. The Black Students' Organization will fire the frat houses and sear the sororities. Weathermen in the meteorology lab, safety pins in the computers, blood on the blackboards. Professors' notes'll be burned, they'll rip the railings in the cafeteria and pour weed-killer on the AstroTurf. What, are you kidding me? Mass arrests are coming. The night school students are spoiling for a fight."

"The night school students?"

"They want the professors to take naps. They ain't fresh in the evening classes. They need shaves, they say, their suits ain't pressed."

"Listen, who is this?"

"*Mene, mene, tekel, upharsin.* If you don't read your student newspaper, try your Bible. It's Alexander Main, the Phoenician bailbond salesman. Listen to me, Doctor, the University of Cincinnati is a streetcar college. You don't know what passion is till you've smelled it on the breath of the lower classes. Your kid from the middle class, he's fucking around, his heart ain't in it. His heart's in the jukebox, his deposit's down on a youth fare to Europe. Think, where does the big-time trouble come from? S.F. State, City College. It's your greaseballs and Chicanos, Chancellor. I got my ear to the ground. The University of Cincinnati is the biggest municipal university in the country. She's coming in like an oil well, it's going to blow. Already I smell smoke. State troopers are coming, the Guard. Fort Benning is keeping the engines warmed. Are you ready for all this, Doctor? Where you gonna be when the lights go out? I'm telling you straight, you heard it here first, I think they got their eye on upwards of twenty-five hundred kids. What'll your forty-five-grand-a-year job be worth you got twenty-five hundred students in jail who can't make bond?"

"Where do you get this stuff? I never heard anything like this."

"No. Sure not. I sit at the blower. All alone by the telephone, waiting for a ring, a ting-a-ling. I thought by now you'd have made your arrangements. But no, every day I come back from lunch I ask my secretary, Mr. Crainpool, 'The chancellor ring yet, Mr. Crainpool?' Mr. Crainpool says no. I call the phone company. 'Is this line in working order?' They tell me hang up, they'll call back. The Bells of St. Mary's, Chancellor! Loud. Clear. Could wake the dead. I know in my heart it's only the service department of Ohio Bell, but I think no, maybe this time it's the chancellor of the University of Cincinnati calling to do a deal. I wave Mr. Crainpool aside. 'I'll get it, Mr. Crainpool,' I say, 'it could be the big one.' I pick up the phone. 'This six-seven-eight, five-oh-one-two?' All hope founders, zing go the strings of my heart. 'Everything's A-OK,' I tell him. 'Check,' he says. 'Roger and out,' I offer.

"But you know something? I lied, I told a fib to the fucking service department of Ohio Bell. Because it ain't A-OK. *Pas de doing* with the university. The chancellor is not making his arrangements. You play golf, Doctor? What's your handicap? Wait, I'll tell you. *Your handicap is that when this place goes sky-high you won't know where to turn!* Do the deal, my dear Doctor of Philosophy. Twenty-five hundred kids at an average bond of three hundred dollars. That's three-quarters of a million dollars, Doc. Who's going to approve that kind of dough? Your trustees? With *their* politics? 'Let the bastards rot,' they'll say. Right. And from that moment on the world can forget the University of Cincinnati. After all you did. All that work down the drain.

"All right, let's be serious, let's be serious business people. *I* can't take on twenty-five hundred kids by myself. It's not the money; I could probably raise that. A bondsman has tie-ins with insurance companies, loan associations, sometimes he can even get banks to pick up some of his paper. The sky just could be the limit in certain circumstances. So it ain't the money. It's the *number*. How can I keep an eye on two thousand, five hundred crazies? I *can't*. Humanly impossible. Statistically out of the

question. I'm sorry; that's it, it's useless to argue. But I'll tell you
what I *will* do. I'll spring five hundred. It's asking a lot, but I'll
do it. I'm overextending, but don't concern yourself. I'll want a
retainer from the university. A buck a head."

"This is incredible. Are you actually a bondsman?"

"Thirty-eight years in the same location. Centrally located,
convenient to all courts and many jails. Look, here's what I'm
doing. I'm having a contract drawn up. Mr. Crainpool will hand-
carry it to the university. If you like what you see, sign it. If
not don't, and you haven't spent a dime. You'll have the speci-
men contract inside twenty-four hours. That's pressing me, but
we have to get off our duffs, Chancellor, the sky is falling."

I hang up, slip the contract I've already drawn up out of my
desk, sign it, have Mr. Crainpool witness it and tell him to pop
it by the university on his way to work tomorrow. Mr. Crainpool lives out that way. A respectful, very soft-sell letter accom-
panies the document spelling out our mutual undertakings.
Chances are nothing will come of it, but in these times who can
tell? I *do* take the campus newspaper; something like what I
outlined to the chancellor *could* happen. A bright bondsman
stays on top of things.

"What's on, Mr. Crainpool? Anything come up while I was
at court?"

"No."

"Nothing at all? Sometimes the merest inquiry or the most
innocuous information can lead to the biggest action."

"No, sir."

"Where's all this fucking crime in the streets I keep hearing
about? I sometimes think the people around here aren't pulling
their oar."

"No, sir."

"They're letting us down, Mr. Crainpool."

"Yes, sir."

"You remember when Covington was wide open?"

"Oh, yes."

"That's what this reminds me of."

Covington is across the Ohio River in Kentucky. Till they

cleaned it up a few years ago it used to be the wildest town in America. Gambling, strip joints, after-hours places, whorehouses, the lot. It may have been the only small town in the country with its own press bureau. Articles used to come out regularly in the men's magazines—"Covington, Kentucky: Sin City, U.S.A." It was terrific. It was terrific, but it was an optical illusion. Organized crime, you could starve to death. The only licensed bondsman in town used to complain to me. He'd cross the river and sing the blues. I told him when he first moved out there, "Harry, you're wasting your time in the suburbs. They'll never amount to a hill of shit. That's syndicate money, that's family. That's no place for the little man."

"Button your sweater, Mr. Crainpool, please. How many times do I have to tell you?"

I like him to look cold. It gives him the look of a clerk in Dickens and lends tone to the place. I even made him a high stool he can sit on when a client comes into the shop. He slips on these arm garters and a little green eyeshade. I try to get him to wear a muffler but he's allergic.

"You're supposed to call Edna," Mr. Crainpool says.

"Right, Mr. Crainpool. Thank you."

There's no need for Mr. Crainpool to dial it for me; I remember the number. Oh, my flat Phoenician head, my definitive, paradigmatic eyes like the cutouts in masks—all my archaeological features like the beaked profiles of birds, the ledges of my lids deep as window sills, my ears, pressed back as a hairdo: all this *information* in me, my face built for remembering, my black eyes that can hold accusation and grudge in them, commodious, flexible as the infinity of configurations in the interiors of airplanes. Of course I remember the number.

"Is Edna up, Mrs. Shea? . . . What, don't recognize my voice yet? And meself after callin' yer daughter these many times these many months? . . . Well, if you don't, you don't. You're a good woman, Mrs. Shea, sad fortune gave you your daughter and your cross. . . . What's that? . . . No no, 'tisn't Fatha, Mrs. Shea, 'tis Mr. Main. *Through whose good offices your daughter sleeps under your roof instead of in some godless cell, or walks where you and me both know she oughtn't!* Be so good as to wake her for me, Mrs. . . . Edna? Alexander, Edna. Mother tells me you were in bed. Been taking those pills then, have you, Edna? Good, sweetheart. How many have you got left? . . . What's that? . . . Then go see at once, you filthy pig. Wait. Put Mom on the extension. . . . Mrs. Shea, hasn't Edna gone through the bottle Mr. Crainpool left? How many? . . . As much as that? Edna, you fiend, Mummy tells Uncle Al you've still got twelve tabs in the bottle. You haven't been taking your medicine, dear. . . . Oh, la, you answer pretty good for a girl who's supposed to be doped up. You *haven't* been taking the pills, Eddy. Never mind putting on that where-am-I voice for me. You came to the phone too quick. You want me after you, girl? You want me to have you fixed? You want your tongue rolled in the acid bath, or the knife taken to your taste buds? *That'd* fix you pretty good, wouldn't it, dearie? Don't you know even the first thing about appetite—a girl with one like yours? Think, sweetheart, if you beat this rap and they let you out in the streets again, you wouldn't even be able to smell a playground. You'd rub up against the first diamond wire fence you came to. Pathetic, pathetic, child. You'd wait for recess and find when the whistle blows it's only some factory you've been hanging round."

"They make me sleepy," Edna whines. "I can't think. They make me goofy."

"Mnephenedrin? They relax you, doll. They keep you away from the bus stations and off the superhighways, and Uncle Al doesn't have to worry about you. Enjoy the pills. Pretend you're on vacation."

"I get nervous."

"All right, Edna, if you're not going to cooperate I'll have to send Mr. Crainpool out with the cold serum. You're leaving me no alternative. One injection and your nose will run till your trial comes up. Your head will be stuffed. Your throat will tickle like poison ivy. You want that, darling?"

"I'm not going off anywhere."

"Mama, you still on the phone?"

"I'm here."

"*Two* pills for Edna today. One with her orange juice, another tonight. Drop it in the back of her mouth yourself so you can see she's really swallowing it. All right, Edna, listen dear, it's only another two weeks. Do as I say. You think all I'm trying to do is protect an investment? Kid, I like your style. I take an interest in your case. You're a credit to the deviates, darling. I don't want to see a really innovative cookie like you shut up with a lot of tough broads. They *menstruate*, Edna. Every babe in the Ohio whoresgow—that's my name for it, daughter, the whoresgow—has blood on her. An odor so strong it would come right through Mr. Crainpool's serum. I'm telling you, Eddy, the state gives out sanitary napkins. The toilets are choked with 'em. More egg in the air than at all the breakfast tables in the world. You want to go to a place like that? Now stop that crying, Edna; don't go soft, kid. I'm just laying the cards out on the table for you, covering aspects you might have missed. You've got a good lawyer. With your psychiatric record you don't have a thing to worry about. Chances are they won't even lock you up; you'll be an outpatient right in Cincinnati. Do you know where the clinic *is*, Edna? I've saved the best for the last, dear. Do you have any idea at all where they *built* that clinic? *Right next to a nursery school!* . . . Of course I'm not kidding, sure I'm telling the truth. Take your pill, doll. Go back to bed. In a couple of weeks we'll wake you and take you to court. Okay? Say okay, sweetheart. Tell me okay."

"Okay."

"Good. That's a promise, Edna. That's a bond, honeybunch. Sleep now, sweetie. Night night. . . . Mama, are you still there? The orange juice, Mama. Go get it for her please."

Mr. Crainpool grins slyly when I replace the receiver. "There's no such serum," he says.

"Botheration, Mr. Crainpool, this is intolerable! Listening to my private conversation, were you?"

"Wasn't private, was a business call."

"Blow on your hands, sir. Button your sweater. Look cold."

"It's almost April."

"Out there, Mr. Crainpool." I point to the Venetian blinds, so tightly shut that their louvers make a solid creamy wall. "Out there it's almost April. In here it's the Dark Ages. There's capital punishment, men languish in prison for debt, hang for a stolen horse, poaching, a loaf filched for love. Severed heads, could you but see them, perch taking the weather on the flagstaffs above Riverfront Stadium, and not the pennants of the National League. The executioner's head like a black bullet in its hood. Yes and class divides like the surgeon. It Moseses us left and right. You eat too much, Mr. Crainpool, you're too well-fed. Easy on the starch and sauces, sir. Make yourself wan and drawn, if you'd be so kind."

Mr. Crainpool chuckles. His master is a strange old codger.

"Cool the cackle, Crainpool. I'm talking about image. How would tapers look in here, do you suppose? A bit much, you think? Eh? Oh well, you may be right. We must learn to make do with what's given—fluorescent tubing, running water and the rulings of the late, unlamented Warren Court."

The door opens and a little bell sounds. Like in a bakery or an old candy store. I don't suppose much of this registers on my clients, but perhaps I get to them subliminally.

Mr. Crainpool, per his training, scratches arduously in a ledger. I look up casually and greet the newcomer, a man in a checkered sports coat, loud matching shirt and tie, new style cuffs on his flaring trousers. He has a sort of crew cut and looks for all the world like an off-duty cop. (I cast no aspersions. I *like* cops, but they do look vacuous sometimes. That air they have of concentration that comes from having to remember their lines, the unnatural vocabulary they're lumbered with, that abject, dispassionate diction of the trade, having to say words like "Negro" and "alleged" and "suspect," speaking as they do increasingly these days for Xerox and the tape recorder, for bookkeeping and the public record. And that sense of direction cops have, having always to be oriented, going about like human compasses, knowing the avenues, forced to think in terms of east and south, his left, my right—that's what does it.) So this fellow looks abstracted. We often get them in here. They tip us off about raids and sometimes consult us about the nature of the charges to be brought. One man's collusion is another man's professional courtesy. (But the cops don't really like *us*. They envy us our powers of arrest, stronger even than their own. And we don't have to deal with the technicalities of extradition, and carry guns lightly as credit cards.)

"Top of the morning," I tell him pleasantly.

"Top of the morning yourself." This man is not a policeman.

"Raise the blinds please, Mr. Crainpool. A little sunshine on the tough here. You had me fooled, son."

"You the Phoenician?"

"I am Mr. Alexander Main, the bailbusinessman."

"I'm from out of state."

"You're lost?"

"I'm Mafia, Pops."

"Mafia, wow."

"Wow? This is how you talk to a mobster?"

"One call on the hot line and you'll never talk out of the side of your mouth again. Me and the Don of all the Dons are like that. I call him Donny. Behave yourself. Nice folks don't come in off the street on a bright and sunny morning and say 'I'm Mafia, Pops.' Who are you, son? Where are you from?"

"Chicago. They call me 'the Golfer.' "

"The Golfer, eh? What do you shoot?"

"*People*," we both say together. I turn to Mr. Crainpool. "Mr. Crainpool, do you hear this dialogue? What a business this is! The nearer the bone you go, lifewise and deathwise, the saltier the talk. Peppery. You could flavor meat with our exchanges."

It's true what I tell Crainpool. I'm called on to make colorful conversation in my trade. Don't think I enjoy it. I'm a serious man; such patter is distasteful to me. When day is done I like nothing better than to ask my neighbor how he's feeling, to hear he's well and tell him same here, to trade what we know about the weather, to be agreeable and aloof and dull. Leave poetry to the poets, style to the window trimmers. I'm old. I should have grandchildren. But I turn back to the young man who will tire one day, should he outlive his apprenticeship, of such cheap excitements. We're doing business. He's come from Chicago and expects his money's worth. "All right," I tell him, "you're Mafia. What do you want, you gonna put a jukebox in here? I got to change the beer I been using thirty years? What?"

"There's a man in town. We don't know where he is, but the pigs do. He'll be picked up. We want you to spring for him."

"What? On *your* recognizance? Do you hear this, Mr. Crainpool? I put up my money—*if* the man is even bailable—then the Golfer here takes him out in a hole-in-one, and when the yobbo doesn't show up for his trial I'm out of pocket."

"You won't be out of pocket. The cops don't know what they're getting. His bond won't be set higher than a few thousand—five thousand. We advance you the cash forfeiture. You make five hundred bucks."

"Young fellow, no. I don't need the business."

"Mr. Main, it's Command Performanceville," he says softly.

Oh, he's very sinister. "Why didn't you say Command Performanceville in the first place? Command Performanceville's another story. For Command Performanceville my commission is thirty percent."

"Drinks all around," he says agreeably. "I'll put you in the picture."

"I read the book, I seen the picture. Your man downtown calls my man downtown who tells me your lad is under arrest. It's strictly offside vis-a-vis the other bondsmen, but I get to him first, arrange the bail, and he steps out into the sunshine a free man."

"A hundred percent."

"That will be sixty-five hundred dollars please."

"C.O.D."

"C.O.*D.*?"

"Phoenician, Mr. Main, I'm a sporty young man. I drive fast cars fast. How would it look I was picked up for speeding and the cops found sixty-five hundred bucks on me? Use your *keppeleh*. Did we know you drive such a hard bargain?"

"I drive hard bargains hard."

"Of course, of course. You'll be paid. The handle plus thirty percent. You'll get registered mail. Who's more honest than a syndicate man?"

"Then why do you speed?" I ask gloomily.

But there's reason on the young fellow's side. We shake and he leaves. The little bakery bell jingles behind him. Mr. Crainpool looks at me reproachfully, sorrow in his eyes like the toothache. "Something on your mind, Jiminy Cricket?"

"No, sir."

"What would happen if I refused? Fetterman would do it, or Klein. Adams would. Does Macy tell Gimbel?"

"It's only fifteen hundred dollars after the forfeit."

"Oh ho. I see where it is with you. It's all right to finger a man, just make sure you get a good price. Mr. Crainpool, kid, my finger comes cheap. If they ask how I do it, say it's my terrific turnover."

"Yes, sir."

"We would rather be a banker in a fine suit. We would rather conduct discreet business over drinks at the club. Heart to heart, man to man, gentlemen's agreements and a handshake between friends. We would prefer silver at our temples and a portrait in oils in the marble lobby. *But . . .*"

Even Crainpool gets the benefit of my colorful rhythms. This is what is distasteful, not the high hand and the strong arm. The rhetoric. To be laconic, taciturn, the quiet type. To speak modestly and thank my clients for their custom. Nothing can make up for this, not the viciousness or the seamy excitements or my collective, licey knowledge of the world. Boy oh boy, what goes on. My thoughts explode in words. I tell Crainpool.

"Do you know, Mr. Crainpool, the progress of the liver fluke through a cow's intestine to a human being? *That's* a picture. The trematode worm forms itself in shit, is discharged in a cow's stool. It can't crawl, it can't fly. All its mobility is concentrated toward one end, the act of boring. So, good nature's corkscrew that it is, it infiltrates the foundation of a blade of grass. Everything else in the cow pat dies off—every microbe, every virus. Just the flatworm, rising out of its matrix of shit like a befouled Phoenix to nest in the basement of a single blade of grass, only that survives. Even the cow moves on, wants distance between its manure and its lunch. Well, the rains come, the sun shines, the grass grows. The fluke hasn't hurt it; it's only along for the ride. Till finally it's at the top, which is the only part of the grass that the sheep will touch—his heart of artichoke and palm. A connoisseur, the sheep. And that's all that that trematode has been waiting for, some nasty radar in him that Reveres his logy instincts and tells him the sheep are coming, the sheep are coming. Lying in ambush all that time till the grass is high enough to munch. Then the paralyzed little creature goes crazy. It hasn't stirred its ass all the while it's been on the grass, mind, but now suddenly it leaps out of its wheelchair and walks, runs, does fucking triples, commandos the sheep's liver, where it's wanted to be all along, you see. Swimming the mile, doing the decathlon, dancing, dining, diamonds shining, making right for the liver, riding there like an act of vengeance, like a bronco-buster, spoiling the sheep's piss, poisoning the ground the sick sheep shits. Only now it's metamorphosed, now it's some viper butterfly to sting the heels of the barefoot kid on one of those fucking calendars of ours. Nature's nasty marathon, its stations of the cross and inside job.

"And the same with people. What the liver fluke can do man can do. The fix is in, takes two to tango, all crime's a coopera-tion. This I wanted to see. I've seen it, show me something else. Phooey. A Phoenician's phooey on it all."

Crainpool listens and nods, but his eyes are glazing. Not much interested in the overview, my Mr. Crainpool, not much feeling for the morphology of our business.

I dreamed of Oyp and Glyp again last night. Perhaps I should tell Crainpool. Would cheer him up. Well, I won't, don't. Bother Crainpool's moods. I'll be his Nature as Nature is mine. Ah, Na-ture, who can send us so many dreams, which do you choose? Do we dream of feasts? Three-star Michelin picnics on a check-ered cloth on soft, spongy zoysia, wicker work baskets with wine in linen and gorgeous chicken sandwiches on a windless day? Of beautiful women yielding to us in lovely water, or riding behind us bareback on horses in splendid country? Do we hear wit in our sleep, or does Nature deposit millions in our account or furnish our houses as we would wish them? Does She show us new colors or sound new notes or whisper good news? Would She grant us a view of the stars close up, or entertain us with the contemplation of beasts? Where is there to be found in dreams new masterpieces to study or even the slow motion of the ordinary cinema? No. She is too niggardly, gives us rag-shop, rubbish, engineers trivial enigma we forget on rising. Better altogether to leave us dreamless—but no, not Nature. She sends us Oyp and Glyp. I can't really remember where they were in my dream, but it was someplace high, I think, mountains (though the view was not spectacular), above Nature's three-mile limit, smug, warm behind their beards—they do not have beards in life; they'd grown them there, though these were matted ice and hair, an awful aspic. I saw them from below. (I was not even with them.) Such heights no place for a Phoenician; God gave us men to match our mountains. Oyp and Glyp. They're alive. Alive and loose and flouting my extradiitionary will. But there's my comfort if the dream speaks true. They are still to-gether, and to find one is to find both. It wasn't so with Evans, it wasn't so with Stern, it wasn't so with Trace. The Phoeni-cian's scattered, his Diaspora'd enemies drifting outward like the universe. It took years to find them. I put them together like a collection.

"Will there be any special instructions for me today, sir?"

"Do your accounts. Update your inventory. Bookkeep me my criminals. Advance the calendars. Mullins has run out of post-ponements. We can pull off November now."

"Yes, sir."

"Destroy it. Don't just leave it lying about as you did Oc-tober."

"No, sir."

"I want November off my walls and out of here."

"I'm rather fond," Crainpool says slyly, "of the angler in hip boots. He looks like my brother."

"Sure, kid, take it." I think Crainpool keeps a scrapbook of the pictures on my calendars. That angler doesn't look like his brother. He has no brother. I think Crainpool associates the pic-tures with the month's crimes in some mnemonic way. November would be a rapist and three car thieves, a pair of armed assaults, a little breaking and entering, a dangerous driver and a berk who threw away a suitcase of traffic tickets. Crainpool's Wanted poster Americana. Perhaps he's right, perhaps there's more connection than I've thought about between the pictures on those calendars and the life of crime. "It's all yours, sirrah, a fringe benefit."

"Yes, sir, thank you."

"Stay by the phones, it's a telethon. When that cop calls, tell him I'm at the jail. Have him leave a message with Lou who the guy is I'm supposed to see."

"Sir?"

"Yes, Mr. Crainpool?"

"Shouldn't you take the call yourself? The officer might be reluctant to pass on such information through a fellow police-man."

"Reluctant? You forget the liver fluke, sir. Where would the liver fluke be if he attended the cow's compunction or the sheep's scruple? Screw his sensibilities and reluctances. I'm down at the jail." I take my hat and go out. The little bakery bell tinkles pleasantly and I smile. I have made my joyful noise in the world.

The jailhouse is two miles from municipal court—a big reason for that referendum next year—and I call there regularly. I like the idea of having places to be to conduct my business. I have the route salesman's heart. It gets me outside. There are many such places: the jail (and its interview rooms where I consult with my clients), the courthouse, police headquarters, various law offices, the chambers of certain judges, even the main post office (one of the best ways to trace a jumper is to keep in touch with the postal authorities; sooner or later some of them send in one of those change-of-address cards requesting that their mail be redirected to a particular P.O. box in a distant city), the homes and apartments of their relatives, and, when I'm on the road tracing these mugs, the world itself. I don't drive—I know how but I don't—and always take public transportation (you might spot someone you're looking for or overhear something you need to know; you can't do this in a closed car).

The jailhouse is my favorite. It relaxes me to go there. There's a lot of shit and sycophancy in this business. It's "Yes, Your Honor" and "No, Your Honor" even when the guy is on your payroll. The lawyers are worse; they think we're scum. I keep half the town's lawyers in booze, but have yet to be invited to have a drink with one. I always send a nice present when their kids get married but have never been within goddamn hailing distance of one of those weddings. So the jail relaxes me. It's all cops there. Cops and robbers. And though I'm as deferential to the guards as I am to the biggest judge or hot-shot pol, somehow I don't mind so much.

It's a big facility, eleven stories high with rough gray stone and bars so black and thick you can make them out even on the top story, law and order's parallel lines. I love the jail. It's a building which constantly hums, murmurs, the cons at the windows of the lower floors ragging the pedestrians or shouting obscenities across the areaway to the women's block. And the woman shouting back, soliciting Johns from the eighth floor. The invitations and promises tumbling all that way somehow lose their viciousness, space moderating the human voice. It's as though they were all outside at recess and the rest of us indoors with flus and colds.

Some old gal spots me getting off the bus. (Whores must have incredible vision.) "Dey's dat nice Mr. Bondsman," she yells. "Hidy, lover. You still got dat golden prick on you? Man got a golden weewee," she explains to the street.

"Whut you sayin', fool? *Him?* Ain' nuthin' weewee 'bout it. It de Trans'lantic Cable. You kin get J'rus'lem on it. One time I call up Poland, talk to de Prince."

"Dat de hot line den in dat white man's pan's?"

"Yeah, dass ri', dass it all ri'."

"If dat so," another voice adds, "let dat boy get up de vigorish an' get us all a partner."

"You means a pardon."

"Shit, fool, I know what I means. I means a *partner.* I gettin' *tired* dis ole cellmate dey gimme. She ain' no bad *lookin'* girl, ya unnerstan', but she got fingernails on her like de railroad spikes. She makin' my po' ole hole *bleed.*"

A crowd has gathered in the street to listen. Another face has come to the window and takes the place of the woman who has just spoken. "Dat ain' blood, honey, dass gism. Dis gal got fo'ty years ub de gism packed up her crack. I jus' heppin' her to get it out. She got so much gism we habbin' us snowball fights up heah." The men laugh.

I squint against the sun and look up at the women, staring into their eclipse. I can't recognize them, though I go with whores from time to time. If they know me it's because I've become part of the jail's unofficial personnel, as the lawyers have. They wouldn't dare speak this way to the guards, or even to the prison's cooks and bakers. Nor, I've noticed, do they tease each other's visitors. Only strangers and those of us who can help them.

The girls have had their turn. Now it's the men's chance at me. An enormous black face appears at a barred window on the third floor. He sticks his arms through the bars and holds them out in front of him, suddenly turning his head and bending, pressing his ear against the bars as if he's listening to them. He makes some sort of imaginary adjustment on the bars with the fingers of his right hand, then strums them with his left. He begins to sing in a loud, terrible voice.

> "I got de blooooooz,
> I got de blooooooz,
> Oh boy oh boy, do I got de blooooooz!
> I got de blues in de mornin'
> I got de blues in de ebenin',
> I eben got de blues in de afternoooooon.
> I got de blooooooz,
> I got de mornin', ebenin', afternoon blues.
> I got de blues in Febr'ary,
> I got de blues in fall,
> I got de blooooooz on Thursday, April twelfth."

A white face appears in the cell next to his. "I'm in a jungle," he screams. "I'm in a fucking jungle. I'm locked up in a fucking jungle with a bunch of fucking coons. I feel like Dr. David Fucking Livingstone."

The black man opens his fingers and turns fiercely to the white man. "You made me drop my guitar, you pink-toed bastard. How in hell I supposed to practice without I got a guitar? How they gonna scubber me I ain't got my twenty-string guitar? It's useless to me now all busted up on the *ce*ment. You think they treat Leadbelly this way?"

"Use your accordion," someone calls. "Let them discover you on the accordion." There are many white faces at the windows now.

The singer disappears, returns, thrusts his arms through the bars again and starts to make crazy, waving, squeezing movements.

> *"Lady ub Spain, ah adores you,*
> *Lady ub Spain, ah adores you."*

He breaks off. "It ain't the same," he says disconsolately.

"Then take up track!" a prisoner shouts. They laugh.

Below them I applaud. "Very funny, ladies," I call. "Very amusing, gentlemen."

"You liked it?"

"Oh, yes. 'Vastly entertaining dot dot dot.' 'Four stars dot dot dot—Alexander Main, Cincinnati bailbondsman.' You've got a big hit, kids. Boffo!"

"You think they'll hold us over?"

"Months. Years." I do a two-step, a little shuffle. I break into song:

> *"There's no business like show business,*
> *Like no business I know.*
> *One day they are saying you will not go far,*
> *Next day on your dressing room they hang . . . you."*

"Sheeeit."

"You think so?" I hold my palms out and up to them. I turn them over. "You see that? Recognize that? Any you people re-member what this stuff is? Sunshine. Look, watch this." I breathe deep. "Fresh air. Smells good. I'll tell you something else. I ever need to take a crap I get to lock the door. No lids. Sit on a toilet seat like a kid's inner tube. I go out to lunch they hand me a menu. There's a napkin on my lap so I shouldn't get crumbs on my suit. After lunch, I feel like it I walk in the park, sit on a bench, look at the girls. If I wanted I could throw a ball over a wall and chase it. I could walk a mile for a Camel. I got a radio next to my bed pulls in *all* the stations and there's never any interference on the TV from the electric chair."

"Go peddle your papers, motherfucker."

"He is."

"I am."

"Sheeeit."

"There are seven million arrests in the United States annually—I'm giving you the latest year for which we have statistics—a hundred and sixty thousand people in the jails, prisons, pens and work farms at any given moment. I'm giving you the latest moment for which we have statistics."

"Sheeeit."

"Eighty thousand of you monkeys are in a pretrial or preconviction stage. *Eighty thousand.* Do you follow what I'm telling you? One out of every two could be out this afternoon if he went bail. I'm coming inside. I've arranged with the guards to see as many of you as I can. They'll be no trouble. Just call the guard and tell him you want to see Mr. Main." I have a sudden inspiration. "Tell the screw to take you to the visitors' room. What the hell, I'll do the lot of you. This town's been kind of boring with you mothers off the streets." There are catcalls but I shout above them. "I talk this way in the public streets because this ain't privilege but constitutional rights we're discussing. Don't ask me how it happens, but you creeps have constitutional rights. God Bless America and I'll see you in a few minutes."

The screens in the visitors' room give it the look of high summer. I wave to the guards, chipper Phoenician that I am. An act of the purest good will because it makes no difference to these sober, side-armed fellows. They have no more regard for me than for their charges. The public makes a mistake when it assumes that all its officials are on the take. Many of these men, low fellows bribed by their very jobs, don't get a penny off me.

"Give us a fiver, Phoenician," one hisses before the men arrive. "You'll never miss it, sir."

"I never heard that," I tell him, waving the paper container of coffee at him that I got from the machine. "You never said it and I never heard it. Now, where are my boys and girls? Whatever can be keeping them? If there's been any infringement of their constitutional rights—"

"Naw, naw," Poslosky, the chief guard, says. "Nothing like that."

They begin to file through a thick door on the other side of the screening. "Paul, they're on the other side. I want to go in there with them."

"Aw, Phoenician, you know the regulations. You shouldn't be here at all. You're supposed to see them in the interview rooms. I'd get in trouble."

"All right, kid, you're down for five percent of whatever I take in, but we got to go backstage."

"Phoenician, I mean it, you could cost me my job one day."

"Good. Terrific. Then you'll come work for me. What do you say? You'll be my field representative in the southwest in charge of wetbacks and Indians. I'll turn you into a *real* policeman. A hundred fifty bucks for every jumper you kill. I'm getting old, Paulie, slowing down. You don't know what all those Big-Boys and Burger-Chefs do to a man's stomach when he's out on the road looking for the bail jumpers. What's going to happen to the business when I'm gone?" I put my arm around his shoulder and we go out of the room and into the corridor.

"I shouldn't be taking you back there," Poslosky tells me, "I mean it's really off-limits."

I steer him toward a barred gate. The guard there stands up when he sees me. "Hey, Phoenician, I got a message for you."

"Not now, Lou."

"I think it's important, I kinda recognized the voice. A chief, I think. About some guy named Morgan."

"Later, Lou, please. I'm running late. Open the gate." He presses the button and the gate slides open. "Lou, I'll get back to you." We go through another gate and pause before a thick metal door. "Open it," I tell Poslosky.

"No kidding, Phoenician, civilians strictly ain't allowed back here."

"*Civilians?* That's the way you talk to a man who's been in the war against crime all his life? Unlock the fucking door, I'm reviewing the troops."

Inside, in addition to the guards, there are seven men and four women. I hadn't expected a crowd, but it's a poor showing. I rub my hands. "Most bondsmen wouldn't take this trouble," I tell them. "What can I say? It's the way I'm built. Painstaking attention to detail. We try harder." I recognize no one. Most of them have probably been refused bail already. Others couldn't find anyone who would put it up for them. They mill about listlessly. Some have come just to get out of their cells. I go up to one. "How's the grub?"

"I've tasted worse."

"My compliments to the chef. Beat it, I wouldn't touch you. All right, anybody else like the food here? No? Who's been refused bail? Come on, come on, don't waste my time." I grab a nigger. "Hey, didn't I already turn you down for bail?"

"No, sir, Cap'n, I never got no hearing."

"No hearing, eh?"

"No, sir."

"Must have been pretty bad, what you did, if you didn't get a hearing. What'd you do, slice up on someone."

"No, sir."

"Shoot? Chain whip? Don't stand there and tell me you used poison. Dropped a little something extra in the soul food?"

"I didn't do none them things."

"Well, my bad man, you must have done something pretty awful if you never got a hearing."

"They say I slep' with my child."

"Who says that?"

"My wife. She swore the complaint."

"And you want to get out of here."

"Yes, sir."

"Bad?"

"I can taste it."

"Yeah, taste it, I know what you mean. How old's your daughter? This *is* a daughter we're talking about? They don't say you buggered your boy?"

"No, sir, my daughter."

"Well, you look to me to be a young man. What are you—twenty-six, twenty-seven?"

"I be twenty-eight the Fourth of July."

"Yankee Doodle Dandy. How old's the kid?"

"She nine, sir."

"Now you told me you were married. This isn't some woman you're living with. You two are legally married?"

"Oh, yes."

"Ever been divorced? I check all this stuff out. It won't help you to lie."

"No, never. My wife and me been married since we both seventeen."

"So this little girl—what's the little girl's name?"

"Ruth."

"So Ruth is your and your wife's blood daughter?"

"That's right."

"She go to school?"

" '*Course* she go to school. What the hell you talking about?"

"Take it easy, Romeo. What school does she go to, what grade's she in?"

"O'Keefe School, she in the fourth grade."

"O'Keefe's a white school."

"They buses her."

"What are her marks?"

"She smart, she get *good* scores."

"Ever been to a P.T.A. meeting?"

"Sure I been. Ruth the president of her class."

"The president of her class, eh? Tell me, what school did she go to before they started busing her to O'Keefe?"

"Lamont School."

"She do pretty well over there?"

"She on the honor roll."

"Your wife work?"

"She cleans."

"What do you do?"

"I work in my cousin's car wash."

"This cousin—he your cousin or your wife's cousin?"

"He *my* cousin. My wife's people don't amount to much."

"Okay. Give me the name of your lawyer. I'll see to it you get bail."

"Hey. You means I gets out of here?"

"Sure."

"What it cost me?"

"That bother you?"

"I just works in a car wash."

"Well, it's a pretty serious charge. I'd say they'll set your bail at two thousand. It costs you ten percent of that, two hundred. You got two hundred dollars?"

"In the bank."

"You give me a signed note saying I can draw two hundred dollars out of your account."

"I gives you that you gets me out of here?"

"All there is to it. There's just some papers you have to sign."

"Papers."

"You people shit your pants when you hear papers. Don't worry. I ain't selling livingroom bedroom suites or color TV's. I'm Alexander Main, the freedom man. The Great Emancipator. No. These papers have nothing to do with money. They simply state that you waive extradition proceedings and consent to the application of such force as may be necessary to effect your return should you make an effort to jump bail."

"What's all that?"

"That if you try to get away I can kill you."

"I ain't gonna try to get away."

"Of course not. You're a *good* risk. That's why I'm going your bond."

"Gimme that paper. Where do I sign?" He fixes his signature laboriously, as if he were pinning it there.

"Fine. You're as good as out."

"I wants to thank you."

"Sure. I understand. It's true love, the real thing. You miss that kid." I turn to the others. "Next. Who's next? Step right up, ladies and gentlemen, it's A. Main, the freedom man, selling you respite for ten percent down. Tired of the same old routine? Ass got cornhole blisters? Long to get back in the blue suede shoes? Bailbonds, bailbonds here. Bailbond, mister?"

"Yeah."

"What're you in for?"

"He's on remand for murder, Phoenician," Poslosky says.

"Murder? Who says murder? Is that true, son?" The kid, a dark, sullen-looking mug just out of his teens, stares back at me. You could skate on his eyes. "Come on, boy, think of me as you would a doctor. If I'm going to help you, you've got to put your balls in my hand and cough."

"He killed a fourteen-year-old for winking at his girl."

"He killed an enemy, an affair of honor. Since when is it murder to kill an enemy in an affair of honor? Not guilty. It's the unwritten law."

"They weren't even engaged, Phoenician, they didn't even go steady. It was their first date," Poslosky says. "All the kid did was wink."

"It's the unwritten law. This is America. Since when is there one unwritten law for the married and another unwritten law for the single?"

"He set the boy on fire," Poslosky whispers.

"Arson is a bailable offense. I see no reason why this man should be held without bond. It was an enemy he set fire to in an affair of honor. The word gets about in these things. What are the chances of someone else winking at his date? The risk's negligible. Are you highly connected, son?"

"Highly connected?"

"Are your people rich?"

"Nah."

"Not so fast, son. Hold on there. You'd be surprised what constitutes an estate. Is Father living?"

"Yeah."

"That's a start, that's a *good* start. Does he own his home?"

"He's paying it off."

"Where is this house?"

"Brackman Street."

"Above or below the fourteen hundred block?"

"Below. Six Brackman Street."

"Six, you say? River property? Six is river property."

"Yeah."

"Don't say 'yeah' as if this were some vacant lot we're talking about. This is bona fide river property."

"It's an old house."

"On an older river. What size lot?"

"I never measured."

"When you cut Dad's grass—just give me an estimate on this— how long does it take you to go from the front to the back, from one side to the other? Do you use a power mower or a manual? Just give me a rough estimate."

"I never cut no grass."

"Too big a job? That could be in your favor if it was too big a job."

"Yeah, it was too big a job."

I whistle. "How many bedrooms?"

"Two."

"Two? Only two on an enormous estate like that? . . . Are you an only child? This could be important."

"Yeah, there's just me."

"Better and better. Look, son, think carefully, try to remember, is Mom dead or alive?"

"Yeah, I remember. I'm an only child and Mom's dead."

"Son, you're an heir. You're a son, son."

"The old man hates my guts."

"There are deathbed reunions. The ball game isn't over till the last man is out. All right, let's inventory this thing. We've got a good piece of riverfront property, a magnificent two-bedroom house and an only child. Now. Tell me. You look a stocky, sturdy guy. You take after your father? You built like Pop?"

"I'm taller. We weigh about the same."

I squeeze the flab around his belly, palm his gut like a tit. "A hundred ninety? One ninety-five?"

He shakes me off. "One seventy-two." The fat fuck lies.

"We'll call it one eighty. How old's your daddy?"

"I don't know, he don't invite me to his birthday parties."

"Easy, son, easy. Pa in his sixties? Fifties?"

"I don't know. Fifties."

"He smoke?"

"Yeah."

"Well, that's good. I'll tell you the truth, I'd have been a little worried if you'd told me he was in his sixties because that would have meant he's beaten the actuarial tables. There's no telling how long you can go once you've beaten the actuarial tables, but in his fifties, and a smoker, that's something else . . . All right, is there insurance?"

"Who knows?"

"Fair enough. Is he self-employed or does he work for someone?"

"He's a baker. He's got a little bakery."

"Hey. You didn't say anything about a bakery. That's terrific."

"It's a dump."

"It's a small business. It's a small business and it's insured. Okay, up to now we've been talking about potential collateral. What would you say he's worth, right now, alive? Any stocks or bonds?"

"I don't know."

"Come on. Do you ever see him reading the financial pages? Does he rail at Wall Street?"

"No."

"All right. Does he read the sports section? Following scores often indicates an interest in the fluctuation of dollars."

"He reads the funnies."

"I'm beginning to get a picture. Owns a piece of riverfront property which at today's prices could be worth fifty or sixty thousand to a developer. He has a small business which means he probably banks his money. He an immigrant?"

"Yeah."

"Sicily? Italy?"

"Yeah, Sicily, Italy."

"An immigrant. Came to this country in the late twenties as a youngster. Saw the stock market crash and learned a good lesson. Worked and saved till he owned his own small bakery. Banks his money, likes to see it grow—watch the numbers get bigger. Sure. By this time there could be thirty or forty thousand in his account. At the inside your pop's worth a hundred grand, not counting any possible insurance."

"Gee."

"Plus maybe a car, probably a small delivery truck." The kid nods. "The equipment at the bakery, of course. The industrial ovens alone could be ten or fifteen thousand dollars."

"Gosh."

"That kind never throws anything out. The old-country furniture might be worth another couple grand. These are optimum figures. All in all between a hundred and seventeen and a hundred and twenty-three thousand dollars. Round it off at a hundred twenty."

"Christ."

"This is a great country, sonny. But those were optimum estimates. In my business you've got to be conservative. It might not be more than ninety thousand."

"That old bastard sitting on ninety thousand bucks."

"Wait, wait, I'm still figuring. Now, you know, when you come right down to it Poslosky here is right. You're in for a capital offense, and while my arguments for your release might go over with the judge, the bond would have to be a high one."

"How high?"

"Fifty to seventy-five thousand dollars."

"That's a lot."

"We could swing that. I just showed you."

"It ain't *my* money, it's his."

"I could talk to him, bring him around."

"Will you do that?"

"No."

"What do you mean no? What's all this about?"

"You're a shitty risk."

"What are you talking about? I acted in anger. Like you said yourself, people will steer clear of me. It couldn't happen again."

"That's not it."

"What? What then?"

"You never cut the grass. You haven't got good ties to the community. Next, who's next here?"

There's a tall, good-looking white man in his late thirties. Well dressed, he's the only one in the room not in prison garb. I go up to him. "Sir, it looks to me as if we might have a case of false arrest here. Excuse me, I just want to take a swig of this coffee, I think it's getting cold . . . Now. What's a nice girl like you doing in a place like this?" He walks abruptly away from me and I follow. "Don't get sore, that's just my way of scraping acquaintance. Please don't be mad at me."

"I'm not talking to this creep," he tells Poslosky.

"This is the bondsman," Poslosky says. "If you want to get out you're going to have to work with him."

"I'll take my business elsewhere."

"Why is this man dressed like this, Lieutenant?"

"Maybe he hasn't been processed yet, Phoenician."

"He just came in," the guard from his cellblock volunteers. "I brought him down to see the bondsman. I'll get him fixed up as soon as we go back."

"Like hell," the chap says. "You're not getting me in one of those outfits. I haven't been convicted of anything. I can wear my own clothes."

"Shut up, bigmouth," Poslosky says.

"Hold on, Lieutenant," I say mildly, "he's right. He knows his law. The law states that a prisoner may wear his own clothes while he's waiting to be brought to trial."

"Well, sure," Poslosky sputters, "but—"

"As long as they're neat and presentable."

"I know, but—"

I throw the remainder of my coffee at the guy's suit. "There," I say, "now they're not neat and presentable."

Poslosky roars with laughter and the guy starts for me. Almost has me, too, but the guards grab him. "All right," I say, "I think he's going to be a good sport about this. You can let him go. He won't touch me. You won't touch me, will you, Morgan?"

"If you know who I am and still did that, you're a fool," Morgan says.

I turn to Poslosky. "That's it for today, Lieutenant, I think. I'll get back to you about the golliwogg once the bank releases his dough. They can go back. All but Morgan. I'll go Morgan's bail. We'll work something out so it's processed immediately."

"You haven't asked any questions. You don't even know what he's in for."

"Morgan? Morgan's all right. Morgan's a good risk. I know a little something about the case and I give you my assurance he's bondable."

"I'm not going with this guy."

"We can't keep you once your bail's been paid."

"I don't want it paid."

"The state has no rights in it," I tell him quietly. "If you're bondable, you're out."

"I'll jump bail." Poslosky looks at me.

"Nah. That's exuberance talking, the flush of freedom. The guy's got terrific community ties. Roots like beets. Bring him along, then." This is a violation of procedure and Poslosky visibly balks. Morgan's guard stands up against his man like a Siamese twin. Sotto voce I say to Poslosky: "Ontday ooyay ohnay oohay oovyay otgay?"

"Oohay?"

I whisper into his ear and remind him of the message Lou said he had for me. I offer a few Phoenician flourishes. Poslosky looks over at Morgan who by this time is almost cuddling his guard.

"Well, if he's such a big shot—"

"Shh."

"Well, why's he so reluctant to leave?"

I take him aside. "Poslosky, you have an inquiring mind. I like that in a policeman. All we know for sure is that City Hall wants him the hell out of this place. My best guess is that he's a plant from the *Enquirer* here to do an exposé on conditions."

"The son of a bitch, I'll exposé his head."

"No, that would be playing into his hands. Look, I don't know any more about it than you. I heard something was up and I'm just putting two and two together from the message Lou tried to pass me. I bet Lou tells us we're to zip down with the guy in a paddy wagon to Judge Ehrlinger's chambers, arrange a quick *pro forma* bond and get him the hell off our backs before his suit dries. They give it a twelve-minute investigation and charges are dropped this afternoon. If he's held a minute longer than necessary I wouldn't want to be in your shoes."

"All right, we'll see what Lou has to say." Poslosky tells the guard to hold on to the prisoner and we step outside to speak to Lou.

Word-for-word, I swear to you. My people haven't been in this business thousands of years for nothing! Morgan, the wagon, Ehrlinger—Ehrlinger, a hack, is special-duty magistrate this week —everything. Poslosky is electrified. He gets on Lou's phone and arranges for a wagon and a couple of guards to be waiting when we come out with the prisoner. Inside five minutes we're on our way. I sit up front with the driver. Poslosky himself helps me into the wagon and closes the door for me. He shakes my hand through the open window.

"Thanks, Phoenician."

I lean out. "Lieutenant," I tell him coolly, "I'm no goddamn do-gooder. If conditions in this jail are ever exposed, the Bail Commission will be letting everyone but the murderers out on their own recognizance. Those Commission bastards are cutting my throat as it is."

"The revolving door," Poslosky sighs.

"Too true. We're goners, Poz, they're wiping us out. Cops, bondsmen."

"The fucking Supreme Court," Poslosky says, "the fucking Miranda decision."

"Yeah, Pus. Gee, kid, I could stick around here talking philosophy with you all day, but we better get that mother downtown before Ehrlinger wets himself."

"Yeah. So long, Phoenician."

At the courthouse Morgan walks between me and the cop to Ehrlinger's chambers. I study him closely but can't tell how much his anger is antagonism to me or appreciation of his situation. "You know," I tell him amiably, "I'm pretty ashamed of what I did back there. What a temper. I want you to send me the cleaning bill for your suit. I'll pay."

"Shit, if the coffee stains don't come out, you'll buy me a new goddamn suit."

He knows from nothing. "Sure," I say, "I promise."

A judge's chambers, even Ehrlinger's, give me a hard-on of the spirit. All that oak paneling—brown is your color of civilization—dark as bark, those long earthen fillets of wood like a room made out of cellos, the faint oily odor of care (I remember the smell), the deep brass fittings like metals in museums, the lovely heavy leathers adumbrating strap, blood sports—geez, it's terrific. The desk big as a piano, and the deep, clean ashtrays on its wide top. And the souvenirs. These guys have been officers in wars, served on commissions. Their official surfaces trail a spoor of the public history: a President's pen ammunitions a marble bore, Nuremberg memorabilia, a political cartoonist's original caricature framed on the desk in love's egotistic inversion, the flier's short snorter aspicked in paperweight; toys, some pal industrialist's miniature prototype—all respectability's groovy junk. And cloudy, obscure prints on the walls, deft hunts and European capitals in old centuries, downtown London before the fire, Berlin's Inns of Court. A fat globe of the world rises like an immense soft-boiled egg in an eggcup, girdled by a wide wooden orbit that catwalks its equatorial waist. Red calf spines of lawbooks glow behind glass. Only the flag distracts—an absurd bouquet drooping from a queer umbrella stand on three claw feet with metallic, undifferentiated toes. The judge's black robe is snagged on a hatrack.

Ehrlinger is at his desk pretending to write an opinion when the clerk admits us. The man has been a district judge for years, will never rise higher, but he is absolutely incorruptible, so inflexible that he is never more dangerous than now when, sitting in his capacity as the week's special-duty magistrate—who hears *in camera* special pleadings that violate the court calendar—he is asked to alter the conventions.

Like many humorless men, Ehrlinger loves to be entertained. I play the fool for him and he likes me for it.

"Yes?" He looks toward us annoyed and glances at Morgan's papers that the clerk has just placed on his desk. "Can't this wait? This man's just been arrested. The police can hold him for twenty-four hours. Why couldn't he have his bail hearing tomorrow with everyone else?"

"Influence," I break in quickly. "You know these crooks, Your Honor. They have friends in low places."

"Oh, it's you, Phoenician, is it?"

"Yes, Your Honor."

"Well, let's get on with it, then."

"Wait just a moment, Your Honor. There's something I've always wanted to do, sir."

"What? What's that?"

"No, no don't pay any attention to me, sir. Just go on writing that precedent-making opinion."

"Here, what's all this about then?"

I rush to the hatrack where Ehrlinger's robe is hanging. I lift its hem, draw it back and lean in under it, manipulating my right arm free of the robe and holding it up. Still bent down and hidden in the garment I pivot toward the judge. "Hold it." I clench my exposed hand into a fist. "There! Got your picture, Your Honor!" I creep back out of the robe and stand up beaming.

"Oh, Phoenician," Ehrlinger says. "Tarnation, sir, a man your age. All right, now, all right," he says like Ted Mack on *The Amateur Hour*, "that will do. Let's see what we've got here." He turns back to the file and I wink at Morgan. Ehrlinger studies the file for a moment and looks back up. "Well," he says, "according to this there have been no previous arrests. Is that right?"

"Yes, sir." Morgan says.

Ehrlinger grins. "Punched him, did you?"

"I'm afraid I did, sir."

"Fetched him a good one?"

"I guess so, Your Honor."

"Well, strictly speaking, you're supposed to keep your hands to yourself, and since these students had a permit for their rally it was quite proper for the police to bind you over."

"What's this?" I ask.

"Still—" Ehrlinger says.

"When I heard him urging those kids to burn their draft cards—"

"Couldn't control yourself."

"No, sir."

"Wait a minute."

"Well, when I was your age I'd like to think I'd have done the same."

"Hold on."

"He was a pimply, long-haired freak. To tell you the truth, Your Honor, it was more like slugging a girl."

"Well, you can't say he didn't have it coming."

"I'm even kind of ashamed."

"Jesus!"

"Broke his jaw, did you?"

"I'm afraid so, sir."

"Under the circumstances it would be hypocritical of me to *congratulate* you, Mr. Morgan, and the law's the law. There were a lot of witnesses at that rally. I'm afraid you'll have to appear."

"I know that, Your Honor."

"Still, I'll try not to make it *too* hard on you. We'll set a fifty-dollar bond."

"Thank you, Your Honor. I didn't anticipate any of this, so I don't happen to have that much cash on me."

"I understand."

"Fifty dollars? *Fifty?*"

"I'm glad you brought him by, Phoenician. You showed good judgment. There's no sense in a man like this having to spend even an extra minute in jail."

"He broke his jaw!" I shout.

"Yes," the judge says.

I turn to Morgan. "He was making a speech?"

"Yeah," Morgan says, "terrible things."

"A rabble-rouser?"

"Until I clipped him."

"Judge, this man broke a boy's jaw. No matter what you or I may think of the young man's politics, it's perfectly apparent that the kid was a student leader, a public speaker. Who can tell what disastrous effect Morgan's punch might have on that young fellow's future platform performances? Suppose he meant to go into radio? Or be a singer? To let Mr. Morgan off on a pledge of just fifty dollars—why it's . . . it's condoning, it's tantamount to a dereliction of duty."

"Always having me on, Phoenician," Ehrlinger says blandly. "That's humor, so it's all right, but blatantly to try to up the ante at a patriot's expense just to line your pockets with a few paltry dollars, that's something else. No. To be perfectly frank, Phoenician, I know as well as you do that the bail in these circumstances is five hundred dollars. It's my little joke on *you*."

It's useless. "Sure. That's a good one, Your Honor."

"Just turn your documents over to the clerk on the way out. Your appearance is in three weeks, Mr. Morgan. Will that be all right?"

"Yes, Your Honor. Thank you."

Outside I take out my checkbook. "Wait a minute," Morgan says, "what are you doing?"

"Writing a check."

"Hold on," he says uncomfortably, "money doesn't change hands unless I fail to appear."

"Yes, that's right. Sign here, please. By my penciled x." He's glaring at me now, but he signs the forms and I give them to the clerk together with the check. We step into the elevator together.

"Your fee's what? Ten percent? Here's your five bucks." He holds the bill out stiffly to me but I make no motion to take it. I study him carefully. "What is it, the suit? It don't cost five bucks to clean a suit. Give me two-fifty change." I hand him two dollars and fifty cents and he tries to give me the five-dollar bill again. "Go on," he says, "take it."

"It's been taken care of."

"What do you mean it's been taken care of?"

"It's been taken care of. There's a gentleman waiting for you outside. A professional golfer I think he said."

Morgan's face drains. "What for?" he asks hoarsely.

"How should I know? Maybe he needs you to fill out a foursome."

"You son of a bitch," he screams, "you sold me out!"

"That's right. I pick up a cool twelve fifty on the deal."

"Cocksucker!"

He comes for me and I draw my gun and press the emergency button. The elevator jerks to a stop. "You're Mafia and you don't carry cash and you don't pack a gun. Me, I'm an honest man and am lumbered with both. All right, I figure we've both been screwed. That's why I'm doing you this favor."

"Some favor."

"You *bet* some favor. I was supposed to get fifteen hundred bucks for you. How the hell could I know all the cops wanted you for was for smacking some goddamn hippie? Painstaking attention to detail, we try harder. Bygones are bygones. The favor is I warned you."

"The guy's outside, you said. What am I supposed to do?"

"It's a courthouse here. Confess a crime. Expose yourself to a meter maid. Up to you. I'm getting out on three. You're not." I press three. We stop and the door opens. "*Vaya con Dios*, Uncle Sam." As I step out I bang a button, but before it can shut I lean my weight against the door. "One more thing. If you *should* happen to get away from that palooka, just remember your appearance is in three weeks. I've got fifty bucks tied up in you. If you don't show up, *I'll* come get you." I release the door, it closes behind me and we're quits.

2.

The bailbondsmen of Cincinnati, Ohio, eat their lunch across the Ohio River in what is now an enormous restaurant a mile south of Covington, Kentucky. Called The Grace and Favor, its name sounds like an English pub, but it bears no resemblance to one. Built in the early twenties, it has had several avatars: speak-easy, night club, gambling casino; briefly a dance hall during the big-band era and then a roadhouse when that style went out after the war; a night club again in the fifties until the public had learned by heart on television the songs and routines of the stars who appeared there, then a sort of caterer's hall where the Jews of Cincinnati bar mitzvah'd their sons and sprang for the enormous weddings of their daughters; a place where the Republican Party sponsored $1,000-a-plate dinners and the Democrats $25- and $50-a-ticket closed-circuit viewings of rallies staged in Hollywood and New York, with a cash bar available—until, in the mid-sixties, it finally became a restaurant, though it had always had a kitchen, food being a necessary concomitant of such places, prepared to serve at a moment's notice the high roller's steak and the gunman's lobster.

Probably because of its various incarnations, The Grace and Favor enjoyed a certain geisha ambiguity: no matter what its function at any given moment, there were always people around who remembered when it had had another; who saw a dance floor where the tables and banquettes now stood, or remembered the crap tables and chemin de fer and roulette where the dance floor used to be; who could still see the queer metallic aisles and pews formed by the rows of slot machines; who could conjure up through the altered walls and windows and raised platform (which was once space sunk feet beneath the ordinary sea level of the surrounding room) prior configurations, where coppers' bullets, shattering mirrors, might have brought seven years bad luck had not the management seen to it that no such continuity was likely in the place's chameleon transitions. But no one, save the émigré English gangster who built it and who was now an old man, had witnessed all of it, though some, even some here at the long table reserved for the bondsmen, had been there at the beginning. There had been lacunae. They'd had to leave town, perhaps, or been called to war, or suffered strokes; one thing or another had taken them away at a time when the establishment was undergoing one of its many transformations. Now, in per-

haps its most effete phase, as a restaurant for Cincinnati businessmen and clubwomen, it did its biggest business at lunch. (It was
genuinely immense. Its main room alone could handle 500 diners
without giving the appearance of crowding them.) The new
Interstate Federal Highway that led across the new bridge that
spanned the Ohio River and actually provided it (since advertising is banned along federal highways) with its own broad grass-
green reflecting sign ("Grace and Favor ½ Mi.") and exit ramp
(no one, not even the most cynical of the bondsmen, knew how
this had been finagled, though the speculation was that perhaps
one of those $1,000-a-plate dinners had made it possible) made it
as accessible as any restaurant in Cincinnati.

The bondsmen came in taxis, five or six to a cab, and rubbed
their loud, heavily padded, sports-jacketed shoulders—they
dressed in a sort of mid-fifties style, like customers in delicatessens
on Sunday mornings—with the furred shoulders of the clubwomen and sober-suited buyers from the downtown stores. The
London broil for $1.50 was a specialty. It was what they all ate,
the distinction in their appetites if not their characters apparent
only in the way they wanted it prepared and what they chose
to gulp it down with.

The Phoenician was not with them today, and since word of
Ehrlinger's joke had already been leaked, some of the bondsmen
were disappointed that he was not there to take their ragging.
None made any comment, however. This was not their usual
social gathering. It was a new departure, more or less a formal
business meeting, scheduled weeks ago. They had never had a
business meeting and were a little uncertain how to begin. In the
trade all their adult lives, these were men who had never tired
of the infinite eccentricity that came their way, who by the
simple process of constant witness had become expert raconteurs,
sheer access to "material" democratizing any differences in
imagination and delivery that might once have existed between
them. They looked around the table at each other, their glance
finally settling on Lester Adams, a tall, speckled, taciturn bondsman in his seventies.

Adams had got into bailbonds in the thirties when his farm
was taken from him by the banks. He had come to Cincinnati to

look for work and found $100 in the street on his first day in the
big city. He was on his way to the courthouse (his small village
of Bend, Ohio, had no jail, though it had a J.P. who functioned
also as a law enforcement officer and Lost and Found service) to
return it, carrying it openly in his hand because he had never
seen such traffic before and was a little afraid he might be run
over by a truck and the money found concealed on his person
and people would wonder what a simple, destitute farmer like
himself was doing with a hundred dollars cash in his pockets.
He was looking for the Lost and Found, which was, he reasoned
by analogy, in the immense courthouse. He waved the bill in front
of him as he came down the corridors, snapping it like a flag of
safe passage, the ostentation of the gesture only slightly less pain-
ful to him than his fear that people might think he came by it
wrongfully, until he was stopped by a lawyer who was looking
for a bondsman to put up $75 bail for his client.

The lawyer, who had seen Adams waving his money, touched
his sleeve to get his attention. "Bondsman," the lawyer said, and
Adams, thinking the man had said "Bendsman" and that it was a
question, immediately answered "Yes." The lawyer explained
his client's circumstances and Adams, who hadn't followed a
word of what the man was saying but who was chagrined not to
have recognized a fellow townsman, thought: In the big city not
a whole day and whole night and so shook that I not only don't
remember this feller though we come from the same village but
don't even recognize that he looks familiar to me, and nodded
in agreement to everything the lawyer said, figuring out only
as the lawyer went on and it was too late, and that it was his own
pleasant nodding that had *made* it too late, that his old friend
seemed to want to borrow seventy-five dollars of the farmer's
found hundred to help out a friend of his own—possibly, Adams
imagined, another fellow Bendsman. When the lawyer's client
was produced, he thought: Yep. I'm in worse trouble than I
thought, for this feller don't look no more familiar to me than
the first. Not in the big city a whole day and whole night and
already I can't remember nobody. Spoiled, he thought, cursing
himself, spoiled rotten, bigger headed 'n a sow's belly.

So he was already prepared to turn over the hundred dollars

to the lawyer and the twenty-five dollars change to the Lost and Found as soon as he could get away from him and find it when the lawyer said, "What about the form?"

Adams shook his head sadly. "Ain't got no farm. Lost the farm."

"Never mind," the lawyer said, "I'll be right back." He was as good as his word. In a few moments he was back with a piece of paper. "This'll do," he said. "I got it from the clerk. Here. Sign."

And though Adams couldn't read very well he could write his name all right—wasn't that how he'd lost the farm in the first place?—and he imagined that this was something to do with the loan, it not seeming at all strange to him that in the big city, where everything else was turned around, it was the lender who should fix his name to an IOU rather than the borrower. Then he saw that it was going to be all right when the lawyer's client signed too. "When do I give the seventy-five dollars?" he asked.

"What?" said the lawyer. "Don't worry, he isn't going anywhere. Hey," said the lawyer, "Baxter, pay the man." And Baxter, the lawyer's friend and fellow townsman, handed Lester Adams $7.50 for which Lester didn't even thank him, so concerned was he that not only could he not place the lawyer and the lawyer's friend, but couldn't even remember Baxter now that he knew his name.

It was all over in a few minutes; Baxter and the lawyer left the building and Adams was standing there with one hundred and seven dollars and fifty cents. He was so confused by now that he couldn't move, and others approached him—all asking, it seemed, to borrow money. Under no obligation to these new borrowers since none claimed kinship with him, he was still too good-natured and too timid to have to tell them that he himself had no money and so he refused no one, and when he left the courthouse that day he had not only the hundred found dollars but eighty-four *additional* dollars that the new borrowers had pressed on him!

Now Lester Adams was no dope. He knew a good thing when he saw one, and though he did not understand what had happened he understood that there had been a misunderstanding. When the corridors finally cleared, he approached one of the policemen and told him the story from the beginning and asked him if he could make anything out of it. The policeman couldn't stop laughing for fifteen minutes, but when he finally did he explained it all to Adams, careful to omit nothing, not the most trivial detail, since the cop felt that only the truth, the whole truth and nothing but the truth, could drive home to the farmer what an outrageous hick he was, and this, meant as cruelty, was the best lesson anyone could ever have had about the ins and outs of bailbondery.

"I'll be damned," Adams said to all the policeman had told him, "I'll be goddamned. That's some business! Why, I'll bet you dollars to doughnuts that in a wicked city like Cincinnati there's always some feller or other in trouble." With some of his one hundred eighty-four dollars he hired a private tutor, and inside two months he had not only improved his reading skills but could read and understand the most complicated legal documents, and inside three he was licensed by the State of Ohio to set himself up in the bailbond business, and by the fourth he had already had to go out after Baxter, the original borrower, shoot him in the leg, and bring him back by force to the courthouse to stand trial as best he could on one leg. In the years since he had killed eleven men, was no longer a hick and could tell stories of depravity that curled hair.

Taciturn still, yet his imagination so greased by daily contact with the surreal that over the years his character had seemed to turn itself inside out as you would reverse trousers to sew their seams, it was Lester Adams who opened the conference. "They're killing us, gentlemen. The social scientists and New Left coalitions and civil libertarians. The Supreme Court—and don't kid yourselves, the Burger Court not only is not all that different from the Warren Court but in certain respects is even more dangerous, because where the Warren guys merely built up the rights of the indigent, this so-called conservative crew is inventing rights for the fat cats. Anybody here who wouldn't rather go bail for the president of GM than Pete the Tramp? All that's happened is that now they have a legacy. With a legacy these strict constructionists are going to wall up our assholes. History is stubborn; once its mind is made up it's made up. Compassion is an historical inevitability and we have no better chance of bringing back laissez-faire than we do public whippings.

"So they're killing us. The 1966 Federal Bail Reform Act which gave federal courts the discretion to act as their own bondsmen and accept a ten-percent bond up front has already put us out of kidnapping, skyjackings and political assassinations. It's put us out of bank stickups where the robbers have crossed state lines. It's pushed us off antitrust, and it's going to take the big antipollution cases that are coming up right out of our fucking mouths. Crime, gentlemen, is increasingly political. It's thrown us out of the more apocalyptic riots and raised the bridge on espionage—which admittedly has never been big for us—and it has the potential to squeeze us out of narcotics, to say nothing of the new pattern of conspiracy prosecutions which I see emerging. With all these grass-roots Legal Defense Funds, this could have been the most lucrative fiddle of all.

"Mark my words. As crime turns increasingly against the state and the people get the wind up, all that's going to be left for us poor bastards are the petty thieves, wife beaters and dog poisoners. The chicken stealers—that's our meat. Vagrants. Shit, colleagues, even abortion's legal today. Five and dime, gentlemen, penny ante times, a métier of small potatoes like a little Ireland. In fact, there's some doubt in my mind that even this will be permitted us. As heart wins the battle of history and bail commissions throughout the length and breadth of the land each day secure releases for 'good risks,' we're going to be left with only the two- and three-time losers. You'd do better to take a flier in a Bronx uranium mine. We're dead ducks, fellows, law's dirty old men."

"We know all that," Barney Fetterman said. "We know all that. What do we do?"

Ted Caccerone stood up. He had a Coca-Cola in his hand. There was A-1 sauce on the side of his mouth, and crumbs from the open-faced bun on which his London broil had lain. "We undersell. We cut our fee to seven and a half percent."

"A gas war," Art Klein said, "we'll have a fucking gas war."

"We won't be so quick to shoot," Paulie Shannon said. "Somebody jumps bail on us we bring him back alive, we talk him down like an expert in the control tower, we come on like social workers, we change our hard-guy image."

"We take turns at the courthouse, we draw a number, stand on line, everything courteous. We get rules, choreography. Like in gin rummy the dealer gives the other guy first shot at the face card."

"Who's in?" Adams asked.

"I am," said Shannon.

"Me too," said Klein.

"It'll have to be worked out," Ted Caccerone said, "but I guess I can go along."

"Something has to be done, that's for sure," Walter Mexico said. "Some sort of committee ought to study some of these suggestions we've been hearing, formalize them, and then we can put it to a vote."

"Would you chair such a committee?" Adams asked.

"Sure, why not?"

"Where's the Phoenician?" Barney Fetterman said.

"It's got to be rationalized," C. M. Smith said. "Blunt the competition, is that what we're saying?"

"Just about," said Lester Adams.

"Lapels shouldn't come off in our fingers in the corridor, is that the idea? Okay, who's going to be on the committee?"

"We're the committee," Adams said, "this is the committee."

"Where's that Phoenician?"

"We don't jump the gun," said Paulie Shannon, "we pool our resources. I think it's the only way. I'm glad this is your thinking. I think a lot's been accomplished today."

"But we've all got to commit ourselves to this, that's the important thing. Otherwise it's no good. We've got to behave like brothers. Where's that goddamn Phoenician?"

"That fucker. He's off beating our time."

"He plays Sooner with us we'll wipe him."

"Where *is* the son of a bitch?"

3.

Alexander nods to the guard. The old man frowns, bored as ever. Main notes his shoes, the heavy, cumbersome shoe shape like some pure idea of foot in a child's drawing. The broad black leather facing, a taut vault of hide, a sausage, all its tensions resolved as if ribbed by steel or some hideous flush fist of foot. The shine speaks for itself. There is discipline in it, duty, and he wonders if there is a changing room somewhere where the men polish these stout casings, get them that lusterless, evenly faded black that has no equivalent in nature.

The shoes are made to go with the heavy serge of the uniform, the now formless trousers that may have been formless when new, the long drop to the dark ankles, black themselves, black on black on black, undifferentiated as the cloths in a stage illusion. Alexander wonders if the guard has back trouble, if he soaks his feet in hot salt water. These oiled and bare wood floors, pale as match sticks, faintly dipping, uneven. Marbles set down on them would tumble erratically, collect in some unpredictable pool of gravity. This same force would suck at the man's feet, pulling at them painfully through the solid soles as he stood all day in his area. Alexander senses the old man's crotchets, his distaste for stragglers, his ambiguous desires for female art students whose backs, propelled forward in their chairs, reveal an orbit of the elastic tops of underwear above their blue jeans, sliver of the moon, cantaloupe slice of pantie, square inches of backflesh forgotten behind them in their young concentration like Cinderella's slipper. Does he even see the exhibits? Has he a favorite? Or is his concern only for the glass cases themselves, for whistling, loud talk and no smoking?

As he often does, Main feels an odd envy of the man, of his circumscribed conditions. It suddenly strikes him that the guard is the only person on his Christmas list who is not a lawyer or judge, cop or custodial officer, clerk of the court or prison official. And though the guard gets nothing that Main has especially picked out for him, only the box of good cigars or bottle of Scotch or top-grade Florentine leather wallets bought in bulk for his least important contacts, this makes him, he supposes, his friend. A friendship that is entirely one way, for to the extent that he considers Main at all, the man almost certainly thinks of him as a crank. There must be others, drawn as he is, to this place, or to some other like it. Though Alexander has never seen them, has seen only the schoolchildren and illicit lovers and the vague flirts and lonely, overanxious men.

He loves the cool, big room, its antiquated radiators and old-fashioned exhibit cases, its antiquated space, the corny visual aids, the large type on the yellowing cards by the exhibits. He loves the teeth.

"Afternoon," Main tells the guard.

The man nods and Main steps away from him and goes toward the case. "These specimens," reads the legend, "were obtained from drugstores in the Far East. The apothecaries regarded them as 'dragon's teeth,' no matter what they really were. The teeth shown here probably came from cave deposits in the Karst of South China, for they are like the teeth of the Middle Pleistocene animals found in the region."

He sees the tooth of the giant panda, large as a small seashell, the impression across its broad grinding surface like a curled fetus. Next to it a pair of molars from an orang-utan, the shape and shade of old dice, three deep holes in each like a goblin's face, history throwing a six. There's the dentin of a wild pig, dark as root beer, the pulp chambers in cross section like the white veins in liver. He sees the enormous tooth of a rhinoceros, taking the card's word for it. It does not even resemble a tooth; it is deep, chambered as a lock. In another case there is a comb of kangaroo jaw, four teeth blooming from the bone like cactus.

He moves along a ledge of the extinct, peers at the camel-like jaw of the *Macrauchenia Patachonica*: "a member," says the card, "of the peculiar South American ungulate orders. This genus was camel-like but others were horse-like. Thus the litopterns show parallelism with the more familiar true camels and horses." The keyboard of teeth float in the petrified gum like tulip bulbs. And the lower jaw of a ground sloth, relative of the *Megatherium*, the teeth driven like stakes deep into the bone, all shapes, one a figure eight worn down to the ground, another like a tree stump, a third like a pipe, a fourth with a crown the texture of target cork. The teeth are in terrible disrepair. (They died this way, Alexander thinks, biting their pain.) A root thicker than the wire in a coat hanger rises a full inch above the awful terraces of decay which surround it. There are teeth long and thick and curved as tusks—these were inside a mouth, Main thinks—huge as jai alai bats.

As always, Alexander ignores the skeletons, the carefully wrought xylophonic carcasses, immense scaffoldings of spine, he supposes, from a hundred animals, so that what he sees is some ancient committee of beast he finds it difficult to believe in (though he is fascinated by the individual parts: the shield-like pelvis, the separate vertebrae, long as the hilts of swords, a hinged jaw like the underedge of a key). Comically a megathere squats upright pawing a prop tree, its odd squat like some plantigrade, prehistoric crap. No. It is the teeth. The tiny spines in the skull of a young jaguar, curiously white, sharp as toenail. Skin still adheres to the palate, the concentric tracery distinct and fine as what he touches with his tongue at the roof of his own mouth. It is teeth that he comes back again and again to see, as if these were the distillate of the animal's soul, the cutting, biting edge of its passion and life.

He is thinking in geological time now, in thousands of millions of years—thinking Pre-Cambrian, Cambrian, Ordovician, Silurian, Devonian, Carboniferous, Permian, Triassic, Jurassic, Cretaceous, saddened at the sixty-million-year-old threshold of his own immediate past, Paleocene, Eocene, Oligocene, Miocene, Pliocene, Quaternary. From seaweeds, younger only than the earth's crust, through invertebrate animals, fishes, land plants, amphibians, reptiles, mammals, birds and men. He is weeping.

The guard approaches him. "Are you all right, sir?"

"What? Oh. Yeah," the Phoenician says, "I'm a sentimental old fool." He starts past the guard, his friend.

"I was wondering something," the guard says.

"What's that?"

"Well, it's just that you spend so much time here."

"Yeah, well," he tells the keeper, "I'll tell you why that is. I'm a dentist."

He was late for lunch. (As so often on museum days, his sense of time—he is an early riser, beats others to appointments, brisk as a candidate when it is time for the next, goes late to bed, paper work in the toilet, on the bus home, carrying no brief case but all pockets stuffed with correspondence, pens, notepaper, stamps ready in his wallet—turned tragic, pulling long faces, the past slowing his blood, thickening it, stopping his watch.) He did not even have time to go back to the office.

The bus stop he'd chosen, looking back over his shoulder as he walked from one the two blocks to the next, was outside a drugstore. A woman waited with a shopping bag.

"Missus," Alexander said, "have you been waiting long?"

"About ten minutes."

"Just miss a bus?"

"It was pulling away when I came out of Kroger's."

If he hurried he would have just enough time to call Crainpool.

"Crainpool?"

"Yes, sir."

"What's up?"

"It's been very quiet."

"No messages?"

"The man who was in earlier stopped by."

"What? The mobster?"

"He said Mr. Morgan gave him the slip. He holds you responsible."

"Does he, now? Has there been an afternoon mail?"

"Yes, sir."

"Well?"

"There was nothing from Chile, nothing from Iran." Crain-pool chuckled.

"East Germany?"

"No word from East Germany."

The Phoenician cracks down the receiver so hard that the drugstore clerk looks up at him. Loose, he thinks, fugitives at large—the phrase, as always, chilling, raising goosebumps. He thinks of swamps, caves, passes in mountains. Loose. At large. He thinks of settlements so inland in terrains so forbidding that the inhabitants have no language. The chatter of apes, perhaps, the signals of birds. As always, the idea of such remoteness abstracts his face, neutralizes his features, a sort of paralysis of the attention. People watching him wish to help.

"Is there something you wanted, sir?" the clerk asks. At large, loose.

"Hmn?"

"Is there anything I can get you?" *Loose.*

"What have you got that's binding?" He sees his bus outside and rushes to board it.

They are in Hilgemann's Restaurant at the girl's request. At his they have chosen to remain indoors rather than to dine outside in the beer garden. Though it's warm enough, the long bare vines snaking among the trellis make him nervous. He could never have been a farmer; he is a bailbondsman because he can exercise some control over his crops of criminals, his staggered harvests so nearly continuous that he feels he does not deal in time at all. (His calendars are only a sort of map, like the precinct maps in police stations.) So they are inside, in an Ohio approximation of Bavaria, leashed to reality by the sealed blue hemispheres of Diners Club, American Express's bland centurion and Master Charge's interlocking gold and orange circles decaled on the window like bright postage. He sees airy clubs, spades and hearts between the spindles of the heavy, low-backed captain's chairs, notices the sweet intrusion of a stuffed deer's head —no teeth there—and the elaborate plaster-of-Paris mugs that hang from their handles above the bar and that gravity arranges

in identical angles, a fringe of falling men, with here and there
a lidded pewter beer mug like a tiny hookah or an early, complicated steam engine. Once Herr Hilgemann offered to present
the Phoenician with his own, and to have his name inscribed on
it. "I'm not a joiner," he told him. He sees without appetite the
heavy portions of thick, stringy meats—flank and chuck and pot
roasts, and sanded schnitzels, worms of anchovy curled on them
like springs. Thick gravies wound the table linen. There are con-
structs of pastry, geometric lattices of chocolate, baked bridges
of caramel, fretworks of crust, flake, cherries in cross section
like the intimate slivers of biopsy. Among these moist ruins Main
chews the sandwich he cannot taste; he does not want the fear-
ful cutlery in his mouth, those heavy tines.

He is amazed at the girl's appetite. The lunch, as Miss Krementz might have guessed, is unnecessary; this could have been
handled in the office, or on the phone. He might have asked her,
as he had asked others, to write a composition for him: "Why
I Think ——— ——— Will Not Jump Bail."

He doesn't even feel like explaining it to her. He feels like
taking a nap, like dreaming of fugitives, for though they are his
nightmares, at least in his dreams he is with them, learning their
plans, seeing them in their new settings and fresh disguises.

"All right," he says, and puts down his sandwich. By the time
he is ready to speak he has already decided against her boyfriend.
"Arson's one of the highest bonds there is. It's a very high bond.
You set fire to a building—"

"But he *didn't*."

Alexander shrugs. "You set fire to a building you bring the
insurance companies into it. They're the ones who determine
the prices; not me. I admit it isn't fair. Every sort of minority
pressure group exists in this country, but who gives a second
thought to the arsonist? Fire Power! I'm just thinking out loud."

"His lawyer says we've got to get him out, that there's too
great a presumption of guilt if he stays in before the trial."

"That's true."

"Well, what do you say? Have you made up your mind?"

"I have to give you a test."

"A test."

"It's routine."

"What do I have to do? Hey, wait a minute, I'm not looking for a part in your picture. Don't get any funny ideas."

"What, the crap you eat? You'd blow me out of bed."

"Okay, I just wanted that understood. I'll give you a cashier's check. We'll go to the bank and have it drawn up."

"You have to pass the test."

"I have to pass the test."

"It's a very stupid test."

"All right. Let's get it over with."

"It's not scientific. It isn't for an educated person like yourself."

"Go ahead."

"Actually it's an insult to your intelligence."

"*Try* me, for God's sake."

"How much do you love Mr. Hunsicker?"

"What?"

"How much do you love him? Do you love him a bunch?"

"Certainly. Of course I do."

"A *whole* bunch?"

"Yes. What is this?"

"Oodles and oodles?"

"This is crazy."

"Do you?"

"Yes."

"Show me with your hands."

"With my *hands*?"

"Just spread them out real wide and show me."

She opens her arms. She might be a fisherman demonstrating the length of a large bass.

"That's *all*?"

"No. More. Much more."

"Show me."

She opens her arms so wide Alexander can hear her shoulder blades crack. Her tits come forward into her food.

"That's not so much," he says.

"You're making a fool of me. There isn't any test."

"I can't do it. He's a marked man. Your boyfriend's ruined.
You shouldn't think badly of him. Innocent men are sometimes
lousier risks than guilty. How do I know if he sets fires? I like
the prosecution's case, but that doesn't mean anything; they
could still lose. The thing is, in your boyfriend's state of mind
he doesn't think they will. I saw him. He's very depressed that
this has happened to him. I don't think he'll go the course. Too
much money is involved; it's too big a risk."

"Why did you put me through all this?"

"You got a good lunch, what are you kicking? What did the
other bondsmen's food taste like? You want dessert?"

"I want to get out of here."

"I'll get the check in a minute. No, you were thinking a little
earlier I was trying to put the make on you. I ask you, what
chance would a person like myself have with a girl like you?"

"None. Thanks for the lovely lunch. See you."

"Yeah. My wife is dead, did you know that?"

"I'm sorry to hear that. That's like, you know, tough shit."

"Right. That's just what I told her when we learned she was
dying."

"You really are one dreadful son of a bitch."

"No. What are you saying? What do you know about it?
You want dessert? How about some of that creamy shit with
the nuts?"

"You actually think you can get me to go to bed with you."

"One lunch? You set some value on yourself. I never remar-
ried." She makes no move to leave. Perhaps she thinks he will
still do a deal with her. "I play the field, go with the whores
now and again to get my rocks off. Cincinnati has some lulus. Do
anything for money, some of those girls. Now if one of my
whores died, I'd put money in the jukebox and sit at the bar
with my hat on my head like Walter Winchell."

"You must have loved her very much, your wife," Miss
Krementz says levelly.

"Yes, well, she was very ordinary, very plain. We married
each other in our middle years. You know what I couldn't stand

about being married? The picnics. All those trips to the damn
beach. With the blankets and the towels and the sandwiches in
wax paper. Warm Coca-Cola. Wearing swim trunks. Being barefoot on the pebbles, or the sand in my shoes if I kept them on.
It wasn't any better in the backyard. Stretched out in Bermudas on the folding lawn furniture. I come from a desert people,
a hot culture, sand in my blood like lymph, but it's as if I was
running a temperature the whole time I was married, as if your
Mr. Hunsicker did a job on me with the oily rags. Sweat on
my belly like the fat on soup. My jockstrap was grimy, it gave
me a rash. Sundays. We were together four years but all I
remember are the fucking Sundays. Lounging around. Trying to
figure out things to do, bored at the barbecue and settled at the
fence like a lost ball.

"Not only Bermudas—pajamas. Do you know how much I
hated pajamas by the time it was over? I *like* pajamas, I always
did. Who wants to lie with his great red balls over the place,
with his cock drifting like a weather vane or the needle on a
compass? No, I'm a pajama guy. In motels, hotels, I love a pair
of pajamas. But they have to be starched, they have to be fresh.
I like a crease in them like the morning paper. But when my
wife was living I wore them for a week, a guy who never slept
in the same pajamas two nights running, soiled as handkerchiefs
and smelly as socks.

"I don't know, a year is supposed to have four seasons. I only
recall the heat waves, being uncomfortable, doing stuff I never
wanted to do, that *she* never wanted to do. Nobody could *want*
to do that crap. People need to be comfortable, but you get two
people together and all of a sudden there's got to be plans, activities, you bust your ass figuring new ways to get stuck in the
traffic. Her leukemia went my bail. Now I jerk off or go to the
whores, specialists like the one man in Boston who can do this
terrific operation. Or I give myself a treat and get one of those
pricey call girls from the university. The ordinary is out forever.

"I see guys like me in restaurants—like the two of us here—
old goats with tall blond bimbos with bangs on their foreheads
like a cornice and terrific tans. You wonder, father and daughter? Uncle and niece? Never. They're guys from out of town

with the nerve actually to ask bellboys where the action is. Why am I telling you all this?"

"Why *are* you telling me all this? What makes you think I'm interested in your life?"

"You're not? Don't you want to know how people live? What's the matter with you? What are you, twenty-five years old? How much can a kid like you have seen? You got a fever too? Did Mr. Hunsicker shove wadded newspaper up your ass and spritz it with charcoal lighter? All right, we'll skip the love life. This is how I feel on this fine spring day: like I could only recover with drugs the sense of my possibilities. Like I've never been to the laundry in my life. You eat like a horse and I'm full. This is the reason I asked you to lunch and turned down your buddy's bond. To lay this on you. Now you know some of how I feel. It isn't privileged information; a lot know this much about me. There's more, but I'll spare you. Say, you got any pictures of yourself? You're a beautiful girl. I'd like to have your snapshot. I'll give you four dollars for it."

"You're crazy."

"The hell I am. Crazy people are excited. You think I'm excited? Then I can't have been making myself clear. Listen, I'll tell you something. If we had this conversation yesterday I might have made the bond. Maybe not, maybe yes. Something came up. I crossed a scary man today. I was slipshod. My altiloquent style takes too much energy. I'm the best in the business, but I'm seven thousand years old and slowing down. Also I missed an important meeting with my colleagues. They're planning ways to beat history, natural selection, doing in progress over a suggestion box and London broil in Covington, Kentucky. They think I'm against them. I'm not against them; I'm ahead of them. *London broil!* Those damn fools. They're chewing extinction and don't know it. London broil. A half-hour ride all the way to Kentucky and they eat London broil. And you know why? You want a sign of the fucking times? *Because Kentucky fried chicken ain't been on the menu for years!*"

He took out his wallet, put seven dollars on the plate beside the bill and stood up. "What sign are you? Do they still ask that? What sign are you?"

"Me? Sagittarius."

"Sagittarius, yeah?"

"What sign are you?"

"Pliocene."

The Phoenician put the girl in a taxi. He had the beginning of a hard-on.

Stepping out of the bright cool sunshine, Alexander Main opens the door to his office, jiggling the gay sleigh bells above his door. "Get to work, Mr. Crainpool," he calls out absently to the arm-gartered man. "Get to work, you idle scoundrel. While the cat's away, is it? If you've finished what you were doing, find something else. We don't pay out our good money . . . 'ello, 'ello," he says in his inspector's voice. The mug from Chicago is sitting at his desk. "Who's been sitting in my chair?" the Phoenician asks dully.

"Where's Morgan? What did you tell him?"

"Listen, type, you owe me money. The bail came to something under the five thousand you mentioned."

"Where is he?"

"You want to know where he is?"

"That's right."

"He got away from you?"

"You told him I was outside."

"Let me understand. He got away from you and we're back at square one?"

"Yeah, right."

"Then I'm still on the payroll?"

"Where is he?"

"I'm still on the payroll?"

"You know where he is?"

"Yes?"

"If you can produce him."

"Let's see. The bond came to fifty bucks. Thirty percent for fingering him is another fifteen. That makes it sixty-five dollars I'm owed."

The gangster takes out his wallet and lays two twenties, two tens and a five down on his blotter.

"Very well." He takes the bond agreement from his pocket and shows it to him. "Yes. Municipal court. Room nine. His appearance is in three weeks."

"You're something else, brother." He shoves one of the tens back in his pocket.

"Welsher!" Main shouts. "Do you see, Crainpool, how this soldier contrives to worm out of our agreement? Indian giver!"

"Oh, you're *really* something else," he says. "You're just lucky I'm a professional and that no one's paying me to do you. I don't play benefits. But I'm going to have long talks with my superiors about you. Oh, yes, I'm going to make detailed reports about *you*, Mister." His tone changes and he looks at Alexander with something like surprise. "Fifty bucks? His bond was only fifty bucks? Shit, don't they know anything in this burg?"

"A backwater."

"Okay, bad information. We got this call he was busted and they sent me down."

"What the hell, a day in the country for you."

"Sure, right."

"An outing, a little fresh air. Come back and see us now you know the way."

"Right," he says. "In three weeks."

He goes out.

"Well, Mr. Crainpool, was that exciting enough for you?"

"I've seen better."

"Yes. And you'll see better yet."

"Will I?"

"Twenty-twenty, sir, close calls and closest. Now then, what have you got for me?"

Crainpool points to a calendar. "Tomorrow's the first."

"Yes. I'll call on Avila, I think."

"You're always the one who gets to go out," he whines.

"Yes," I say, "that's the thing about freedom."

Avila's offices are downtown. He is not a criminal but a divorce lawyer, and his place of business reflects this. It is in with the good stores and better office buildings in that three- or four-block section of the city that is our Fifth Avenue.

The day is a reproach to my heart, as though, like all old men on a splendid day, I precede Nature, am there by sufferance, time's professional courtesy. I have left my topcoat behind, but no matter. God sees through me, knows it's only old Alexander Main down there in His high-rent Cincinnati, no boy, no boulevardier, only the sullied Phoenician with sin and history like shit in his gut. God sees through my bright caps, knows what's beneath them, sees right down to the gums, the pink base of my being, the cloudy tracings in which the teeth stand parallel as staves. And under the gums the cementum-sheathed roots hooking bone, seeking wild handhold and purchase like some apraxic mountaineer. God knows my jaws.

Still, here I am. If nothing else my money entitles me. (I have written my will. I am to be buried with my cash. It will line my coffin like salad, so that one day the archaeologists will find me, lightning will strike, the earth move, the state push through a thruway, the new ice age bulldoze me a thousand miles south, scientists of some distant time catalog me, my bones like leftovers in the wormy lettuce of my fortune, Alexander's ragtime bond, gone surety for himself, in on bail. Perhaps, if they still exist, space will be found for me in the case of some future museum, the fingertips of schoolboys on my glass, smudging the watch face of my crystal isolation.) Meanwhile I usurp pleasure from the fine day, shudder in the faint chill of the spring breeze blowing through Cincinnati's Lego boulevards, in our Lego America. Down the big street I go where the skin of one building merges with the skin of the next in Siamese connection, a long Chinese wall of architecture, past an outdoor café with a little low white fence propped on the wide white street like a playpen that must be folded each night and taken in from the weather. Awning shows. As if Cincinnati were a port city, some sailcloth town. A waiter moves in and out among the tables, not in uniform but in a light gray suit, wearing an old boy's tie beneath a vest crisscrossed with watch chain and trophied with the keys of elective societies.

I gaze in at the clean store windows—there's our century's real art, in its window trimming—like sets for a perfected life. I enjoy other people's good taste. Things arc set off, isolated in high fashion's splendid cages—a beautiful desk and beautiful chair off-center in an immense window. In another, on a luscious rug, across the arm of a superb Wassily chair, is a Braemar cashmere, pale green as the open spaces on dollar bills. A kiosk bristles with bright announcement—a Ukrainian dance troupe, Lipizzaner horses, the Black Theater of Prague, the Stones, the Black Watch—the posters projected on the tall cylinder like foreign countries painted on a globe. I am surprised they are printed in English and not French. Even the air smells French—chestnuts, Gauloises and gasoline. Ahead of me a girl steers down the street with her hand deep inside the back of her boyfriend's trousers, using his ass as a tiller.

I pass another sidewalk café. An elegant woman sits beside a man who wears the whitest turtleneck I have ever seen. His cavalry twill trousers are custom-made, bespoke *slacks*. Elbows on the table, the two lean toward each other in intense affinity over their empty coffee cups. I look down to read the message in the crumbs of their brioches on the white cloth, a Morse code of dough and crust. Further on, workmen in ladder trucks lift Easter decorations into the thin trees, long strips of gold foil in light rigid frames, exactly the size and appearance of bedsprings. When I passed here two days ago they were up only to Pogue's Department Store; now they have gone another two blocks, inching their way the long length of the avenue like a golden blight.

I enter the new office block and refer to the huge directory that takes up almost the entire width of one black marble wall. I locate the number of Avila's suite—I have never been here before—and tell the operator I want the eighteenth floor. He stops the car between floors, turns to me and takes a crude wooden box from his pocket. There is a sort of Hawaiian scene painted on it. He is going to show me a magic trick. "You smoke?" Without waiting for me to answer, he lifts the lid and demonstrates that the box is empty; then he opens it again and there are four cigarettes in it. They look stale and have lost tobacco at both ends. He laughs. He has plastic hearing tubes in his ears like tiny drains. "Maybe I get you one of this. Three dollar."

"Say, do that one again."

"You smoke?" He lifts the lid and the box is empty. He opens it again and there are the four stale cigarettes. "Three dollar. I get you one?"

"Nah, it's a trick," I tell him.

Avila's suite of rooms is as much a stage set as the store windows. Behind the façade of the steel and glass skyscraper the architect has contrived dormers, queer shapes to the rooms, here let in and there let out like a suit off the rack. I am eighteen stories above the street, but I could be on the second floor of someone's two-story colonial in the suburbs. On the walls of the anteroom (I have no appointment; the secretary has asked me to wait) are great blown-up photographs, grainy as money, large as flags. The furniture here is not like office furniture at all. I recall the waiter's good suit. It's too much for me—spring, style, the future.

The secretary says I may go in and I head down a corridor like a hallway of bedrooms. Avila greets me outside a door, a man in his mid-thirties, jacketless in black trousers and vest, long lengths of bright white shirt-sleeve dropping through its armholes like acetylene. He shakes my hand and leads me by it into his office—how passive I have become—which looks as if it has been decorated by emptying three or four of those store windows. His desk is a drawerless slab of white marble five feet long and a yard deep on legs of Rhodesian chrome. At the wall to my right is an antique breakfront, old lawbooks behind golden grillwork like a priest crosshatched in a confessional. A cigarette lighter on his desk like a silver brick. A large round standless lamp white as a shirt-front bubbles on the marble, and the carpet, long pelts of creamy wool, has the appearance of bleached floorboard. An eighteenth-century French console table doubles itself against a mirror. Only the chair I sit on is invisible to me. Taste. Taste everywhere. A tasteful office in a city pickled in taste.

Avila does not go behind his desk but takes a seat at the other end of the room in a chair upholstered in nubby handwoven linen. He wears his clothes well. I see him sockless as a Kennedy in wet tennis shoes; I imagine his rich man's articulated ankles. I see him on his low, wide bed, the giant strawberry print of his king-size sheets. I see him pluck parking tickets from the windshield of his sports car; I see him hand them to his secretary to pay.

"Look," he says, "I wasn't expecting you. As a matter of fact, I was just going downstairs for a trim." He has an actor's indeterminate haircut. "The barber's right in the building. Why don't you come with me? We can chat while I'm in the chair."

It's out before I can think. "But it's perfect. Nothing needs to be done to it."

"Oh," he laughs, "appearance is nine tenths of the law. I have a standing appointment with my barber every day at this time. A divorce lawyer depends a lot upon transference. Like a psychiatrist."

We are in the same elevator I have just come up in, but the man who showed me the trick is gone, sucked into history. It bothers me that I will never see him again. I don't know how I know this.

The barbershop is dazzling. Long slabs of yellow Formica jut out the length of one mirrored wall and the width of another like quick-lunch counters in a restaurant. It's a beauty parlor here, bright as a plastic surgeon's consulting room. Boxes of Kleenex, jewelers' trays of combs, dop kits, big pink sponges, blue satin barber sheets, magnums of cologne, an assortment of brushes with tufts sleek as swatches of mink and chinchilla, a definitive collection of Band-Aids, eyebrow pencils like the city desk at *Women's Wear Daily*. There are laquers, shallow dishes of tint, a stand of Q-Tips upright in a clear box like a forest above the snowline. There are nests of wig, surgical adhesive, pots of mascara, blushers, eyelash curlers set on their sides and curving into each other like spoons in a service for eight. There are logjams of emery board, hot stringents and cold creams, fingernail clippers like tools in a surgery. Triple strands of fluorescent tube marquee the mirrors. I am excited here: I wish I could smell the lotions and shampoos and suddenly I lift a Max Factor pan stick and lick it with my tongue as if it were a kid's push-up ice cream.

Avila sits amused and content in a barber chair and a woman in white slacks makes a few passes at him with her scissors and comb. As she steps back to appraise him, I accuse him of his handsomeness; I tell him that his bone structure is his fate.

"What? No. I am very nondescript."

I see myself caromed off the mirrors, fractured in space like a break shot in pool. I see the checkered reflection of my checkered jacket. It is expensive, even new, but it is gross. I have no taste, only hunger. I have never been fashionable, and it's astonishing to me that so much has happened in the world. The changes I perceive leave me breathless. I am more astonished by what remains to happen. I have erratic, sudden premonitions of new packaging techniques—breakfast cereal in spray cans, insulated boxes of frozen beer, egg yolk in squeezable tubes. Avila's barber sheet could be a shroud. I can't stand looking at myself, so I pop into an empty chair at Avila's side.

A barber sets his newspaper aside. He approaches me. "Haircut?"

"Leave me be," I say too loudly. "Can we talk here?" I ask Avila.

"Of course we can," he tells me mildly.

" 'Of course we can.' Counselor, counselor, what a style you have! Yes, I like it. Niggerizing the neighborhood, spilling confidence like soup." Going on the offensive shakes off a little of my passivity. "What a professional ethic you got there! 'Can we talk?' 'Of course. What, is it a public library that we should lower our voices?' Right. Smell that fart? *I* claim that. That came out of Alexander's ragtime asshole, Main's brown bellows. Why should I deny the obvious? No two men's farts smell alike in the entire universe. Like snowflakes and fingerprints. Learned counsel's point is well taken. We can talk here."

"What are you on about?"

"Yes, well, we never did business till now, or you'd know my thoroughness, my eye for detail, my fastidious methods. I take more pains than aspirin. Tomorrow is April first, lest we forget."

"Yes?"

"Yes. Withers is to appear in court." I raise my voice so that everyone in the shop can hear. "*That's Withers, the banker. Eugene Withers who could not make good on his alimony payments of twenty-five hundred dollars a month and who was thirty thousand dollars in arrears when our paths crossed in the courts. Eugene Withers, the president of Ohio First Federal Savings Bank, lest we forget. Incidentally, if any of you barbers, manicurists or shoeshine guys do business with him I would suggest a small run on his bank. Pass it on. Withers.*"

"What's the matter with you?" Avila says. "Where do you think you are?"

"He's not in town."

"Well, he's probably upstate on business. Why don't you wait for me in my office?"

"You know this for fact that he's upstate on business? I'm not his ex-wife. I have no fond memories of President Withers in bed to tide me over while the arrears pile up. I call and call his bank. 'Not here,' they say, 'we'll take a message.' Where upstate is he? I'll put in a little person-to-person."

"Charleen, call the guard, please," Avila tells his barber. "I want this man out of here."

"The guard? Call the guard? Charleen, dear, guards are my bread and butter. From baby sitters to electrocutioners, they're all in my pocket, Charleen. Andy Frain stood up at my wedding. Call, call him, we're old friends. Now, lawyer, the man's trial is tomorrow. I want to be there to meet his train, his boat, his private plane. If he doesn't show, I'll look him up. See my gun? You want me to make him an April Fool?"

"You'd better leave, I think."

"You give me a number where I can reach him."

"I'll see to it that your license is revoked."

"*My* license? How are you going to do that? How are you going to revoke carte blanche? You think the system's an Indian giver? Listen, LL.D., you could be disbarred easier. Poor Withers. Twenty-five hundred a month. Some lawyer. Twenty-five hundred a month for a broad who went down on every depositor in Ohio First Federal Savings. She gave it away to every guy who opened an account. *In all the branches.* Or are you talking

about my license for the gun? I got papers on it like a natural-
ized citizen or the warrantee on your toaster. I got instruments
for it like General Eisenhower's honorable discharge."

The man stares at me; he's never seen such a performance in
all his fancy practice. But suddenly I have run out of steam. I
finish lamely. "Make sure he's around. See to Withers."

In the lobby I wait for each of the elevators to appear. I
promise myself that should the old man be in one of them I will
buy his trick, but the man is gone.

Back on the street. He's tired. He's made very little money for
a Monday. It's late, but not late enough to call the desk ser-
geants. When *is* the best time to call? Midnight when they've
closed the books? *Too* late. The others will have skimmed the
cream. The only sure thing would be to buy all the desk ser-
geants, but that would be prohibitive. Best to make it almost a
social call, work it that way. Too much money shouldn't change
hands. If bondsmen had a trade journal I'd write a paper on it.
This afternoon in Covington they voted to cooperate. Threats
were made in my absence. My little leverage is leaking.

The street has changed. Not so much money here, not as much
taste, but even more style. The shops burst with an egoism of
the present tense, the bright letters of the bright wood signs
molded in a sausage calligraphy like those quick, clever strokes
that leg and backbone animals in balloon-blowing acts. Or black,
no capitals, a svelte, spare geometry of case. He remembers these
shops, could tell you stories, recalls like a perfect witness their
former, failed incarnations. The woman's shoe store, Bootique,
was once Kefauver's campaign headquarters, then a bookie joint
with empty cigar boxes and tire irons half-heartedly showing
form's flag in a casual, lip-service hypocrisy in the front window.
After that nothing at all for a time—though once, initially, Ty-
son's Liquors, as he still thinks of it, really. Most of the shops
won't last the year. But never till now, the witness thinks, so
uniform, locked into style's faddish contagion, a terminal domino

theory. What discrepancies he perceives between will and doom, these tenants' signs like life's campaign buttons. He looks for reasons but sees only the irrational, a self-conscious hedonism. The signs, these shops, this business and that enterprise, this landscape, seasonal as the pictures on one of his calendars, are all jokes. The toy shop, with its expensive Creative Playthings and Chinese boxes and big stuffed animals and folk dolls and folk tops and folk sticks and folk hoops and folk balls and miniature green and black boilers of real steam engines for curator kids who never existed, is called—in rainbow letters, yes, it *is* the rainbow sequence: yellow catching green, green blue and so on, on the glass—"Kinder Garden." And the butcher shop, sawdust on the floor like cereal and the butchers in boaters, and skinned, unrefrigerated rabbits, plucked chickens and carcasses upside down on hooks that could hold coats, is "The Meating House." A fabric shop: "Knits and Bolts." An Italian restaurant: "Pizza Resistance." "Sole Food": a fish 'n chips. "Diaspora Travel." A head shop: "Headquarters." A cinema: "The Last Picture Show." "Save Face": a beauty parlor. A health food store: "Mother Nature's." "The Basic Premise": a realtor. A carry-out chicken place: "Marcho Pollo." "Rock 'n Roll": a lapidary and bakery. A tie shop: "Get Knotted." A rug store: "Underfoot." "*Cap-tain's Courageous*": a men's hat shop. A watch repairman's: "Time Out." "Howard Johnson's." (How the hell did that get there?) Even a small moving company: "Gutenberg's Movable Types."

They spoke of the breakdown of law and order, of crime in the streets, but what a discipline was in these streets, what a knuckling under and catering to the times. It is beyond his capacity to conjure up the future, he cannot even imagine what the safety razors will look like twenty-years from now, or a snow shovel. He passes a drugstore and sees a sign on the window: "Established 1961." He laughs before he realizes that it is no joke. If it were a question of just this one neighborhood— but it isn't; it's spread now even to the shopping centers, even to the ghettos. In his own area—"Alexander Main, Licensed Bail-bond Broker"—he has seen wide-windowed tour buses, the sightseers' attention close-order-drilled by the tour guide. What can they be looking at? Survivors for a lousy generation and a half? In history already? So soon? He's not young. He's seen good times and bad, but never times like these, time itself doing in a season what once it had taken a decade to accomplish. Shall he get paint? Send Crainpool to the window with a brush? Have him paint in . . . what? "Bail Out?" "I Been Working on the Bailbond?" "A Surety Thing?" It's as if he lives trapped in the neck of an hourglass. Style, he thinks. As a young man he wanted it, hoped that when he wakened it would be there like French in his mouth. Now he sees it as a symptom of a ruinous disease.

He needs sleep, a nap. He pushes past the strollers and lovers and shoppers—it's past three, the high school kids are out, the students from the university are—moving in the garishly dressed crowd like someone hurrying down an escalator. He brushes the arm of a young man in an ordinary white shirt with a master sergeant's chevrons sewn to the sleeve. He dodges a girl in an ammunition belt, kids in flags, yarmulkes, the girls braless, their nipples erect, puckering their T-shirts as if they moved in per-petual excitation, the genitals of the young men askew, crushed packages in their tight jeans, both sexes horny, literally, their sex antlered inside their binding clothes. He sees colors which till now have never been printed on cloth. He sees all the good-looking young who seem some new species in their furred shoes, their boots, bags suspended from the shoulders of the young men, oddly courierizing them. The girls in pants, the ground rounds and roasts of their behinds, the lifting tension of their crotches making it appear as if they are actually suspended in their trousers, like parachutists perhaps, sunk in them up to their hips and the small of their backs. There is something strangely military about this crowd. Perhaps it is the stripy patterns of their clothes, like the tricolors of decorations.

The Phoenician yawns and a young man turns to him. "Hey uncle, I dig your sport coat."

"What, this?"

"No, it's nice."

"You think this is nice? You should see my doorman's uniform."

"You got a doorman's uniform? Wow."

"Yeah, well my daughter's getting married Sunday and I'm giving her away."

"Getting *married*? No shit?"

He talks to him as if asleep. (So accustomed am I to chatter, to giving as good as I get, coming on strongest, dialogue alive on my teeth like plaque. How long has it been since I've had a conversation? A long time. Since my wife died.)

He spots a taxi rank—black, right-hand-drive Austins imported from London: "Guv's Taxi Company, Ltd."—and goes over to the first cab, gets in and sinks back into the leather seat.

"Cor blimey, Guv, where to?"

He does not want to return to the office, does not want to go home. "Take me," he says, inspired, "to a swell hotel."

A doorman opens the cab for him and he steps out, pays the driver, goes through the revolving doors and checks in. He remembers he has no pajamas and asks the room clerk if there's a men's store in the hotel.

He tells the salesman he takes a D.

"Any particular style, sir?"

"Crisp. Linen. Crisp."

He pays for the pajamas and returns to the desk to pick up his key.

"Luggage, sir?"

He holds up the new pajamas. The clerk hesitates. "What do you want? You want me to pay in advance? What's the damage?" He looks down at the card he has just signed. "Twenty-eight bucks? Here." He pushes the bills toward the man who at first does not pick them up. "What is it, you think I'm a troublemaker, a suicide? Furthest thing from my mind. Gimme my key. Gimme my key or I'll get the manager." The clerk extends the key and a bellboy steps forward. The Phoenician puts his hand in his pocket, takes out a dollar and gives it to the bellboy.

"Save you a trip," he says and, holding his new pajamas, moves off in the direction of the elevators.

He loves a hotel room. This one is large, new. He is on the twenty-third floor. Through the wide clean Thermopane he can see the ball park, the clipped chemical grass, bright, glowing as emerald, green as eyeshade, has a perfect view into the stadium's open skull, the variously colored stands folded like nervous system along its sides. Cincinnati beneath him like a crescent of jawbone, the buildings dental, gray as neglect, the Ohio juicing the town like saliva. It is a corner room and commands the south and west; he can see Kentucky. He does not draw the drapes, bunched tight, coiled on a recessed track that runs along the ceiling above the windows, pleats on pleats in a loose reserve, a collapsed bellows of fabric. The blue drapes match the blue bedspread which looks as if it has never been used—looks new, as everything in this room does: the deep modern chairs, webbed as baseball gloves and with seats like the pockets in catchers' mitts, the two-foot-high cherrywood strips set into two beige walls textured as taut canvas, the aluminum grill of the heating and air-conditioning unit flush with the top of the long window seat by the enormous western wall of glass. He admires the desk (of the same smooth cherrywood) that levitates against a wall, its drawers suspended, hanging in air like holsters. He sits in the red low-backed chair and moves his lap into position beneath the desk, opening a drawer, seeing with satisfaction the stack of thick white stationery, the golden logotype of the letterhead, the two ballpoint pens, the yellow Western Union blanks. He clears the menu, textured and greasy as a playing card, from the surface of the desk, removes the tented cards that announce check-out time and give instructions about the operation of the TV, and places them in a drawer beside the treated shoe-polishing cloth and folded paper laundry bag with its tough kite string and green laundry ticket, a framed gum reinforcement hole at the top. He trails his fingers in the pile of brochures, shuffling them like a magician preparing a card trick. He closes the drawers which move back silently along their grooves. On the right the smooth wooden desk—the wood in this room does not feel like wood, it is level as glass—becomes a chest of drawers, then a treaded slab on which to place suitcases. There are five lamps in the room: on the desk, on the chest, beside his bed, on a low white table; a chrome floorlamp with a tall narrow shade. The television swivels on a chrome stem before the southern window. He turns it on, and from his bed the figures on the screen seem to stand in the sky. He reaches over to the control panel—there is an electric clock, a radio, a speaker like a patch of brown canvas, rows of switches, buttons—and clicks it off. He walks into the bathroom, sees plastic jewel cases of soap, towels of different size and thickness like a complicated terry-cloth cutlery or a pantry of flag. He runs his hand along the rail angled like the trajectory of a banister above the tub, and touches the beautiful basin with its queer fittings. Like a dignitary cutting a ribbon, he tears the paper strip that packages the toilet seat. He pees long and hard into the bowl, drilling his urine solidly into the faintly blue water.

He loves a hotel room.

I love a hotel room. This is in my blood. Oasis in my Phoenician genes, way station in my ancient heart.

He returns to the bed and picks up the phone by the nightstand, first pulling out the tray at the base of the phone to study the information on the card there. He dials.

"Room service? Mr. Main in two-three-four-one. How late do you serve? . . . Excellent . . . No, nothing now, thank you. I may get hungry around three this morning."

He dials a different number. "Is this the housekeeper? . . . Housekeeper, if I should want some laundry done, could you . . . What? . . . Oh, I want the valet, do I?"

"Valet? Have you same-day service? . . . What about dry cleaning? . . . Thank you very much, valet."

"Message desk? Are there any messages for Mr. Main in two-three-four-one? . . . Yes, dear, would you please? . . . The red light? Where might that be? . . . Yes, I see it . . . No, it *isn't* flashing. I thought it might be broken. Could you test it, please? . . . Yes, there it goes now. What's the message?"

And the bar and the garage and the Avis desk. He makes inquiries about a baby sitter and calls the cashier and asks about cashing a check. He finds out, too, that he can leave his watch and valuables in the hotel safe.

Then he dials nine-nine. "Who," he asks, "is the house doctor? . . . I see. Can you tell me anything about him? . . . Well, like where did he intern? . . . Could you find this information out and call me back? Or leave a message with the message desk? Or give me his room number and I'll do it myself . . . Isn't that nice, we're on the same floor."

He calls the doctor. The man has interned with the Sheraton chain.

And one last call. "Operator, this is Alexander Main in two-three-four-one. I want to leave a call for seven A.M. . . . Thank you. Goodnight to you, too, sweetheart." It is not yet four in the afternoon.

He did not ring up for theater tickets or dial the florist. He didn't call the hairdresser or ring 32 to request a Remington shaver or 64 to find out about an interpreter. He didn't put a call through to rail and air reservations or to the hall porter to inquire about kenneling his pet. He never rang the secretarial service. But he was reassured that these services and others were available, that he sat in his room linked, hooked up as a President to his needs, oddly loved, certainly trusted, his cash and checkbook and cards like letters of credit to the world. He could have anything he wanted—carpenters to build him boxes, models from stores to show him new fashions, women, passport photographers, even locksmiths. He was totally self-contained, desert-islanded but not deserted, certainly not lonely, his options open, more dilated here than at home or at work or in the street. How silly of the hotel to call him its guest. His credit established he was something far more privileged and potent.

In this mood he showered, not bothering to close the stall, careless of the water he deflected against the mirrors and walls, of the puddles he made on the tiled floor. Private, possessed by his privacy. In this mood rubs himself dry with the enormous bath towel and leaves it crumpled in a heap beneath the sink, takes one by one the pins from his new pajamas, their odor of freshness like the smell of health, their new resins like a pollen of haberdash. He draws the drapes, touching them, feeling their heavy, opaque lining, pulling them so tight that it might be a half-hour beyond dusk instead of barely four o'clock. He goes to the door to leave his shoes in the corridor for the porter to polish, already anticipating the morning when he will hook them in like a croupier. He removes the bedspread, tosses it in a corner, feels the cool bleached sheets, white as letterhead, the soft blanket. He sleeps. I sleep. He dreams. I dream.

4.

He smells the gold before he sees it, a vague, involuntary pinch of nostrils, some pepper reflex. He feels the gold before he sees it, coarse-grained as the friction strip on a matchbook. He tastes the gold, warm, faintly curried, greasy as magnets, drawing his tongue like a poultice, carbonating his saliva. He *hears* the gold, its hum of precious engined molecules, its rare hiss just beyond range. It must be all around him. Its heaviness thickens the air, himself, stranding his stance, sucking at his legs and feet like ground beside a precipice.

He hears noises, hopes it is animals, knows it is men. No one has actually said anything. (It is this silence which is so minatory. Animals, forgetting themselves, would chatter.) He hears —what? Exploration. The silences presiding decision. Then a stone shoved against, the pressure of a shoulder against a wall, its resettling like elastic relaxing to its neutral length. Then taps, randomly scientific, reasoned, and shortly abandoned, a fury of the indiscriminate and something giving way, some rolled stone blossoming sesame; the source of the sounds abruptly shift, ventriloquized, higher, further off. But he takes no comfort from this, for if the noises are now more different, they are more

regular too, the scuffle gone out of them, and he hears . . . foot-
steps. And their proximity again adjusts.

He knows where he is—in some payload of labyrinth, maze's
choice darkmeat like the eye of a hurricane—and that he is
subterranean, in some architectonic cul-de-sac, an archipelago
of walls and red-herringed ectopic space. He pictures the stone
baffles and barricades, the inverted, earthen, conical screw of
tunnel, wedges and bottlenecks and groins of space, all the false
spurs, all the difficult dark. And through it all he hears them,
now far, now near, unraveling the puzzle of place as if they
were walking along a map, taking no confidence when momentarily he thinks he hears them where he has heard them moments before. Soon they are close enough for him to distinguish
their tools, their levers and scrapers and mallets and spades, and
to hear, too, in the aftermath of their progress, a queer dragged
rustling. Then hears seals popping, stone scraped, wooden beams
lifted and shoved back along grooves, some final hammering and
the adjustment of stone tumblers in some huge lock. It is as if
he hides in a hollow—the linchpin center, say, of a cube puzzle
on a counter in a drugstore.

He sees their light before he sees them, refracted, rolling off
the walls like a sand dune, breaking like a wave, caught, con-
firming as it comes the gold surfaces he had smelled, felt, tasted
and heard before he had seen. He calls out, "Don't hurt me.
I'm your bondsman." They keep coming. They are here.

In addition to the dish of blazing oil one of them carries, they
have brought torches, and these they now ignite, planting them
in standards already there. The torches mitigate the gloom, but
it is the contents of the chamber which dispel it, laserizing the
light, unfurling it like flags in wind and flinging down impression in a brilliant tattoo.

"Can you see anything?" one asks.

"Yes," says the other, "wonderful things."

Their first impression is aesthetic, then, the Phoenician thinks.
He stands beside the tomb robbers, sharing their awe. It gives
him a queer feeling. No criminal himself, this is the first time
he has ever been tempted. He's a little nauseous. Yet he is

thrilled, privileged; something stupendous is about to happen. This is what he sees:

First the giant sarcophagus, the carniverous stone high as a man and long and wide as a car, a goddess in nude profile at each corner—Isis, Nepthys, Neith and Selkit—their arms spread like traffic cops', their hands almost touching, death's and state's holy ring-a-rosy, an electric net of intersecting wings stretched like necklaces between them. Articulated tiers of carefully wrought scales and feathers hang from their armpits and along their outstretched arms, and bloom behind their breasts and cunts and asses like webs. Hieratic columns are etched behind these like sums in a foreign mathematics. The Phoenician squints but cannot read them, can make out only water fowl and horse, owl and implement, musical instruments, boat and bowl and fish and wheat, and an incoherent zigzag of joined m's like an illegible signature or a level lightning. He is furious with himself. This is how he has felt staring into museum cases.

There is architecture on the walls, chemistry, astronomy. White Osiris sits on a throne in the air beneath a high hat like a bowling pin. Anubis, the black-headed jackal, stands behind him, resting a red, avuncular hand on his shoulder while bird-faced Horus looks on. Two of the gods trail hairdos like the comb of a cock.

One thief points to a wall; the other walks up to it and rubs his hand along a gilt bas-relief of two figures, a man and a woman, who sit in profile on a couch. The man clutches a sheath of arrows in his hand like a batter in a batter's box, the woman a small fan of arrowheads. The tomb robber fondles the woman's headdress.

"Geez," says this perfectly ordinary, human young man, no ghoul or monster but only one of the locals seen everywhere around Thebes and Karnak and Luxor these days, with none of the vandal's malice or nonconformist's zeal, out of work perhaps, for these are hard times, the slaves getting all the plum jobs, having the construction trades sewn up—and welcome to it, too, he thinks. The Phoenician notices something funny with one of the man's hands. It's clear he can be no apprentice to an artisan, and to judge from his sharp, cheap, city clothes there is nothing of the farmer about him. "It's like it was knit right there on the wall or something."

"Come on, don't stand there gawping or I'll have your guts for garters. We've got work to do," says the first, an older man, the pro in the outfit, the Phoenician thinks, down from played out Giza or Saqqara probably, or Heliopolis, lured by rumors of these new untapped fields in the south—maybe an escaped slave's drunken tale, confirmed by a primitive, illiterate map drawn by the slave himself, who may even have been killed for it, for this one looks a tough customer. Yet there's something dedicated about him as well. Tough as he is, he was just as taken aback by that first sight of the tomb, his dry runs through the reamed ruins of Imhotep's masterpiece or his posed tourist attitudes at the sites of the crumbling mastabas not having prepared him for anything like this.

No. All he'd been truly prepared for (treasure being merely a concept to one who'd stood in plenty of treasure houses but had seen no treasure, or seen it only piecemeal, behind ropes in public rooms or flashing by quickly in a parade, or seen it only as a proposal, looking over a shoulder at the draftsman's roughs and sketches on a drawing board; real collective treasure, a Pharaoh's fortune, being just something one has heard of in rumors, third- and fourth-hand accounts that lost detail and sank deeper into wild myth each time they passed from mouth to mouth, as geography is merely a concept to one who has never traveled) were the architect's mazes and torils and culs-de-sac, the dim blind alleys and traps and suckers' avenues that led nowhere and kept him busy till the sun came up and the hired priests that guarded the tombs were flashed into wakefulness. Such impediments had turned him into the scout or hunter or Indian he was preparing himself to become by forcing him to discriminate between the real spoor and the counterfeit, testing himself in each of Lower Egypt's violated pyramids, hanging back, then straying from the rest of his party who rushed forward with the guide to view the now empty storerooms and holy chambers and chapels where the Pharaoh's painted double stood in mimic life in the picture-book rooms viewing his faded family album, fooled into feasting on images of food, hunting cartoon deer and fishing cartoon fish from cartoon rivers, copulating with cartoons and waiting for the dead man's soul to invade the ka's body like a virus. (And perhaps it *could* have happened, except that the tomb robbers always got there first, breaking the chain of expectation, spoiling eternity with the fierce needs of the present.) Hanging back from the rest of his party to wander those useless funhouse corridors and minefield spaces, an illiterate who has trained himself to read a stone's insincerity, a musician of structure with perfect pitch for the false note, who fell to this place like water guided by gravity or a magnetized needle ignoring every direction but north.

"We'll do the amphoras first," the older tomb robber says.

"The amphoras?"

"Those big alabaster jugs. Come on, have you got the waterskins?" The rustling I heard, thinks the Phoenician. "All right, give them here. Tip it. Careful, careful, you're spilling it." The Phoenician smells the precious perfumes, sees a glowing prism on the floor of the tomb, a puddle of spilled perfume reflecting light from the burning torches. It smells of the colors themselves, of red and yellow and blue and all the declensions of the spectrum, and is trampled by the first thief's sandals so that it looks as if he is standing in a broken, burning nimbus. "Tip it back. I'll get the other waterskin ready."

"Why mess with this stuff? It'll only weigh us down. Let's just take what we came for and clear off."

"I'm the one who decides what we came for. You're just the bearer. What do you know about the traders in Rosetta and Avaris? A Pharaoh's unguents and liquors, that's what's wanted. Tip the other one."

"This one's heavy. It's too heavy."

"Get your back into it. Shove, shove. Heave ho."

"It's too heavy, I tell you."

"Here, hold the skin. I'll try. Woof, you're right; it *is* heavy. All right, we'll just have to go into it. Hand me the iron bar. Give me the mallet. I'll tap this fucker like a maple tree." The older thief kneels and fixes the sharp end of the bar halfway down the length of the tall cask. "Move that standard over," he snaps, "I can't see what the hell I'm doing."

The second thief moves a candelabra of torches to within a yard of the kneeling tomb robber. Behind the sarcophagus a wall shines suddenly, and the Phoenician can see a panel decorated with the twelve sacred baboons of the night. They sit on their brown, swollen genitals as on basketballs, decorous and pacific as ladies on seats in public toilets. Silver furred over their blue bodies and silver banged above their long doggy profiles, they contemplate symbols that look like the detached slides of slide trombones. There are black squares, brown, brown and black moons like slivers of overturned melon, silhouettes of thick cleavers, pairs of pillars in the same black and brown alternatives, a mysterious geometric alphabet, dark herons, one-legged chiaroscuro runners and odd wingless fowl that float in long vertical columns like figures in strange bankbooks.

What's going on here, the Phoenician wonders, for whom fine print and subordinate legal clause, loophole and condition and contractual exigency are as clear and straightforward as the exit signs on superhighways. Then he sees the fine translucent alabaster vessel with its gorgeous banded layers—teeth and checks and regiments of painted slaves, friezes of pumpkin and rows of something like nails in colors he has never seen and does not recognize but which remind him of vast latitudes of campaign ribbon. It is here, just beneath the first buxom curve of the high jug, that the first tomb robber means to make the puncture.

"Spread the lip on that skin wide as you can. Here, stand right here, we want to catch as much of this gism as we can. I'll try to do the hole clean but the goddamn thing may shatter. Whatever happens don't let the flame anywhere near this shit or we'll go up like sunshine."

The Phoenician moves against a wall, his back, he imagines, grazing the strange painted symbols. He feels an odd warmth through the cloth of his shirt. Is it brown craftsmen in white kilts preparing funerary furniture, sawing wood, one man holding the piece steady while the other leans toward him awkwardly, his saw extended like the bow of a cello? Long-eared Anubis in his jackal's head bending over the mummy on its couch, touching the chest, making the embalmist's final adjustments like someone straightening a pal's tie? Osiris, fastidious as a hostess, checking the offerings on the dead man's table, the decoy food and painted drink? The wailing, grieving women of the house, their breasts bared, arms raised in a semaphore of grief, dust on their heads and in the limp springs of their hair? His flesh takes their electric impression.

"Get ready to catch the juice. It'll come out like high tide."

He makes one deft, powerful stroke. The thick shaft goes in neat as a needle, but he was wrong to have worried about the flow. The amber liquid, whatever it is, is viscous, slow and thick as glue. It comes in measured plops, filling the chamber with a sweet sick smell, the odor of vital essence, a human butter lined with brine and the scraped, rendered slimes and marrows. A Pharoah's liquors indeed, stuff of his godhead, ejaculatory final ethers. The Phoenician and the two tomb robbers reel and sway in a sort of instant drunkenness that sobers as it stuns.

"Wow," says the kid, "those Rosetta and Avaris traders must be cuckoo. Who'd want this crap around?"

The older man giggles. "Collectors, man. Souvenir hounds. First editioners. That lot."

"One sip and you're dead."

"They don't drink it, fool; it ain't any apéritif. They put it in their cellars with the rest of the hard stuff." He dips his finger into it and holds it under his nose for a second. "A very good dynasty. *Yech.*" He wipes his hand off on his clothes. "There, that's enough, close the skin, plug it. I've got to stuff something into this bunghole or the smell will put us out." Closest to the source, the older tomb robber starts to gag. "Quick, get me a rag, a strip of that weave. Over there. On top of that chest in the treasury. Hurry up, will you?"

"That's no rag. That's cloth-of-gold. That's priceless."

"I'm puking my guts out and the connoisseur here gives me an estimate. Stand aside, I'll get it myself." He gropes toward the chest, stumbles over a low couch, blunders momentarily against the brake on a golden chariot which skitters across the floor and crashes into a wall. Recovering his balance he rips the cloth from the top of the chest, knocking a gilded alabaster statuette of the king to the stone floor and shattering it.

"You got good moves," the other tomb robber says. "Jesus."

"Forget it. Just plug that hole so we can get to work." The young tomb robber shrugs, crumples the cloth and stuffs it into the amphora's open wound. It protrudes from the hole, a golden run of gut. The Phoenician thinks of the gold weave sopping up the Pharaoh's sublime jams and gravies, an inside-out alchemy that turns gold to dressing. But the smell is stanched and the air clears. What little lies uncollected on the floor is defused when the second tomb robber thinks to pour some of the perfume from the first waterskin over it. "You didn't use too much, did you?" the older thief asks.

"A couple drops. We can fill her up again from the first whatdoyoucallit, amphora."

"Okay. Go ahead, pour. Hold it, that's got it. Good man. Here, set these skins in the antechamber where we can pick them up again when we leave." They seem pleased to discover that they can cooperate. With a lift of his chin the second tomb robber indicates a gold life sign like a giant key ring that lies on a funerary chair. The older man nods, the kid scoops it up to place with the waterskins in the antechamber, and then both of them simultaneously rub their hands together. They are giddy with greed, high on their mutual visions of untapped plunder, their initial reserve and caution turned by their preliminary success. They know that they are already rich men. They move through the tomb expansively, magnanimous as high rollers.

"The crowbars?" the second tomb robber suggests.

"Crowbars it is," says the first. "No, not that. Use this." He strides up to the sculpted, life-size double and wrenches the shepherd's crook from where it rests like a riding crop on a ledge of hip and along a rail of upturned palm.

"That's class," the second says. "Is it real gold, you think?"

"Thirty three thousand-karat."

They start the short stroll to the sarcophagus, but their initial jauntiness fades as they approach. They come up to it much as they might to a living Pharaoh, tentative, as if each hides behind his own presence, concentrating, queerly chaste, made innocent by the magnitude of the violence they are about to do.

They move silently toward opposite ends and silently raise their tools to the sealed lid. The older man seeks a purchase for the flat wedge of his crowbar, tilts at the seam experimentally, pumping in brief arcs as he would prime a tire jack. It slips out and the second thief swears.

"Easy, old son. This ain't no beer can."

"Let me try."

"No, hold on. I'm not even budging it. You come on over to my side. Maybe if we both try." The second thief stands behind the first, gets a grip on the long handle as if he were holding a rope in a tug of war. "When I give the signal, push in and up."

"Wait up," the young one says, "I better wipe my hands first. They're all slippery from that Pharaoh grease. Okay. What we really need is a block and tackle."

"We ain't got any damn block and tackle."

"What's this stuff?"

"I don't know—yellow quartzite probably. You set? Push . . . in and *up*."

"No good. It's like trying to drive a spike with your bare hands."

"Get the mallet."

"Are you kidding? It'd take months to chisel a hole in that thing with the mallet. Why don't you give it a karate chop?"

"Shut up. Give me a minute to think."

The boy, satirically deferential, retires to a throne chair from which he first removes a small ivory casket. He puts it on the floor and props his feet on it. "I don't know," he says, "we've already got more than *I* ever bargained for. There must be half a million bucks worth of junk right in this casket I'm resting my tootsies on. Why don't we just grab what we can and scarper?"

But if the first thief has even heard him he gives no indication. He is walking around the sarcophagus, touching it here, tapping it there, looking for invisible levers. He is the complete cynic who has trained himself all his life to think in an idiom of Achilles vulnerabilities. He simply does not trust walls. He has a cryptographer's imagination. In his fingers there is a touch for weak link like a blind man's for Braille. He is a piano tuner of a man who in some other age or different circumstances might have found the Northwest Passage or the source of the Mississippi. He makes his slow, halting circuit of the sarcophagus. "It's bonded solid," he says.

"Yeah," says the second tomb robber, "I could have told you that. Let's scarper, mate."

"But it's still on its original platform."

"Its original platform."

"Look down here. See? The nine inches at the bottom are gilded wood. They must have moved the thing in on rollers, then pulled the rollers out and left it."

"No shit," the kid says wearily, "so that's how they did it. The pyramids, now that's some engineering feat. I mean when you think of the unsophisticated equipment they had. And all the patience..."

"We brought a file. Get the file." The second tomb robber rises lazily, pokes around in the small pile of tools, finds the file and hands it without interest to the older man. "Bring that torch, hold it down here so's I can see. I want to study the paint . . . Yes . . . No, a little closer. Watch it, don't singe me . . . Yeah, see there, where the gilt bunches like badly hung wallpaper? That's the fault line. That's where the wood's rotting. Where's that mallet? All right."

And he drives the file into the dead center of the dead wood, where it sinks like a knife into tender meat. Stretched out on the floor and working at arm's length, he chips away like a sculptor at the rotting wood. But the file is only a foot long, the sarcophagus wide as a car. He sends the blunt end of the crowbar in after it, pounding at the boxcar connections, trusting as always in the mushy physics by which he lives, the leading edge of the file to be deflected by whatever is hard in there and drawn to whatever is soft. He calls for the second tomb robber's crowbar and fits its blunt end to the protruding wedge of his own. He works in this way for more than an hour—a file, an iron, an iron, the ka's shepherd's crook and the mallet—and is almost through to the other side, but not quite, when he runs out of tools.

"Now what?" the kid asks.

"The bunghole. Bleed me a quart of that stuff. Fetch it in one of those vases."

The older robber takes the substance and butters it along the leading edge of the platform. From time to time, to annul the smell, he has the kid wipe his face with a handkerchief that has been drenched in perfume from the first waterskin. "Now. Clear away anything that can burn. Get the torch." He offers fire to the soaked wood; slowly it scorches, and the gilt blisters like a toasted cheese sandwich, and finally the fire takes hold. The front third of the platform is burning. The smell is horrible. "All right. The tunnel I've made inside the platform should act as a fire-brake." He pulls the shepherd's crook gingerly out of the odd train he has made and quickly substitutes the mallet, shoving it in as far as he can. "Go get the flail out of the double's fist. You should be able to unscrew it. Good. Stand here behind the sarcophagus with me. We'll watch the fire. When it burns through to the tools we'll shove. The front should tip forward fifteen to eighteen inches. That's a tremendous weight. Maybe the shock will jar the goddamn lid loose. Even if it don't, we'll have gravity working for us. We'll worry it like a loose tooth. All right, when I say shove I want you to push up so hard your palms come out your wrists."

The second robber stands by Neith, the first by Selkit watching the flames crawling along the bottom of the platform like fungus, and at exactly the right moment he yells "*Shove!*" and puts all his weight into it. "I said *shove*, you lousy skyver, *shove*." And now they both put all they have into it and the massive sarcophagus falls forward the full eighteen inches, making a sound of metal slamming stone. The shock is all the older man could have wished, for the Phoenician can see the thick lid actually stretch, bounce in some irreparable way that sets off tremors in the stone seam that start at the far ends of the lid and meet each other in a ragged, barely visible line. A crack. Hairline but enough, more than enough for this genius, this Columbus of breakage and entrance who would go through it as if it were a door or gate, whose very nature partakes of something like the quality of gas. He puts his crook down and looks up. "Whatever can I have been thinking of?" he asks abstractedly. "We don't need these toys. Reach in there, mate, and pull our tools out."

"They'll be hot."

"Nah, the breeze cooled 'em off when this big mother fell forward."

The young robber fishes the tools out carefully and the older one picks up his crowbar and mallet. "See? The fire's about burned itself out," he says. "Better let me work at this for a while, kid." Sure enough, he goes—this man who has lived life like a key—for the seal's jugular, playing that hairline crack, driving his mallet and crowbar like a poolsharp, playing the angles, putting actual English on his strokes.

"I think it's coming," the younger man says, and gets up from the throne where he has been resting and takes up his tools. Together they pry and pull and probe and shove, wordless as movers negotiating furniture around the bends in stairs. The lid is loose, and then it's off.

The Phoenician moves away from the wall and comes up behind them. There is no glitter of gold and jewels, only a sort of opaque mass.

"It's empty," the second tomb robber shouts.

"No," says the first. "Those are the palls. You don't know shit about death, kid. Those are just the linen palls. It's Death's hope chest in there, sonny. Here, look." He stirs the palls and reveals a coffin shaped not like a man so much as some trophy of a man, tight and stern and scowling as an Academy Award. Its skin is a tattoo of hieroglyph and chevron. In the dim light the mummiform coffin gives the appearance of someone fat dressed in unflattering swatches of chain mail. Its surfaces break up the light of the torch held down to investigate, disperse it in weird blue and gold tints on the faces of the robbers.

"Pay dirt," the second tomb robber proclaims after a pause.

"Nah," says the older thief, "it's wood. You don't know wood from Shinola." He appears to feel around the side of the coffin with his fingers and apparently presses some button or lever which triggers a springlock, popping the coffin open like a lady's compact. Another mummiform coffin is revealed in hand-in-glove relation to the first.

"The five hundred hats of Bartholomew Cubbins!" says the young tomb robber. He places his hands on the tiled, golden scales of the second coffin, palming its lumpy contours as if he were copping a feel.

"That's just gold-plated wood," the first robber murmurs, "inlaid with glass paste."

So, the Phoenician thinks, not only a mind like a key but a geologist as well. A tailor's affinity for fabric; there's Geiger in him, some litmus vision.

Now the older thief feels around the edges of this coffin, his chin raised and an expression on his face as if he is judging the taste of his food. He is exactly like the attendant in a filling station whose fingers seek a clasp which will raise the hood of your car. He finds it, and the lid of the second coffin snaps into the contours of the first.

The kid tomb robber laughs. "It ain't any Pharaoh's mummy at all, it's a nest of fucking matrioshka dolls."

"Pay dirt," the first tomb robber says. "That's gold, my old son, nothing but gold."

"Did you ever?" The boy whistles.

"It's useless to us. We couldn't even lift it." Nevertheless their eyes travel up the long horizontal shell of the dead king—this priceless golden Easter egg of a Pharaoh which seems to float in its sarcophagus as in a bathtub—taking in each detail, its crossed arms and big golden gloves that grasp the shepherd's crook and flail, Pharaoh's and Osiris' carrot and stick, its great head in three dimensions like some coin of ultimate denomination. They study the weird sphinxy headdress, oddly like hair turbaned in wrapped bath towel. Its open eyes seem not blind so much as distracted, as though its pupils, large and black as handballs, witness something going on extraordinarily high in the sky. Its sweet lips look as if they taste their own goldenness.

"Okay," the older man says, "here we go, then," and again he touches something, and the last veil groans marginally upward, its great weight lying on it like gravity. "Lift, *lift*," the first thief commands, "get the crowbar in, get some leverage. Now prop the lid with your bar. A little more. That's got it. There." The mummy itself, exposed now, lies under the final raised lid as under some gold tent protected from sun, and the Phoenician and the kid see what they have come for: the Pharaoh's funerary mask which has been placed over the head and shoulders of the mummy just as Anubis' jackal's head had been fitted onto his human body. For all the delicately wrought human features of the mask, the mummy is mysteriously bestialized by it.

They stare at the fantastic face, prefigured in each of its protective coffins but only as a paper silhouette prefigures flesh. They have not been prepared for this; all they can do is stare. They are looking at Egypt's most precious materials—gold, lapis lazuli, faïence, quartz and chalcedony. The Phoenician himself cannot take his eyes from the raised lapis lazuli brows that describe an arc from the nose almost to the ears, or from the lapis lazuli lined eyes like the unjoined halves of spectacles. He peers closely at the eyes themselves, stares at the canthi where the angles of the upper and lower lids meet, at the red wattles at the outer and inner edges there, the queer caruncles of God.

The second tomb robber looks at the vulture and cobra, symbols of Upper and Lower Egypt, which seem to grow out of the Pharaoh's forehead, rising spectacularly, ribbed and thick and aloft as the underedge of erections.

The first tomb robber gazes at the long blue faïence beard that looks like a plaited hocky stick. "All right," he says, breaking the spell, "let's get to work."

He takes up a position behind the mummy, and for all his previous delicacy now grabs hold of the mask with both hands and pulls at it roughly. It comes off like a saddle. He puts it down, takes a knife and slashes the bandages.

"Hey, man," says the second tomb robber, "don't *do* that."

The first tomb robber lays the knife in the coffin and tears at the bandages with both hands, opening the Pharaoh like a package. The cloth squeals apart and he plunges his hands inside and pulls out necklaces, gold rings, bracelets, fingerstalls, a scarab brooch, golden pectorals, a spilled piñata of Tiffany implement. "He was gay," he laughs. "This was no king; this was a fucking queen." He reaches inside once more, gropes and brings out a bandaged parcel, holding it up, rapidly unwinding it, tumbling the linen strips like a fisherman dealing line. It is the Pharaoh's natron-dried, embalmed heart. He raises it above his head. "What a good boy am I!" he shouts, and shoves the heart into his garments with the rest of the jewelry. "Now, mate, *now* we scarper!"

"Hoy," says the other.

It is too late. Perhaps the noise of the sarcophagus slamming to the floor had alerted them, or the pounding on the coffin seals, or the older man's shouts, or maybe they'd been tipped off, but when the thieves gathered their booty and made for the ante-chamber the flics were already there, out of breath—they'd been running and, not knowing the way as expertly as the first tomb robber, stumbling—but in sufficient numbers to put escape or even struggle out of the question. The Phoenician looks around for officials, and everywhere among the men shouting orders at each other and pressing forward to get a better look at the haul or to inspect the damage he thinks he can make them out. There are chief inspectors, priests (part clergyman and part guard assigned to protect the tomb), higher-ups, ministers and deputies from the court, important civilians who sat in the highest councils —all the grace and favored, singers, guests, even popular athletes.

It is what he expected. It is a big bust, and his only worry is that harm might come to the tomb robbers through some dumb grandstand play by one of these social commandos before they can be safely hustled out of there. "Hoy," he shouts in the con-fusion, "let's play this one by the books, men. It's too big to blow in the heat of anger."

He needn't have worried. Obviously acting under the highest orders, the police were almost rougher with the spectators than with the suspects. Quickly they collected the evidence, organized the crowd and marshaled them all out of there. They even thought to leave a detail behind until the shrine could be put back together and resealed.

The arrest was swift and correct. A brief announcement was

made to the public and the prisoners were put under special guard. The Phoenician requested that he be permitted to stay with them, but, as he anticipated, this was out of the question. They did permit him to remain in the building where the men were being held, however, a concession that came as something of a surprise. He offered money to the jailer who had told him he would be allowed to stay, but it was politely turned down.

In the morning a guard shook him gently awake on the bench where he had sacked out, and even offered him coffee. "Nice day for a hanging," the fellow said by way of small talk.

"Red sky at night, sailor's delight," the Phoenician answered. "Say, are there many people around?"

"Outside, you mean?"

"Yes."

"The town's packed. You can't get a room. Everybody's very excited."

"What's their mood? Are they upset, are they likely to turn ugly?"

"No, I don't think so. They're leaving this one strictly to the government."

"That's a relief."

"Well," said the guard, "you ain't seen what the government can do when it's worked up."

On the surface, at least, the arraignment was as proper as the arrest. The judge—the Phoenician, circulating, heard talk that he was a fair man—listened impassively to the charges and then requested that the prisoners, Oyp and Glyp, stand.

The Phoenician was astonished. So accustomed had he become to seeing them in their disguises, to recognizing them under their dyed hair, through their patiently grown mustaches and beards and behind their surgical alterations and new postures (Glyp had even trained himself to be left-handed), to discounting the red herrings of their changed diction and the falsetto of their acquired tenor, that he had not known them in their reverted states. He had to laugh. If they'd been snakes they'd have bit me, he thought. I'll be a goddamn purloined letter. Of course it had been dark in the tomb, and most of the time he'd been more interested in what they were doing than in them, and of course they'd been under a good deal of pressure so that their speech rhythms had become those he'd never have anticipated—the iambs and dactyls of action and assault being different in kind from those of evasion—but still and all he was amazed that he'd had no clue at all, not the slightest suspicion, and so their identities staggered him. He was so breathless that when the time came for him to speak he was able to do so only with the most supreme effort, and even then only after the tipstaff, seeing his distress, had brought him a glass of water.

"Your Honor," he said, "I'm Alexander Main, and I wish to go bail for these two."

"There is no question of bail, Mr. Main," the judge said gently.

"There's always a question of bail, Your Honor," he said respectfully. "I appreciate that in the circumstances the bond will necessarily be a high one, but whatever it is I will pay it. I think I can assure the Court, too, that whatever date is fixed upon for the prisoners' appearance they will be here."

"There is no question of bail, Mr. Main."

"Your Honor," he pleaded, "look at these men. They aren't master criminals. They're ordinary. They're banal men. The state hasn't argued in its charges that they've conspired with others to do this thing, or that they acted as agents, or even that they had contacts with or commitments from known fences in their misadventure. Fortunately, no one was killed or even hurt in their abortive attempt. Also, all the property's been recovered; it's been checked against the catalogs and it's all there. Luckily, those pieces which were damaged were the least valuable pieces in the tomb, and I've been given to understand that even these are subject to restoration. I'm told that the cloth-of-gold is even now being dry-cleaned." He paused. "In short, sir," he said slyly, "I think that all we're faced with here is a case of a couple of second-story blokes in under their heads."

The spectators laughed appreciatively at the Phoenician's joke. Even the judge smiled, but when he banged his gavel to restore order all he did was repeat that there was no question of bail.

Main was undeterred. He demanded an explanation of the

fair man. He asked if under Egyptian law tomb robbers were excluded from bail.

A guard moved toward him, but the judge waved him off. "Under Egyptian law, no," he said.

"Are there precedents, then, for such an exclusion?"

"There are no precedents, Mr. Main, because until last night no tomb robbers had ever been apprehended." Now the judge paused. "But since we're on the subject of precedents I would remind you that no precedent ever had a precedent, and that all precedents arise from the oily rags and scraps of tinder condition, law's and experience's spontaneous combustion."

The Phoenician didn't wait for the implication of this to register with the crowd. "Does the State have evidence that Mr. Oyp and Mr. Glyp have been linked with other tomb robberies?" he asked crisply.

"None that has been presented to us."

His next question was dangerous, for he knew the true state of affairs. Hoping that the Egyptians didn't, however, he decided to ask it. "Are these men wanted for other offenses?"

"Not to our knowledge."

"Well then, may we not assume that this is a first offense and that the case is much as I presented it and these two much as I described them—amateurs whose ambitions exceeded their capabilities? I don't mean to prejudice the prosecution's case. Indeed, as the police report states, I was there, an eyewitness. I saw it all and fully expect to be subpoenaed by the prosecution to give my evidence. I intend to go even further." He looked around the hearing room, at the judge, the spectators, and finally directly at Oyp and Glyp themselves. "I shall this day present myself to the police, *voluntarily to assist them in their inquiries.* I shall do this," he pronounced softly, "but under sworn testimony I shall also feel compelled to reveal what is already known to your investigators—that these two did not even bother to bring the proper equipment with them, that they had few tools and those they had massively inadequate to their undertaking. Where was their block and tackle? Where were their drills and blasting caps?

"In view of all this—their amateur status, their faulty preparation and makeshift maneuver, the fact that it was a first offense, that no one was physically harmed, that the suspects were unarmed, that they did not resist arrest, the failure of the State to establish agency or even to locate possible receivers, and the fact that the actual damage they caused to property in dollars and cents (I'm reasoning that the artisans who will be responsible for restoring the *objets d'art* are slaves) barely manages to meet the legal definition of felony, and finally the all-important admission by the court that there is nothing in either Egyptian statute or custom which would justify the withholding of bond in this case —in view of *all* this, I respectfully request that the court fix an appropriate bond forthwith."

The judge glared at him, but when he spoke he was as soft-spoken as before. "Mr. Main," he said patiently, "have you any idea of what bail, if I should agree to set it, would have to be in this case?"

"I have already indicated that I understand it would be high."

"Yes. It would."

"I'll pay it."

"Will you? Whatever the omissions in our law, there is a statute that is relatively specific in these circumstances."

"Your Honor?"

"I will give you the exact wording of the statute . . . Here, this is the pertinent language, I think . . . blah blah de dum blah de dum . . .Oh, yes: 'that the forfeiture be equivalent in value to the value of the *intended* theft.' "

The Phoenician whistled.

"Ignoring the worth of the treasures that were undisturbed in the tomb and fixing a value only on those objects found on the prisoners' persons or waiting to be picked up by them in the antechamber, that would come to—well, I haven't the exact figures, but I should think in the neighborhood of, oh, say twenty billion dollars. That's just a ball park estimate."

"I'll raise it," Main rasped. He didn't see how but he would. People were in debt to him for favors—the nigger, Billy Basket (who only this morning had fallen all over him trying to thank him for going his bond), that other one, the guy who worked in his cousin's car wash. It would only be for a short while. He would stay with Oyp and Glyp. He would hire an army to stay with them. It was true that the Mafia was down on him right now, but there were others, retired guards and nightwatchmen in Cincinnati who would help him baby-sit the two of them. Oyp's and Glyp's freedom would be nominal only, but it was necessary that he buy it for them. "I'll raise it," he repeated.

"Has it occurred to you that your fees alone would cost Mr. Oyp and Mr. Glyp two thousand million dollars? That such a figure might be prohibitive for them?"

"There's *two* of them," Main shouted, "it's only a thousand million apiece!"

"The police report lists them as indigents," the judge said calmly.

The Phoenician glared at the two. Tinhorns, he thought. Cheap no god fucking damn good chiselers, lousy pikers. He swallowed hard. "A personal favor," he said. "It's on the cuff. I waive my fee."

"There is no question of bail," the judge said.

"*Why?*" Main demanded. "Nothing in the statutes prevents it."

"There are laws and there are laws," the judge said, "crimes and crimes. Degrees of guilt like figures on thermometers. There are acts which so far exceed the permissible that to define them in statutes would be to register them in the imagination. And we're talking now of legislators who would have to write these laws, who would subject them to discussion and argument, with all its qualification and demurrer and contingency. We're talking of what would, ideally, occur to the *best* of men. To acknowledge that the best of men, thinking ideally and plotting academically, platonically and picturesquely, could conceive of these actions, would be to admit that ordinary men, with none of the superior man's built-in checks and balances of the heart and mind, could do the same, opening up the unthinkable to refinements, twists, debasing the depraved and declining the corrupt like a verb wheel of evil, some irregularized grammar of the monstrous that would turn the unspeakable into only a sort of French. And what of men who are *not* ordinary? Who live below the timberline of grace? What of *bad* men? What of the vicious, of villains, the ugly customer and the mad-dog killer? What of them? What perversions of the senators' only abstract paradigm of evil would *they* be capable of? What argot and babble and moral solecism and sheer bone-breaking *noise*? What's unthinkable requires no legislation, eschews statute and repudiates law. There's no question of bail."

"*Ostriches*," Main shouted. "You're *ostriches*. You bury your Pharaohs in the sand with their eggs."

"How can the unthinkable be defined?" the judge asked sincerely.

"Unthinkable? What's unthinkable? How many Pharaohs have died? Fifty? A hundred? Their tombs are like slums. Everywhere busted windows and the plumbing ripped out to get cash to buy dope. Everywhere the rats nibble the masterpieces for the lead in the paint. The doors are broke down and the stairs are missing, the furniture's askew and what's too heavy to carry gets broken up. And every generation the neighborhood changing and every dynasty the desert a little less safe at night. Good God, there aren't any playgrounds, kids play wall ball on the Pyramids, write Fuck on the Sphinx. What's unthinkable? Bond these men. *What's unthinkable?*"

"For a crime like theirs?" the judge growled. "Not just breakers and enterers but ghouls, and not just ghouls but ghouls against the state, and not just ghouls against the state but ghouls against God. Handling His things, picking and choosing among His leftovers like junkmen. Derelicts who've never seen the inside of a museum assigning value to God's wardrobe and effects, fingering His empty garments, trying them on. 'Take this, not that, these, not those. How do you think I look in this, Oyp?' 'Not bad, Glyp. Rakish, in fact.' Oyp had Pharaoh's heart in his pocket."

"I told you, Oyp!" Glyp shouted. "I told you not to do that!"

"They siphoned His juices like there was gas rationing. They wiped it up from the floor using His cloth-of-gold as if it was toilet paper. They slashed bandages and let in air, diluting the natron. A dozen embalmers worked an entire season preparing His soil, polishing His seed to last an eternity. They divoted

His course with their knives and crowbars and banged His sarcophagus like boys do drums."

Yes, thinks Main, what a bond this would make! What a feather in my cap!

"They set His platform on fire and tilted it like cheats at pinball. They clumsied His corpse and sat on His throne like Weathermen in an occupied boardroom. They used his Double familiarly and snatched His crook and filched His flail. And not just ghouls against God who goosed and grab-assed above their station, but who stoppered His cycle, who condemned God not even to Hell but to nothingness, who exiled Him, annihilating His soul and sending it to graze in no man's land beyond the twelve-mile limit. Bond them? *Bond them?*"

"There's something else," the Phoenician says. "There's something else, though."

"Please," the judge says, "there can be no bail in this case."

"They're wanted in another state."

"Please?"

"They're wanted in Ohio." He produces the warrant which he always carries and hands it to a bailiff who brings it to the bench.

The judge examines it. "There can be no bond," he says.

"They're fugitives," Main shouts. "I've been hunting them for years."

"No bond."

"They got away from me. They're the only ones who ever did."

"No bond. Bond is refused."

"It couldn't happen again," Main pleads.

"Bond is *refused*!" The judge bangs his gavel, and the Phoenician knows the hearing is over. Then the judge makes an astonishing statement. He instructs the guards to release the prisoners. If there are crimes, he says, that are so unthinkable that no laws can proscribe them, then they must be of such magnitude that no punishment can redress them. Oyp and Glyp were free to go.

The Phoenician trembled. The fugitives were fugitives still,

fugitives once from his scrutiny and control, then from his inter-
cession, and now from earth itself. Fugitives from the bullying
freedom he needed to give them who till now could stand between the law and its violators, having that power vouchsafed to
him, the power to middleman, to doodle people's destiny; the
power, like a natural right, to put killers back on the streets and
return the lunatics to their neighborhoods; the good power to
loose the terrible, to grant freedom where he felt it was due, more
magisterial than a king, controlling the sluices and locks of ordinary life, adjusting at whim the levels and proportions of guilt to
innocence, poisoning the streets with possibility. But Oyp and
Glyp were fugitives from fugitiveness itself, and because they
were, there were limits to his power and his own precious freedom.

He groaned in his bed, chewed a piece of his pillowcase, twisted
in his smooth hotel sheets, moaned, objected, knew helplessness,
awoke and was embarrassed to discover that his dream was not
just a dream but a wet dream. And sure enough, when he
switched on his bedside lamp and looked, there was his cobra
cock and, still spilling from it, the white sweet venom of his
come.
He did not speculate about the dream's meaning. He'd lived
with its meaning for years, since his hair had thinned and his
belly bloomed, since his legs had begun to go and his reflexes
climb down from true, since his aches and since his pains and
his BM's became irregular and he could see into the stream of
his weakened piss. Not that death held any particular horror
for him, nor the cessation of his personality seem an offense
against Nature. Indeed, he might quite welcome that. He was
sick of his slick contempt, his ability to win which had never
left him, his knack of topping the other guy. It took a dream to
beat him, and even then he was the dreamer, the judge no more
than dummy to his ventriloquist. But the other thing, the other
thing. Curiosity was killing the cat. Oyp and Glyp were his only
failures, but Oyp and Glyp in life were as they had been in his
dream: punks, losers. Their collective bond—this was something

which surprised him whenever he remembered it, or contemplated one of those expensive safaris which would take him across the country or out of it when a rumor ripened and fell his way— had been less than eleven hundred dollars. Not masterminds, not arch criminals, just ordinary car thieves. Probably they were already dead, or living through an anonymity that was as close to death as one could come. Split up by now almost certainly, gone their separate sordid ways. Perhaps in some Mexican or Central American jail, too poor or too guilty to obtain lawyers, more sinned against than sinning and, because they were dim, without the mother wit to enlist the help of their embassy, thinking, We're wanted men anyway, why jump out of the frying pan into the fire? Best to stay here, rot for the twenty to thirty years these greasers gave us than get ourselves extradited, go back, make all that fuss, be locked up in Ohio or maybe even some Federal pen because we jumped bail. Doesn't that bring the Feds into it? Shit, we're warm enough here, don't even speak the lingo, which is an advantage since nobody kicks us around too much because we don't understand.

He'd spent five times what he'd lost on them already. And put in how many weeks of sleep dreaming of them?

But now his dreams—this dream—had turned, exalting them. Why, they *were* exalted! Mystery. Mystery. The reason he was a bondsman. The meaning of his life. The way he came to terms with what engined it. Mystery. Why he lived with the cops and the robbers. Why he bothered to eat with his bondsmen colleagues in Covington. Why he was a regular around City Hall, the municipal courts, the Federal halls of justice, on a first-name basis not just with the small-time hoods and criminals of passion but with their families as well, their partners and girl friends. Crime was the single mystery he could get close to. Did he know astronomy? Had he the brains for the higher mathematics or the physics of even thirty or forty years ago? Could he read Spanish or follow a score? Did he know history or even what the symptoms of his own body signified? Could he write a prescription or mix paint?

And it was not true what he told his clients: that their guilt or innocence did not matter to him and that his only consideration was whether they would run or stay put. It mattered very much, almost as much as his power to free them. All that did *not* matter was the verdict, but in his own mind he always reached a verdict, and he was certain that by virtue of his unique relationship it was at least as accurate as the law's. Mystery. Mystery kept him going and curiosity killed him. His limited detective heart made him a Cincinnatian, kept him in this city of exactly the right size. And *still* he bit off more than he could chew, a tapeworm working in his brains. Mystery.

He showered, washing the scum from his long old balls, dried himself with distaste on the already damp towels, disposed of his pajamas in the wastebasket, dressed. Only then, when he was strapping on his watch, did he see the time: it was only eleven o'clock. He picked up his room key, went down in the elevator and left it wordlessly with the night man at the desk.

Hungry, he went into the coffee shop and ordered soup, a ham sandwich, coffee, melon. (What did they taste like? Mystery.) The dream had moved him forcibly. He had already forgotten Oyp and Glyp, as he forgot all clients once he was finished with them. They weren't in it anymore. It was their crime: that was what exalted them, freed them from him, that he couldn't get out of his mind. Why couldn't he, who dreamed the crime, dream the success of his plea to the judge? Mystery. (Did he know the chemistry of even fifty years ago, classics, the future? He didn't even know natural history; without the cards by the specimens in the cases in the museum he could not have told you about the teeth which so fascinated him.) Now a dream precipitated his actions, forced his hand, gave him hunches in the dark like a numbers player.

He paid up and cleared out, turning down the doorman who offered to get a taxi for him. "I've had my taxi ride today," he said. "Where's the bus stop?" Though he knew, of course, knew the routes and times of the last buses, knew the city inside out, knew all the fixed, specific mystery of Cincinnati, Ohio.

He took a Vliet Avenue bus to Rosendale and transferred to the Koch–Demaret which took him up Glad Boulevard and by the park, then past Hebrew Union College and the University of Cincinnati whose tall twin buildings, Physics and Chemistry, faced each other like upended keys. The bus entered a narrow wedge of ghetto. Three blacks in big hats whose wide brims flopped down over their eyes stood down from the curb and waved at a request stop. The Phoenician knew the driver would not stop for them. He wondered how it would work out, what crises and bloodlettings were still to take place, and tried to imagine what assassinations of which leaders yet unborn would have to be endured, and conjured issues, slogans and even men as meaningless and dissociative as scores in a vacuum. He thought in headlines of distant centuries: TRENT REPUDIATES GENNIS, CALLS FOR AMORTIZATION OF EPICENTER. INDIANA WIPPENITES STARCH SCARVES, MARCH ON STATEHOUSE. MERPEN PLEADS HUNDRED AND SEVENTH. REMEMBER NEBRASKA!

But even these were built on analogue. He was depressed by language, the finite slang of his century. SHOTCHKA QUENTZ VISARBLEMENTHS. He needed new endings, new punctuation, a different grammar. There would be people, and they would believe things he could not even imagine. There would be two sides to every question. Trent would be right and Gennis would be right, though in its lifetime the public would never know the whole story. Amortization of the epicenter would be only a short-term solution to whatever problem it had been created to solve. A stopgap, at best only a first halting step. And it was all very well to remember Nebraska, but a time would come when it would be best to forget old wounds. There would be different holidays, epic festivals celebrating heroes who would not be born for a thousand years yet. And in all the countries in the world, on all the calendars the dates of their births would be in *red!* What would they have pulled off? What drugs were coming? What soups and styles, and how would the center line on the highway be made when the paint mines dried up and the pigments rationed? Or legislated against, green outlawed and blue controversial and orange repealed?

How he envied them, the man in the street, the pockmarked dropout of some future millennium, how he was sickened at the thought of the punch lines of jokes he could not understand even if they were patiently explained to him. What answers they would so casually have! Their 90 IQ's would encompass wisdoms that the greatest minds of today could not even begin to comprehend. The more things changed, it was said, the more they remained the same. That was bullshit, just one more justification and excuse, another good word put in for death.

It was a terrible thing Oyp and Glyp had done. How I envy them! How glad I am I was there to see it!

It was his stop. He got off and walked the half-block to the Vernon Manor Hotel.

Although it was a residential hotel, with its wide horseshoe drive and massive quarter moons of carefully tended lawn, its groundfloor ballroom with its sequence of tall leaded windows like five big fingertips, the Vernon Manor had the look of a resort hotel of the Twenties. It might have looked more in place along the shore. Far from downtown, it seemed an awry speculation to the Phoenician whenever he came upon it. He rather liked the hotel, enjoyed the old ladies in their seventies with their clean thin hair that always reminded him of the fish-scale blue one sees in chemical toilets on airplanes. He enjoyed the big white uniformed colored women who pushed their wheelchairs or steadied them on their sticks as they bobbed along, or helped them into their cars and took the wheel to drive them to their doctor appointments. Not all the residents were cripples, but all seemed frail, their survivorship underscoring their frailty, their neatness and grooming a testament to the care they had to take of themselves. They seemed vaguely but limitedly moneyed, on budgets, their strict accountancy signaling necessity rather than a careful husbandry for the benefit of sons and daughters and grandchildren (they seemed as bereft of these as of husbands). It cheered the Phoenician to think of their clever economies, shrewdened them in his eyes. They were like hunters who killed to eat. He pictured them still awake, in front of their television sets or entering figures in ledgers from the financial pages, sipping hot water and lemon to outwit their bowels, warm milk their insomnia. What did they make of the world? (Mystery,

mystery. He did not know them. Old ladies did not come to him for bail.)

In the lobby he moves toward the small bank of elevators where the night porter snoozes in a chair.

"Sir?" the night clerk says.

Main goes up to him, stands by the darkened candy cases, the low revolving tree of post card, the wide magazine rack, tomorrow's *Enquirer*, the headline showing through a window in the yellow vending machine. He looks around at the glass signatures of the signs above the beauty parlor and dress shop, drained of neon and dusty as empty alembic. He glances past the night clerk into the message boxes, the few keys that spill out of their mouths like tongues.

"May I help you?"

"I don't think so."

"You're not a guest?"

"No."

"I'm afraid the dining room is closed. We serve our last meal at ten."

"That's all right, I've eaten."

"Are you visiting someone in the hotel?"

"Yes."

"May I ask if you're expected?"

"I'm not expected."

"It's almost one. I'll have to ring up and announce you."

"Tell Crainpool Mr. Main is downstairs."

The clerk shrugs, goes to the switchboard, plugs into Crainpool's room and speaks softly into the thin prosthetic gear that runs from his ear to his chin. He looks up at Main and frowns. "I'm afraid I woke him. He says he'll be down as soon as he can get dressed."

"I'll go up." The clerk is about to protest, but Alexander has already turned and shaken the porter awake. "Five," he says. He has to repeat himself to the groggy man. In the elevator he glances at the framed menus high on the wall, reads the cheerful Good Morning! from the closed coffee shop. It is old news.

The elevator door opens in a cul-de-sac. There is gray and faded floral carpeting, hard upholstered benches where the old people sit while waiting for the elevator. He turns left and left again and goes down the long corridor past the housekeeper's closets and old-fashioned hollow metal doors that belly the hall. Crainpool's room is at the far end of the corridor. There are hotel offices across from him and a housekeeping closet next door. He turns the knob on Crainpool's door, but it is locked. He bangs on it with his fist.

Crainpool, already in his trousers but still in his pajama tops and an old blue bathrobe, opens it. "Mr. Main."

"It's after hours, Crainpool. We don't have to be so formal after hours."

"Has something happened? Have there been mass arrests on the campus? I was sleeping; I didn't see the eleven o'clock news. Do we have to go downtown? Just give me a minute to put on my clothes."

"Nice place you got here."

"It's comfortable."

"Small, compact, but I expect it meets your requirements. Just get lost in someplace larger."

"Yes, sir."

"Rattle around."

"I guess I would."

"Yet your needs are taken care of." He pounds the swollen metal door. "Hotel has a laundry and dry-cleaning service, I suppose."

"It does, yes, sir, but it's pretty expensive. I don't often use it."

"Wash out a few things in the sink each night, do you? Hang 'em to dry on the rod in the bath?"

"Well, yes, sir, I do."

"Yes. I see. I see you do." He has strolled into the small bathroom. Underwear swims in the sink; two shirts hang on hangers above the tub, dripping water half on the tile and half in the bath; handkerchiefs stretch over the radiators like canvas on Conestoga wagons; a pair of pajamas dry on a wooden rack in the corner.

Main unzips his fly and pees into his employee's toilet. He does not close the door or raise the seat. "These pajamas," he says.

"Sir?"

"I was saying these pajamas," he calls over the splash of his pee, "what happened to the nightshirt I gave you for Christmas? Don't you use it?"

"Well, I thought that was meant as a joke, sir."

He walks back into the room. "A joke? Why would you think it was a joke? And the nightcap, did you think the nightcap was a joke, too?"

"Well, sir—"

"The trouble with you, Crainpool, is that you don't take things seriously. Playful yourself, you assume that everyone else has your sense of humor. A joke! That was a business investment, Mr. Crainpool, a business investment. I took it off my taxes. I thought that nightshirt and cap would solidify your image, help put you in the proper frame of mind for what's wanted. A joke indeed! Like the garters, I suppose. Like the quill pens and the high stool. I've taken a great many pains, Mr. Crainpool—and gone to considerable expense, too, I might add—to reinforce your clerk's ambience, to clericalize you. Yet you persist in your taste for the newfangled. I suppose you've been thinking in terms of electric typewriters and Xerox machines. What's next, sir, conference telephones, gadgets that take your calls? 'Mr. Crainpool is unavailable right now. Your message will be recorded and played back for him when he returns. Please begin speaking when you hear the electronic bleep . . . Bleep.' "

"No, sir."

" 'No, sir.' *You're damned right, sir, no sir.* And what happens to the thick ledgers with the careful rulings inked down the center of the page? The big gray and black cardboard boxes with their snaps and clasps and their colors running like a melted zebra? To the huge checkbooks like a family album? What do we do, throw *them* all out, I suppose?"

"I'm sorry, sir," Crainpool says, trying not to giggle.

"Yes, sir. I should think you would be. It isn't as if I've tried to trespass in your private life . . . Well, have I?"

"No, sir."

"No. You didn't see the eleven o'clock news, you said. That implies that you have a television. Television is provided, is it not? You needn't answer; I see it. Television is provided. Three networks and an educational channel at your disposal. There is the telephone. I see an air-conditioning unit. I rode up here in an elevator."

"Yes, sir."

"I was under no *obligation* to provide you with such lavish mod cons. None of the advantages you enjoy—there's the electric light, there's the flush toilet—were actually *coming* to you."

"No, sir."

"My first thought was to set you up in a boardinghouse. Such places still exist, you know, though admittedly they are scarcer now than when you first came into service."

"Yes, sir." Crainpool is trying very hard to keep a straight face.

"Go on, go on, continue dressing."

"Then we're going downtown?"

"Then I thought, *no*, though a boardinghouse would be the proper place for you and would go a long way towards bringing out those qualities in you which I was looking for, it might have certain drawbacks. You might not have liked your neighbors— or you might have liked some of them *too* much, fallen in with the wrong sort, made yourself vulnerable at the dinner hour or in the lounge on Sunday. You'd have had to share a bath, don't forget."

"Yes, sir." Crainpool is buttoning his shirt.

"You wouldn't have had your own phone. You'd have been roused at all hours to take other people's messages. The walls in such places are paper thin. A fellow roomer's radio could have kept you up half the night."

"Yes, sir, I suppose that's true, sir."

"Then I found this place for you, didn't I?"

"You did."

"Yes. Then I found this place for you. A quiet residential hotel. Genteel. Yet with all the latest up-to-the-minute features you could possibly wish. Say, I like that carpet in the hall. Do all the floors have it?"

"Some do, but the patterns vary, I think."

"You *think*. Only what you see when the elevator opens to take on a passenger. I take it, then, that you have no close friends in the hotel. Only the odd nodding acquaintance in the lobby and coffee shop."

"That's about it, sir." He has begun to put on his tie.

"So I thought. No, don't bother about the tie."

"I'll just get my jacket, sir." He puts on his jacket and looks at the Phoenician. "I'm ready."

"Ready?"

"To go downtown with you."

"No, no, it's after business hours; I already told you that. Shop's closed. You'll have to remember these things, Mr. Crainpool."

"We're *not* going downtown?"

"We're not."

"I see." Crainpool leaves the hall where he has been waiting for the Phoenician and returns to the center of the room. "Would you like to sit down, sir?"

"Thank you, Crainpool. Too bad there's only the one chair."

Crainpool sits primly on his bed. "To what do I owe this honor?" he says at last.

"To bad dreams. To my poor scores in the hard subjects. To your vulnerable history."

Crainpool blushes and it is the first time in years. Their cat-and-mouse had settled years before into a rhetoric, glancing off Crainpool like punch lines rained down on fools in comedy turns, touching him as little. Over the years he has become a stunt man, his bruises routinized, his flexible rubber bones deep-sea'd fathoms beneath his skin and his nerves and pride Atlan-tisized, lost continented. The blush is not embarrassment but fear, and Main recognizes it because he has seen it once before.

"Aren't you satisfied with my work, Mr. Main?"

"Perfectly."

Now his face goes redder still, and Main sees ideas squeezing in his brain like turds. "Oyp and Glyp," he says breathlessly, "you found Oyp and Glyp."

"Oyp and Glyp are dead."

"Dead?"

"Or captured. Split up, perhaps. Gone straight, could be. Married with kids. Working in factories or fueling jets on the runway. With the Highway Department, waving red flags to stop the traffic while the road's being fixed. Or selling door-to-door, or moving *The Watchtower*. Hired hands, maybe, or taken up cooking. In Dobb's House management, Dairy Queen. Studying the motel trade."

"You have information?"

"Who has information? Nah, they're dead."

"Have you given up on them, sir?"

"The bailbondsman's statute of limitations, Mr. Crainpool, the Phoenician's sanctuary, Main's pardon—they have it all."

"Gee."

"That surprise you?"

"I thought you'd found them, or even just one of them."

"Never find 'em. They're vanished. Cut my losses like a tailor. God told me that in a vision."

"Yes, sir. Good advice."

"What, that? That's how He answers all prayer."

"Oh," Crainpool says. "That lawyer called, Avila. He told me to tell you that Mr. Withers is back and that he'll appear as scheduled."

"Anything else?"

"Just before I closed up, the desk sergeant from the Fourth District called in with some leads about the arraignments. I tried to reach you at home."

"Something interesting?"

"Well, they've picked up a suspect for that bank robbery. They think they have enough evidence to hold him. I left a message with your answering service and asked the girl to call before you left in the morning."

"All right."

"Would you like some coffee, sir? There's only the hot plate, and it's just instant, but I could make some if you'd like."

"You're losing the thread."

"Sir?"

"You're losing the thread. Of the conversation. I make this extraordinary late-night visit and an absolutely unique allusion to your past to which you duly react, and now you're losing the thread of the conversation. You're not out of the woods yet, you know, Mr. Crainpool."

"I know that, sir," he says shyly.

"That's better. Tell me, Crainpool, did you blush like that when you beat up your wife and put her in hospital?"

"I didn't have the opportunity to study myself, sir."

"No, of course you didn't. Did you have the opportunity when you heard three weeks later, and you were already out on my bond, that there was a fire in her ward and that she'd burned to death?"

"Mr. Main," Crainpool says, "that was sixteen years ago. You spoke of the statute of limitations."

"Certainly. And you'll be able to take whatever advantage of it you can once I turn you over to the police. Be sure to mention it to them. Tell your lawyer."

"You're turning me in? Jesus, Phoenician, that was sixteen years ago that happened. I've been your goddamn slave *eleven* years. You're turning me in?"

"Which among us craps jellybeans, Mr. Crainpool?"

"Sixteen years and you're turning me in?"

"No, lad, I'm killing you. I'm going to kill you."

"The statute of—"

"That's between you and the State of Ohio. We have a contract." He pats his breast pocket. "Nothing about any old statute of limitations in this. You jumped my bail. Do I have to read it to you? Good God, man, you've worked for me eleven years. You've seen thousands of these contracts, you have the relevant clauses by heart, all that stuff about consenting to the application of such force as may be necessary to effect your return."

Crainpool jumps up from the bed. "Let's go," he says crisply and smiles. "*I consent!*" He begins to laugh. "I consent, I consent. Draw your gun and stick it in my ear, I consent!"

The Phoenician studies him. "You're putting up an even bigger struggle than I anticipated. Best sit back down, son. Sit down, honey."

"But I *consent*," Crainpool whines.

"My life should retain credibility," the Phoenician says.

"Listen, Mr. Main," the man pleads, "let me off."

"Hush, Crainpool." He looks at his man. "Tell me what you're thinking."

"What I'm *thinking*? I'm scared stiff."

"Please," Main says reassuringly, "be calm, take time. Nothing will happen yet. What are you thinking?"

The frightened man begins to speak, but hesitates. "Yes?" Main coaches.

"That our arrangement wasn't such a bad one," Crainpool says finally.

The Phoenician sighs, disappointed. "You're trivial, you're a trivial man," he says. "Me too. Well-a-day, Crainpool, me too. All I can think to do right now is satisfy you. I put myself in your shoes and I think, 'He's mad, he won't do it, he'll never get away with it.' I'd want scenario, demand explanation like a last cigarette, civilized denouement like a detective's professional courtesy in the drawing room and even the murderer's glass filled. Do you feel any of that?"

"I do. Yes. A little. I do."

Main looks at Crainpool suspiciously. "I hope you do. There are conventions, ceremonies. The mechanics are explained but never the mysteries. Foh. Look at me. I'm a parade. At bottom I've a flatfoot's heart: *This is how I broke the case.* You need to know anything like that?"

"Sure," Crainpool says.

"You're not just stalling for time, are you?"

"Not entirely."

"Because to tell the truth I haven't made my mind up yet. Not absolutely. I'm more likely to kill you than not, but nothing's been finalized."

"How'd you break the case, sir?"

"*Don't patronize me, you son of a bitch!*"

"Take it easy."

The Phoenician stands. "You won't rush me, will you?"

"No."

"You won't fling the pillows at me?"

"I'm wanted, I'm a wanted man. You didn't break in. The clerk called and I agreed to see you."

"That's right. Look, kid, stall. Stall for time, don't make sudden moves."

"All right," Crainpool says kindly, "how do you think you can get away with a thing like this?"

"That's it, that's the way. Good," the Phoenician says, "good."

And he begins to tell him, feeding him detail, inventing his plausible arrangements as he goes along, reassuring himself as he annihilates loophole, shutting off Crainpool's harbors and posting guards at his roadblocks, at his gangways and airline check-in counters, watching Crainpool's trains. And it is all true, even if it is only a sort of foreign language he has learned to speak, the flashy grammar of body contact, a shoptalk of which he is weary because no one has yet bested him at it, least of all this dim Crainpool. And he sees that the man takes it all in, held, not just stalling but actually *interested*, a disciple to his own destroyer. *Puppy!* The Phoenician punishes him with strategy, game plan, pressing Crainpool's nose to the blackboard where the y's and x's of opposition spray chalk in Crainpool's spread, admiring nostrils. It's what has held him all these years, kept him in town while the Phoenician was off rounding up jumpers; not only what kept him when Main wasn't looking, but what brought him to the office earlier than usual at such times, and what held him there later, after hours, waiting for a phone call that would check up on him, wanting to hear even if only at long distance what normally he got in person, feeding on comeuppance, humiliation, wisecrack, connoisseur of the Phoenician's abuse. I am his life's work, the Phoenician thinks. I have rehabilitated him. He has gone straight man.

So he pours it on, showers Crainpool with spurious inevitability, moves him to object only to shut him off at the pass.

"Such force as may be necessary to effect my *return*," Crainpool says triumphantly.

"Asshole. I'll return you. You're a fucking deposit bottle."

"Suppose I shout? Suppose I shout, 'Don't shoot, Mr. Main, I surrender'?"

"You fucked up fucking fuck. *I* shout louder. 'Call the police,' I shout, 'Crainpool's got my gun.'"

"Shmuck. What *about* the police? Why didn't you bring them to arrest me?"

"First principles. Shmuck yourself, I'm a bondsman. My reputation depends upon doing my own enforcing."

"You *harbored* me. Eleven years you *harbored* me."

"I harbored somebody who called himself Crainpool. In the five years it took me to catch up with you, you'd aged beyond recognition. You'd lost hair. You were seventy-five pounds lighter than when you jumped my bond. Your mama wouldn't have known you."

"The perfect crime," Crainpool says appreciatively.

"You're in season. It isn't even crime."

The man nods; he is satisfied that it can be done. Probably he'd never doubted it. But he still doesn't understand why. "I was your slave," he says.

"I paid top dollar. You got annual raises, paid vacations, fringe benefits. The first bondsman's clerk in the State of Ohio with his own retirement plan."

"I don't want to die," Crainpool says. "My God, Mr. Main, why would you do this?"

"Because," he says quietly, "you're the only man in the world I'm allowed to kill." He has drawn his gun.

Crainpool begins to whimper, and the Phoenician is moved. He owes this forlorn man more than the fringe benefit of his theatrics. "How," he asks, "can there be indifference? How can there be suicides? Why are there old men? Help me, Crainpool. Why is life so lovely? The night sweeter than the day and the day more joyous than the night? Who alive can grieve? How dare there be good weather, seasons when the world is at room temperature? Where are my muscles, my smooth skin? Why doesn't desire die? Why is it that it's the one thing which remains intact, that has some fucking strangle hold on immortality? Who sabotaged us and gave our will insomnia? Why am I more interested in others than others are interested in me? What am I to make of their scents, their firm bodies and their healthy hair? Of the snatches of conversation I overhear, the endearments passed like bread? Who wired this tension in me between ego and detachment? Why do I have this curiosity like a game leg? How can I cross-examine the universe when it jumps my bond?"

He begins to feel a little of what he has been saying. Crainpool is alive too, and his determination to kill him momentarily wavers. He sees it as a stunt, one more thing to impress this man who has lived eleven years with and for such impressions and who would, in the instant he squeezed the trigger (first the wild warning shot overhead or out the window to establish alibi—Crainpool would understand, having lived so long in ringside connection to technique, a first-nighter in aisle and orchestra to the Phoenician's thousand performances, would perhaps even roar "Author, author. Bravo, bravo" to his own death—to make the point that in this small room, in these close quarters, he could not possibly have missed his man and had given him a chance to come quietly), probably smile, appreciation riding his lips like dessert, recognition sparking campfires in his eyes.

"Look at me, Mr. Crainpool. I take all the papers. I. F. Stone wrote me newsletters. I have *Scientific American*. *The Journal of the American Medical Association* is on the floor by my bed. *National Geographic* is in the toilet, *American Heritage* next to the toaster. Time-Life gives me the prepublication discount. *Au courant* I am as a deb with my nose for trend and influence and my insider's thousand knowledges. What does it mean? Everything I don't know and will never know leans on me like a mountain range. It creams me, Crainpool. It potches my brains and rattles my teeth."

"You, Mr. Main? You're a smart man. I wish I had a tenth your brains."

"Yeah. Same here. I wish I had a tenth yours—anyone's, everyone's. I'd fatten on your memory and experience like a starver, suck at your inputs and engrams as at sweet fruit. What's the future going to be like, Mr. Crainpool? What will people whistle a hundred years from now? What snatch of song will run through the beautician's head as she leans forward over a customer's hair? Tell me and I'll let you go. What will the priorities be? What ruins will yet be uncovered, what treasures from what sunk ships will rise from which seas? What cities will be built and destroyed and uncovered again? Whose teeth will come up in the earthquake and go in the case?"

"I don't understand."

"Me too. *Nothing.* Me too. The ocean beds are squeezing together, did you know that? They tow the continents like tugboats. Asia will be a day's hike from Australia, and a man standing in Italy will cast a shadow in Yugoslavia. Nations shall be resolved like a jigsaw, Mr. Crainpool, and what we call land will one day form a perfect circle, a globe within a globe that sits on the oceans like a skullcap. What a seashore that will be! Like a wet nimbus, Crainpool! Who'll drive the Golden Spike that first day? What language will he speak?"

He fires the first shot. It goes out Crainpool's open window and clears the four-story building across the way. "That will merely wake some of them," he says. "Wait, you'll hear." They listen together and can barely make out the sound of one or two doors opening down the corridor. Somewhere a window scrapes open.

"Is everything all right?" someone shouts from the dark street.

The Phoenician levels the gun at Crainpool's chest in case he calls out. "No," he whispers. Then to Crainpool in his previous tone, but more excited, "But that's just the world, the earth. Have you considered astronomy, have you given any thought to physics?"

"No," Crainpool says dryly. His voice is parched.

"Physics breaks my heart, astronomy gives me the blue balls. I dassn't bother with mathematics. I better not think about chemistry."

"No."

"You asshole, Mr. Crainpool. We're blind. We ought to have white canes and dark glasses. There should be pencils in our caps. We should sit in the weather against tall buildings and use the caps as offices. Listen, listen to me. They've proof that all life is merely four simple compounds arranged on a spiral string of sugars and phosphates. We're necklaces, Crainpool, sugar and spice and everything nice. We're fucking *candy*. And your cocksucker and muffdiver are only guys with a sweet tooth. Listen, listen, there's a theory now that certain things move faster than light. They think that atoms were lighter millions of years ago, gravity stronger. We live in a universe that puts on weight, that builds its body like a Sumo."

"I don't follow."

"I don't lead."

"Please, Mr. Main—"

He is talking very quickly now. "I hear tell that matter enters our universe from another universe. That we get our physical laws from some universe in another country. That gravity comes like the post, imported like teak and coffee beans. Physical law like an unfavorable balance of payments. Our ways are not their ways, Mr. Crainpool. Jesus, atoms, atoms and the crap between stars."

"Why are you killing me?"

"*Hush.* Einstein's theory posited objects of infinite density within an infinitely small space. You see? Their atoms would be so fat and their gravity so dense that not even light could escape from them. *That* was a darkness, fella. Can you imagine such a darkness? That was a darkness so dark it was invisible. You could read your newspaper through it. Listen, listen to me. Wheeler and Ruffini predicted that by their x-rays we would know them —are you keeping up, are you getting any of this?—that they'd give themselves away circling visible stars, nibbling at them with their infinite gravity, drawing at them, giving the stars a toothache."

"I don't know why you want to kill—"

"They've been *seen*! In recent months. They've been detected. The black holes in the universe."

"I don't want you to shoot me, Mr. Main."

"And for every black hole there's a *white* hole. That's what Hjellming thinks, how he accounts for the quasars. Are you reading me, Crainpool? The universes are leaking into each other. There's this transfusion of law in the sky. I'm honest, I'm an

honest man. Upright and respectable here in this universe I in-
habit. I'm honest, but the fucking laws are leaking, the physical
constants bleeding into each other like madras. God Himself
nothing but a slow leak, some holy puncture, Nature's and reality's sacred flat. Matter and anti-matter. Inside our universe is
another. Dig? Chinese boxes of universes. When I kill you in
your room here tonight, maybe that's virtue next-door. You
think?"

"Why? Please, Mr. Main, *why*?"

"Shut up about why. I don't *know* why!"

Crainpool changes his tactics. He stops whining and becomes
almost angry. "You always have to have the last word," he says.
"You always have to do things big, don't you? Big shot. You'd
kill me for nothing, for the sake of your style."

"My style? Nah."

"You would. You think you're so hot."

"Me? No, I'm catching cold, I'm in a draft, I've got this chill.
Brr, Crainpool, it's the Ice Age in me, record snowfalls and not
enough antifreeze in the world to grow a calory. My atoms, my
gross thick atoms. Can you see me? Can you make me out?"

"I see you. I make you out. Like you said—you're a parade."

"Don't believe everything they tell you, killer. I don't give a
fart for me. You can have my personality for a Green Stamp.
My ego wore out years ago. Call Goodwill Industries, I'll put it
in a box on the front porch they can pick it up. Crainpool,
dummy, this isn't heroics, it ain't no grandstand here. I'm a functional illiterate, I don't know my ass from my elbow mystery-
wise. If I can't stand being a fool, it's got nothing to do with
pride. Screw the bubble reputation, I say, fuck fame and shove
I. Gobble genes and blast being. I pass."

Crainpool has had to strain to hear this last, leaning so far forward that he can almost pluck the gun from Main's lap. "Then
it makes no sense to kill me," he says.

"All I wanted," Main says so quietly that the clerk has to
watch his lips to understand him, "was to know things. I'm honest, I'm an honest man. I took delight in the impersonal. I've
lived with curiosity like the seven-year itch. That's what at-

tracted me to you guys, you mugs and malefactors, you villains and cutpurses. Who done it? What's the motive? *Cherchez la femme*. What's that? What does crime come to at last? Nothing. Crummy hornbook, lousy primer. Slim volume, Crainpool, pot fucking boiler, publisher's remainder. You taught me nothing, mister. And where did I get the idea that by getting next to aberration I could . . . But what hurts, I mean what really *hurts*, is that if I had a brain as big as the Ritz I still wouldn't know anything. We die dropouts. All of us. Disadvantaged and under-achievers. I have questions. I'm up to *here* with questions. I never needed to be happy; I only needed to know. Simple stuff. A dopey kid of the next century could tell me. If I could only live long enough I would sit at his feet as if he was Socrates and he'd tell me . . . What? Whether Dubuque ever made it into the majors. If there's crab grass on distant planets. Who won the war and what they were supposed to be fighting for and old Uncle Tom Cobbly and all. He'd rattle off the damn fool slo-gans of his time and I'd take them in like the Ten Commandments. What do I do with my wonder, I wonder?"

Crainpool stands up. He squeezes himself between Main and the bed and walks toward the door. "Please," he says, "I'll see you in the office. Go on home, Mr. Main, get some sleep." He opens the door for him.

"What?"

"It's pretty late, Mr. Main."

"You off the hook?"

"I think so."

"Out of the woods?"

"That's the chance I'm taking."

"And you'll see me in the office."

"Yes."

"In the morning."

"Yes, sir."

The Phoenician smiles wearily. "You let me talk myself out, do your stalling for you."

"You're a reasonable man, Mr. Main. You're a reasonable man, Alex."

"Oyp and Glyp are dead."

"Well, as you say, who can know what happened? I'm glad you closed the books on them. It was time."

"That's right."

"You had a perfect record otherwise."

"Sure."

"They don't change that."

"No."

"Do you want me to call a taxi for you?"

"Do you think they're really dead? I mean, I've got no actual *proof*. It's just a feeling."

"You know those two. If they were alive we'd probably have heard something. We were bound to. Leopards don't change their spots."

"I guess." He raises his pistol and aims it at Crainpool's hand which is still on the door. "There was always someone to hunt," he says. "A mystery I was good at. My line of country. But if Oyp and Glyp are dead—"

"Come on, Mr. Main, don't—"

He fires and the bullet chips the knuckles of Crainpool's hand. Astonished, the clerk raises the hand to his mouth and stares wild-eyed at the Phoenician. The blood makes it appear that he has been eating cherry pie.

"Run," the Phoenician commands, hisses. "Run, you bastard."

"What?"

"*Run*. Down the stairway. Run, *run*."

"What are you doing?"

He raises the pistol again, and Crainpool turns and flees. The Phoenician walks into the corridor. Doors are ajar down the long line of rooms. Oddly they give the hallway the appearance of stalled traffic. Old women stand before them in nightgowns, their hands at their hearts. The Phoenician can just make out Crainpool's back as he shoves open the door to the emergency stairway. "OYP," he shouts, "AND GLYP," he shouts, "ARE DEAD," he shouts. He starts after the clerk in his old man's gravid trot. "LONG," he roars, "LIVE CRAINPOOL!"

He hurries to the stairwell through the door that Crainpool

has just moved through. He is panting; the hand that holds the pistol shakes. He leans over the railing and sees a blur of Crainpool as the younger, faster man reaches the bottom stair. He points the pistol downward and fires without looking. Ah, he's missed. Good. He puts the gun in his jacket and walks lazily down the stairs. He enters the lobby and, feigning breathlessness, calls to the night clerk behind his counter. "Did you—did you see him?"

"What the hell's happening?"

"Did you *see* him?" He taps his pocket. "I've got a warrant for his arrest. Did you see which way he went?"

The clerk shakes his head. "He went out. I don't know. He went out. He was bleeding," he says. "His hand was all blood, his mouth."

"Yeah, he was too fast for me. I missed. I catch him I'm going to fuck all over him."

He goes through the revolving doors and out into the street. The air is lovely. He looks left and right. Which way, he wonders. North? To the suburbs? East towards the railroad tracks? Or did he double back? Head downtown maybe? To the street where he himself had walked that afternoon? Where the people were more like film stars than the film stars were, as everybody was these days, handsomeness creeping up the avenues of the world like the golden bedsprings in the Cincinnati trees?

The Making of Ashenden

I 'V E   B E E N spared a lot, one of the blessed of the earth, at least one of its lucky, that privileged handful of the dramatically prospering, the sort whose secrets are asked, like the hundred-year-old man. There is no secret, of course; most of what happens to us is simple accident. Highish birth and a smooth network of appropriate connection like a tea service written into the will. But surely something in the blood too, locked into good fortune's dominant genes like a blast ripening in a time bomb. Set to go off, my good looks and intelligence, yet exceptional still, take *away* my mouthful of silver spoon and lapful of luxury. Something my own, not passed on or handed down, something seized, wrested—my good character, hopefully, my taste perhaps. What's mine, what's mine? Say taste—the soul's harmless appetite.

I've money, I'm rich. The heir to four fortunes. Grandfather on Mother's side was a Newpert. The family held some good real estate in Rhode Island until they sold it for many times what they gave for it. Grandmother on Father's side was a Salts, whose bottled mineral water, once available only through prescription and believed indispensable in the cure of all fevers, was the first product ever to be reviewed by the Food and Drug Administration, a famous and controversial case. The government found it to contain nothing that was actually *detrimental* to human beings, and it went public, so to speak. Available now over the counter, the Salts made more money from it than ever.

Mother was an Oh. *Her* mother was the chemical engineer who first discovered a feasible way to store oxygen in tanks. And Father was Noel Ashenden, who though he did not actually invent the matchbook, went into the field when it was still a not very flourishing novelty, and whose slogan, almost a poem, "Close Cover Before Striking" (a simple stroke, as Father liked to say), obvious only after someone else has already thought of it (the Patent Office refused to issue a patent on what it claimed was merely an instruction, but Father's company had the message on its matchbooks before his competitors even knew what was happening), removed the hazard from book matches and turned the industry and Father's firm particularly into a flaming success overnight—Father's joke, not mine. Later, when the inroads of Ronson and Zippo threatened the business, Father went into seclusion for six months and when he returned to us he had produced another slogan: "For Our Matchless Friends." It saved the industry a second time and was the second and last piece of work in Father's life.

There are people who gather in the spas and watering places of this world who pooh-pooh our fortune. Après ski, cozy in their wools, handsome before their open hearths, they scandalize amongst themselves in whispers. "Imagine," they say, "saved from ruin because of some cornball sentiment available in every bar and grill and truck stop in the country. It's not, not . . ."

Not what? Snobs! Phooey on the First Families. On railroad, steel mill, automotive, public utility, banking and shipping fortunes, on all hermetic legacy, morganatic and blockbuster bloodlines that change the maps and landscapes and alter the mobility patterns, your jungle wheeling and downtown dealing a stone's throw from warfare. I come of good stock—real estate, mineral water, oxygen, matchbooks: earth, water, air and fire, the old elementals of the material universe, a bellybutton economics, a linchpin one.

It is as I see it a perfect genealogy, and if I can be bought and sold a hundred times over by a thousand men in this country—people in your own town could do it, providents and trailers of hunch, I bless them, who got into this or went into that when it was eight cents a share—I am satisfied with my thirteen or fourteen million. Wealth is not after all the point. The genealogy is. That bridge-trick nexus that brought New-

pert to Oh, Salts to Ashenden and Ashenden to Oh, love's lucky
longshots which, paying off, permitted me as they permit every
human life! (I have this simple, harmless paranoia of the good-
natured man, this cheerful awe.) Forgive my enthusiasm, that
I go on like some secular patriot wrapped in the simple flag of
self, a professional descendant, every day the closed-for-the-
holiday banks and post offices of the heart. And why not? Aren't
my circumstances superb? Whose are better? No boast, no boast.
I've had it easy, served up on all life's silver platters like a sa-
trap. And if my money is managed for me and I do no work—
less work even than Father, who at least came up with those
two slogans, the latter in a six-month solitude that must have been
hell for that gregarious man ("For Our Matchless Friends": no
slogan finally but a broken code, an extension of his own hos-
pitable being, simply the Promethean gift of fire to a guest)—
at least I am not "spoiled" and have in me still alive the nerve
endings of gratitude. If it's miserly to count one's blessings,
Brewster Ashenden's a miser.

This will give you some idea of what I'm like:

On Having an Account in a Swiss Bank: I never had one,
and suggest you stay away from them too. Oh, the mystery and
romance is all very well, but never forget that your Swiss bank
offers no premiums, whereas for opening a savings account for
$5,000 or more at First National City Bank of New York or
other fine institutions you get wonderful premiums—picnic
hampers, Scotch coolers, Polaroid cameras, Hudson's Bay blankets from L. L. Bean, electric shavers, even lawn furniture. My
managers always leave me a million or so to play with, and
this is how I do it. I suppose I've received hundreds of such
bonuses. Usually I give them to friends or as gifts at Christmas
to doormen and other loosely connected personnel of the household, but often I keep them and use them myself. I'm not stingy.
Of course I can afford to buy any of these things—and I do,
I enjoy making purchases—but somehow nothing brings the joy
of existence home to me more than these premiums. Something
from nothing—the two-suiter from Chase Manhattan and my
own existence, luggage a bonus and life a bonus too. Like having

a film star next to you on your flight from the Coast. There are treats of high order, adventure like cash in the street.

Let's enjoy ourselves, I say; let's have fun. Lord, let us live in the sand by the surf of the sea and play till cows come home. We'll have a house on the Vineyard and a brownstone in the Seventies and a *pied-à-terre* in a world capital when something big is about to break. (Put the Cardinal in the back bedroom where the sun gilds the bay at afternoon tea and give us the courage to stand up to secret police at the door, to top all threats with threats of our own, the nicknames of mayors and ministers, the fast comeback at the front stairs, authority on us like the funny squiggle the counterfeiters miss.) Re-Columbus us. Engage us with the overlooked, a knowledge of optics, say, or a gift for the tides. (My pal, the heir to most of the vegetables in inland Nebraska, has become a superb amateur oceanographer. The marine studies people invite him to Wood's Hole each year. He has a wave named for him.) Make us good at things, the countertenor and the German language, and teach us to be as easy in our amateur standing as the best man at a roommate's wedding. Give us hard tummies behind the cummerbund and long swimmer's muscles under the hound's tooth so that we may enjoy our long life. And may all our stocks rise to the occasion of our best possibilities, and our humanness be bullish too.

Speaking personally I am glad to be a heroic man.

I am pleased that I am attractive to women but grateful I'm no bounder. Though I'm touched when married women fall in love with me, as frequently they do, I am rarely to blame. I never encourage these fits and do my best to get them over their derangements so as not to lose the friendships of their husbands when they are known to me, or the neutral friendship of the ladies themselves. This happens less than you might think, however, for whenever I am a houseguest of a married friend I usually make it a point to bring along a girl. These girls are from all walks of life—models, show girls, starlets, actresses, tennis professionals, singers, heiresses and the daughters of the diplomats of most of the nations of the free world. *All* walks.

They tend, however, to conform to a single physical type, and are almost always tall, tan, slender and blond, the girl from Ipanema as a wag friend of mine has it. They are always sensitive and intelligent and good at sailing and the Australian crawl. They are never blemished in any way, for even something like a tiny beauty mark on the inside of a thigh or above the shoulder blade is enough to put me off, and their breaths must be as sweet at three in the morning as they are at noon. (I never see a woman who is dieting for diet sours the breath.) Arm hair, of course, is repellent to me though a soft blond down is now and then acceptable. I know I sound a prig. I'm not. I am—well, classical, drawn by perfection as to some magnetic, Platonic pole, idealism and beauty's true North.

But if I'm demanding about the type I fall in love with— I *do* fall in love, I'm not Don Juan—I try to be charming to all women, the flawed as well as the unflawed. I know that times have changed and that less is expected of gentlemen these days, that there's more "openness" between the sexes and that in the main, this is a healthy development. Still, in certain respects I am old-fashioned—I'm the first to admit it—and not only find myself incapable of strong language in the presence of a lady (I rarely use it myself at any time, even a "damn" even a "hell") but become enraged when someone else uses it and immediately want to call him out. I'm the same if there's a child about or a man over the age of fifty-seven if he is not vigorous. The leopard cannot change his spots. I'm a gentleman, an opener of doors and doffer of hats and after you firster, meek in the elevator and kind to the help. I maintain a fund which I use for the abortions of girls other men have gotten into trouble; if the young lady prefers, I have a heart-to-heart with the young man. And although I've no sisters, I have a brother's temperament, all good counsel and real concern. Even without a sister of my own—or a brother either for that matter; I'm an only child—I lend an ear and do for other fellows' sisses the moral forks.

Still, there's fun in me, and danger too. I'm this orphan now but that's recent (Father and Mother died early this year, Mother first and Father a few days later—Father, too, was courteous to

women), and I'm afraid that when they were alive I gave my
parents some grisly moments with my exploits, put their hearts
in their mouths and gray in their hair. I have been a fighter pilot
for the RAF (I saw some action at Suez) and a mercenary on
the *Biafran* side, as well as a sort of free-lance spy against some
of your South American and Greek juntas. (I'm not political, but
the average generalissimo cheats at cards. It's curious, I've
noticed that though they steal the picture cards they rarely play
them; I suppose it's a class thing—your military man would
rather beat you with a nine than a king.) I am Johnny-on-the-
spot at disasters—I was in Managua for the earthquake—lending
a hand, pulling my oar, the sort of man who knocks your teeth
out if he catches you abusing the water ration in the lifeboat
and then turns around and offers his own meager mouthful to a
woman or a man over fifty-seven. Chavez is my friend and the
Chicago Seven, though I had to stop seeing them because of the
foul language. (I love Jerry Rubin too much to tear his head
off, and I could see that's what it would come to.) And here and
there I've had Mafiosi for friends—wonderful family men, the
Cosa Nostra, I respect that. And the astronauts, of course; I
spent a weightless weekend with them in an anti-gravity chamber
in Houston one time, coming down only to take a long-distance
phone call from a girl in trouble. And, let's see, sixty hours in the
bathysphere with Cousteau, fathoms below where the ordinary
fish run. So I have been weightless and I have been gravid, falling
in free-fall like a spider down its filament and paid out in rappel.
And in the Prix de this and Prix de t'other, all the classic combats
of moving parts (my own moving parts loose as a toy yet to be
assembled), uninsurable at last, taking a stunt man's risks, a
darer gone first, blinded in the world's uncharted caves and
deafened beneath its waterfalls, the earth itself a sort of Jungle
Gym finally, my playground, swimming at your own risk.

Last winter I fought a duel. I saw a man whipping his dog and
called him out. Pistols at fourteen paces. The fellow—a prince, a
wastrel—could get no one to act as his second so I did it myself,
giving him pointers, calling the adjustments for windage, and at
last standing still for him as one of those FBI paper silhouettes,

my vitals (we were on a beach, I wore no shirt, just my bathing suit, the sun, rising over his shoulder, spotlighting me) clear as marked meat on a butcher's diagram, my Valentine heart vaulting toward the barrel of his pistol. He fired and missed and I threw my pistol into the sea. He wept, and I took him back to the house and gave him a good price for his dog. And running with the bulls at Pamplona—not in front of them, *with* them— and strolling at two a.m. through the Casbah like a fellow down Main Street, and standing on top of a patrol car in Harlem talk- ing through the bull horn to the sniper. And dumb things too.

Father called me home from Tel Aviv a few weeks before he died.

He was sitting on a new bed in his room wearing only his pajama tops. He hadn't shaved, the gray stubble latticing his lower face in an old man's way, like some snood of mortality. There was a glass in his hand, his one-hundred-dollar bill rolled tight around the condensation. (He always fingered one, a tic.)

"Say hello to your mother."

I hadn't seen her. Like many people who have learned the secret of living together, Father and Mother slept in separate suites, but now twin beds, Father in one, Mother in the other, had re- placed Father's fourposter. A nightstand stood between them— I remembered it from Grandmother Newpert's summer house in Edgarton—on which, arranged like two entrenched armies, were two sets of medicines, Father's bright ceremonial pills and May Day capsules, and Mother's liquids in their antique apothe- cary bottles (she supplied the druggist with these bottles herself, insisting out of her willful aesthetic sense that all her prescrip- tions be placed in them), with their water glasses and a shiny artillery of teaspoons. Mother herself seemed to be sleeping. Perhaps that's why I hadn't noticed her, or perhaps it was the angle, Father's bed being the closer as I walked into the room. Or perhaps it was her condition itself, sickness an effacement. I hesitated.

"It's all right," Father said. "She's awake. You're not disturb- ing her."

"Her eyes are closed," I said softly to Father.

"I have been seeing double in the morning, Brewster darling," Mother said. "It gives me megrim to open them."

"Mother, you naughty slugabed," I teased. Sometimes being a gentleman can be a pain in the you-know-where, to oneself as well as to others. Well, it's often fatuous, and in emergency it always is, as anything is in emergency short of an uncivilized scream, but what can you do, a code is a code. One dresses for dinner in the jungle and surrenders one's sword to the enemy and says thank you very much and refuses the blindfold. "Shame on you, sweetheart, the sun up these several hours and you still tucked in."

"It's cancer, Son," Father said in a low tone not meant for Mother.

"Lazybones," I scolded, swallowing hard.

"Oh, I *do* want to see you, Brewster," Mother said. "Perhaps if I opened just *one* little eye—"

"Not at all, you sweet dear. If you must lie in bed all day I think it best that you do some honest sleeping. I'll still be here when you finally decide to get up."

"There, that's better," Mother said, opening her right eye and scowling at me.

"Please, honeybunch, you'll see double and get megrim."

"Brewster, it's lovely. It makes you twice as handsome, twice as tall."

"Please, Mother—"

"Let her, Brew. This is a deathbed."

"Father!"

"Why are you so shocked, Brewster? It had to happen someday."

"I think I'll close it now."

"Really, Father, a *death*bed . . ."

"Since it upsets him so."

"Well, death*beds* then."

"But I reserve the right to open it again whenever I choose. If a cat can look at a king . . ."

"Father, aren't you being—that's right, darling, shut it, shut it tight—the slightest bit melodramatic?"

"Oh, for Lord's sake, Brew, don't be prissy. Mother and I are going, she of cancer, I of everything. Rather than waste the little time we have left together, we might try to get certain things straight."

"When Father called you back from overseas he arranged with Mrs. Lucas to have these twin deathbeds set up in here."

Mrs. Lucas is the housekeeper. She used to give me my baths when I was a child. I always try to remember to bring her a picnic hamper or some other especially nice premium from the bank when I come home for a visit. Over the years Mrs. Lucas has had *chaises longues*, card tables, hammocks and many powerful flashlights from me—a small fortune in merchandise.

"What were you doing in the Middle East in the first place? Those people aren't your sort, Brew."

"He did it for you, darling. He thought that by putting both deathbeds in the same room you wouldn't have to shuffle back and forth between one chamber and the next. It's a time-space thing, Noel said. Isn't that right, Noel?"

"Something like that. Yes, Nora."

"Father, the Jewish are darned impressive. They run their military like a small family business. The Arabs can't touch them."

"Arabs, Jews. In my time a country club was a country club. I don't understand anything anymore."

"Don't quarrel, Noel, Brew. Brew, you're the reason we decided to have deathbeds in the first place. Well, my family has always had them, of course. None of this hole-and-corner hospital stuff for them. I don't speak against hospitals, mind you, they're all very well if you're going to get better, but, goodness, if you're really dying it's so much more pleasant for the immediate family if they can be saved from those drafty, smelly hospital corridors. Grandmother Oh herself, though she invented the oxygen tank, refused the tent when her time came if it meant going to a hospital."

"Brr."

"Are you addressing me, Father?"

"What? No, no, I have a chill."

"Let me help you." I lifted his legs into the bed gently, took the glass out of his hand and set it down, unpeeling the $100 bill as if it were a beer label. I placed his head back on the pillow and, smoothing the sheets, started to cover him when he grinned.

"Close cover before striking," he said hoarsely. That broke the ice and we all laughed.

"Nothing important ever gets said in a hospital," Father said after a while. "There's too much distraction. The room, the gadgets, the flowers and who sent what, the nurses coming in for one thing or another. Nothing important gets said."

I nodded.

"Mother's right, Brewster. The deathbed has been a tradition in our family. This twin bed business is a little vulgar, perhaps, but it can't be helped. We'll have a deathbed vigil. It's a leisure thing. It's elegant."

"Please, Father, let's not have any more of this morbid stuff about dying," I said, getting the upper hand on myself. "It's my notion you're both goldbricking, that you'll be out on the links again in no time, your handicap lower than ever."

"It's heart, Brew," Father said gloomily. "It's Ménière's disease. It's TB and a touch of MS that hangs on like a summer cold. It's a spot of Black Lung."

"Black Lung?"

"Do you know how many matches I've struck in my time?"

"I wouldn't be surprised, Father, if there were another slogan in you yet. 'I Would Rather Light an Ashenden Match Than Curse the Darkness.' How's that?"

"Too literary. What the smoker wants is something short and sweet. No, there'll be no more slogans. Let others carry on my work. I'm tired."

"There's this Israeli ace," I said as a stopgap, "Izzy Heskovitz, who's . . ."

"What's this about a duel, Brewster?" Father asked.

"Oh, did you hear about that? I should have thought the Prince would have wanted it hushed up, after what happened."

"After what happened? He thinks you're mad. And so do I. Exposing yourself like that, offering a target like a statesman in an open car, then tossing your pistol into the sea. It was irresponsible. Were you trying to kill yourself?"

"It was a question of honor."

"With you, Brewster, everything is a question of honor."

"Everything is."

"Stuff and nonsense."

"I'm looking for myself."

"Brewster, you are probably the last young man in America still looking for himself," Father said. "As a man who has a certain experience with slogans, I have some sense of when they have lost their currency."

"Father, you are probably the last *old* man in America to take to a deathbed."

"Touché, Brew. He's got you there, Noel," Mother said.

"Thank you, Mother, but all I intended was to point out that obsolescence runs in our family. I am the earth, water, fire and air heir. Let the neon, tin and tungsten scions prepare themselves for the newfangled. I have pride and I have honor. My word is my bond and I'll marry a virgin. And I agree with you, Father, about the sanctity of the deathbed, though I shall continue, out of chivalry and delicacy, to maintain the imposture that this . . . these"—I took in the twin beds—"is . . . are . . . not that . . . those."

"You're marvelous, Brewster. I . . ."

"Is something wrong, Father?"

"I . . . we . . . your mother and I . . ."

"Father?"

"I love you, Son."

"I love *you*, sir," I told him. I turned to Mother. She had opened one eye again. It was wet and darting from one side to the other like an eye in REM sleep. I understood that she was trying to choose my real image from the two that stood before her. In a moment her eye had decided. It stared off, focused about four yards to my right. I smiled to reassure her that she had chosen correctly and edged slowly to my right, an Indian in reverse, unhiding, trying to appear in her line of sight like a magician's volunteer in an illusion. "And all I have to say to *you*, you great silly, is that if you're not out of bed soon I'll not answer for your zinnias and foxgloves. I noticed when the taxi brought me up the drive that Franklin, as usual, has managed to make a botch of the front beds."

"Franklin is old, Son," Mother said. "He isn't well."

"Franklin's a rogue, Mother. I don't know why you encourage him. I'm certain he's going to try to trade Mrs. Lucas the three hundred feet of lovely rubber garden hose I brought him for her Scotch cooler so that he can have a place to hide his liquor."

Mother closed her eye; Father grinned. I wrung out Father's hundred-dollar bill and handed it back to him. Excusing myself, I promised to return when they had rested. "Brr," Father said.

"Were you speaking to me, Father?"

"It's the chill again," he said.

I went to my room, called up their doctors and had long, discouraging talks with them. Then I phoned some specialist friends of mine at Mass General and a good man at Barnes in St. Louis and got some additional opinions. I asked about Franklin, too.

I kept the vigil. It was awful, but satisfying, too, in a way. It lasted five weeks and in that time we had truth and we had banter, and right up to the end each of us was able to tell the difference. Only once, a few days after Mother's death (her vision returned at the end: "I can see, Brewster," she said, "I can see far and I can see straight." These were not her last words; I'll not tell you her last words, for they were meant only for Father and myself, though I have written them down elsewhere to preserve for my children should I ever have them) did Father's spirits flag. He had gotten up from his bed to attend the funeral —through a signal courtesy to an out-of-stater, the Governor of Massachusetts permitted Mother to be buried on Copp's Hill Burying Ground near the Old North Church in Boston—and we had just returned to the house. Mrs. Lucas and Franklin were weeping, and I helped Father upstairs and back into his death-bed. He was too weak to put his pajamas on. "You know, Brew," he said, "I sure wish you hadn't thrown that d——d pistol into the ocean."

"Oh Father," I said, "never mind. Tomorrow when you're

stronger we'll go to town and buy a fresh brace and stroll the woods and shoot the birds from their trees just as we used to."

He was dead in his own tree a few days later. I sensed it coming and had moved into the room with him, where I lay next to him all night in the twin bed, only Grandmother New-pert's nightstand between us, Mother's effects—the lovely old apothecary bottles and her drinking glass and medicine spoons—having been cleared away. I was awake the entire night, hanging on his broken breath and old man's groans like a detective in films on the croaks of a victim. I listened for a message from the coma and tried to parse delirium as if it were only a sort of French. Shall a man of honor and pride still searching for him-self in his late thirties deny the sibyl in a goner's gasps? (I even asked one or two questions, pressing him in his terminal pain, pursuing him through the mazes of his dissolution, his death-bed my Ouija board.)

Then, once, just before dawn, a bird twittered in the garden and Father came out of it. For fifteen minutes he talked sense, speaking rapidly and with an astonishing cogency that was more mysterious somehow than all his moans and nightmares. He spoke of ways to expedite the probating of the two wills, of flaws in the nature of his estate, instructing me where to consolidate and where to trim. He told me the names of what lawyers to trust, which brokers to fire. In five minutes he laid down principles which would guarantee our fortune for a hundred years. Then, at the end, there was something personal, but after what had gone before, I thought it a touch lame, like a P.S. inquiring about your family's health at the end of a business letter. He wished me well and hoped I would find some nice girl, settle down, and raise fine children. I was to give them his love.

I thought this was the end, but in a few moments he came round again.

"Franklin *is* a rogue," he said. "For many years now he and Mrs. Lucas have been carrying on an affair below stairs. That time during the war when Mrs. Lucas was supposed to have gone to stay with her sister in Delaware she really went away to have Franklin's child. The scoundrel refused to marry her and would have had money from us to abort the poor thing. It was Mrs. Lucas who wouldn't hear of it, but the baby died anyway. Mrs. Lucas loves him. It's for her sake we never let him go when he screwed up in the garden."

Those were Father's last words. Then he beckoned me to rise from my bed and approach him. He put out his right hand. I shook it and he died. The hundred-dollar bill he always held came off in my palm when the final paroxysm splayed his fingers.

The grief of the rich is clubby, expensive. (I don't mean *my* grief. My grief was a long gloom, persistent as grudge.) We are born weekenders anyway, but in death we are particularly good to each other, traveling thousands of miles to funerals, flying up from Rio or jamming the oceanic cables with our expensive consolation. (Those wires from the President to the important bereaved—that's our style, too.) We say it with flowers, wreaths, memorial libraries, offering the wing of a hospital as casually as someone else a chicken leg at a picnic. And why not? There aren't that many of us—never mind that there are a thousand who can buy and sell me. Scarcer we are than the Eskimaux, vanishing Americans who got rich slow.

So I did not wonder at the crowds who turned up at Mother's funeral and then went away the long distances only to return a few days later for Father's. Or at the clothes. Couturiers of Paris and London and New York—those three splendid cities, listed always together and making a sound on the page like a label on scent—taxed to the breaking point to come up with dresses in death's delicious high fashion, the rich taking big casualties that season, two new mourning originals in less than two weeks and the fitter in fits. The men splendid in their decent dark. Suits cunnngly not black, *off* black, proper, the longitudes of their decency in their wiry pinstripes, a gent's torso bound up in vest and crisscrossed by watch chains and Phi Beta Kappa keys in the innocent para-militarism of the civilian respectable, men somehow more vital at the graveside in the burdensome clothes than in Bermudas on beaches or dinner jackets in hotel suites with cocktails in their hands, the band playing on the beach below and the telephone ringing.

And all the women were beautiful, gorgeous, grieving's colors good for them, aloof mantles which made them seem (though I knew better) unattainable, virgins again, yet sexy still as secret drinkers. God, how I lusted when I was with them! I could barely put two words together for them or accept their condolences without feeling my importunate, inopportune blood thicken, my senses as ticklish as if Persian whores had gotten to them. Which added to my gloom, of course, because I was dishonoring my parents in their death as I never had while they lived.

Only the necessity to cope saved me from some sacrilege. (Oh, the confidence of lust! Surely that's the basis of its evil. The assumptions it permits one, glossing reality like a boy in the dark, touching himself and thinking of his mother's bridge guests.) Somehow, however, I managed to see my tailor, somehow got the arrangements made, somehow wrote the necessary checks and visited the near-at-hand safe-deposit boxes before they were red-flagged, somehow got through the inventories, spoke to the obituary people at the *Times*, prepared the eulogies somehow, and fielded all the questions of the well-meaning that are asked at times like these.

"Will there be a foundation, do you suppose, Ashenden?" asked an old friend of the family who had himself been an heir for as long as we had known him. (And oh, the effect of that "Ashenden"! It was the first time one had been thus addressed, at least officially, since one's roommates at boarding school and college, thinking of their own inheritances, had used it.)

"I don't know, sir. It's too early to tell. I shall have to wait until the estate is properly probated before I can be certain what there is."

"Of course, of course," he said, "but it's never too soon to start *thinking* about a foundation, fixing your goals."

"Yes, sir."

"Let me give you a little advice on that score. The arts. There are those who swear by diseases and the various social ills, but I'm not one of them. And of the arts I think the *performing* arts give you your best return. You get invited backstage."

"I'll have to look into it."

"Look into it."

And one of Mother's friends wondered if marriage was in the offing. "Now you really *are* eligible, Brewster," she said. "Oh, you were before, of course, but now you must certainly feel a bit of pressure to put your affairs in order and began to think about the next generation."

It was a rude thing to say (though something like these had been almost Father's last words to me), but the truth was I did feel it. Perhaps that was what my shameful lust had been about, nature's way of pointing me to my duty. My search for myself seemed trivial child's play now. Honor did subsist in doing right by the generations. I know what you're thinking: Who's this impostor, this namby with no will of his own? If he's so rich, why ain't he smart? Meaning glacial, indifferent, unconscious of the swath of world he cuts as the blade of what it leaves bleeding —the cosmos as rich man's butter pat. Listen, disdain's easy, a mug's game, but look close at anything and you'll break your heart.

I was inconsolable, grave at the graveside, beside myself like a fulfillment of Mother's prophetic double vision.

"People lose parents," a Securities and Exchange Commission cousin told me. (Yes, yes, it's nothing, only nature bottoming out.) "Sons lose mothers," he said, his gray hair trimmed that morning, wet looking. "Fathers die."

"Don't look," I said wildly, "shut an eye. I am beside myself."

I keened like a widow, a refugee from hardest times, a daughter with the Cossacks, a son chopped in the thresher. I would go about in black, I thought, and be superstitious. My features will thicken and no one will know how old I am.

"There, there," he told me, "there, there."

"There, there. There, there," said this one and that.

My pals did not know what to make of me.

"My God, Ashenden," one said, a roommate from boarding school, "have you seen the will? Is it awful?"

"I've been left everything," I told him coolly.

He nudged me in the ribs. I would have called him out had I not been in mourning.

Only the sight of Mrs. Lucas saved me. The thought of that
brave woman's travail enabled me to control myself at last. I no
longer wept openly and settled into a silent, stand-offish grim-
ness, despair like an ingrown toenail on a man of fashion.

The weekends began.

All my adult life I have been a guest in other people's houses,
following the sun and seasons like a migratory bird, an instinct in
me, the rich man's cunning feel for ripeness, some oyster-in-an-r-
month notion working there which knows without reference to
anything outside itself when to pack the tennis racket, when to
bring along the German field glasses to look at a friend's birds,
the telescope to stare at his stars, the wet suit to swim in beneath
his waters when the exotic fish are running. It's not in the *Times*
when the black dinner jacket comes off and the white one goes
on; it's something surer, subtler, the delicate guidance system of
the privileged, my playboy astronomy.

The weekends began, and the midweeks and week- and two-
week stretches in the country. I was very grateful to my friends'
sense of what I needed then. Where I was welcome before, I
was now actively pursued. My friends were marvelous, and not
a mean motive between them. If I can't say as much for myself.

In the luggage now with the bandboxes of equipment, the
riding boots and golf clubs and hiker's gear, was a lover's wardrobe: shirts like the breasts of birds, custom ties that camouflaged
themselves against their backgrounds or stood out like dye in the
sea, ascots like bunting for the throat's centennial, the handmade
jackets and perfect trousers and tack room leathers. I dressed to
kill, slay should I meet her, the mother of my children. (These
were my mourning togs, mind.) And if I brought the best that
could be had, it was not out of vanity but only respect for that
phantom girl who would be so exquisite herself, so refined and
blessed with taste that it would have been as dangerous for her to
look at the undistinguished as for another to stare directly into
the eclipse. So it was actually humility that made me dress as I did,
simple self-effacement, the old knight's old modesty, shyness so
capitulative that prostration was only a kind of militant attention,
a death-defying leap to the earth. And since I had never met her,
nor knew her name, nor had a clue to where she might be, I

traveled alone, for the first time taking along no guest of the guest. Which my friends put down to decency, the thirty- or sixty- or ninety-day celibacy of the orphaned. But it wasn't that.

It was a strange period of my life. My friends, innocent of my intentions and honoring what they supposed to be my bereavement, omitted to invite any girls for me at all, and I found myself on this odd bachelor circuit, several times meeting the same male guest I had met at someone else's house a few weeks before. We crossed each other's paths like traveling salesmen with identical territories. And I rode and hunted and fished and stayed up all hours playing whist or backgammon or chess with my hosts or the other male guest, settled before fires with sherry and cognac, oddly domestic, as if what I owed the generations was a debt already paid, a trip in the time machine, keeping late hours in libraries until the odor of leather actually became offensive to me. On the few occasions I retired early it was at my host's instructions. (I am an obedient guest.) The next morning there was to be an excursion in the four-wheel drive to investigate property he had acquired in backwoods forty miles off—a lodge, an abandoned watchtower, twice an old lighthouse. And always, nodding my approval if the purchase had been made or giving my judicious advice if it hadn't, I had this sense that I'd had the night before in the library: that the property in question was *my* property, that I was already what I was dressed to become.

I was not bored; I was distraught.

A strange thing happened. It occurred to me that perhaps my old fastidiousness regarding the inviolability of a friend's wife was wrong, morally wrong. Had not these women made overtures, dropped hints, left doors ajar so that returning to my room with a book I could see them in nightgowns beside bedlamps; hadn't they smiled sweetly and raised arms? Perhaps I had been a prig, had placed too high a value on myself by insisting on the virginity of my intended. Perhaps it was my fate to figure in a divorce. I decided that henceforth I must not be so stand-offish with my friends' wives.

So I stroked their knees beneath the whist table and put down their alarm to surprise. I begged off going on the excursions and stayed home with them when my friend and the other guest climbed into the jeep. I followed the wife all about the house and cornered her in stairwells and gardens.

"I'm no prig," I told Nan Bridge, and clasped her breast and bit her ear.

"What the hell do you think you're doing, buster?" she shouted.

"Four months ago I would have called you out for that," I told her lamely and left her house that afternoon and went to the next three days early, determined to be more careful.

I was staying with Courtney and Buffy Surface in Connecticut. Claiming a tennis elbow, I excused myself from the doubles early in the first set. Courtney and I were partners against Buffy and Oscar Bobrinage, the other houseguest. My plan was for Buffy to drop out and join me. I sat under a wide umbrella in the garden, and in a few minutes someone came up behind me. "Where does it hurt? I'll rub it for you."

"No thank you, Oscar."

"No trouble, Brewster."

"I've a heating pad from Chase Manhattan in my suitcase, Osc," I told him dejectedly.

That night I was more obvious. I left the library and mentioned as casually as I could that I was going out for a bit of air. It has been my observation that the predisposition for encounter precedes encounter, that one must set oneself as one would a table. I never stroll the strand in moonlight except when I'm about the heart's business, or cross bridges toward dawn unless I mean to save the suicides. There are natural laws, magnetism. A wish pulls fate.

I passed the gazebo and wondered about the colors of the flowers in the dark, the queer consolidation of noon's bright pigment, yellow sunk in on yellow a thousand times as if struck by gravity. I thought of popular songs, their tunes and words. I meant for once to do away with polite conversation should Buffy appear, to stun her with my need and force. (Of all my friends Buffy was the most royally aloof. She had maddening ways of turning aside any question or statement that was the least bit threatening.)

I heard the soft crunch of gravel. "Oscar?"

"No, it's Buffy. Were you loking for Oscar?"

"I thought he might be looking for me."

"*Voilà du joli,*" Buffy said. She knew the idioms of eleven modern languages.

I gazed into her eyes. "How are you and Courtney, Buffy?"

"*Mon dieu! ¿Qué pasa? Il est onze heures et demi,*" she said.

"Buffy, how are you and *Courtney*?"

"Courtney's been off erythromycin five days now and General Parker says there's no sign of redness. God bless wonder drugs. *Darauf kannst du Gift nehmen.*"

"Do you ever think of Madrid, Buffy?" Once, in a night club in Madrid on New Year's Eve she had kissed me. It was before she and Courtney met, but my memory of such things is long lasting and profound. I never forget the blandest intimacy. "*Do* you?"

"Oh, Brewster, I have every hope that when Juan Carlos is restored the people will accept him."

"Buffy, we kissed each other on New Year's Eve in Madrid in 1966 before you ever heard of Courtney Surface."

"*Autres temps, autres moeurs.*"

"I can't accept that, Buff. Forgive me, dear, but when I left the game this morning you stayed behind to finish out the set *against* Courtney. Yes, and before that you were Oscar's partner. Doesn't this indicate to you a certain aberrant competitiveness between you and your husband?"

"Oh, but darling, we play for *money*. *Pisica blândă pgarie rău*. Didn't you know that? We earn each other's birthday presents. We've an agreement: we don't buy a gift unless we win the money for it from the other fellow. I'll tell you something, *entre nous*. I get ripped off because I throw games. I do. I take dives. I go into the tank. *Damit kannst du keinen Blumentopf verlieren*. Isn't that *awful*? Aren't I *terrible*? But that's how Courtney got the money together to buy me Nancy's Treehouse. Have you seen her? She's the *most* marvelous beast. I was just going out to the stables to check on her when I ran into you. If you'd like to accompany me come along *lo más pronto posible*."

"No."

"*De gustibus.*"

"That's *not* a modern language, Buffy."

"People *grow*, darling."

"Buffy, as your houseguest I *demand* that you listen to me. I am almost forty years old and I am one of the three or four dozen truly civilized men in the world and I have been left a fortune. A fortune! And though I have always had the use of the money, I have never till now had the control of it. Up to now I have been an adventurer. The adventures, God save me, were meant to teach me life. Danger builds strong bodies twelve ways, I thought. Action and respite have been the pattern of my existence, Buffy. Through shot and shell on hands and knees one day, and breakfast in bed at the Claridge the next. I have lived my life a fighter pilot, beefed up like a gladiator, like a stuffed goose, like a Thanksgiving turkey. I am this civilized . . . *thing*. Trained and skilled and good. I mean *good*, Buffy, a strict observer till night before last of every commandment there is. Plus an eleventh—honor thy world, I mean. I've done that. I'm versed in it, up to my ears in it as you are in idioms. I was an environmentalist a decade before it was an issue. When I first noticed the deer were scrawnier than they'd been when I was a boy and the water in the rivers where I swam no longer tasted like peaches.

"I've been a scholar of the world—oh, an amateur, I grant you, but a scholar just the same. I understand things. I know literature and math and science and art. I know *everything*. How paper is made, glass blown, marble carved, things about furniture, stuff about cheese. This isn't a boast. With forty years to do it in and nothing to distract you like earning a living or raising a family, you can learn almost all there is *to* learn if you leave out the mystery and the ambiguity. If you omit the riddles and finesse the existential.

"No, *wait*! I'm perfectly aware that I'm barking up the wrong tree—do you have that idiom, my dear?—but looky, looky, I'm speaking my heart. I'm in mourning, Buff. Here's how I do it. By changing my life. By taking this precious, solipsistic civilization of mine—Buffy, listen to me, dear; *it's not enough that there are only three or four dozen truly civilized men in the world*—this precious civilization of mine and passing it on to sons, daughters, all I can get."

"*Was ist los?*" she said miserably.

"Time and tide."

"*Pauvre garçon.*"

"Buffy, *pauvre garçon* me no *pauvres garçons.*"

She looked at me for a moment with as much feeling as I had looked at her. "Jane Löes Lipton."

"What?"

"Jane Löes Lipton. A friend of my sister Milly."

"What about her?"

"Ah."

"Ah?"

"She'll be Comte de Survillieur's houseguest this month. Do you know the Comte?"

"We did a hitch together in the Foreign Legion."

"Go. Pack. I'll phone Paris. Perhaps Milly can get you an invitation. *In bocca al lupo.*"

I missed her at the Comte de Survillieur's, and again at Liège, and once more at Cap Thérèse and the Oktoberfest at München. All Europe was talking about her—the fabulous Jane Löes Lipton. One had only to mention her name to elicit one of those round Henry James "Ah's." Nor did it surprise me that until the evening in Buffy Surface's garden I had never heard of her: I had been out of society for three or four months. These things happen quickly, these brush fires of personality, some girl suddenly taken up and turned into a household word (if you can call a seventy-room castle a household or "Ah" a word). Once or twice I had seen an old woman or even a child given this treatment. Normally I avoided such persons. When their fame was justified at all it was usually predicated on some quirkishness, nothing more substantial than some lisp of the character—a commitment to astrology, perhaps, or a knack for mimicry, or skill at bridge. I despise society, but who else will deal with me? I can't run loose in the street with the sailors or drink with the whores. I would put off everyone but a peer.

Still . . . Jane Löes Lipton. Ah. I hadn't met her, but from what I could gather from my peers' collective inarticulateness when it came to Miss (that much was established) Lipton, she was an "authentic," an "original," a "beauty," a "prize." And it was intriguing, too, how I happened to keep missing her, for once invited to the Comte's—where I behaved; where, recovering my senses, I no longer coveted my neighbor's wife and re-dedicated myself to carrying on the good work of my genes and environment in honorable ways—I had joined a regular touring company of the rich and favored. We were like the Ice Capades, like an old-time circus, occasionally taking on personnel, once in a while dropping someone off—a car pool of the heavily leisured. How I happened, as I say, to keep on missing her though we were on the same circuit now, going around—no metaphor but a literal description—in the same circles—and it is *too* a small world, at our heights, way up there where true North consolidates and collects like fog, it is—was uncanny, purest contretemps, a melodrama of bad timing. We were on the same guest lists, often the same floors or wings (dowagers showed me house plans, duchesses did; I saw the seating arrangements and croquet combinations), co-sponsors of the same charity balls and dinners. Twice it was I who fell out of lockstep and had to stay longer than I expected or leave a few days early, but every other time it was Jane who canceled out at the last minute. Was this her claim on them, I wondered? A Monroeish tempera-ment, some pathological inability to keep appointments, honor commitments (though always her check for charity arrived, folded in her letter of regret), the old high school strategy of playing hard to get? No. And try to imagine how *this* struck me, know-ing what you do about me, when I heard it. "Miss Löes Lipton called to say she will not be able to join your Lordship this weekend due to an emergency outbreak of cholera among the children at the Sisters of Cecilia Mission in Lobos de Afuera." That was the message the Duke's secretary brought him at Liège.

"She's Catholic?" I asked.

"What? Jane? Good Lord, I shouldn't think so."

Then, at Cap Thérèse, I learned that she had again begged off.

I expressed disappointment and inquired of Mrs. Steppington whether Miss Lipton were ill.

"Ah, Jane. Ill? Jane's strong as a horse. No, dear boy, there was a plane crash at Dar es Salaam and Jane went there to help the survivors. She's visiting in hospital with them now. For those of them who have children—mostly wogs, I expect—she's volunteered to act as a sort of governess. I can almost see her, going about with a lot of nig-nog kids in tow, teaching them French, telling them the Greek myths, carrying them to whatever museums they have in such places, giving them lectures in art history, then fetching them watercolors—and oils too, I shouldn't doubt—so they can have a go at it. Oh, it *will* be a bore not having her with us. She's a frightfully good sailor and I had hoped to get her to wear my silks in the regatta."

Though it was two in the morning in Paris, I went to my room and called the Comte de Survillieur.

"Comte. Why couldn't Jane Löes Lipton make it month before last?"

"What's that?" The connection was bad.

"Why did Miss Löes Lipton fail to show up when she was expected at Deux Oiseaux?"

"Who?"

"Jane Löes Lipton."

"Ah."

"Why wasn't she there?"

"Who's this?"

"Brewster Ashenden. I apologize for ringing up so late, but I have to know."

"Indians."

"Indians?"

"Yes. American Indians I think it was. Had to do some special pleading for them in Washington when a bill came up before your Congress."

"HR eleven seventy-four."

"*Qu'est-ce que c'est?*"

"The bill. Law now. So Jane was into HR eleven seventy-four."

"Ah, what isn't Jane into? You know, I think she's become

something of a snob? She has no time for her old friends since undertaking these crusades of hers. She told the Comtesse as much —something about finding herself."

"She said *that*?"

"Well, she was more poetic, possibly, but that's how it came down to me. I know what *you're* after," the Comte said roguishly. "You're in love with her."

"I've never even met her."

"You're in love with her. Half Europe is. But unless you're a black or redskin, or have arranged in some other way to cripple yourself, you haven't a chance. Arse over tip in love, *mon cher* old comrade."

We rang off.

In the following weeks I heard that Jane Löes Lipton had turned up in Hanoi to see if there weren't some way of getting negotiations off dead center; that she had published a book that broke the code in Oriental rugs; that she had directed an underground movie in Sweden which despite its frank language and graphic detail was so sensitive it was to be distributed with a G rating; and that she was back in America visiting outdoor fairs and buying up paintings depicting clowns and rowboats turned over on beaches for a show she was putting together for the Metropolitan entitled "Shopping Center Primitive: Collectors' Items for the Twenty-Third Century." One man said she could be seen in Dacca on Bangladesh Television in a series called "Cooking Nutritious Meals on the Pavement for Large Families from Garbage and Without Fire," and another that she had become a sort of spiritual adviser to the statesmen of overdeveloped nations. Newspapers reported her on the scene wherever the earth quaked or the ships foundered or the forests burned.

Certainly she could not have had so many avatars. Certainly most was rumor, speculation knit from Jane's motives and sympathies. Yet I heard people never known to lie, Rock-of-Gibraltarish types who didn't get the point of jokes, swear to their testimony. Where there's smoke there's fire. If most was exaggerated, much was true.

Ah, Jane, Candy Striper to the Cosmos, Gray Lady of the

Ineffable, when would I meet you, swap traveler's tales of what was to be found in those hot jungles of self-seeking, those voyages to the center of the soul and other uncharted places, the steeps and deeps and lost coves and far shelves of being? Ah, Jane, oh Löes Lipton, half Europe loves you.

I went to London and stayed in the Bottom, the tall new hotel there. Lonely as Frank Sinatra on an album cover I went up to their revolving cocktail lounge on the fiftieth floor, the Top of the Bottom, and ran into Freddy Plympton.

"She's here."

"Jane Löes Lipton? I've heard *that* one before." (We hadn't been talking of her. How did I know that's who he meant? I don't know, I knew.)

"No, no, she is, at my country place. She's there now. She's exhausted, poor dear, and tells me her doctor has commanded her to resign temporarily from all volunteer fire departments. So she's here. I've got her. She's with Lady Plympton right this moment. I had to come to town on business or I'd be with her. I'm going back in the morning. Ever meet her? Want to come down?"

"She's there? She's really there?"

"Want to come down?"

There's been too much pedigree in this account, I think. (Be kind. Put it down to metaphysics, not vanity. In asking Who? I'm wondering What? Even the trees have names, the rocks and clouds and grasses do. The world's a picture post card sent from a far hotel. "Here's my room, this is what the stamps in this country look like, that's the strange color of the sand here, the people all wear these curious hats.") Bear with me.

Freddy Plympton is noble. The family is old—whose isn't, eh? we were none of us born yesterday; look it up in *Burke's Peerage* where it gets three pages, in *Debrett* where it gets four—and his great estate, Duluth, is one of the finest in England. Though he could build a grander if he chose. Freddy's real wealth comes from the gambling casinos he owns. He is an entrepreneur of chance, a fortune teller. The biggest gaming palaces and highest stakes in Europe, to say nothing of hotels in Aruba and boats beyond the twelve-mile limit and a piece of the action in church bingo basements and punchboards all over the world, the newsprint for which is supplied from his own forests in Norway and is printed on his own presses. Starting from scratch, from choosing odds-or-evens for cash with his roommate at Harrow, a sheikh's son with a finger missing from his left hand—he was left-handed —which made him constitutionally unable to play the game ("He thought 'even,' you see," Freddy explains), taking the boy, neither of them more than fourteen, to the cleaners in the third form. It, the young sheikh's deformity, was Freddy's initial lesson in what it means to have the house odds in your favor and taught him never to enter any contest in which he did not have the edge.

Freddy has one passion, and it is not gambling. "Gambling's my work, old bean," he says. (He uses these corny aristocratic epithets. They make him seem fatuous but are as functional to his profession as a drawl to a hired gun.) "I'm no gambler at all, actually. I'm this sort of mathematician. Please don't gamble with me, please don't accept my bets. We're friends and I'm ruthless. Not vicious—ruthless. I will never surrender an advantage. Since I know the odds and respect them, to ignore them would be a sort of cheating, and since I'm honorable I couldn't think of that. Don't play with me. We're friends. I was never the sheikh's friend, never the friend of any of those feet-off-the-ground *Fleugenmensch* sons of rich men I lived with at Harrow and Cambridge and who gave me my stake. Where I was meditative they were speculative. I like you, as I like anyone who doesn't confuse his need with his evidence. Let's never gamble. Promise. *Promise?*"

So he has a passion, but it isn't gambling. It's animals— beasts, rather. Duluth contains perhaps the most superb private zoo in the world, a huge game park, larger than Whipsnade and much more dangerous. Where Whipsnade hedges with moats and illusions, at Duluth the animals are given absolute freedom. An enormous, camouflaged electrified fence, the largest in the world, runs about the entire estate. ("We control the current. The jolt merely braces the larger animals and only stuns the smaller, puts them unconscious. I've installed an auxiliary electrical plant for when there are power failures") Although from time to time a few of the animals have fought and occasionally killed each other, an attempt has been made to introduce as near perfect an ecological balance as possible, vegetarians and carnivores who find the flesh of the beasts with whom they must live inimical, some almost religious constraint in the jaws and digestion, some once-burned, twice-sorry instinct passed on from generation to generation that protects and preserves his herds.

It was an ancestor of Plympton's who began the park, and as a result of the care he and his successors put into selecting and arranging the animals, some of the most incredible and lovely juxtapositions in the world are to be found there. (Freddy told me that Henri Rousseau painted his "Sleeping Gypsy" while he was a guest on the estate.) From the beginning a single rule has determined the constituency of the zoo: all the beasts collected there must have appeared on the Plympton heraldry. Lions, bears, elephants, unicorns ("a pure white rhinoceros actually"), leopards, jackals ("One old boy helped to do in Becket, old boy"), pandas, camels, sheep and apes. The family is an old one, the list long.

Though Plympton and I had known each other for years— we're the same age—this was the first time I had been invited to Duluth. I drove down with him the next morning, and of course it was not of the fabulous game park that I was thinking— I was not sure I even approved of it—but of Jane. I gave myself away with my questions.

"She's ill, you say?"

"Did I? I thought I said tired. What she told me, anyway. Looks ruddy healthy, in fact. Tanner than I've ever seen her."

"Is she alone?"

"What, is there a *man* with her, you mean? No, no, Ashenden. She's quite singular."

"How did she happen to drop in on you?"

"I'm not in it at all, dear chap. I'm a businessman and game-keeper. My life's quite full. I suppose that may actually have had something to do with it, in fact. She called from Heathrow day before yesterday. Said she was in England and wanted some-place to rest. Lord, I hope she's not put off by my bringing you down. Never thought of that aspect of it before."

"I won't bother her."

"No, of course you won't," he said smiling. "Sorry I suggested that. Just thinking out loud. A man concerned with animals must always be conscious of who goes into the cage with whom. It's a social science, zoology is, very helpful in making up parties. I suppose mine, when I trouble to give them, are among the most *gemütlich* in Europe. Indeed, now I think of it, I must have realized as soon as I saw you last night that you'd be acceptable to Jane, or I'd never have asked you. Have you known her long?"

"We've never met."

"What, never met and so keen?" I smiled lamely and Freddy patted my knee. "I understand. I do. I feel you hoping. And I quite approve. Just don't confuse your hope with your evidence." He studied me for a moment. "But then you wouldn't, would you, or I'd not be so fond of you."

"You do understand quite a lot, Freddy."

"Who, me? I'm objective, is all. Yearning, I can smell yearning a mile off."

"I shall have to shower."

"Not at all, not at all. It stinks only when untempered by reason. In your case I smell reason a mile off, too. Eminently suitable, eminently," he pronounced. "I wouldn't bet against it," he added seriously, and I felt so good about this last that I had to change the subject. I questioned him about Duluth, which till then I hadn't even thought of. Now, almost super-stitiously, I refused to think about Jane. Every time he gave me an opening I closed it, choosing, as one does who has so much at stake and success seems within his grasp, to steer clear of the single thing that is of any interest to him. We spoke trivially the whole time, and my excitement and happiness were incandescent.

"How many miles do you get to the gallon in this Bentley of yours, Plympton?" I asked, and even before he could answer I turned to look out the window and exclaim, "Look, look at the grass, so green it is. That's your English climate for you. If rain's the price a nation must pay to achieve a grass that green, then one must just as well pay up and be still about it. Who's your tailor? I'm thinking of having some things made."

When we left the M-4 and came to the turnoff that would bring us at last to Duluth I put my hand on Plympton's sleeve. "Freddy, listen, I know I must sound like a fool, but could you just introduce us and give me some time alone with her? We've so many friends in common—and perhaps other things as well—that I know there won't be any awkwardness. My God, I've been pursuing her for months. Who knows when I'll have such an opportunity again? I know my hope's showing, and I hope—look, there I go again—you won't despise me for it, but I have to talk to her. I have to."

"Then you shall," he said, and we turned onto the road that took us across the perimeter of the estate and drove for five miles and came to a gate where a gatekeeper greeted Lord Plympton and a chauffeur who seemed to materialize out of the woods got in and took the wheel while Freddy and I moved to the back seat, and we drove together through the lovely grounds for another fifteen or twenty minutes and passed through another gate, though I did not see it until we were almost on it—the queer, camouflaged electric fence—and through the windows I could hear the coughing of apes and the roar of lions and the bleating of lambs and the wheezes and grunts and trebles and basses of a hundred beasts—though I saw none—and at last, passing through a final gate, came to the long, curving, beautiful driveway of the beautiful house and servants came to take our bags and others to open doors and an older woman in a long gown—Plympton kissed her and introduced her as his wife, the Lady Plympton I'd never met ("She came with guanacos on her crest, dear fellow, with the funny panda and the gravid slug. I married her—ha ha—to fill out the set"), and he bolted upstairs beckoning me to follow. "Come on, come on," he said, "can't wait to get here, then hangs back like a boy at his first ball," and I bounded up the stairs behind him, and overtook him. "Wherever are you going? You don't know the way. Go on, go on, left, left," he called. "When you come to the end of the hall turn right into the Richard Five wing. It's the first apartment past the Ballroom of Time. You'll see the clocks," and I left him behind, only to come to the door, *her* door, and stop outside it.

Plympton came up behind me. "I knew you wouldn't," he said, and knocked on the door gently, "Jane," he called softly. "Jane? Are you decent, darling?"

"Yes," she said. Her voice was beautiful.

"Shall I push open the door?"

"Yes," she said, "would you just?"

He shoved me gently inside, but did not cross the threshold himself. "Here's Brewster Ashenden for you," he said, and turned and left.

I could not see her clearly. No lights were on and the curtains were still drawn. I stood in the center of the room and waited for a command. I was physically excited, a fact which I trusted the darkness to shield from Jane. Neither of us said anything.

Then I spoke boldly. "He's right. I trust he's right. I pray he is."

"He?"

"Plympton. 'Here's Brewster Ashenden for you,' he said."

"Did he? That was presumptuous of him, then."

"I am Brewster Ashenden of the earth, air, fire and water Ashendens and this moment is very important to me. I'm first among eligible men, Miss Löes Lipton. Though that sounds a boast, it is not. I have heard of your beauty and your character. Perhaps you have heard something of mine."

"I never listen to gossip. And anyway hearsay is inadmissible in court . . . ship."

I knew she was going to say that. *It was exactly what I would have replied had she made the speech I had just made!* Do you know what it means to have so profound a confirmation—to have, that is, all one's notions, beliefs, hunches and hypotheses suddenly and entirely endorsed? My God, I was like Columbus standing in the New round World, like the Wrights right and aloft over Kitty Hawk! For someone like myself it was like having my name cleared! I'm talking about redemption. *To be right!* That's everything in life, you know. To be right, absolutely right, one hundred percent correct in all the essentials, that's all we want. And whoever is? Brewster Ashenden—once. I had so much to tell her.

I began to talk, a mile a minute, filling her in, breathlessly bringing her up to date, a Greek stranger's after-dinner talk in a king's gold palace on an inaccessible island in a red and distant sea. A necessary entertainment. Until then I had not known my life had been a story.

Then, though I could not see it in the dark room, she held up her hand for me to stop. It was exactly where I would have held up *my* hand had Jane been speaking.

"Yes," she said of my life, "it was the same with me."

Neither of us could speak for a time. Then, gaily, "Oh, Brewster, think of all the—"

"—coastlines?" I said.

"Yes," she said, "yes. All the coastlines, bays, sounds, capes and peninsulas, the world's beaches scribbled round all the countries and continents and islands. All the Cannes and Hamptons yet to be. Shores in Norway like a golden lovely dust. Spain's wild hairline, Portugal's long face like an impression on coins. The nubbed antlers of Scandinavia and the great South American porterhouse. The French teapot and Italian boot and Australia like a Scottie in profile."

"Asia running like a watercolor, dripping Japan and all the rest," we said together.

"Yes, yes," she said. "God, I love the world."

"There's no place like it."

"Let me wash up on seashores and eat the local specialties, one fish giving way to another every two or three hundred miles along the great continuous coasts like an exquisite, delicious evolution. Thank God for money and jet airplanes. Let me out at the outpost. Do you feel that way?"

"What, are you kidding? An earth, fire, air and water guy like me? I do, I do."

"Family's important," she said.

"You bet it is."

She giggled. "My grandfather, a New Yorker, was told to go west for his health. Grandfather hated newspapers, he didn't trust them and said all news—even of wars, heavy weather and the closing markets—was just cheap gossip. He thought all they were good for, since he held that calendars were vulgar, was the date printed at the top of the page. In Arizona he had the New York *Times* sent to him daily, though of course it always arrived a day or two late. So for him the eleventh was the ninth or the tenth, and he went through the last four years of his life a day or two behind actual time. Grandfather's Christmas and New Year's were celebrated after everyone else's. He went to church on Easter Tuesday."

"Easter Tuesday, that's very funny."

"I love the idiosyncratic; it is all that constitutes integrity. Difference, nuance, hues and shade. Spectra, Brewster. That's why we travel, perhaps, why we're found on all this planet's exotic strands, cherishing peculiarities, finding lost causes, chipping in to save the primitive wherever it occurs—"

"Listen to her talk. Is that a sweetheart?"

"—refusing to let it die, though the old ways are the worst ways and unhealthy, bad for the teeth and the balanced diet and the comfort and the longevity. Is that selfish?"

"I think so."

"Yes," she said pensively. "Of course it is. All taste's a cruelty at last. We impede history with our Sierra Clubs and our closed societies. We'll have to answer for that, I suppose. Oh, well . . . Brewster, do you have uncles? Tell me about your uncles."

"I had an Uncle Clifford who believed that disease could be communicated only by a draft when one was traveling at high speeds. He wore a paper bag over his head even in a closed car. He cut out holes for the eyes, for despite his odd notion he dearly loved to travel and watch the scenery go by. Even going up in elevators he wore his paper bag, though he strolled at ease through the contagion wards of hospitals dispensing charity to the poor."

"Marvelous."

"Yes."

"Brewster, this is important. Do you know things? People should know facts."

"I know them."

"I knew you knew them."

"I love you, Miss Löes Lipton."

"Jane," she said.

"Jane."

She was weeping. I didn't try to comfort her, but stood silently in place until she was through. I knew she was going to tell me to open the curtains, for this part of the interview was finished.

"Open the curtains, Brewster."

I went to the bay and pulled the drawstring and light came into the room and flooded it and I turned to the chair in which Jane was sitting and saw her face for the first time. She looked exactly as I knew she would look, though I had never seen a photograph of her or yet been to any of the houses in which her portraits were hung. All that was different was that there was a darkish region under her eyes and her skin had an odd tan.

"Oh," I said, "you've a spot of *lupus erythematosus* there, don't you?"

"You *do* know things, Brewster."

"I recognized the wolflike shadow across the eyes."

"It's always fatal."

"I know."

"The body develops antibodies against itself."

"I know."

"It's as if I were allergic to my own chemistry."

"I know, I know." I went toward her blinded by my tears. I kissed her, her lips and the intelligent, wolfish mask across her beautiful face. "How much time is there?" I asked.

Jane shrugged.

"It isn't fair. It isn't."

"Yes. Well," she said.

"Marry me, Jane."

She shook her head.

"You've got to."

"No," she said.

"Because of this fatal disease? That doesn't matter to me. I beg your pardon, Jane, if that sounds callous. I don't mean that your mortality doesn't matter to me. I mean that now that I've found you I can't let you go, no matter how little time you might have left."

"Do you think that's why I refused you? Because I'm going to die? Everyone dies. I refuse you because of what you are and because of what I am."

"But we're the same. We know each other inside out."

"No. There's a vast gulf between us."

"No, Jane. I know what you're going to say before you say it, what you're going to do before you do it."

"No."

"Yes. I swear. Yes." She smiled, and the wolf mask signal of her disease made her uncanny. "You mean because I don't know why you refuse me? Is that what you mean?" She nodded. "Then you see I *do* know. I knew that it was because I didn't know why you refused me. Oh, I'm so confused. I'm—wait. Oh. Is it what I think it is?" She nodded. "Oh, my God. Jane, *please*. I wasn't thinking. You let me go on. I was too hasty in telling you my life. It's because you're pure and I'm not. That's it, isn't it? Isn't that it?" She nodded. "Jane, I'm a *man*," I pleaded. "It's different with a man. Listen," I said, "I *can* be pure. I can be again. I *will* be."

"There isn't time."

"There *is*, there *is*."

"If I thought there were . . . Oh, Brewster, if I really thought there *were*—" she said, and broke off.

"There *is*. I make a vow. I make a holy vow." I crossed my heart.

She studied me. "I believe you," she said finally. "That is, I believe you seriously *wish* to undo what you have done to yourself. I believe in your penitent spirit, I mean. No. Don't kiss me. You must be continent henceforth. Then . . ."

"We'll see?"

"We'll see."

"The next time, Jane, the next time you see me, I swear I will have met your conditions."

I bowed and left and was told where I was to sleep by a grinning Plympton. He asked if, now that I had seen Jane, I would like to go with him on a tour of the estate.

"Not just yet, Freddy, I think."

"Jane gave you something to think about, did she?"

"Something like that."

Was ever any man set such a task by a woman? To undo defilement and regain innocence, to take an historical corruption and will it annulled, whisking it out of time as if it were a damaged egg going by on a conveyor belt. And not given years—Jane's disease was progressive, the mask a manifestation of one of its last stages—nor deserts to do it in. Not telling beads or contemplating from some Himalayan hillside God's extensive Oneness. No, nor chanting a long, cunning train of boxcar mantras as it moves across the mind's trestle and over the soul's deep, dangerous drop. No, no, and no question either of simply distributing the wealth or embracing the leper or going about in rags (I still wore my mourning togs, that lover's wardrobe, those Savile Row whippery flags of self) or doing those bows and scrapes that were only courtesy's moral minuet, and no time, no time at all for the long Yoga life, the self's spring cleaning that could drag on years. What had to be done had to be done now, in these comfortable Victorian quarters on a velvet love seat or in the high fourposter, naked cherubs climbing the bedposts, the burnished dimples of their wooden behinds glistening in the light from the fresh laid fire. By a gilded chamber pot, beneath a silken awning, next to a window with one of the loveliest views in England.

That, at least, I could change. I drew the thick drapes across the bayed glass and, influenced perhaps by the firelight and the Baker Street ambience, got out my carpet slippers and red smoking jacket. I really had to laugh. This won't do, I thought. How do you expect to bring about these important structural changes and get that dear dying girl to marry you if the first

thing you do is to impersonate Sherlock Holmes? Next you'll
be smoking opium and scratching on a fiddle. Get down to it,
Ashenden, get down to it.

But it was pointless to scold when no alternative presented
itself to me. How *did* one get down to it? How does one unde-
file the defiled? What acts of *kosher* and exorcism? Religion
(though I am not *irreligious*) struck me as beside the point. It
was Jane I had offended, not God. What good would it have
done to pray for His forgiveness? And what sacrilege to have
prayed for hers! Anyway, I understood that I already had her
forgiveness. Jane wanted a virgin. In the few hours that remained I had to become one.

I thought pure thoughts for three hours. Images of my mother:
one summer day when I was a child and we collected berries
together for beach plum jelly; a time in winter when I held a
simple cat's cradle of wool which my mother was carding. I
thought of my tall father in a Paris park when I was ten, and
of the pictures we posed each other for, waiting for the sun to
come out before we tripped the shutter. And recollected mornings in chapel in school in New England—I was seven, I was
eight—the chaplain describing the lovely landscapes of Heaven
and I, believing, wanting to die. I recalled the voices of guides
in museums I toured with my classmates, and thought about
World's Fairs I had attended. The '36 Olympics, sitting on the
bench beside the New Zealand pole vaulter. I remembered perfect picnics, Saturday matinees in Broadway theaters, looking
out the window lying awake in comfortable compartment berths
on trains, horseback riding on a fall morning in mountains, sailing with Father. All the idylls. I remembered, that is, my virginity, sorting out for the first time in years the decent pleasures
of comfort and wonder and respect. But—and I was enjoying
myself, I could feel the smile on my face—what did it amount
to? I was no better than a gangster pleading his innocence because he had once *been* innocent.

I thought *impure* thoughts, reading off my long-time bachelor's hundred conquests, parsing past, puberty and old fantasy,
reliving all the engrams of lust in gazebo, band shell, yacht and

penthouse, night beaches at low tide, rooms, suites, shower stalls, bedrooms on crack trains, at the carpeted turnings of stairs, and once in a taxi and once on a butcher's block at dawn in Les Halles—all the bachelor's emergency landing fields, all his makeshift landscapes, propinquitous to grandeur and history, in Flanders Fields, rooms with views, by this ocean or by that, this tall building or that public monument, my backstage love-making tangential as a town at the edge of a map. Oh love's landmarks, oh its milestones, sex altering place like sunset. Oh the beds and oh the walls, the floors and bridges—and me a gentleman!—the surfaces softened by Eros, contour stones and foam rubber floors of forests, everywhere but the sky itself a zone for dalliance, my waterfalls of sperm, our Laguardias of hum and droned groan. Recalling the settings first, the circumstances, peopling them only afterwards and even then only piecemeal, a jigsaw, Jack-the-Ripper memory of hatcheck girl thigh and night club singer throat and heiress breast, the salty hairs of channel swimmers and buttocks of horseback riders and knuckles of pianists and strapless tans of models—sex like flesh's crossword, this limb and that private like the fragments in a multiple choice. And only after that gradually joining arm to shoulder, shoulder to neck, neck to face, Ezekielizing my partners, dem bones, dem bones gon' walk aroun'.

Yes? No. The smile was *still* on my face. And there in that Victorian counting house, I, lust's miser, its Midas, touching gold and having it gold still, an ancient Pelagian, could not overcome my old unholy gratitude for flesh, and so lost innocence again, even as I resisted, the blood rushing where it would, filling the locks of my body. "Make me clean," I prayed, "help me to make one perfect act of contrition, break my nasty history's hold on me, pull a fast one at this eleventh hour."

A strange thing happened. The impure thoughts left me and my blood retreated and I began to remember those original idylls, my calendar youth, the picnic and berry hunts, and all those placid times before fires, dozing on a couch, my head in Mother's lap and her hands in my hair like rain on the roof and, My God, my little weewee was stiff, and it was stiff now too!

It was what I'd prayed for: shame like a thermal inversion, the self-loathing that *is* purity. The sailing lessons and horseback rides and lectures and daytrips came back tainted. I saw how pleased I'd been, how smug. Why, I'm free, I thought, and was. "I've licked it, Jane," I said. "I'm pure, holy as a wafer, my heart pink as rare meat. I was crap. Look at me now."

If she won't have me, I thought, it's not my fault. I rushed out to show myself to her and tell her what I'd discovered. I ran over it again to see if I had it straight. "Jane," I'd say, "I'm bad, unsavory from the word go, hold your nose. To be good subsists in such understanding. So innocence is knowledge, not its lack. See, morality's easy, clear, what's the mystery?" But when I stepped outside my suite the house was dark. Time had left me behind. The long night of the soul goes by in a minute. It must have been three or four in the morning. I couldn't wake Jane; she was dying of *lupus erythematosus* and needed her rest. I didn't know where Plympton slept or I would have roused him. Too exhilarated by my virtue to sleep, I went outside.

But it was not "outside" as you and I know it. Say rather it was a condition, like the out-of-doors in a photograph, the colors fixed and temperature unfelt, simply not factors, the wind stilled and the air light, and so wide somehow that he could walk without touching it. It was as if he moved in an enormous diorama of nature, a crèche of the elements. Brewster Ashenden was rich. He had lain on his back on Ontario turf farms and played the greens of St. Andrews and Burning Tree, but he had never felt anything like Duluth's perfect grass, soft and springy as theater seats, and even in moonlight green as billiard cloth. The moon, perfectly round and bright as a tennis shoe—he could make out its craters, like the eternally curving seams of a Spalding—enabled him to see perfectly, the night no more than the vaguest atmosphere, distant objects gyroscopically stilled like things glimpsed through the whirling blades of a fan.

What he saw was like the landscapes behind madonnas in classical paintings—one missed only the carefully drawn pillars and far, tiny palaces—blue-hilled horizons, knolls at the end of space, complex shores that trailed eccentrically about flat, blackish planes of water with boulders rising from them. He thought he perceived distant fields, a mild husbandry, the hay in, the crops a sloping green and blue debris in the open fields, here and there ledges keyholed with caves, trees in the middle distance as straight as the land they grew from. It was a geography of eclectic styles and landscapes, even the sky a hybrid—here clear and black and starred, there roiling with a brusque signature of cloud or piled in strata like folded linen or the interior of rock.

He walked away from the castle, pulled toward the odd, distant galleries. His mood was a fusion of virtue and wonder. He felt solitary but not lonely, and if he remembered that he walked unprotected through the largest game preserve this side of the Kenyan savannah, there was nothing in his bold step to indicate this. He strode powerfully toward those vistas he had seen stretching away in every direction from the manor. Never had he seemed to himself so fulfilled, and never, unless in dreams, had such seeming distances been so easily negotiated, the scenery changing every hundred yards or so, the hills that had appeared so remote easily climbed and giving way at their crests to tiny valleys and plains or thick, sudden clots of jungle. This trick of perspective was astonishing, reminding him of cunning golf courses, sudden doglegs, sand traps, unexpected waterholes. Everything was as distinctively charactered as foreign countries, natural borders. He remembered miniature golf courses to which he had been taken as a child, each hole dominated by some monolithic feature, a windmill, perhaps, a gingerbread house, a bridge, complicated networks of banked plains that turned on themselves, culs-de-sac. He thought that Duluth might be deceptively large or deceptively small, and he several miles or only a few thousand feet from the main house—which had already disappeared behind him.

As he came, effortlessly as in any paradise, to each seamed, successive landscape, the ease of his arrivals added to his sense of strength, and each increment of strength to his sense of purity, so that his exercise fed his feelings about his heart and happiness. Though he had that day made the long drive from London, had his interview with Jane (as exhausting as it was stimulating) and done the hardest thinking of his life, though he had not slept (even in London he had tossed and turned all night, kept awake by the prospect of finally meeting Jane) in perhaps forty hours, he wasn't tired. He wondered if he would ever be tired again. Or less gay than now. For what he felt, he was certain, was not mood but something deeper, a stability, as the out-of-doors was, as space was. He could make plans. If Jane would have him (she would; they had spoken code this afternoon, signaled each other a high language of commitment, no small talk but the cryptic, sacred speech of government flashing its secret observations over mountains and under seas, the serious ventriloquism of outpost), they could plan not to plan, simply to live, to be. In his joy he had forgotten her death, her rare, personal disease in which self fled self in ultimate allergy. *Lupus erythematosus.* It was not catching, but he would catch it. He would catch *her.* There was no need to survive her. Together they would grow the wolf mask across their eyes, death's big spreading butterfly. It didn't matter. They'd have their morality together, the blessed link-up between appropriate humans, anything permissible between consenting man and consenting woman—anything, any bold or timid configuration, whatever the one craved and the other yielded, whatever whatsoever, love's sanctified arrangements, not excluding the deathbed itself. What need had he to survive her—though he'd probably not die until she did—now that he had at last a vehicle for his taste, his marriage?

He was in a sort of clearing. Though he knew he had not retraced his steps nor circled around, it seemed familiar. He stood on uneven ground and could see a line of low frigid mountains in the distance. High above him and to his right the great tear of the moon, like the drain of day, sucked light. At his feet there appeared the remains of—what? A feast? A picnic? He bent down to investigate and found a few clay shards of an old jug, a bit of yellow wood like the facing on some stringed instrument and a swatch of faded, faintly Biblical cloth, broadly striped as the robe of a prophet. As he fingered this debris he smelled what was unmistakably bowel.

"Have I stepped in something?" He stood and raised his shoe, but his glance slid off it to the ground where he saw two undisturbed lumps, round as hamburger, of congealing lion waste. It came to him at once. "I *knew* it was familiar! 'The Sleeping Gypsy.' This is where it was painted!" He looked suspiciously at the mangled mandolin facing, the smashed jug and the tough cloth, which he now perceived had been forcibly torn. My God, he thought, the lion must have eaten the poor fellow. The picture had been painted almost seventy-five years earlier, but he understood from his reading that lions often returned to the scenes of their most splendid kills, somehow passing on to succeeding generations this odd, historical instinct of theirs. Nervously he edged away, and though the odor of lion dung still stung his nostrils, it was gradually replaced by more neutral smells. Clearly, however, he was near the beasts.

He turned but still could not see the castle. He was not yet frightened. From what he had already seen of Duluth he understood that it was a series of cunningly stitched enclaves, of formal, transistorized prospects that swallowed each other transitionlessly. It seemed to be the antithesis of a maze, a surface of turned corners that opened up on fresh surprises. He thought of himself as walking along an enormous Möbius strip, and sooner or later he would automatically be brought back to his starting point. If he was a little uneasy it was only because of the proximity of the animals, whose presence he felt and smelled rather than saw or heard.

Meanwhile, quickening his pace, he came with increasing frequency to experience a series of déjà vus, puzzling at first but then suddenly and disappointingly explicable. He had hoped, as scenes became familiar to him, that he was already retracing his steps, but a few seconds' perusal of each place indicated otherwise. These were not places he had ever been, only places he had seen. Certainly, he thought, the paintings! Here's Cranach the Elder's "Stag Hunt." Unmistakably. And a few moments later—I'll be darned, Jean Honoré Fragonard's "A Game of Hot Cockles." And then Watteau's "Embarking for Cythera," will you look at that? There was E. Melvin Bolstad's "Sunday in the Country" and then El Greco's "View of Toledo" without Toledo. Astonishing, Ashenden thought, really worthwhile. Uh oh, I don't think I care for that Constable, he thought; why'd they use that? Perhaps because it was here. Gosh, isn't that a Thomas Hart Benton? However did they manage that odd rolling effect? That's really lovely. I'll have to ask Plympton the name of his landscaper. Jane and I will certainly be able to use him once we're settled. Now he was more determined than ever to get rid of Franklin.

And so it went. He strolled through wide-windowed Wyeths and gay, open-doored Dufys and through Hoppers—I'll have to come back and see that one with the sun on it—scratchy Segonzacs and dappled Renoirs and faintly heaving Cézannes, and across twilled Van Gogh grasses and faint Utrillo fields and precise Audubon fens, and one perfect, wild Bosch dell. It was thrilling. I am in art, thought Brewster Ashenden, pleased to have been prepared for it by his education and taste.

He continued on until he came to a small jewel of a pond mounted in a setting of scalloped shoreline with low thin trees that came up almost to the water. It was the Botticelli "Birth of Venus," which, like El Greco's "View of Toledo" without Toledo, was without either Venus Zephyr, Chloris, or the Hour of Spring. Nevertheless it was delightful, and he took a seat on a mound of earth and rested, thinking of Jane and listening to the sea in a large shell he had found on the beach.

"I'm glad," he said, speaking from the impulse of his mood now that his wanderings were done and the prospect of his—their—death had become a part of his taste and filled his eyes with tears, "I'm glad to have lived in the age of jet travel, and to have had the money for tickets." He grew contemplative. "There has never been a time in my life," he said, "when I have not had my own passport, and never a period of more than four months when I was not immune to all the indigenous diseases of place for which there are shots. I am grateful—not that I'd ever lord it over my forebears—that I did not live in the time of sailing ships. Noble as those barks were, they were slow, slow. And Dramamine not invented. This, for all its problems, is the best age to be rich in. I've seen a lot in my time."

Then, though he couldn't have told you the connection, Ashenden said a strange thing for someone at that moment and in that setting. "*I am not a jerk*," he said, "I am not so easily written off. Profound guys like me often seem naïve. Perhaps I'm a fool of the gods. That remains to be seen. But answers are mostly simple, wisdom is." He was melancholy now and rose, as if by changing position he hoped to shake off this new turn in his mood. He looked once more at the odd pool and spoke a sort of valedictory. "This is a nice place. Jane would enjoy it. I wish I still had those two folding chairs the Bank of America gave me for opening an account of five thousand dollars. We could come here tomorrow on a picnic."

He did not know whether to go around the pond or cut through the thin trees, but finally determined not to go deeper into the forest. Though he suspected the animals must be all around him, it was very quiet and he wondered again about them. They would be asleep, of course, but didn't his presence mean anything to them? Had their queer captivity and the unusual circumstances in which they lived so accustomed them to man that one could walk among them without disturbing them at all? But I am in art, he thought, and thus in nature too, and perhaps I've already caught Jane's illness and the wolf mask is working someplace under my skin, making me no more significant here than the presence of the trees or the angles of the hills.

Walking around the other side of the pond, he noticed that the trees had changed. They were sparser, more ordinary. Ahead he spied a bluff and moved toward it. Soon he was again in a sort of clearing and here he smelled the smells.

The odor of beasts is itself a kind of meat—a dream avatar of alien sirloin, strange chops and necks, oblique joints and hidden livers and secret roasts. There are nude juices in it, and licy furs, and all the flesh's vegetation. It is friction which rubs the fleshly chemistry, releasing it, sending skyhigh the queer subversive gasses of oblique life forms. It is noxious. Separated as we are from animals in zoos by glass cages and fenced-off moats, and by the counter odors of human crowds, melting ice cream, peanut shells crushed underfoot, snow cones, mustard, butts of bun —all the detritus of a Sunday outing—we rarely smell it. What gets through is dissipated, for a beast in civilization does not even smell like a beast in the wild. Already evolution has begun its gentling work, as though the animals might actually feel compunction, some subtle, aggravating modesty. But in Plympton's jungle the smells were uninhibited, biological, profane. Their acidity brought tears to Ashenden's eyes and he had to rub them.

When he took his hands away he saw where he was. He had entered, he knew, the last of the pictures. Although he could not at first identify it, much was familiar. The vegetation, for example, was unmistakably Rousseau, with here and there a Gauguin calabash or stringy palm. There were other palms, hybrid as the setting itself, queer gigantic leaves flying from conventional European trunks. The odor was fierce but he couldn't leave. At his feet were thick Rousseauvian candelabras of grass, and before him vertical pagoda clusters of enormous flowers, branches dangerously bent under the weight of heavy leaves like the notched ears of elephants. Everywhere were fernlike trees, articulated as spine or rib cage, a wide net of the greenly skeletal and the crossed swords of tall grasses. There were rusts and tawns and huge wigwam shapes and shadows like the entrances to caves, black as yawns. The odor was even more overpowering than before, and had he not seen the vegetation he would have thought himself at the fermented source of the winish world. Yet the leaves and grasses and bushes and flowers were ripe. He reached out and touched a leaf in a low branch and licked his hand: it was sweet. Still, the place stank. The smell was acrid, actually hot. Here the forest was made impenetrable by its very odor and he started to back off. Unable either to turn away from it completely or to look at it directly, he was forced to squint, and immediately he had a striking perception.

Seen through his almost closed eyes, the trees and vegetation lost their weird precision and articulation and became conventional, transformed into an ordinary arbor. Only then, half blinded, he saw at last where he was. It was Edward Hicks's "The Peaceable Kingdom," and unquestionably the painter had himself been squinting when he painted it. It was one of Ashenden's favorite paintings, and he was thrilled to be where lion and fox and leopard and lamb and musk ox and goat and tiger and steer had all lain together. The animals were gone now but must have been here shortly before. He guessed that the odor was the collective conflagration of their bowels, their guts' bonfire. I'll have to be careful where I step, he thought, and an enormous bear came out of the woods toward him.

It was a Kamchatkan Brown from the northeastern peninsula of the U.S.S.R. between the Bering and Okhotsk seas, and though it was not yet full grown it weighed perhaps seven hundred pounds and was already taller than Ashenden. It was female, and what he had been smelling was its estrus, not shit but lust, not bowel but love's gassy chemistry, the atoms and hormones and molecules of passion, vapors of impulse and the endocrinous spray of desire. What he had been smelling was secret, underground rivers flowing from hidden sources of intimate gland, and what the bear smelled on Brewster was the same.

Ashenden did not know this; indeed, he did not even know that it was female, or what sort of bear it was. Nor did he know that where he stood was not the setting for Hicks's painting (that was actually in a part of the estate where he had not yet been), but had he discovered his mistake he would still have told you that he was in art, that his error had been one of grace, ego's flashy optimism, its heroic awe. He would have been proud of having given the benefit of the doubt to the world, his precious blank check to possibility.

All this changed with the sudden appearance of the bear. Not *all*. He still believed—this in split seconds, more a reaction than a belief, a first impression chemical as the she-bear's musk—that the confrontation was noble, a challenge (there's going to be a hell of a contest, he thought), a coming to grips of disparate principles. In these first split seconds operating on that edge of instinct which is still the will, he believed not that the bear was emblematic, or even that he was, but that the two of them there in the clearing—remember, he thought he stood in "The Peaceable Kingdom"—somehow made for symbolism, or at least for meaning. As the bear came closer, however, he was disabused of even this thin hope, and in that sense the contest was already over and the bear had won.

He was terrified, but it must be said that there was in his terror (an emotion entirely new to him, nothing like his grief for his parents nor his early anxieties about the value of his usefulness or life's, nor even his fears that he would never find Jane Löes Lipton, and so inexpert at terror, so boyish with it that he was actually like someone experiencing a new drive) a determination to survive that was rooted in principle, as though he dedicated his survival to Jane, reserving his life as a holdup victim withholds the photographs of loved ones. Even as the bear came closer this did not leave him. So there was something noble and generous even in his decision to bolt. He turned and fled. The bear would have closed the gap between them and been on him in seconds had he not stopped. Fortunately, however, he realized almost as soon as he began his sprint that he could never outrun it. (This was the first time, incidentally, that he thought of the bear as *bear*, the first time he used his man's knowledge of his adversary.) He remembered that bears could cruise at thirty miles an hour, that they could climb trees. (And even if they couldn't would any of those frail branches already bowed under their enormous leaves have supported his weight?) The brief data he recalled drove him to have more. (This also reflex, subliminal, as he jockeyed for room and position in the clearing, a rough bowl shape perhaps fifty feet across, as his eye sought possible exits, narrow places in the trees that the bear might have difficulty negotiating, as he considered the water—but of course they swam, too—a hundred yards off through a slender neck of path like a firebreak in the jungle.) He turned and faced the bear and it stopped short. They were no more than fifteen feet from each other.

It suddenly occurred to him that perhaps the bear was tame. "Easy, Ivan," he crooned, "easy boy, easy Ivan," and the bear hearing his voice, a gentle, low, masculine voice, whined. Misconstruing the response, recalling another fact, that bears have weak eyesight, at the same time that he failed to recall its corollary, that they have keen hearing and a sharp sense of smell like perfect pitch, Ashenden took it to be the bear's normal conversational tone with Plympton. "No, no, Ivan," he said, "it isn't Freddy, it's not your master. Freddy's sleeping. I'm Brewster, I'm your master's friend, old Bruin. I'm Brewster Ashenden. I won't hurt you, fellow." The bear, excited by Ashenden's playful tone, whined once more, and Brewster, who had admitted he wasn't Plympton out of that same stockpile of gentlemanly forthrightness that forbade deception of any creature, even this bear, moved cautiously closer so that the animal might see him better and correct any false impression it might still have of him.

It was Ashenden's false impression that was corrected. He halted before he reached the bear (he was ten feet away and had just remembered its keen hearing and honed smell) and knew, not from anything it did, not from any bearish lurch or bearish bearing, that it was not tame. This is what he saw:

A black patent-leather snout like an electric socket.

A long and even elegant run of purplish tongue, mottled, seasoned as rare delicatessen meat, that lolled idiotic inches out of the side of its mouth.

A commitment of claw (they were nonretractile, he remembered) the color of the heads of hammers.

A low black piping of lip.

A shallow mouth, a logjam of teeth.

Its solemn oval of face, direct and expressionless as a goblin's.

Ears, high on its head and discrete as antlers.

Its stolid, plantigrade stance, a flash as it took a step toward him of the underside of its smooth, hairless paws, vaguely like the bottoms of carpet slippers.

A battering ram of head and neck, pendent from a hump of muscle on its back, high as a bull's or buffalo's.

The coarse shag upholstery of its blunt body, greasy as furniture.

He knew it was not tame even when it settled dog fashion

on the ground and its short, thick limbs seemed to disappear, its body hiding in its body. And he whirled suddenly and ran again and the bear was after him. Over his shoulder he could see, despite its speed, the slow, ponderous meshing of muscle and fat behind its fur like children rustling a curtain, and while he was still looking at this the bear felled him. He was not sure whether it had raised its paw or butted him or collided with him, but he was sent sprawling—a grand, amusing, almost painless fall.

He found himself on the ground, his limbs spraddled, like someone old and sitting on a beach, and it was terrible to Ashenden that for all his sudden speed and the advantage of surprise and the fact that the bear had been settled dog fashion and even the distance he had been sent flying, he was no more than a few feet from the place where he had begun his run.

Actually, it took him several seconds before he realized that he no longer saw the bear.

"Thank God," he said, "I'm saved," and with a lightning stroke the bear reached down from behind Ashenden's back and tore away his fly, including the underwear. Then, just as quickly, it was in front of him. "Hey," Ashenden cried, bringing his legs together and covering himself with his hands. The tear in his trousers was exactly like the inside seam along the thigh and crotch of riding pants.

"əəŋ̑g," said the bear in the International Phonetic Alphabet.

Brewster scrambled to his knees while the bear watched him. "ŏŏhwm."

"All right," Ashenden said, "back off!" His voice was as sharp and commanding as he could make it. "Back *off*, I said!"

"кнаēr кнŏŏnn."

"Go," he commanded. "Go on. Shoo. Shoo, you." And still barking orders at it—he had adopted the masterful, no-nonsense style of the animal trainer—he rose to his feet and actually shoved the bear as hard as he could. Surprisingly it yielded and Brewster, encouraged, punched it with all his considerable strength on the side of its head. It shook itself briefly and, as if it meant to do no more than simply alter its position, dropped to the ground, rolled over—the movement like the practiced effort of a cripple, clumsy yet incredibly powerful—and sat up. It was sitting in much the same position as Ashenden's a moment before, and it was only then that he saw its sex billowing the heavy curtain of hair that hung above its groin: a swollen, grotesque ring of vulva the color and texture of an ear and crosshatched with long loose hairs; a distended pucker of vagina, a black tunnel of oviduct, an inner tube of cunt. Suddenly the she-bear strummed itself with a brusque downbeat of claw and moaned. Ashenden moved back and the bear made another gesture, oddly whorish and insistent. It was as if it beckoned Ashenden across a barrier not of animal and man but of language— Chinese, say, and Rumanian. Again it made its strange movement, and this time barked its moan, a command, a grammar of high complication, of difficult, irregular case and gender and tense, a classic of aberrant syntax. Which was exactly as Ashenden took it, like a student of language who for the first time finds himself hearing in real and ordinary life a unique textbook usage. O God, he thought, I understand Bear!

He did not know what to do, and felt in his pockets for weapons and scanned the ground for rocks. The bear, watching him, emitted a queer growl and Ashenden understood *that*, too. She had mistaken his rapid, reflexive frisking for courtship, and perhaps his hurried glances at the ground for some stagy, bumpkin shyness.

"Look here," Ashenden said, "I'm a man and you're a bear," and it was precisely as he had addressed those wives of his hosts and fellow guests who had made overtures to him, exactly as he might put off all those girls whose station in life, inferior to his own, made them ineligible. There was reproof in his declaration, yet also an acknowledgment that he was flattered, and even, to soften his rejection, a touch of gallant regret. He turned as he might have turned in a drawing room or at the landing of a staircase, but the bear roared and Ashenden, terrorized, turned back to face it. If before he had made blunders of grace, now, inspired by his opportunities—close calls arbitrarily exalted or debased men—he corrected them and made a remarkable speech.

"You're in rut. There are evidently no male bears here. Listen, you look familiar. I've seen your kind in circuses. You must be Kamchatkan. You stand on your hind legs in the center ring and wear an apron and a dowdy hat with flowers on it that stand up stiff as pipes. You wheel a cub in a carriage and do jointed, clumsy curtseys, and the muzzle's just for show, reassurance, state law and municipal ordinance and an increment of the awful to suggest your beastliness as the apron and hat your matronliness. Your decals are on the walls of playrooms and nurseries and in the anterooms of pediatricians' offices. So there must be something domestic in you to begin with, and it is to that which I now appeal, madam."

The bear, seated and whimpering throughout Ashenden's speech, was in a frenzy now, still of noise, not yet of motion, though it strummed its genitalia like a guitar, and Brewster, the concomitant insights of danger on him like prophecy, shuddered, understanding that though he now appreciated his situation he had still made one mistake. No, he thought, *not* madam. If there were no male bears—and wouldn't there be if she were in estrus?—it was because the bear was not yet full-grown and had not till now needed mates. It was this which alarmed him more than anything he had yet realized. It meant that these feelings were new to her, horrid sensations of mad need, ecstasy *in extremis*. She would kill him.

The bear shook itself and came toward him, and Brewster realized that he would have to wrestle it. Oh Jesus, he thought, is this how I'm to be purified? Is *this* the test? Oh, Lord, first I was in art and now I am in allegory. Jane, I swear, I shall this day be with you in Paradise! When the bear was inches away it threw itself up on its hind legs and the two embraced each other, the tall man and the slightly taller bear, and Brewster, surprised at how light the bear's paws seemed on his shoulders, forgot his fear and began to ruminate. See how strong I am, how easily I support this beast. But then I am beast too, he thought. There's wolf in me now, and that gives me strength. What this means, he thought, is that my life has been too crammed with civilization.

Meanwhile they went round and round like partners in a slow

dance. I have been too proud of my humanism, perhaps, and all along not paid enough attention to the base. This is probably a good lesson for me. I'm very privileged. I think I won't be too gentle with poor dying Jane. That would be wrong. On her deathbed we'll roll in the hay. Yes, he thought, there must be positions not too uncomfortable for dying persons. I'll find out what these are and send her out in style. We must not be too fastidious about ourselves, or stuck-up because we aren't dogs.

All the time he was thinking this he and the bear continued to circle, though Ashenden had almost forgotten where he was, and with whom. But then the bear leaned on him with all her weight and he began to buckle, his dreamy confidence and the thought of his strength deserting him. The bear whipped its paw behind Ashenden's back to keep him from falling, and it was like being dipped, supported in a dance, the she-bear leading and Brewster balanced against the huge beamy strength of her paw. With her free paw she snagged one sleeve of Ashenden's Harris tweed jacket and started to drag his hand toward her cunt.

He kneed her stomach and kicked at her crotch.

"ärng."

"Let go," he cried, "let go of me," but the bear, provoked by the pleasure of Ashenden's harmless, off-balance blows and homing in on itself, continued to pull at his arm caught in the sling of his sleeve, and in seconds had plunged Brewster's hand into her wet nest.

There was a quality of steamy mound, a transitional texture between skin and meat, as if the bear's twat were something butchered perhaps, a mysterious cut tumid with blood and the color of a strawberry ice-cream soda, a sexual steak. Those were its lips. He had grazed them with his knuckles going in, and the bear jerked forward, a shudder of flesh, a spasm, a bump, a grind. Frenzied, it drew his hand on. He made a fist but the bear groaned and tugged more fiercely at Ashenden's sleeve. He was inside. It was like being up to his wrist in dung, in a hot jello of baking brick fretted with awful straw. The bear's vaginal muscles contracted; the pressure was terrific, and the bones in his hand massively cramped. He tried to pull his fist out but

it was welded to the bear's cunt. Then the bear's muscles relaxed and he forced his fist open inside her, his hand opening in
a thick medium of mucoid strings, wet gutty filaments, moist
pipes like the fingers for terrible gloves. Appalled, he pulled
back with all his might and his wrist and hand, greased by bear,
slid out, trailing a horrible suction, a concupiscent comet. He
waved the hand in front of his face and the stink came off his
fingertips like flames from a shaken candelabra, an odor of metal
fruit, of something boiled years, of the center of the earth,
filthy laundry, powerful as the stench of jewels and rare metals,
of atoms and the waves of light.

"Oh Jesus," he said, gagging, "oh Jesus, oh God."

"û(r)m," the bear said, "wrənff."

Brewster sank to his knees in a position of prayer and the
bear abruptly sat, its stubby legs spread, her swollen cunt in her
lap like a bouquet of flowers.

It was as if he had looked up the dress of someone old. He
couldn't look away and the bear, making powerful internal adjustments, obscenely posed, flexing her muscular rut, shivering,
her genitalia suddenly and invisibly engined, a performance coy
and proud. Finally he managed to turn his head, and with an
almost lazy power and swiftness the bear reached out with one
paw and plucked his cock out of his torn trousers. Ashenden
winced—not in pain, the paw's blow had been gentle and as
accurate as a surgical thrust, his penis hooked, almost comfortable, a heel in a shoe, snug in the bear's curved claws smooth and
cool as piano keys—and looked down.

"OERƏKH."

His penis was erect. "That's Jane's, not yours!" he shouted.
"My left hand doesn't know what my right hand is doing!"

The bear snorted and swiped with the broad edge of her fore-
paw against each side of Ashenden's peter. Her fur, lanolized by
estrus, was incredibly soft, the two swift strokes gestures of forbidden brunette possibility.

*And of all the things he'd said and thought and felt that night,
this was the most reasonable, the most elegantly strategic: that
he would have to satisfy the bear, make love to the bear, fuck
the bear. And this was the challenge which had at last defined*

itself, the test he'd longed for and was now to have. Here was the problem: *Not whether it was possible for a mere man of something less than one hundred and eighty pounds to make love to an enormous monster of almost half a ton; not whether a normal man like himself could negotiate the barbarous terrains of the beast or bring the bear off before it killed him; but merely how he, Brewster Ashenden of the air, water, fire and earth Ashendens, one of the most fastidious men alive, could bring himself to do it—how, in short, he could get it up for a bear!*

But he had forgotten, and now remembered: it was *already* up. And if he had told the bear it was for Jane and not for it, he had spoken in frenzy, in terror and error and shock. It occurred to him that he had not been thinking of Jane at all, that she was as distant from his mind at this moment as the warranties he possessed for all the electric blankets, clock radios and space heaters he'd picked up for opening accounts in banks, as distant as the owner's manuals stuffed into drawers for all that stuff, as forgotten as all the tennis matches he'd played on the grass courts of his friends, as the faults in those matches, as all the strolls to fences and nets to retrieve opponents' balls, the miles he'd walked doing such things. Then why was he hard? And he thought of hanged men, of bowels slipped *in extremis,* of the erectile pressures of the doomed, of men in electric chairs or sinking in ships or singed in burning buildings, of men struck by lightning in open fields, and of all the random, irrelevant erections he'd had as an adolescent (once as he leaned forward to pick up a bowling ball in the basement alley of a friend from boarding school), hardness there when you woke up in the morning, pressures on the kidney that triggered the organ next to it, that signaled the one next to *it,* that gave the blood its go-ahead, the invisible nexus of conditions. "That's Jane's" he'd said, "not yours. My left hand doesn't know what my right hand is doing." Oh, God. It *didn't.* He'd lied to a bear! He'd brought Jane's name into it like a lout in a parlor car. There was sin around like weather, like knots in shoes.

"*What the hell am I talking about?*" he yelled, and charged the bear.

And it leaned back from its sitting position and went down on its back slowly, slowly, its body sighing backward, ajar as a door stirred by wind, and Ashenden belly-flopped on top of it—with its paws in the air he was a foot taller than the bear at either end, and this contributed to his sin, as if it were some child he tumbled—pressed on its swollen pussy as over a barrel. He felt nothing.

His erection had withered. The bear growled contemptuously. "*Foreplay, foreplay,*" Brewster hissed, and plunged his hand inside the bear. I'm doing this to save my life, he thought. I'm doing this to pass tests. This is what I call a challenge and a half.

The bear permitted the introduction of his hand and hugged him firmly, yet with a kind of reserve as though conscious of Ashenden's eggshell mortality. His free hand was around her neck while the other moved around inside the bear insinuatingly. He felt a clit like a baseball. One hand high and one low, his head, mouth closed, buried in the mound of fur just to the side of the bear's neck, he was like a man doing the Australian crawl.

The bear shifted. Still locked together, the two of them rolled over and over through the peaceable kingdom. For Ashenden it was like being run over, but she permitted him to come out on top. His hand had taken a terrific wrenching however, and he knew he had to get it out before it swelled and he was unable to move it. Jesus, I've stubbed my hand, he thought, and began to withdraw it gently, gingerly, through a booby-trapped channel of obstacle grown agonizing by his injury, a minefield of pain. The bear lay stock still as he reeled in his hand, climbing out of her cunt as up a rope. (Perhaps this feels good to her, he thought tenderly.) At last, love's Little Jack Horner, it was out and Ashenden, his hand bent at almost a right angle to his wrist, felt disarmed. What he had counted on—without realizing he counted on it—was no longer available to him. He would not be able to manipulate the bear, would not be able to get away with merely jerking it off. It was another illusion stripped away. He would have to screw the animal conventionally.

Come on, he urged his cock, wax, grow, *grow*. He pleaded with his penis, taking it in his good hand and rubbing it desperately, polishing it like an heirloom, Aladdinizing it uselessly. Meanwhile, tears in his own, he looked deep into the bear's eyes and stalled by blowing crazy kisses to it off his broken hand, saying foolish things, making it incredible promises, keeping up a lame chatter like the pepper talk around an infield.

"Just a minute. Hold on a sec. I'm almost ready. It's going to be something. It's really . . . I've just got to . . . Look, there's really nothing to worry about. Everything's going to work out fine. I'm going to be a man for you, darling. Just give me a chance, will you? Listen," he said, "I love you. I don't think I can live without you. I want you to marry me." He didn't know what he was saying, unconsciously selecting, with a sort of sexual guile he hadn't known he possessed, phrases from love, the compromising sales talk of romantic stall. He had been maidenized, a game, scared bride at the bedside. Then he began to hear himself, to listen to what he was saying. He'd never spoken this way to a woman in his life. Where did he get this stuff? Where did it come from? It was the shallow language of two-timers, of drummers with farm girls, of whores holding out and gigolos holding in, the conversation of cuckoldry, of all amorous greed. It was base and cheap and tremendously exciting and suddenly Ashenden felt a stirring, the beginning of a faint lust. He moved to the spark like an arsonist and gazed steadily at the enormous hulk of impatient bear, at its black eyes cute as checkers on a snowman. Yes, he thought, afraid he'd lose it, *yes. I am the wuver of the teddy bear, big bwown bear's wittle white man.*

He unbuckled his pants and let them drop and stepped out of his underwear feeling moonlight on his ass. He moved out of his jacket and tore off his shirt, his undershirt. He ran up against the bear. He slapped at it with his dick. He turned his back to it and moved the spread cheeks of his behind up and down the pelt. He climbed it, impaling himself on the strange softness of the enormous toy. He kissed it.

Pet, pet, he thought. *"Pet,"* he moaned, his eyes closed now. "My pet, my pet." Yes, he thought, yes. And remembered, sud-

denly, *saw*, all the animals he had ever petted, all the furry under-
bellies, writhing, inviting his nails, all the babies whose rubbery
behinds he'd squeezed, the little girls he'd drawn toward him and
held between his knees to comfort or tell a secret to, their hair
tickling his face, all small boys whose heads he'd rubbed and
cheeks pinched between his fingers. We are all sodomites, he
thought. There is disparity at the source of love. We are all
sodomites, all pederasts, all dikes and queens and mother fuckers.

"Hey bear," he whispered, "d'ja ever notice how all the short,
bald, fat men get all the tall, good-looking blondes?" He was
stiffening fast. "Hey bear, ma'am," he said, leaning naked against
her fur, bare-assed and upright on a bear rug, "there's something
darling in a difference. Why me—take *me*. There's somethin'
darlin' in a difference, how else would water come to fire or
earth to air?" He cupped his hand over one of its cute little
ears and rubbed his palm gently over the bristling fur as over the
breast buds of a twelve-year-old-girl. "My life, if you want to
know, has been a sodomy. What fingers in what pies, what toes
in what seas! I have the tourist's imagination, the day-tripper's
vision. Fleeing the ordinary, crossing state lines, greedy at
Customs and impatient for the red stamps on my passports like
lipstick kisses on an envelope from a kid in the summer camp.
Yes, and there's wolf in me too now. God, how I honor a difference and crave the unusual, life like a link of mixed boxcars."
He put a finger in the lining of the bear's silken ear. He kissed
its mouth and vaulted his tongue over her teeth, probing with it
for the roof of her mouth. Then the bear's tongue was in his
throat, not horrible, only strange, the cunning length and marvelous flexibility an avatar of flesh, as if life were in it like an essence
sealed in a tube, and even the breath, the taste of living, rutting
bear, delicious to him as the taste of poisons vouchsafed not to
kill him, as the taste of a pal's bowel or a parent's fats and
privates.

He mooned with the giant bear, insinuating it backwards,
guiding it as he would a horse with subtle pressures, squeezes,
words and hugs. The bear responded, but you do not screw a
bear as you would a woman and, seeing what he was about to

do, she suddenly resisted. Now he was the horse—this too—and the bear the guide, and she crouched, a sort of semi-squat, and somehow shifted her cunt, sending it down her body and up behind her as a tap dancer sends a top hat down the length of her arm. With her head stretching out, pushing up and outward like the thrust of a shriek, cantilevering impossibly and looking over her shoulder, she signaled Ashenden behind her.

He entered her from the rear, and oddly he had never felt so male, so much the man, as when he was inside her. Their position reinforced this, the bear before him, stooped, gymnastically leaning forward as in the beginning of a handstand, and he behind as if he drove sled dogs. He might have been upright in a chariot, some Greek combination of man and bear exiled in stars for a broken rule. So good was it all that he did not even pause to wonder how he fit. He fit, that's all. Whether swollen beyond ordinary length himself or adjusted to by some stretch-sock principle of bear cunt (like a ring in a dime store that snugs any finger), he fit. "He fit, he fit and that was it," he crooned happily, and moved this way and that in the warm syrups of the beast, united with her, ecstatic, transcendent, not knowing where his cock left off and the bear began. Not deadened, however, not like a novocained presence of tongue in the mouth or the alien feel of a scar, in fact never so filled with sensation, every nerve in his body alive with delight, even his broken hand, even that, the nerves rearing, it seemed, hind-legged almost, revolting under their impossible burden of pleasure, vertiginous at the prospect of such orgasm, counseling Ashenden to back off, go slow, back off or the nerves would burst, a new lovely energy like love's atoms split. And even before he came, he felt addicted, hooked; where would his next high come from, he wondered almost in despair, and how you gonna keep 'em down on the farm, and what awfulness must follow such rising expectations?

And they went at it for ten minutes more and he and the bear came together.

"uəōōŏŏŭ(r)reñg hwhu ä ä ch ouhw ouhw nnng," said the bear.

"uəōōŏŏŭ(r)reñg hwhu ä ä chch *ouhw* ouhw *nnñg*!" groaned Ashenden, and fell out of the bear and lay on his back and looked at the stars.

And he lay like that for half an hour, catching his breath, feeling his nerves coalesce, consolidating once more as a man, his hard-on declining, his flesh turning back into flesh, the pleasure lifting slow as fever. And thinking. So. I'm a sodomite. But not just any ordinary sodomite with a taste for sheep or a thing for cows, some carnivore's harmless extension of appetite that drives him to sleep with what he eats. No. I'm kinky for bears.

And then, when he was ready, when at last he could once more feel his injured hand, he pushed himself up on his elbows and looked around. The bear was gone, though he thought he saw its shape reclined beside a tree. He stood up and looked down and examined himself. When he put his clothes back on, they hung on him like flayed skin and he was conscious of vague with-drawal symptoms in his nuts. He moved into the moonlight. His penis looked as if it had been dipped in blood. Had it still been erect the blood might perhaps have gone unnoticed, a faint flush; no longer distended, it seemed horrid, wet, thick as paint. He cupped his hand beneath himself and caught one drop in his palm. He shook his head. "My God," he said, "I haven't just screwed a bear, I've fucked a virgin!"

Now his old honor came back to chide him. He thought of Jane dying in the castle, of the wolf mask binding her eyes like a dark handkerchief on the vision of a condemned prisoner, of it binding his own and of the tan beard across his face like a robber's bandanna. Ashenden shuddered. But perhaps it was not contagious unless from love and honor's self-inflicted homeo-pathy. Surely he would not *have* to die with her. All he had to do was tell her that he had failed the test, that he had not met her conditions. Then he knew that he would never tell her this, that he would tell her nothing, that he would not even see her, that tomorrow—today, in an hour or so when the sun was up— he would have Plympton's man take him to the station, that he would board a train, go to London, rest there for a day or two, take in a show, perhaps go to the zoo, book passage to someplace far, someplace wild, further and wilder than he had ever been, look it over, get its feel, with an idea of maybe settling down one day. He'd better get started. He had to change.

He remembered that he was still exposed and thought to cover himself lest someone see him, but first he'd better wipe the blood off his penis. There was a fresh handkerchief in his pocket, and he took it out, unfolded it and strolled over to the pond. He dipped the handkerchief in the water and rubbed himself briskly, his organ suddenly tingling with a new surge of pleasure, but a pleasure mitigated by twinges of pain. There was soreness, a bruise. He placed the handkerchief back in his pocket and handled himself lightly, as one goes over a tire to find a puncture. There was a small cut on the underside of his penis that he must have acquired from the bear. Then the blood could have been mine, he thought. Maybe *I* was the virgin. Maybe *I* was. It was good news. Though he was a little sad. *Post-coitum tristesse*, he thought. It'll pass.

He started back through art to the house, but first he looked over his shoulder for a last glimpse of the sleeping bear. And he thought again of how grand it had been, and wondered if it was possible that something might come of it. And seeing ahead, speculating about the generations that would follow his own, he thought, Air. Water, he thought. Fire, Earth, he thought . . . And *honey*.

The Condominium

"NO DREAM," he would write, "not a vision, not even a reverie. No fancy nor aspiration either. No crummy goal nor lousy aim. Something harder, acknowledged. More real than any of these. Something two-in-the-bush realer than any bird. Right up there with death and taxes.

"A place to live, to be. Out of what vortical history came spinning this notion of a second skin? From what incipit, fundamental gene of nakedness came, laboring like a lung, insistent as the logical sequences of a heartbeat, the body's syllogisms, this demand for rind and integument and pelt? (Small wonder our daddies were tailors, needlers and threaders, or that our mothers threw up an archaeology on the dining room table, first the wood, varnished and glossed and waxed, then thick baize pads, next a linoleum, then a plain cloth and then a crocheted, a sheet of plastic over all with a bowl of fruit, a dish of candy, a vase of flowers, and none of this for protection and even less for ornament, but just out of dedication to weight as a principle, a tropism in the bones for mass and hide.) Out of what frightful trauma of exclusion arose this need, what base expulsion from what cave during which incredible spell of rotten weather?

"And never land, never real estate, the land grant unheard of, unimagined and unnecessary (what could you do with land?), even the notion of a 'promised land' merely religion, poetry. No. No great Mosaic East India Company tracts in the background, no primogenitive tradition of estates, properties, patents and dominions. Not land, not dirt, only what land and dirt threw up, its lumbers and sands and clays and ores and stones—its ingredients, like a recipe for cement."

"His father," he would write, "met his mother at 'camp.' There were tents but this may have been before tents. Somewhere there was a photograph of young men in bedrolls, his father and his shrouded pals like disaster victims laid out in a line in the sun. And the girls—Floradora, Gibson, Bloomer, whatever the Twenties term for their type may have been—with already about them a sepia hunt of nostalgia puffing their knickers, thickening their socks, bagging their sweaters, complicating their curls. Weekend fraternities—'The River Rats,' 'The Crusoe Club,' 'The Peninsula Club'—and sororities—'The Blueschasers,' 'The Flappers,' 'The Go-to-Hell-God-Damnits'—of the white-collar working class down to New Jersey on the train from New York, the city. He had spent more than half his summers there, but had no fixed memory of the place because it was always changing. When he was a boy it was like living on a sound stage, some studio town going up before his eyes. He watched the carpenters, the Phil-Gas, the diggers of septic tanks, all the electricians, all the Dugan's and Breyer's Ice Cream and Borden's Milk and Nehi Soda people opening up routes, signing up customers, civilizing this wilderness as ever any missionaries or conquistadors civilized theirs. He saw electricity come in, city water, mail (the rural delivery boxes like the tunnels for toy trains, PATERSON MORNING CALL or BERGEN MESSENGER stenciled on the tin tunnels like names for the trains).

"So the tents came down (never having actually seen the tents, he nevertheless sensed them, or rather their absence, knowing that he walked not through fields and cleared woods but along lots and parcels, and that antecedent to these there would have to have been sites) and the bungalows went up, each summer some new section of the colony developed, the new bungalows put up in pairs or fours or half-dozens, as though speculators and contractors were incapable of dealing in anything but even numbers, their insistence on the careful geometric arrangements like architecture's on some principle of equilibrium, a vaguely military hedging against the failure of their enterprise. Only his and a few of the other bungalows owned, or anyway mortgaged, not rented, by his parents and a handful of collateral old-timers, 'pioneers'—some of them relatives, all of them friends—as they styled themselves, had been put up independently. (And didn't he feel proud, aristocratic even, with the distinction imposed by ownership?)

"The bungalows went up and he went to meet the Friday night trains on the hill that brought the droves of what were still called campers for their weekend in the country. Saw with the gradual development the appearance of the fabulous 'extras'—handball courts, an entire ball field with wooden bases, two or three tennis courts and, one summer (it had gone up over the winter) an actual outdoor roller-skating rink, which later, when the bungalows were finally purchased, the developers would fail to maintain so that he would see it literally reclaimed, the shuffleboard court inset within the oval rink the first to go, the painted numbers fading, fading, gone like a dissolve in films, then weeds springing up irresistibly through cracks in the cement that had not been there the year before and the once smooth white concrete overrun with sudden wolf-man growths and sproutings, the rink itself collapsing piecemeal, drowning in ivies, nettles, briars and poisonous-looking trees. Eventually not a handball court was left standing, not a tennis court, nor a single dock for canoes, the rollers rusted, jammed, as if the renters, now owners themselves, had no interest in the out-of-doors at all, had repudiated it, as if life were meant to be lived inside and the games they once played as bachelor boys and bachelor girls—'The Good Sports,' 'The Merry Maidens'—were over, literally, the scores frozen, more final than Olympic records. (Though he and his cousins and friends still used the courts, their skills damaged by the disrepair.)

"But—this was the period of transition before the renters became owners—the developers themselves were now the aristocracy. Men like Klein and Charney, rarely seen and imbued with power and magic like emperors of Japan, not just through money or force (he'd seen Charney, an old, crippled millionaire driven in a limousine by a black man who smoked cigars, parked in front of his eight bungalows to collect the rents shyly offered up to him through the barely opened window of his car) but through ownership itself: men with houses, power to evict. That many of the bungalows stood vacant during the war didn't detract from this power but reinforced it, as though men with empty houses were even more powerful than men with full ones. (Klein he'd also seen, a fat man like the Captain in the Katzenjammer Kids, walrus mustache and all, who always wore a khaki shirt.)"

("And what, incidentally," he would write in the margin, "was all this crap? This stroll down memory lane? I didn't care a fart for my childhood, was more moved by someone else's—anyone's. Why, I was the kid who went to bed early, whose mother had me in the sack at seven o'clock, even in summer, whom daylight saving failed to save, imposing on me instead with its bright eight-thirties a sense—some of this was wartime, remember—of having worked night shifts, swing shifts, putting him—me—at odds, possibly forever, with the light.")

"Later, the war over now, the bungalows were winterized. Roofs came down and insulation tucked into them. Porches were enclosed, rooms added on, showers moved inside, money spent. There were almost no bachelors left, though even when they were still around he had already begun to forget who went with whom, seeing the following summer what were still familiar faces in now unfamiliar conjunctions (realizing only later what had happened —winter with its cozy betrayals—and just as light stood for something hostile, so cold began to seem mysterious). Only his parents' place, one of the first to go up, remained untouched, bungalows his had once dwarfed dwarfing his, bursting their boundaries, inching forward toward the road in a sort of architectural horse race, assuming complicated shapes, the original shell disappearing, swallowed in second and even third growth. Yet no one lived there in winter, or only a handful. The rest were small-time Kleins and Charneys themselves now, landlords casting their nets to catch the overflow from Pompton Lakes (where oddly violent industries had begun to spring up—a munitions factory, a quarry, a training camp for professional boxers, roadhouses that were said to be gambling casinos) but landing instead vague gypsy types, self-proclaimed migrants following nameless crops in unmarked seasons, New Jersey hillbillies with Italian names. As though—

he understood what was going on: men of forty plotting their retirements twenty-five years hence where they had been thirty —being a landlord was a necessary first step in becoming a home-owner, as a knowledge of the names of the presidents and their incumbencies was a necessary first step in becoming a citizen. A gradual breaking-in period, in the three summer months they occupied the bungalows themselves learning the bugs of furnace and washing machine and garbage disposal before one dared live amongst such things oneself for any extended period. Meanwhile, in winter, they continued to live in apartments, marking time, getting down payments together, even moving from apartment to apartment as though this too were good practice.

"His parents stopped going in the summer, or went for only a couple of weeks every third or fourth year. The building had stopped entirely. Now, in its hodgepodge of composition roofs and variously synthetic fronts—imitation brick, tile, aluminum siding—it looked like a tub of mixed fonts waiting to be melted down. It was finished. It was awful. High, dangerous grasses grew in the infield, the outfield was a no man's land, the river too low to swim in, the once presentable Ramapo Mountains behind them gone bald from too much blasting in the quarry. The bunga-lows, now houses of a sort, were locked into a permanent shabbi-ness which no paint or extravagance of metal awning could dis-guise."

"Meanwhile," he would write later in his preliminary notes, "in the early Sixties, a word went out: CONDOMINIUM.

"At first one thought it was a metal alloy, or perhaps a new element. Maybe it was used to fashion industrial diamonds. There were those who thought it had to do with big business, interna-tional stuff—combines, cartels. Others thought it was a sort of prophylactic. It was strange that the very people who would later become most intimate with the term should at first have had so vague a notion of what it meant. Only after doctors tell him does the patient know the name of his disease. Condominium. (Kon'-də-min'-ē-əm.)

"Perhaps it strikes you as strange that these should suddenly have become so popular. After all, the concept is not entirely new; there had been cooperatives for years. But a closer investigation reveals it's not that mysterious. Myth is more persistent than staph. Accuse others of what you're guilty of yourself and go scot-free. The Jews, say the gentiles, are too clannish; they stick together. Yet the cooperative was a gentile device, an arrangement whereby individuals owned their own apartments but could not sell them unless they had permission from the other owners. There were few Jews in cooperatives. He did not know any. Participation in a co-op was often restricted and the constituency of a building monolithic. The condominium, on the other hand, simply grants each owner a recordable deed, enabling him to sell, mortgage or otherwise dispose of his property in any way he sees fit, independent of the will and advices of the other owners in the building. It is this last fact which makes all the difference, driving home the last implication of ownership, giving dominion (con-*domini*-um) over possession, reserving to the possessor the ultimate rights of belonging, extravagantly excluding all other men's say-so, finessing all putative ownership's tithe and obligation and easements, both Platonic and legal, making it unique, total, proprietorship in depth and in fact.

"So Klein and Charney—who weren't Jewish—lived again. (The two old men, their last bungalows sold, died in the same summer within a month and a half of each other in 1953.) It was an *age* of developers, fast talkers who had the ear of bankers, insurance companies, financiers, boards of directors—all those mysterious resources where the money was, all those who sat in judgment of the feasible, who, like odds-makers, actuaries of the probable, made the determinations and fine distinctions, running up the flagpoles of the possible this probability and that likelihood, weighing needs and tastes and trends and fixing priority like hoods a horse race. Solomons of the daily life who, surer than legislators or artists, give its look to whatever age they live in wherever they happen to live it. This was the ear the developers had, this the power they had managed to tap.

"There were trial runs, pilot projects. Condominiums went up in Florida and Arizona, existing side by side with the retirement communities, the Sun Cities like reservations for a dying species in nature, the high-rises rising high in the yeasty sun, cities of the plain, sketching skylines where none existed before, the face of nature instantly changed by fiat and ukase—not like Oakland, New Jersey, where it had taken years—here a lake put in and stocked as you'd lay a golf course, there a series of canals and inlets like the interesting underedge of a key. Marinas constructed for people who got seasick and golf courses for duffers who didn't know doglegs from birdies (and the courses actually *fixed*, shaving a dozen strokes off the game of even the lousiest player, gravity improving the lie, the water holes and sand traps more optical illusion than obstacle, the customer is always right), 'country clubs,' airstrips for the charter flights on converted bombers that bussed potential investors down from Chicago, Cleveland, New York and St. Louis, shopping centers, medical centers, swimming pools and even, in those deserts, gardens.

"It was Oakland, N.J., all over again, but an Oakland blessed by money this time, an Oakland of surfeit, manifesting an unseen but individual will, an individual yet collective style so that the final result approached, in appearance at least, American fiefs and kingdoms, an impression underscored by the pennants on staffs which outlined the approaches to these places and which, along with the flags of the states (one for each state represented in the ownership), waved a sort of visible fanfare, a cracking clothy panoply, suggested actual nationhood, a city-state perhaps, like ancient Florence or old Siena. And the private police too, the security guards in sentry boxes and shelters like little tollbooths along the perimeters and outposts who if they did not actually salute at least smiled a sort of obeisance to every potential buyer and waved him through as if he carried the privileges and immunities of a funeral procession or official cortege." ("Yes," he would write excitedly, *"Federal! National!* Isle this, Cape that, Lake the other, topography built into identity even if topography, a product of blast and bulldozing, was collateral with the development itself. Ha!")

Then a few days later he would write: "But the developers were wrong; they'd missed their marks, people who had even less interest in the spurious trappings of nationhood than they had in fishing the stocked man-made lakes or kidding themselves on the tampered greens which bore as much relation to real golf as the ringing bells and falling tin soldiers of a shooting gallery to real warfare. The dream house stood vacant, the planned community went unattended. Even the sun went unattended, the customers seeking shade, air conditioning, the great indoors. You rejected nationhood for neighborhood!

"So it was no surprise to him—who had seen the river wither, the skating rink turn in upon itself, the handball courts crumble and the base paths choke with weeds; who had watched the dissolution of all the communal apparatus, the Junglegym given back to the jungle and even the sidewalks sink—that the attractive nuisances of play were ignored, used only by the occasional grandchild or prospective customer a salesman took fishing. They weren't wanted. What was wanted was the basic living space: the bath and a half, two-bedroom, Pullman kitchen, living-dining room area where you could put forty years of furniture. Oh, yes, oh yes, indeedy, and perhaps a California or Florida room where the color TV could go, and certainly an outside balcony for the potted plants. But primarily the space, the apartment itself.

"A place to live, to be!"

He was thirty-seven. Single. A famous heart patient. A schoolboy.

And he could answer certain hypothetical questions one often hears about but are rarely put. He could tell you without hesitation—and give reasons—which ten books he would take with him to a desert island. And which ten people could come with him. He could tell you, breaking it down to the penny, how he would dispose of $1,000,000,000 in twenty-four hours. He knew precisely the dozen persons, living or dead, he would most like to meet, and could discourse on what historical era he would prefer to have lived in. Not only that; he could cite the great dead man he would be willing to change places with and the living man *or* woman he would be if he could be one person other than himself. He knew what age he would be if he had the power to alter his real age. Also he could tell you creditably whether or not he would do it all over again if he could. (He wouldn't.) He could name his favorite American city and his favorite foreign country. He was a whiz on *all* the desert isle stuff: not only which ten books or companions but which three films, what single food, which five inventions. If everything in the world had to be just one color, he knew which he'd choose. Finally, he could tell you what his three wishes would be if a powerful magician granted them to him.

It was one of his four or five lectures, and out of habit he still tried to keep the lists up to date, though with the falling off of demand and his all but official retirement—his agency had probably dropped him from its rolls; he didn't know—his interest in his lists had become academic. Perhaps he was waiting for someone to put these questions to him seriously, an eventuality he reckoned might take place just after the powerful magician appeared. At any rate, he no longer actively pursued replacements, brooding uneasily about them like someone with a name or forgotten word on the tip of his tongue, and there was something anachronistic about some of his lists. He had no substitute, for example, for the "fun person" he would prefer to emergency-land on a jet with—Baby Jane Holzer.

He received the news by telephone. This was what he kept it for, he supposed: incoming and outgoing emergencies. (And also for the correct time and temperature, and to call movie houses to find out when the last feature went on.) He didn't recognize the man's voice, only its general tone: gentle but with a certain imperfectly concealed excitement. The way his name might be pronounced by a process server. The man used his first name—Marshall—and told him his father had died.

He flew across the country to Chicago. No fun person sat beside him in the plane, but he found the jet an appropriate and even dignified way to go to a funeral. Rather than urgency and speed he had an impression of stately motion, and from somewhere outside himself, outside perhaps even the plane, he saw himself in profile, his seat upright, his hands forward in his lap, the black seat belt which he kept fastened a decorous sash of mourning. Soberly he decided to purchase a drink and gravely ordered, impersonally as he could, from the passing stewardess.

The sight of the clouds and of a sky as gray as the sea was a fitting approximation of death's mood in him. He was comforted by the serious presence of businessmen. They would have wills (he himself was an intestate heart patient), irrevocable trusts, safe-deposit boxes, ledgers in which—he imagined tiny writing—they had listed their holdings, a loving, responsible inventory written with Parker pens of their stocks and bonds, the occasional flier (Canadian mining stocks, small backwoods railroads), posthumous earnests of their humor which leavened their blue-chip probity. He supposed many of them to be lawyers, and it was this notion that brought his first forceful recognition that he was an heir. Strangely, there seemed nothing greedy in this awareness. If anything, it made his father's death even more solemn, as if the transfer of property were a signal of the gravest succession, a rite like a twenty-first birthday— he was thirty-seven but something about his life (he was a schoolboy) had kept him childish, driven him further and further into kidhood—or a sad ceremony of the state. It was just that formal and historical. He would be a wise steward. This occurred to him with the stern idealism of a pledge, an oath of office.

He asked the stewardess for pencil and paper, and when she brought them he lowered the tray table on the seat in front of him and sketched his expectations as a sentimental act, a eulogy to his father. Working with figures that were at least fifteen years old (and at that based on things he'd overheard, occasional glimpses of bankbooks, his recollection of the high insurance premiums his father paid, scraps of memory of the man's moods, the odd time or two he'd boasted of holding a stock that had split two or three for one), he put together an estimate of his inheritance—perhaps one hundred and twenty-five thousand dollars. He knew there was a sixty-thousand-dollar exemption but was not certain it applied to sons. What the death duties might be he had no idea, but he wished to be conservative—this would be the first token of the piety of that wise stewardship— and allowed himself an extravagant conservatism. Say the government took half; say funeral expenses and outstanding debts came to another ten thousand dollars. He would have about fifty thousand. It was no fortune, but he was proud of his father. It was more by several hundred percent than he himself could have left. He wept for his father and himself.

At O'Hare his mood changed. There was no one to meet him (who could have? he was an only child, his father's brothers were dead; his dad's sister, a chronic arthritic, lived in a wheelchair in Brooklyn; other than himself and a handful of eastern cousins on his mother's side no one survived), and he saw how fatuous he had been on the plane, betrayed by the air that held him up, the jet's great speed, his vulnerability just then to the seeming perfection of the people who had surrounded him. If they were lawyers why weren't they traveling in first class? He was thankful he hadn't struck up conversations with them and asked them his questions about death taxes, or offered, as he had been almost prepared to do, to hire them on the spot.

He got into a cab. The driver didn't—or pretended he didn't —know the way. "Does Kedzie cut through that far north? I don't know if Kedzie cuts through that far north." And so they spent time not on expressways or even main streets, but in neighborhoods, narrow one-way streets, cruising unfamiliar sections of the city he had once lived in, passing discrete yellow brick bungalows—brick everywhere, the brick interests powerful in Chicago, brick bullies, you couldn't put up a wooden garage— in the ethnic western edges of the city. Am I being taken for a ride, he wondered, staring gloomily from the driver's neck to the vicious meter. Six dollars and forty-five cents and no sight of land, no birds or green jetsam. Alarmed, he began a crazy, uneasy monologue, throwing out street names for the cabby's benefit, making up facts, cluing him in that he was no stranger here.

"Cabanne. In the old days this was the red-light district. It was outside the city limits and Big Bill Thompson couldn't do a thing about it. That's interesting about Big Bill. You'd think from his name he was a giant or something. Actually he stood only a little over five and a half feet. They called him that because the smallest banknote he carried was a hundred-dollar bill. Oh look, they've torn down the animal hospital on Lucas and Woodward."

The cabby glanced out the window. "Yeah, they needed the space for a vacant lot."

Then he got tough. "Come on," he said, "find out where we are. Ask at a gas station."

He'd been there before it was finished, when all that had existed were three massive foundations like partially excavated ruins and a few Nissen huts (the archeologists might have stayed there) for the sales office and models of the layouts of the apartments. The buildings were up now, an eleven-story center building and two flanking high-rises. Pallidly bricked and lightly mortised—from a distance the walls had the look of pages on which messages have been rubbed out—and lacking ornament, they seemed severe as Russian universities. A modern fountain stood dead center before the main building like a conventionally hung picture. The place seemed encumbered by signs: instructions to tradesmen regarding deliveries, notices about visitor parking, an old hoarding with the names of all the firms that had had anything to do with the construction of Harris Towers, another with an enormous arrow directing prospects to the main office, others that pointed the way to the garages and pools, warnings to trespassers. The names of the buildings, derived from their positions and printed in thick, raised letters on wide brasses, reassured him. (He was a sucker for all stark address. A restaurant that took its name from its street number and spelled it out, writing a cursive *Fifty-Seven* for 57, was, for him, a piece of elegance that approached the artistic.)

He got out at South Tower but couldn't get beyond the front door. There was no doorman, but a sort of complicated telephone arrangement had been set up in the outside hall. Where the dial would normally have been was a plastic window with numbers that appeared in it when you turned a knob at its side, like a routing device at the check-in desk of motels. These were the apartment numbers, he guessed. Lifting the phone from its

cradle probably signaled the apartment whose number appeared
in the plastic window. There was no directory. He spun the
knob all the way around hoping that the superintendent might
be listed but the numbers were stolid as code. Remembering only
that his father's apartment was on the fifteenth floor, he made
a fifteenth-floor number appear in the window and lifted the
phone.

"Yes?"

"Hello?"

"Yes?"

"Hello? I'm in the lobby. I'm Phil Preminger's son, Marshall.
I flew in for the funeral. I don't remember my father's apartment number."

"Yes?"

"Can you hear me?"

"I can hear you. Yes?"

"Well, I don't have his apartment number. Could you let me
in? Someone from this building called, but I never got his name.
He may have given it to me but in the excitement it didn't register."

"I don't know who called you."

"Do you know my father's apartment? Maybe the man who
called me is still up there."

"I'm not at liberty to give out that information."

"I just flew fifteen hundred miles. What am I supposed to do?
Did you know my father?"

"I knew Philip Preminger. I was very sorry to hear Philip
Preminger died."

"Thank you."

"We had pleasant chats beside the pool."

"The man who called me said he was a neighbor."

"We are all neighbors."

"Could you ring the bell? I've got luggage. Maybe I could
leave my luggage with you while I find out what to do."

Suddenly her voice turned hard. "Listen," she said, "you may
be who you say you are. If you are, you are. What did you say
your name was?"

"Marshall Preminger."

"Just a minute." Whoever it was had evidently left the phone. In a moment she was back. "All right, what's your father's sister's name?"

"My father's sister?"

"What's her name? Your aunt."

"Faye."

"Last name?"

"Faye Saiger."

"All right. When's the interment?"

"Sunday. He said Sunday, the thirteenth. What is all this?"

"What is all this? This proves you could be a fake. Everything you told me is in today's *Tribune*. You find out from the notices if there's survivors, then you come and clean out the place before the body is even in the ground. You have the address of every condominium in the city. You figure they're all old people in them."

"This happens?"

"Everything happens. They shouldn't print those things."

"Look," he said, "I'm Marshall Preminger. Phil was my father. What am I going to do with my luggage? What apartment did he live in? Where's the interment?"

"Read the *Trib*."

"Don't you see? If I had the paper I wouldn't have to ask you. I'd know."

"Verisimilitude."

"What?"

"It's a trick."

"I'll go to the office. They'll tell me."

"I apologize in advance if you're really his son. I'm sorry for your trouble. I'm just protecting him."

"If I'm not who I say I am," he said slyly, "I could wait until someone comes out. I could wait until someone comes out and then go in."

"Sure," she said, "they try that too. We look you over from behind the glass. If you seem suspicious we get help."

He went to the office, identified himself and asked for the key. The salesmen were out. The boss was at lunch. The girl was a little nervous. His father's was the first death in Harris Towers and she wasn't sure about the legalities. He still held his suitcase—he felt marvelous now that he could be seen—a man from the world in a wrinkled summer suit, a modified Panama hat with a narrow, striped barber-pole band. Where did he get his power? From his long sideburns, his salesman features, from his tie which, loosened in the taxi, hung from his neck like the whistle of a coach, from his spongy composition soles, from his being thirty-seven and fit, it must appear, as a fiddle, in the prime of his life. From his loss, his primogenitive aspect. People would sympathize, say they loved his dad. That would be their word; his, in that outfit, would be Pop.

"The legalities," he said, "don't start until Pop's body's in the ground. You don't even *think* of the legalities till the rabbi goes home. I've talked on long-distance telephones. I haven't slept. I've been in the sky in airplanes." He rubbed his face, hoping she would pick up the rasp of stubble, hoping his beard had darkened. "I haven't shaved." The cab had not been air-condi-tioned. A grand ring of sweat stained the underarms of his suit, round and wide as pawprints. "I need a shower." Potency spilled from his disreputable circumstances, his fleshy thighed, big-assed good looks, like an M.C.'s in a night club. "The legalities begin when no one's crying. Give me the key."

She gave it to him. He went back to South Tower.

The lobby was gorgeous, red flock on the walls, narrow smoked mirrors ceiling-to-floor, black low leather-and-chrome sofas and chairs, short glass tables on thick carpet the color of blood. There were tubular lamps and a huge chandelier with staggered, concentric rings of tiny bulbs that reminded him of the one on *The Glen Campbell Goodtime Comedy Hour*. It was astonishing after the low-rent government housing impres-sion he'd had from the outside. It was as if he'd been admitted to some plush speakeasy or tasty Mafioso palace buried in ware-house gut. He put it down to security, inconspicuous consump-tion, and rode up to his father's floor, where the corridors swept back from the elevator at modest angles like the wings on air-planes and the red flock had been replaced by gold.

He let himself into 15E. "Hello?" No one was there. It had

not really occurred to him that he would be alone in the apartment. He removed his jacket and placed it across the back of a chair, deciding that for the time being he would confine himself to the living room. He sat, prim as a guest asked to wait on the couch, then rose and walked to the enormous television and turned it on. It was color. The Saturday morning cartoon shows looked splendid, everything in bright, solid colors like plastic sculpture in museums. He watched for twenty minutes, expecting the phone to ring. Once it did and he turned the volume down guiltily, but it was a wrong number. He jabbed off the set.

Judging by the living room, his father's apartment was not what he expected. There were no pictures of his mother or himself, and he recognized no pieces from the old place. Everything was new and expensive and in marvelous taste, the apartment of a bachelor twenty years younger than his father (himself if he could have afforded it?) or of a couple without children. The lobby could have served as a model. Leather, chrome, glass. Swedish stuff, Finnish, the low geometry of high countries. Elsewhere there might be pieces he'd recognize, but he couldn't leave the living room. He thought his father might still be in the bedroom.

In an hour he went into the kitchen. Brown built-ins, a refrigerator, a hooded electric stove, a line of cupboards—everything the color of new shoes. He took ice water from the spigot on the refrigerator by putting his mouth directly under the faucet. Leaving the kitchen he investigated the rest of the apartment, the rooms falling to him quickly now, like towns at the close of a war. Here and there were things he recognized, though almost nothing from the time he still lived with his parents; just things he'd seen on visits when, first sonless, then wifeless, his father had made his subsequent moves.

Only the spare bedroom was the same, furnished with the twin beds and blond furniture of his high school days. Under the thick glass on his desk were photographs of himself and of friends whose names he'd forgotten, and the only picture in the entire apartment of his mother. He was not moved, either by the photos—he recognized them all, remembered when they'd been taken, how he'd felt posing; no time had passed; how could he be moved?—or by the preserved quality of his old room, his though he'd never spent a single night in it or even seen it before he walked into it just now for the first time.

In his father's room the bed was empty, carefully made, high as a chest of drawers under its tufted spread and fluffed pillows. Another television, a black Sony with a dark screen, sat on a chrome stand facing it. Under so well made a bed the linen would be smooth and fresh. (Where were the neighbors who'd removed the dead man's sheets and pillowcases and punched his pillows like a bread dough?) On impulse he disturbed one corner of the bedspread near the headboard. The pillowcase was a print, a single enormous Audubon bluejay. He drew the spread the rest of the way down and raised the blanket: another bluejay, big on the king-size bed as a pony. He touched the percale, smooth as paper in a dictionary. My God, he thought, this sheet must cost four hundred dollars. He rushed back to the spare bedroom— his room—and pulled the spread back from one of the twin beds. White, muslin, it did not seem even to have been ironed. Naked, he would have bruised his body on it. Carefully he retucked both the beds, thinking of his Egyptian father, pharaohed up to the eyes in treasure. It seemed a shame he had to be interred elsewhere. Then he recalled that he didn't know where they had taken the body.

Though he had grown up in Chicago he'd lived remarkably free of death—the blessing of a small family—and couldn't think of the name of a single Jewish cemetery. His mother had died when he was on a lecture tour eight years before. She'd been visiting her sister who still had a bungalow in New Jersey, and was buried in the family plot in Hackensack, literally at her parents' feet. His father had gotten his itinerary from his agent (those were the good old days; he'd had an agent, an itinerary) and called him in Salt Lake City, and he'd flown to Newark, flown to his mother's death as he'd flown to his father's. His maiden aunt had been willing, even anxious, to surrender her rights in her sister, the notion that the man had lain with her sister exalting his father and making her fear him. It was his father who'd insisted on Hackensack. "Someone would have to sit with her in the baggage car. Don't ask me to do that. I'd throw myself under the wheels." If it occurred to them that Marshall might sit with his mother, they hadn't said anything. "I'll come back," his father promised, "when it's my time I'll come back to be with her." Irritated, he used the absence of his mother's photographs to unburden himself of the pledge his father had made and which he had only just now remembered.

He went to the extension phone in his father's bedroom expecting to find a space on the dial for the office or even a "7" for room service, but it was an ordinary phone. (Though actually it wasn't. It was a custom job in a felt-lined box like a case for dueling pistols. If its lid hadn't been raised he would never have noticed it.) He had to hunt around for a directory (he found it in an antique sword case, a rebuilt McCormack Plaza phoenixy on the front cover) and look up the number of Harris Towers. A salesman told him that the girl he had spoken to and who had promised to find out where they had taken his father had gone to lunch. Leaving the apartment, he went downstairs, the key to someone else's apartment in his pocket somehow reassuring and making him feel lucky. He walked four blocks to a drugstore and looked up the details of his father's burial in the *Tribune*.

The body was at Pfizer's Funeral Home in a coffin the color of the appliances in his father's kitchen. The coffin was open and he saw that his father had grown long hair, sideburns, a mustache. The effect—the shirt beneath his Edwardian blazer was a wallpaper print, his tie, cut from the same cloth, almost invisible against it—was oddly healthy, obscurely powerful. "It sounds crazy," a director whispered, "but hippies make a terrific appearance in a box." It was true; his father seemed to glow. He looked marvelous, solider in death than in life, though Marshall hadn't seen him since he'd grown his new hair and bought his new wardrobe.

He felt no particular grief, only a curious letdown, and wanted to explore this. The only person there he knew was Joe Cane, a business associate of his father. "Don't get me wrong," Marshall said. They had gone outside to smoke. "I loved him a lot. I'm fucked up like a jigsaw puzzle, but he had nothing to do with that. My life is largely unexamined, Joe, but he was a sensible guy. He didn't give me bad times. And he gave me good advice. He was against my going into the lecture business. Even in my senior year at college, I was pulling three hundred, sometimes four hundred bucks for a lecture. It started as a gag, you know. I wrote a parody of a travel lecture—'Mysterious Minneapolis'— and my roommate sent a copy of it to this bureau. That's how I first got started with them. Pop came up when I did it in St. Paul and laughed harder than anybody, but afterwards he told me not to count on it."

"He should never have retired," Cane said, a tiny well-dressed man who looked the same now as he had in the Forties. Cane reminded Marshall of Roosevelt. Thinner, he had the old President's handsome sobriety and looked always a little worried. Marshall respected him. He appeared a talisman of responsibility and competence. The manager of the Chicago office of the firm for which his father traveled, he had always seemed mysterious. He had lived in an orphanage until he was seventeen. (Cane was not his name, Joe wasn't. He had become that person—this was the mystery—out of some other person.) He was totally self-made. There were Book-of-the-Month Club selections in his house and on the desk in his office.

"He was tired out, Joe. The road exhausted him."

"He could have worked in the office. He could have written his own ticket."

"He was a salesman."

"He could have sold from the office. The costume jewelry business isn't what it was, but buyers still come to Chicago. He could have hired college boys to work his territory and seen the buyers here. He could have used the telephone more. Lots of men do it."

"I don't know."

"It was jealousy. He didn't want anybody to think he was working for me. He couldn't stand me. I loved Phil, but he always had a resentment against me."

"That's silly. Why would he be jealous? He was a very dynamic man."

"He was the Wabash Cannonball, but he was jealous. Always. I was an executive and he was a salesman. I didn't make more money. He made more money, though I got more benefits. As an executive I was entitled to extra stock options. He resented that."

"He loved being a salesman."

"He hated it. He wanted his own desk in his own office and his own secretary, not somebody from the typing pool. He wanted ceremony. When the firm took over the seventh floor of the Great Northern Building I worked my can off to get him that office. New York wanted the space for a showroom. He thought it was me blocking him."

"Jesus, Joe, please don't talk this way about him. You make him sound small."

"Small? He was Yellowstone National Park. Only pipsqueaks like me have decorum and character. Men like Phil are mad and petty and great."

"He was fond of you."

"No. I was fond of him, but he always bad-mouthed me to the New York people. He despised me. May he rest."

"Stick with me, please, Joe. Don't go home early. Get me over the hurdles tonight when his friends show up. Some of them will be people from the South Side and I won't know them anymore. The rest I won't ever have seen. It's going to be rough."

But there were no hurdles. It was not rough, not at least in the sense he'd anticipated. If he felt no grief, then neither did anyone else. They came to the chapel—not a big crowd, but respectable—stood shyly at the coffin for a few moments and then went back to the outer rooms. He recognized many of them, men and women his parents had played cards with when he was a child, and was surprised at his ability to recall their names. When they offered their condolences he offered their names. "Thanks, Rose. Thank you, Jerry. It was good of you to come, Maxine. I was very sorry to hear about Arnold." Their first names odd in his mouth and vaguely forbidden (he'd known them as a child), granting him—Ph.D. manqué, ex-lecturer from the ex-lecture circuit, a man with a large scrapbook almost filled, a man with clippings—a sense of graciousness, a snug sensation of being their host.

The new people, friends his father had made at the condominium, moved with a sort of nervous bustle, more distraught then the others because they had known him less long and more recently. They were the ones who told him that they'd seen him only last Tuesday or Thursday and that he'd seemed fine, tiptop, that he'd done five laps of the pool and hadn't been a bit winded, that they were supposed to play bridge together next week, that they had had a date to go to a restaurant, that he was talking about a trip to Europe, that he was thinking about getting a part-time job. But even these neighbors could register only surprise at sudden, generalized death, their anecdotes about his last days and last plans unremarkable, borrowing their importance from the irony built into all death. He realized that no one was very unhappy, and indeed it developed that several of them—from both camps—had come merely to explain that they would not be able to attend the funeral. His earlier sense of being their host deserted him, and he began to feel that had he been more impressive as a survivor he would somehow have focused their grief. His use of their names was lost on them, and even this, his single resource, was unavailable to him with the new people. He explained a little of this to Joe Cane, thanking him for coming and telling him he could leave now if he wanted. "Don't think I want to steal my father's show," he said, "but it's getting trivial. Nobody's upset, just glum."

Then the big shots came and the chapel cheered up. These were the officials from the condominium: the sales manager, Joe Colper; Shirley Fanon, the corporation's lawyer; Sid Harris, the president himself. They had come together, three wide men in beautiful business suits and sharp shoes. They wore blocky paper yarmulkes which stood high on their heads and somehow gave them the appearance of cantors. They moved vigorous as a backfield in some subtle choreographed way that made it impossible to tell which was the leader. They came down the center aisle and took up positions at the coffin: Colper at the head, Fanon at the foot and Harris in the middle. They looked down on his father like fairies at cribside, and for a moment Marshall thought they would sing. No one approached them, though their celebrity had sparked something in the room, even among his father's old friends. Even Preminger was excited. One of the neighbors told him who they were, but by then he knew; he'd heard his comforters' murmurs, picked up their pleased, congratulatory whispers. "Wasn't that nice?" one said, and his friend had answered, "Gentlemen." It was a word others used too, the presence of the three bringing it out almost reflexively. Preminger wasn't sold yet—he resented this queer gratitude, ubiquitous as pollen—but then they were upon him and he understood.

"Sid Harris," Sid Harris said, and shoved a hard hand at him. "Nice to meet you."

"Nice to meet you," Preminger said, returning the pressure as best he could.

Harris frowned disapprovingly. "Not under these circumstances," he said and dropped Preminger's hand. "My associates," he said, naming them.

"Sorry for your trouble," Colper said.

"Condolences," said Shirley Fanon and winked.

"Ditto, ditto. We're all shook," Harris said. "These things happen. What can I say? Terrible shock, et cetera, et cetera. Look, Marshall—it's Marshall, right?—I'm not small-timing Pop's death. He was a gentleman. Mike's dead, I'm alive, you got me? Life goes on. You know what my rabbi says? 'Fuck death. Live as if it don't exist because it does.' "

"That's some rabbi," Preminger said.

"You'd love him. The Miracle Rabbi of the Chicago Condominiums. Sleeps in a little *sukkah* behind the swimming pool with the inner tubes, water toys and chlorine. Got himself a nice little setup in the filtration *butke* with the towels and the first-aid kit. What the fuck am I talking about? Fanon, you know?" Shirley Fanon shrugged. "Joe Colper?"

"What's that, Boss?"

"What's on my mind?"

"I just got here, Boss," Colper said.

"Must be my grief. Hangs on like a summer cold." He shook his head. "Got to pull myself together. Fanon, help me up off the floor. Colper, take one arm. Marshall, kid, grab another." He sat down at the front of the chief mourners' bench and patted it, inviting Preminger to join him. When he held back, the other two moved in, hustling him toward Harris.

"Hey," he protested, "what is this? This is a memorial chapel. Will you have some respect?" Even to him it sounded as if he were offering them refreshment.

"Fellows, the game's up," Harris said. "He knows who we are."

"The Jewish Mafia," Shirley Fanon said.

"The Kosher Nostra," said Joe Colper.

Preminger looked around desperately. They weren't bothering to keep their voices down. His father's old friends and the people from the condominium were taking it all in. Incredibly, they seemed to approve. He appealed to one man who earlier had claimed to have been very close to his father. The man shrugged. "The owners are clowns," he said.

"Lehrman's got our number," Harris said. "Listen to Lehrman."

"They're *tummlers*."

"A barrel of monkeys?" Harris asked.

"Sure," Lehrman said, "you ought to be on the stage."

"*We're better off*," Harris, Fanon and Colper all said together.

"Come on," Preminger said, "what right have you got to behave like this? You don't know me. You think this shit is charming? That nerve and craziness makes you lovable? What an incredible slant you three have on yourselves. I haven't been in my father's life for years, but that's him dead up there. He grew long hair and bought new clothes and I didn't know about it. We told each other old stuff on the long distance and sent each other shirts on our birthdays. He changed his furniture and went Swedish modern and I sat like a schmuck in a rooming house and lived like a recessive gene, but—"

"That's right," Harris said cheerfully, "let it all out. Cry."

"Go to hell," Preminger said.

"But?" Shirley Fanon reminded him.

"But it's a death. I'm not going to stand by while you turn it -into the cheap heroics of personality." He stared at Harris. "Are you married?" he asked.

"Who ain't married?"

Preminger closed his eyes. "Your wife is growing cancer," he said. "She's a cancer garden. I give her eight months."

"Hey, that's pretty outrageous," one of the neighbors said.

"Name of the game," Preminger said calmly. "That's what this gangster is up to. It's grandstanding from Rod Steiger pictures, it's ethnic crap art."

"Go, go," Harris said.

"Go, go screw yourself." He turned to the people from the condominium who had pressed forward to hear. "What, you think it's hard? This kind of talk? You think it's hard to do? It's *easy*. It makes itself up as you go along. You think it's conversation? It's dialogue. Conversation is hard. I don't do conversation. Like him"—he jerked his thumb toward Harris—"I don't even feel much of this."

"Please," Harris said, rising, "please, neighbors, give us some room. The man's right. Say your last goodbyes to Phil while I apologize to his son." They drifted off, dissolving like extras in movies told to move on by a cop. He sat down wearily and turned to Preminger. "Will you take back what you said about my wife?" he asked softly.

"Oh, please," Preminger said.

"Will you take back what you said about my wife? She ain't in it."

"All right," Preminger told him, sitting down. "I take it back."

"You hit the nail on the head," Harris said. "Didn't he hit the nail on the head, Joe? Shirley, don't you think he . . . Gee, there I go again. But you know something? I'm sick and tired of showing off for these people. The bastards ain't ever satisfied. I put in a shuffleboard, a pool, a solarium. I gave them a party room. They wanted a sauna and I got it for them. They walk around with my hot splinters in their ass. There's a master antenna on the roof you can pull in Milwaukee it looks like a picture in *National Geographic*. Energy, energy—they worship it in other people. *Momzers*. And me, I've got no character. I give 'em what they want. I'm sorry I leaned on you."

"We were both at fault."

Harris sighed. "I'll never forgive myself."

"Forget it."

"No. There's such a thing as a coffin courtesy. I'm a grown man. I haven't even said basic stuff like if there's anything I can do, anything at all, don't hesitate to ask."

"Thank you," Preminger said, "it's kind of you to offer, but really there's nothing."

"That's it, that's it," Harris said. "Will you pray with me?" he asked suddenly.

"Pray?" Startled, Marshall started to rise but Harris restrained him.

"No, no," he said, "We don't have to get on our knees. We'll do it right here on the bench. Everything dignified and comfortable, everything easy."

"Hey, listen—"

"Hey, listen," Harris prayed. "Your servants may not always understand Your timing, God of Abraham, Isaac and Jacob. Sometimes it might seem unfortunate, even perverse. Was there a real need, for example, to take Philly Preminger, a guy in the prime? How old could the man have been? Fifty-eight, fifty-nine? With penicillin and wonder drugs that's a kid, a babe. Was there any call to strike down such a guy? You, who gave him sleek hair, who grew his sideburns and encouraged his mustache, who blessed him with taste in shirts, shoes, bellbottoms and turtlenecks, you couldn't also have given him a stronger heart? Why did you make the chosen people so frail, oh God, give them Achilles heels in their chromosomes, set them up as patsies for cholesterol and Buerger's disease, hit them with bad circulation and a sweet tooth for lox? You could have made us hard blond goyim, but no, not You."

"Look here—"

"Look here, oh Lord," Harris prayed, "the bereaved kid here wants to know. Didn't you owe his daddy the courtesy of a tiny warning attack, a mild stroke, say, just enough to cut down on the grease and kiss off the cigarettes? Here's a man not sixty years old and retired three years and in his condominium it couldn't be two—I can get the exact figures for You when I get back to the office—*a guy who put his deposit down months before we dug the first spadeful for the foundation,* and got his apartment fixed up nice, just the way he wanted it, proud as a bride when the deliveries came, the American of Martinsville, the Swedish of Malmö, who made new friends, the life of the party poolside, a cynosure of the sauna and a gift to the dollies, the widows of Chicago's North Side—*who'll have plenty to say to You themselves, I'll bet, once their eyes are dry and they make sense of what's hit them*—and You knock him down like a tenpin, You make him like a difficult spare. Lead kindly light, amen." He turned, beaming, to Preminger. "Gimme that old time religion," he said. "We got business. You got the will, Shirley?"

The lawyer patted his breast pocket.

"You were my father's lawyer?"

Fanon patted it a second time.

"Don't keep us in suspense," Harris said. He winked at Preminger. "That's how he wins his cases. The juries eat it up."

Fanon reached inside his jacket, pulled out a legal document bound in blue paper. Unfolding it, he took out his glasses, put them on and began to move his lips rapidly, making no sound. "The reading of the will," Joe Colper whispered. Fanon wet his thumb and flipped the page, continuing to read to himself. He looked like a man *davening,* and it seemed the most orthodox thing that had happened that evening.

When Fanon finished, he folded the paper and placed it back inside his jacket pocket.

"Well?" Harris said.

"The boy gets the condominium," Fanon said.

"Airtight?"

"Like a coffee can."

"Will it stand up in court?"

"Like a little soldier."

"What else?"

"Nothing else."

"Let me see that," Marshall said.

The lawyer handed the will over to him. It was very short, a page and a half and most of that merely concerned with authenticating itself. Marshall could see that Fanon was right. He got the condominium and the furnishings. It was his father's signature. "I don't understand," he said. "What about the rest of the estate?"

"There isn't any rest of the estate."

"Well, there *must* be. Insurance policies, stocks. My father was very active in the market."

They looked at him and smiled. "Nope. He cashed his policies. He sold his stocks."

"I figured about a hundred twenty-five thousand. I was being conservative."

Joe Colper put his arm on Preminger's shoulder. "The apartment was forty-five thou. He paid cash. The furnishings must have cost another twenty."

"The man hadn't worked for three years," Fanon said. "Say his food and incidentals cost him ten a year. He had some tastes, your old man. That's ninety-five."

"I figured one hundred twenty-five thousand. That still leaves thirty thousand."

Colper and Fanon shrugged. "Tell him," Harris said, "about maintenance."

"Maintenance?"

"That's the thing sticks in their throat," Colper said.

"He bought a condominium from us," Fanon said. "Where does it say we sold him an elevator?"

"A carpeted lobby," Colper said.

"Game rooms, party rooms, a heated pool, central air conditioning," Fanon said.

"These are 'extras,'" Colper told him.

"Maintenance is three hundred a month," Fanon said.

"Okay," said Harris, "here's the story. I hate to trouble you with details at a terrible time like this, but we've got to face facts. Time and the hour runs through the roughest day. He was behind in the maintenance when he passed. He was broke. I never saw such a guy for spending dough. And he was so cautious when I first knew him. Prudent. Wouldn't you say prudent, Shirley?"

"Very prudent."

"But toward the last—well, toward the last he spent and spent. Call me a cab, keep the change."

"A real sport," Colper said.

"There was drunken sailor in him."

Marshall, who melted when he heard a lowdown, melted. It was as if they'd been up all night together. He felt grotty, intimate, like a man with a shirttail loose at a poker table. "I sound terrible," he said. "I'm not greedy. I'm not a greedy person. I didn't have expectations, I never lived as if I was coming into dough. You sprung this will on me. Naturally I'm surprised."

"Sure," Harris said, "naturally you're surprised. You get a shot like this you fall back on your instincts. Inside every fat man there's a wolf, there's a buzzard, there's a chicken hawk."

"That's human nature," Joe Colper said.

"It's why logic was invented," his father's lawyer said, "to tame surprise and make the world consecutive."

"We understand your . . . lapse," Harris said, "Shit, sonny—"

"I'm thirty-seven."

"Happy birthday. Shit, sonny, I'm your uncle, I like you. Come home and I'll take you to the ball game and get you a hot dog. Listen, there isn't a single one of us who wouldn't give his eyeteeth to behave like you just did. We're not grand characters, we ain't angelfaces. Petty hits us where we live. Let go, relax. What a kick it would be to let the other guy pick up the check in a restaurant! Keep your hands in your pockets, it's cold out. Sit still. What are you reaching around like a fucking contortionist to pay the other guy's toll at the bridge? I'll give you a tip: don't tip. You know the guy who's got it made? The creep in the movies who plays up to the uncle because he thinks there might be an extra buck in the till for him when the old bastard croaks. So don't apologize to *us* for your character. When Counselor Fanon laid the will on you and you gave us that 'Let me see that' and that 'What about the rest of the estate?' I was proud of you. Did you see him, Joe? Shirley? Whining like a baby and his old man dead in the coffin not fifteen feet away."

"Takes guts," Colper said.

"I think we have a young man here who's no hypocrite," Shirley Fanon said.

"I'm not listening to this," Marshall said, and fled to the front where his father's coffin lay open. He looked inside; he might have been watching the sea from the deck of a ship.

"Gee," Harris said, coming up beside him and looking down too, "that's some tan."

"The pool," Fanon said.

"Maybe the pool, maybe the solarium," Colper said.

"Anyway, the little extras that maintenance pays for," Fanon said. "We'll split the difference. He took advantage of all of them. He lived way up on the fifteenth floor and rode shit out of the elevator."

"What do you want?" Marshall asked them.

"We didn't hound him," Harris said. "Don't look at *me* reproachfully. That man lays there dead of his own accord. Voices weren't raised. Nobody nagged him, nobody dunned. No threats were made, we never served a summons. Two times, maybe three, the gentleman's letter went out over my signature, last names and misters."

" 'We feel that you may have overlooked . . .' " Fanon said. " 'If you have already remitted, kindly disregard . . .' "

"Like a four flush was a piece of amnesia," Colper said.

"Like he was an absent-minded professor."

"We knew he was strapped," Fanon said. "That every day the furniture truck came."

"He owed seven months' maintenance," Harris said. "Two thousand one hundred dollars. But who's counting at a time like this?"

"In a week it'll be eight months," Fanon said.

"Let's walk away from the coffin, please," Harris said. He put his hand on Marshall's sleeve. "Appreciate my position, Mr. Preminger. Real estate's involved here. Titles and certificates. A condominium's a delicate thing. Speaking statutorily. Shirley's the legal eagle. Explain to him, Shirl."

Fanon told Preminger that though he would probably get clear title to the place, the will would have to be probated. He named the various steps in the procedure. It could take anywhere from nine months to a year. In the meanwhile the maintenance—which by law he wasn't required to pay until he held clear title—would continue to build up. He could owe them almost six thousand dollars before the condominium was his.

"I'll sell it. I'll put it on the market," Preminger said.

"Well, you can't do that until the will's been probated."

"I'll sublet."

"You'd need dispensation from the court. The dockets are logjammed. Anyway, the money would have to go into escrow. You'd still be responsible for the three hundred every month."

He didn't have that kind of money.

They knew that. They suspected that. Why didn't they do this then? Why didn't they take out an option to buy the unit?

Harris broke in. "Give it to him straight. The heir here wants to hear lump sums."

"We'll give you six thousand dollars for an option," Fanon said. This would wipe out his father's debt, with enough left over to take care of the maintenance payments while the will was being probated. Then, when he had clear title, they would pay him fifty thousand dollars, less the six they had advanced on the option.

"What about the furnishings?"

"Well, that's what the extra five thousand is for."

"That stuff cost my father twenty."

"Go sell it." Harris said. "See what you'd get."

"I'm getting screwed. It's a ridiculous offer. You're offering me fifty thousand for sixty-five thousand dollars' worth of apartment, then taking back six thousand for maintenance." It was true, but strangely he did not feel its truth. He had a sense of the awful depreciation in things. He understood—or rather, understood that there was no understanding—the crazy fluctuations in value. It was as if a spirit resided and moved in objects, tossing and turning, a precarious health in things, irregular, fluxy as pulse and temperature and the blood chemistries. The market went up and it went down. Rhetoric feebly tried to account for the unaccountable, but its arguments were always as whacky as the defenses of alchemy, elaborate as theories of assassination. Value's laws were undiscoverable, undemonstrable finally, as the notion of life on distant planets. (When he was still lecturing, hadn't he once paid a thousand a month for a cottage on Cape Cod which couldn't have cost more than ten thousand to build? In those days, didn't his own fees vary anywhere from one to three hundred dollars a night for the same lecture?) Perhaps nothing more than mood lay at the bottom of it all. They were cheating him, but there was nothing personal in it, and he did not feel badly used. He turned down their offer anyway.

Harris considered him evenly. "You owe me two thousand one hundred dollars. If you have already remitted, kindly disregard."

"I'll pay," Preminger said.

Harris shrugged and took off his yarmulke.

"I'm moving in," Preminger said. It hadn't occurred to him till he said it. He knew his life was changed. "Mr. Fanon?"

"Yes?"

"Were you the one who called me?"

Fanon nodded.

"Did you make these funeral arrangements?"

"That's right."

"Another two thousand?"

"More like three."

"I'll pay," he said. "I'll pay whatever I'm supposed to." He felt valetudinarian. A graceful lassitude. All he wanted was to be in bed in his father's apartment. Thank God, he thought, he had the key. They would have to kill him to take it from him. His life was altered. Later he would make the arrangements. Everything would go smoothly. A life like his, even an altered one, could be lived in Montana or in Chicago. It made no difference.

A limousine called for him on Sunday and took him, the only passenger, to the chapel. Then he rode alone in it to the cemetery. For a time he tried to speak to the driver, miles forward of of him in the strange car, but the man's perfect manners and funereal deference made it difficult. Preminger turned oddly condolent by the man's performance, attempted to reassure him and said a strange thing: "It's all right. I'm not tumbled by grief. My father and I weren't close these last years. I'm from out of town. Someone else made these arrangements. I'm not overcome or anything."

"You don't know what you are," the driver answered.

So instead of talking he took stock of the appointments in the Cadillac, the individual air-conditioning controls, the electric windows and a panel in the door beside him that slid back to reveal a cigar lighter. There were three separate reading lights in the back. What was curious about luxury was the low opinion it gave you of yourself because you had not anticipated your needs as cleverly as people who did not even know you. He could not get used to the stern ideals manifest in the car's appointments. This is what some people *expect*, he thought, and felt depressed not only because he did not expect these things himself but because he could not think of anyone he knew who did. The driver, casually using the strange gauges and controls which to Preminger, spying them from the distant back seat, were as complicated as instruments in remote technologies, seemed unconscious of the car. They could have been riding in a '58 Chevy.

Then he knew what was so awful. How comfortable he was— as if master upholsterers had taken his measure, fitting the car to him more perfectly than any chair he'd ever sat in. The climate was equally perfect, post-card temperature, the low humidity of deep sleep. Subtle adjustments had been made for his clothing, all that he carried in his pockets, where his hair thinned revealing scalp, environment molding itself to him, to the skin of his wrists and his ankles within their light sheath of stocking, to his toes in their woody envelope of shoe. It was as if his chemistry were known, published like secret papers. Someone had a fix on him. Though they rode in silence, the sounds of the thick traffic outside velvetized to mellow plips and hisses, he felt seduced by arguments. He could literally have ridden like this forever. He wanted never to reach the cemetery, always to follow his father's hearse through the traffic of the world, the limousine's headlights shining in broad day, a signal, right of way theirs like something constitutional.

On the way back his mood shifted, and he struggled to recover it, feeling nostalgia for that hour's ride to the cemetery. When the driver opened his door in the driveway of South Tower he told Preminger to wait—it was almost a command—and unlocked the trunk of the car. "This is for you," he said, extending a manila envelope. "The deed to the plot's in there, and the death certificate and contract with the cemetery. Wait a minute." He walked behind the car again. "Here's your *yahrzeit*, here's your bench." He handed Marshall a jelly glass of wax gray as old snow. A tip of wick grew like a poor plant through the surface of the wax. Then he gave him a sort of cardboard bench.

"What's this?"

"For sitting *shivah*," the driver said.

Marshall took the bench and held it up. It was very light. He could see notches marked A and B, dotted lines, a legend that said FOLD HERE. A sort of wood grain was printed on one surface of the cardboard like the corky flecks on a cigarette filter. "It's paper," he said indignantly.

"Low center of gravity," the driver said. "It'll support three hundred pounds."

Upstairs he placed the bench beside the television set in the living room, across from his father's leather couch, and put the *yahrzeit* candle unlit on top of the refrigerator, where he remembered seeing one when his parents mourned. He wondered if he intended to sit *shivah*.

Someone knocked. A woman stood at the front door in a long housecoat, holding a bowl of water. "I apologize," she said breathlessly. "This should have been outside the door when you got back from the cemetery."

"What is it?"

"You wash your hands. You're supposed to do it before you go in the house. It's just a ceremony, it's only a ritual," she said, excusing either him for not knowing or herself for bringing it too late. She held the bowl out to him. "Just splash your hands. To tell you the truth, I need the bowl back." He dipped his hands in the water. "I'll see you later," she said.

Back in the apartment he sat down on the low bench, his knees as high as his chest in a vague gynecological displacement. All around him his father's new furniture glowed seductively. He thought of himself as bereft, shipwrecked, settled at sea on a spar, or on—at last—the desert island of his propositions. He had brought nothing with him; he'd had nothing to bring. Such speculations as those in his lecture were no game (he would amend the lecture), but the dream inventory of the already abandoned. What such people did to pass time, scheduling desires like trains, had somehow filtered down, returned like bottles to civilization. Perhaps he thought as criminals thought, longing out like cards on the table, his lists the ordered priorities of such fellows, the idle bookkeeping of the shitty condition.

Yet even he had options. He could quit his bench, turn the place back into the good hotel it had been the night before—or even accept sixty-two cents on the dollar and get out entirely. Or try for more. (Like all ultimatums and binds, the management's was riddled with loopholes.) How free the will! Till the moment of death how open-ended a man's life! It was at last astonishing that there was so much suffering, so little revenge. Sit *shivah?* Why, he should stand it tiptoe, climb all over it. He was in his father's skin now, plunging into Pop's deepest furniture, but all along the attraction had been that it was someone else's, that he'd been granted the dearest opportunity of his life—to quit it, a suicide who lived to tell the tale. (But to whom?) Wrapping himself in another's life as a child rolls himself in blankets or crawls beneath beds to alter geography. But where *was* everybody? When would the doorbell ring?

Answering his wish, as if his new freedom brought with it special powers, it actually did ring. Just before he opened the door he pulled off his shoes, remembering that he was supposed to mourn in stockinged feet, and rushed to ignite the *yahrzeit.* Dressed now, the woman who had brought him the bowl was standing there. "Are you alone?"

"Yes."

"I have to speak with you."

"Come in."

Closing the door behind her, she stepped into the apartment and looked around. "I'm sorry about your father," she said nervously.

Preminger nodded solemnly. Though he'd never seen her before her brief errand, there was something familiar about her. A large woman in perhaps her early forties, she wore her hair in a weighty golden beehive and seemed as imposing as the hostess in a restaurant, a woman men kidded warily. He could see her with big menus in her hand and wondered if she was a widow. She was the age of the men and women who'd been his parents' friends when he was in high school, in that long-gone postwar prime time when his father earned more than he ever had before or since, when his parents had begun to take vacations in the winter—Miami, cruises to the Caribbean, others that grazed South America's long coast, nibbling Caracas, Tobago, Cayenne. Seeing this woman, he recalled those trips, how proud he'd been of his parents, how proud of the Philco console television and Webcor wire recorder and furniture and fur and stock brochures that had poured into their home in those days, a high tide of goods and services, a full-time maid and a second car, his father's custom suits, his mother's diamonds lifted from their settings and turned into elaborate cocktail rings like the tropical headgear of chorus girls in reviews. It was at this time that there had begun to appear new friends, this woman's age, people met on cruises, in Florida, at "affairs" to which his parents had eagerly gone, bar mitzvahs and weddings—he'd seen the checks, for fifty or a hundred dollars, made out to the sons and daughters of their new friends, children they'd never met—and dinner dances where his father pledged two or three hundred whatever the cause. Proud of *all* the checks his father wrote, of all the charities to which they subscribed—to fight rare diseases, to support interfaith schools, the Haganah, the Red Cross, Schweitzer, Boys Town, the Fund for the Rosenbergs, the Olympic Games Committee, the Democratic Party and Community Chest—proud of his parents' whimsical generosity that bespoke no philosophy save the satisfaction of any need, the payment of any demand.

Indeed, in a curious way he associated their new prosperity (they'd always been prosperous but this was something else) with the appearance of these new friends, a cadre of big handsome men in glowing custom suits, white-on-white shirts. He recalled the monograms stitched into their breast pockets exposed at poker tables, the elaborate thin blue calligraphy closing in on itself in sweeping strokes and loops, their thriving wives. (Had people ever been that happy?) Liquor was served as once fruit had been (though fruit was still served, great overflowing bowls on the coffee and end tables), and coffee cakes baked to order like birthday cakes, and the coffee itself from tall, glistening electric warmers, from Silex and Chemex—it was coffee's Industrial Revolution—a whole range of new and marvelous machines. Prouder still of his parents' hospitality, a streak of it in them a mile wide, that sent him on a hundred errands, around the corner, down to the drugstore to lay in when they'd run out five hundred aspirin for the headache of a single guest, that authorized his rare use of the car to fetch their friends and even their friends' friends from airports and train stations. Where had that hospitality, in his parents so punctilious, gone in him? To what had it been reduced? As the woman stood before him now he could think of nothing so much as of where he would get fruits to give her, coffee, luscious cake to swallow. He felt shamed, consternated, like someone caught out in farce, wondering in these first seconds how he could stall her while he phoned delicatessens, sent messages to appetizer shops to bring back treats.

He threw himself upon her mercy.

"I've nothing to serve you."

"I'm on Weight Watchers."

"I don't even know if there's bouillon. I haven't been cooking."

"It isn't important," she said. "At a time like this it's us who should be doing for you." Suddenly she moved forward and took him in her arms; then, astonishingly, this brisk woman of the earlier errand began to sob hysterically. By stepping forward she had reversed their roles. He pressed her against him, thinking, I can't give her grapes, but I'll stand here and let her hang on. Was this dignity, he wondered? The comforted comforting. Was he Ethel Kennedy reassuring a shaken Andy Williams, Coretta King grim and brave at the peace rallies?

"There, there," he said.

Tall as himself, the woman buried her running nose in his ear. His ear was no tangerine, but surely this was hospitality of a sort too. She gripped him fiercely and moaned and he pressed her harder and patted her back and moved her hair with his hand, and before he knew it he had an erection. Could she feel it? He extricated himself gently. "I'm going back to my mourner's bench," he said. The woman blew her nose in her handkerchief and moved to the neutral corner of his father's sofa. There she continued to sob, though more quietly now. He waited politely and thought, surprising himself, that this had been his first sexual contact in a long time. And with a woman who, though at the most only five or six years older than himself, was in his mind the physical and spiritual counterpart of those guests of his parents when he was in high school, and so through some trick of associative displacement was old enough to be his mother. He recalled how those women had pleased him, inspired his lusts, their laughter over cards overheard through his bedroom door open just a crack (concupiscent, their mah-jongg concentration in its sheer physical huddle; beneath the folding card table their stockinged knees would be touching) sending him signals like whores in daylight gossiping in kitchens or doing their nails, and he blushing simply to overhear recipes recited, as though those treats they prepared for their husbands were code for the exotic movements they made in their beds. He understood why they appealed to him, coming as they did into his parents' lives with his father's rising fortunes, their presence associated with the TV, and the new gadgets and the other merchandise. Perhaps his own low-level sexuality had to do with being broke, his hard-on— another odd displacement only now subsiding—with his being in his father's house again. Which made him an Oedipus of the domestic for whom jealous of his father's place meant just that: *place*.

"May we speak?" she asked.

"Of course."

"I'm sorry," she said. "It was such a shock to all your father's neighbors, to all his . . . friends."

He nodded gravely, hoping to say something that would spark

additional condolences, suddenly needing to hear them, to encourage the proper—all forms of regret were proper, always in season, like basic black—as a necessary aspect of his position, not hiding in commonplaces so much as seeking circuits in them.

He cleared his throat and began.

"Well, one thing—he certainly lived a full life."

"Fifty-nine? Fifty-nine is a full life?"

"I mean he lived life to the brim. Each day was a new possibility. He got pleasure out of things. He never lost his curiosity about life. That's why he retired young, I think. To give himself a chance to feel new things. Always to keep on discovering, keep on learning."

"He didn't know what to do with himself."

"He took pleasure in the apartment. The way he fixed it up."

"The bills beat his brains in."

"He passed in his sleep," he said. "Painlessly?" he added uncertainly.

"Who's to know?" she said. "When your heart falls downstairs you probably feel it pretty good."

"At least he couldn't have suffered *long*," Preminger said.

"He died alone. If you're alone when something like that hits you, you get plenty scared."

Out of commonplaces, Marshall shrugged and sat silently.

"I like to think," she said finally, dropping her devil's advocacy, "that at least his last months weren't entirely all that terrible. There could have been a little sweetness. Toward the end. Frankly, that's why I'm here."

"I see."

"Not the only reason, of course," she added hurriedly. "If there's anything I can do don't hesitate to ask me."

"That's very kind, Mrs.—"

"Riker."

"Mrs. Riker." He'd been in Chicago two days and was beginning to understand that there *were* things people could help him with. "As a matter of fact," he said, "there is something. I don't have my car yet and don't know the neighborhood. Do you drive? Maybe tomorrow or the next day you could take me around to the supermarket and I can lay in some supplies. I mean when *you* go shopping. I don't want you to make a special trip. I could go with you, perhaps."

"Perhaps," she said coolly.

"It's not important," he said, "I just meant if you're stopped at a red light in the lane nearest the sidewalk in a cloudburst and I happen by in the same direction with heavy bundles—"

"Listen," she said, "there could be plenty of people here in a little while. Can we talk?"

He'd forgotten that she'd started to tell him something, and now he waited noncommittally for her to go on.

"I know your car isn't with you," she said. "You flew. Of course there's nothing in the house. Your father ate in restaurants, but I don't think it would be a good idea for us to go shopping together."

"Oh?"

"Come on," she said, "what 'Oh?' You know what I'm talking about. What was between your father and me was no big deal. It isn't as if we *slept* together. It was a flirtation pure and simple. He was a lonely man and he liked to think we were having some sort of, I don't know, adventure. It wasn't vulgar. I didn't encourage him. I didn't lead him on. At no time did I lead him on," she said positively. "You don't believe me?" He just stared at her, his groin warming like toast. "All right," she said, "let's be frank. How much do you know?"

"How much?"

"You've been here two days. *I'm the person who didn't let you in yesterday.* I believed you when you said you were Phil's son. I didn't want you in the apartment till I had a chance to get in here. But damn it, I couldn't find the key."

"I want the key returned," Preminger said icily.

"This is crazy," she said. "You've been alone here two days. A person looks around. He looks for papers, photographs."

"My father is dead," he told her. "Do you think I came to ransack the place?"

"No, of course not. This would be a sentimental thing. Look, how much do you know?"

"I don't know anything," Preminger said miserably.

"I appreciate your position," she said. "Don't think I don't. Look, I'm sorry. There are letters. Did you happen to see them?"

"No."

"Could I have a look around? I think they may be in his desk."

"I'll do it."

"Could I come with you?"

"You think I'll read them?"

"No, of course not. I could help you look. I know what they look like."

"You mean you'd recognize your writing?"

"That's right." She grinned.

"Come on, then," he said.

She went to the right drawer immediately and removed a pale blue box which she slipped into her handbag. Preminger decided she should suffer. "How do I know those are only your letters in there?"

"They are. He kept them in this box."

"I'd have to see."

"They're innocent," she said, "there's nothing in them."

"I'd have to see." He spoke like a landlord, feeling the full weight of the law on his side. He could beat her up now, take the letters from her by force. They were his property, as much a part of his legacy as the furniture. She was trespassing, and if she refused to let him see them he could even kill her. He was stunningly in the right, stunningly protected.

"Hand over the box," said the wise steward, "hand it over by the time I count three or I'll take it away from you. I know my rights. I don't even have to count three. Give me the box or I'll hurt you bad." She looked at him, shocked, and surrendered it. "You can have your letters back," he said, "I won't read them. But first I have to see if there's anything that doesn't belong to you."

"They're my letters," she cried, "they're the letters I wrote him."

"That's as may be. If so, you'll get them back. But there may be wristwatches, jewelry. There may be fountain pens."

"Paper clips," she said, "rubber bands around the envelopes."
It was so. He returned the letters.

"There's nothing in them," she said. "It's a mountain out of
a molehill. Read them if you want to."

"That won't be necessary."

"But there's nothing in them. Just my thoughts, only my
thoughts."

"It's not important. I don't have to know anything about it.
My father was free to live his own life. You are."

"I made you think terrible things," she said, opening the box
and pulling an envelope from the stack. "I'll read one. Does this
sound like we were having an affair? Does this sound dirty?"

"Please."

"You son of a bitch, *you listen to this*." She began to read
rapidly. Everything was as she said. The letters were her thoughts,
letters he might have written a cousin. He understood that on
her part at least there was nothing between them. The subject
never came up. What came up were the movies she'd seen, how
she felt about the war news, where she thought the economy was
headed, her hopes for a better world. It was incredible. They
lived in the same building, on the same floor, yet the letters
could have been written from one pen pal in Australia to another in Alaska.

She read through three of them before stopping. She showed
him the formal signature: Evelyn Riker. "It was an *outlet*," she
cried. "It was only an outlet."

Preminger was confused. "But you have his key."

"He wanted me to have it. He insisted. That was *his* outlet,
that a woman have a key to his apartment. Do you think I ever
used it?"

"Jesus."

"What was so terrible? As long as I had it he could fantasize
that I might use it. It was innocent. We talked by the pool. I
wrote him letters. He gave me his key. Nothing happened. I
can't help what people think."

"I'm sorry I bullied you."

"How could you know what to think?"

The doorbell rang.

"They thought we were mixed up together," she said, looking toward the door.

"I better get that."

"I wanted to be gone when they came. I handled it badly. I can't think straight. In the letters I'm composed, organized. On my feet I can't think straight. They shouldn't see me here."

"Do you want me to hide you?" Preminger asked. "If you want me to hide you I will."

"There are only three floor plans. We know each other's layouts. If the hall toilet was occupied they'd come use the one off the master bedroom and find me."

"I don't have to answer it. Then, after they've gone, you could wait a few minutes and slip out."

"Answer it," she said, "answer it. This is terrible for you. Phil dead and so much crazy excitement. Answer it or I'll bust." They left the bedroom together.

It was two men from Ashkenaz Delicatessen delivering trays, two enormous platters round as old shields.

"I didn't order this stuff," Preminger told them. One of the men, his tray before his belly like a cigarette girl, shrugged. "It's a mistake," Preminger insisted. "Who asked for all this?"

"It's paid for, Mister," the other one said, and again Preminger had a sudden sense of theater, of being on stage, his every step back from the advancing food a piece of alarmed comic business, of conventional blocking in farce. Crazily he felt an overwhelming fondness for the two men, their brusque man-in-the-street manners, their stolid cabby character; he found himself extrapolating their fidelity to their wives, their love of kids, their goofy loyalty to the White Sox. Putting himself in their shoes he thought he understood their surprise at the queer scene—Evelyn still suspiciously sniffing in the corner, his own bare feet, the box of letters, the odd look of the living room, lived in for two days but somehow not as mussed as it should have been, as though the real action had to be going on in the bedroom. Since they worked for a delicatessen they would even have taken in the significance of the vacant cardboard mourner's bench. He had an urgent impulse to behave for them, to rectify their faulty impression. They would know his tourist condition, the unsavory quality of displaced person he gave off, and would have sniffed out all the willful bad timing of his lousy choices. He wanted these decent men in his corner, and would have bent over backwards to demonstrate his piety for them, as he always did in the face of another's.

"It's all right," he said. "Good friends have sent it. We're in mourning here. Deep sorrow has visited this place. I'm not able to go out. My father passed away suddenly. I'm his only son. Everything looks delicious." The men remained impassive, and he wondered if he ought to tip them. No, he decided, guys like this can't be bought. They asked for a ten-dollar deposit on the trays and left.

Evelyn had stopped whimpering; without his noticing she had performed some invisible toilet and reapplied make-up which had smeared when she was crying, her hair and clothes made neat and fresh, the hospital corners of appearance. Unrecovered himself—he still thought of their scene as a debauch—and sick of his sideburns and immodest flash (how should he dress? What was the apparel of his station? where could he get trousers with cuffs, white long-sleeved shirts, correct ties?) he sought to make amends.

Instead he made promises. "Harris wants to buy the place. He offers a ridiculous figure. But I'm not holding out for more. Even if I let him cheat me it would mean more money than I ever had in my life. The money isn't in it. I mean to live here. I can do my dissertation on the kitchen table, use the place like an office. Most of the books I need are in Missoula, but I'm sending for them. Maybe I'll fly out and drive back with the stuff. What I don't have I can get from inter-library loan. As soon as this sitting *shivah* is over I'll get organized. The job market's terrible now—that's why I'm taking my time. Actually, that might even work in my favor, be a blessing in disguise. If I don't rush the thesis it could be publishable. Either way, conditions can't stay like this forever; something has to give. Then, when I've got my doctorate I'll get a job right here in Chicago.

Northwestern, the U of C, Loyola, Marquette—there are plenty of good places. Roosevelt or even Wright Junior College. If I concentrate just on those I should be able to get something."

"What do you owe me? Not even an explanation."

He didn't hear her. He was speaking for the record. "Then, when my life is normal again, when it's routine and respectable, I'll start looking around for a girl. We'll get married, have a kid, live right here on the North Side. I appreciate that I'm starting late. Things are ass-backwards in my life, but I can catch up if I stick with it. I've got the house, the furniture, all I have to do is grow into what's already here. Gee, I'm a pioneer in reverse."

"I wish you every good luck. Like Pat O'Brien's toast on television. 'May the wind always be at your back.'" She giggled. "That would be like standing in a draft."

He looked closely at her. "This sounds pretty lame to you? Like someone terminal making plans? People have no faith in other people's second chances and fresh starts. Things by their nature seem irrevocable. Habit has a full nelson on us, we think. I hear some two-pack-a-day guy, a real cougher, say he's quitting on New Year's or on his birthday, or maybe he throws the cigarette away right in front of me, grinds it out in the ashtray and swears it's his last, and I know he's just kidding himself. How's it any different for me? Is that what you think? What are you, an actuary? I know the odds. I want to tell you something. I'm pretty bouncy, I've come through before this, I've got powers of recuperation pinned on me like a kid's mittens. I had a heart attack when I was thirty-three. It was a close shave and I thought I was a goner, but here I am." He held up his hand. "Present." She had jumped back when he raised his arm. "What did you think I was talking about, climbing Everest? Do I sound like William the Conqueror? Somebody who wants a screen test? I'm talking about ordinary life, H-O scale."

"Listen," she said, "I'd better get going." She started toward the door.

"Gee, who's going to help me eat all this stuff?"

"Oh, there'll be plenty of people. I'll come back later too."

He stood in the doorway as she passed through and watched her as she walked down the hall. She was almost out of sight, at the point where the corridor turned, when he called after her.

"He gave you presents, didn't he? He pissed it all away, my inheritance."

Most of the food disappeared that evening, and all of it was gone by the following afternoon. It had been sent, it turned out, by the Harris Towers Emergency Fund Committee. One of his visitors explained that each month a portion of their maintenance money was shunted into the fund. His guests, who had after all paid for it, were not in the least shy about digging in. Only Preminger, aware of the back maintenance his father owed when he died, felt a freeloader, chewing guiltily and at last preferring to wait until his visitors left before eating anything more. Later he picked ravenously from the marvelous tiered wheel of corned beef and pastrami and sliced turkey laid out like a card trick, his fork flying, occasionally puncturing the bronze-colored cellophane which covered the meats. There were buckets of potato salad tucked away on the trays, logjams of pickles and cartons of coleslaw like a moist confetti. Some women had made coffee, serving it directly from Harris Towers Common Room urns, stainless steel and as large as the equipment in restaurants. They poured it into Styrofoam cups which they took from stacks that rose in high towers like Miami hotels.

Many of his callers were people he recognized neither from the chapel the evening before nor the funeral that morning, and he began to have a sense of the vast population that lived in Harris Towers. A few of them had peculiar names, queer portmanteau conversions of their children's given names, now legally their own, and contrived in a strange incest from the small businesses and manufactories they had lent them to and had now, pleased with their oddly circular memorials, taken back. There was a Wil-Marg (belts) and a Freddy-Lou (blouses). There was a Rob-Roy. Some of the people were quite old, but not as many as he had expected, and though he was younger by several years than the youngest there, they seemed only a fraction of a generation up on him, and the deference these showed to those who were clearly along in years somehow reduced the difference in their ages even more.

He phrased this delicately as he could to one of his guests. "I know," the man said, "most people think a place like this is some kind of Sun City, but I'll tell you something. We haven't even got an emergency room on the premises. A lot of condominiums do, you know. With a twenty-four-hour duty nurse, oxygen, the red telephones, everything. Harris Towers is a condominium with a difference. The clientele's very active. Seventy-two percent of us are still in business." Preminger, his retired father's substitute, was glad he did not drag down the average. "We've got our Golden Agers, but so far they're definitely in the minority. And very few vegetables, very few." He touched Preminger's arm. "Still," he said, "glad to have you aboard. Always use new blood."

In the next few days the weather turned very hot, and the central air conditioning, taxed to the limit, could barely cope. Taking his bench with him, Preminger moved his mourning out onto the balcony to try to catch a fresh breeze; there, facing southeast, he could see Chicago's skyline, the tall apartments of Lake Shore Drive, downtown, Hancock's startling skyscraper. But the heat was absurd, absolute. He stood at the railing and stared down into the cool turquoise of the swimming pool, then and there abandoning his *shivah*.

He had no bathing suit, of course, and walked to the shopping center to buy one. At the entrance to the pool the lifeguard turned him back. "I'm sorry," he said, "but the pool is reserved for the exclusive use of residents and their guests."

"I'm a resident."

The boy took out a mimeographed list. "Your name, sir?"

"Marshall Preminger."

"Oh," he said, setting his list aside, "are you related to Mr. Preminger?"

"I'm his son. I live here now."

"Sir, I'm not doubting your word, but you see in this building the residents all wear blue wristbands. Like the one that woman has on." He pointed to a sort of strap, rather like a garter or the tag worn by patients in hospitals. Other people wore yellow or red bands, but everybody seemed to have one.

"I see other colors too."

"The yellow bands are for guests. It's a code. In this building the guests wear yellow. The red is for visiting residents from another building. In their own pools they might wear yellow bands and the guests would wear blue or red, and their guests yellow."

"I don't have a blue band."

"Sir, all residents are issued a resident band plus two visiting resident and three guest bands."

"I don't have any."

"Sir, your father . . . I was sorry to hear about what happened. I was teaching him to dive. I saw him do a terrific jackknife, and the next day he was dead. Your father never swam without his blue band. Did you look around the apartment?" Preminger shook his head. "That might be a good idea. I'm sure you'll find them."

"I'm certain I will. I'll look for them as soon as I go upstairs."

"Sir," the lifeguard said, "these rules were set up by the residents themselves. I haven't the authority to suspend them." He lowered his voice and spoke confidentially. "Sir, people are watching. You're putting me on the spot. Could you look for the bands now? As a favor to me?"

Preminger shrugged, went back up to the apartment and searched high and low. When he couldn't find them and called the office, they told him that no bands had been turned in. They suggested he look for different colored bands and swim as a visiting resident in one of the other pools. He returned to the pool and, brushing past the lifeguard, jumped into the water. He felt people staring at his naked wrists. It was as if he were skinny-dipping.

"Hey," a fat woman called roughly. "Hey, you!" Preminger continued to swim. The heavy woman went over to the lifeguard and spoke to him and the lifeguard blew his whistle listlessly. Ignoring him, Preminger swam on. The lifeguard, looking sheepish, returned to his post, but the woman followed him and the boy, nodding miserably and setting his pith helmet on the seat beside him, jumped into the water and swam after Preminger.

"Please," he said, "you'll have to leave the pool, Mr. Preminger."

"I can't find the damned bands. I looked everywhere."

"Sir," he said, treading water powerfully and trying to keep his voice gentle, "I'm a college man. I depend on these people for tips. You can petition for a reissue. Why don't you just get out now?"

"It's too goddamn hot," Preminger said stubbornly. "I'm not getting out." He turned away from the boy and swam toward the deep end of the pool. Hearing clean, powerful chops behind him, he realized he was being followed. Though he hadn't raced in years, he tried to get away, but in five strokes the lifeguard caught him.

"Sir," he said, "I'm sorry," and Preminger felt himself captured, the lifeguard's strong arm across his chest and under his chin. It was an official Red Cross lifesaving hold and it was being used against him! Somehow this was more humiliating than anything that had yet happened, and he began to struggle furiously.

"That's right, sir," the boy whispered, "pretend you're drowning."

Preminger considered the proposition.

"Help," he said weakly, "help, help."

"That's it," the kid said softly, then louder, "*it's all right, sir, I've got you.*" He felt himself towed sidestroke toward shore. He closed his eyes to avoid the stares of the others, then felt his body scrape bottom at the shallow end. The lifeguard helped him to stand, and with Preminger's arm around the boy's shoulder they climbed up the steps. When they were out of the pool he coughed a few times and the lifeguard pounded his back.

"Thanks," Preminger said stiffly, "you saved my life. I'll always be in your debt. How can I ever repay you?"

"*Sir, forget it,*" the kid shouted, "*it's my job. It's all in a day's work.*" They shook hands formally and Preminger started back to the apartment.

He passed the fat woman. "Faker," she hissed, "you weren't drownding."

"I was," Preminger said, "I *was* drownding."

Pride, he thought in the apartment afterwards, his chest still constricted from the encounter: the Preminger Curse. There was a floating fury in the low-keyed man, Preminger's underground river. A health factor like a trick knee or a predisposition to allergy. Preminger the Proud, Seismological Preminger, quite simply blew up at a snub or humiliation. He exploded, bunched other men's lapels in his fists, slapped faces like a duelist or slammed out incoherencies like a talker in tongues. Why did underwriters ignore it on forms? He took *that* as a snub!

It was a form of snub that had brought on his heart attack. He had gone to keep an appointment with his agent, in his creased, cuffed slacks and open shirt out of uniform beside the lightly summer suited men who rode with him in the elevator. When the operator shut the doors Preminger had sneezed, a tearing detonation too sudden for handkerchiefs, that had come on him like a mugger and left his nose looping viscous ropes like pulleys of mucus. The others made an alarmed nimbus of space around him, like dancers in night clubs for the turns of a virtuoso, while Preminger, panicking, palmed vast handfuls of the stuff and shoved it into his pockets as though it were money picked up in the street. Then the operator turned to him. He's going to say "Gesundheit," Preminger thought gratefully; he's going to turn it into a joke. "What floor do *you* want?" the man said, and Preminger was on him, his anger bigger than the sneeze itself. "You never asked *them*, you son of a bitch. You ask *them*, you cheap fuckshit, you goddamn errand boy, you ass stink and cunt grease," punching him about the head and shoulders with all his might, leaving sticky wisps of snot where he struck. His heart stopped him before the others could and he collapsed on the floor of the elevator.

Now he took his pulse—twenty-seven for fifteen seconds, four times twenty-seven's a hundred eight—and swallowed two

Valiums. Recognizing his vulnerability he could do nothing about it. On the mourner's bench (despite the fact that he was no longer sitting *shivah,* he continued to go there as to a neutral corner) he cursed the lifeguard, wishing him dead, mutilated, cramped and drowning in his pool, electrocuted by a faulty underwater light. Only his anger, hair of the dog, calmed him, and gradually he steadied down. "I must be nuts," he said aloud. "I'm a crazy." He thought of himself in the elevator in the crummy pants and shirt, his shabby shoes, of pushing past the lifeguard to jump naked-wristed into the swimming pool. Jesus, he thought, if I don't stop violating the dress codes I'm a dead man. Where do I get my fury? he wondered. What nutty notions of my character come on me? What is it with me? Where do I think I am—where three roads meet?

The phone rang. It was Evelyn Riker. She called to tell him that she'd found his father's blue wristband. "It was wrapped around the letters in the box. I was upset or I would have noticed."

"So you heard about that, did you?"

"I heard you almost drowned."

"Yeah."

"I'll put it in an envelope and leave it for you at the office."

"Yeah, thanks."

When he hung up he went to the desk where she'd found the letters. He poked around in it, reaching deep into drawers, and pulled out the five missing red and yellow bands, plus a green band that the lifeguard had not told him about. "This must be the contraband," he said.

The *shivah* had been broken. If he still used the mourner's bench it was out of some vestigial need for the dramatically reflexive. Now he had a signature, a gesture, a theme, something associated with him, if invisibly. (No one saw him on it.) There was something inexplicably counterclockwise in him like a mysterious effect in physics, as personal and offbeat as a sailor hat indoors on a businessman. Watching the color TV from the mourner's bench, his bare feet—for comfort now—extended, he thought that perhaps he could establish a Premingerian trend, a fad, a novelty, a first. He would bring mourner's benches back into the living room. Though, again, no one saw him. He leaped to his feet if the bell rang, if there was a knock on the door, if the telephone sounded, and remained there several minutes after his visitor had gone or the phone had been replaced. What the occasional delivery person, the rare condolence caller from the South Side saw was the vacant bench itself, looking in its woody contact-paper like something left behind after a child's log cabin has been struck. If the style caught on it would be brought back to the world misunderstood, like a Balkan mannerism or Asian idiom. To all eyes he seemed to steer clear, giving a wide berth to the bench.

Two nights following his little drama at the pool, the night his *shivah* would formally have ended had he not already suspended it, he had visitors. Seven men and four women, a jury of his peers manqué. Not individually familiar to him, though he thought he might have seen a few of them and one or two might even have been in his house, he recognized even before they spoke that they had come as a group. His behind still tingled with the austere, ghostly caress of the hard mourner's bench and he felt a sort of mixed curiosity and low-intensity outrage at the sight of them. How dare these people, so patently a band (the fact that there were so many of them was a sure sign that they had not *all* been able to make it—and, oh, he thought, what low time is it in my life that I have taken to counting my guests?— who clearly would have had to have *arranged* this call, who didn't look like brothers and sisters or husbands and wives or fathers and daughters), take it for granted, after their own elaborate arrangements with each other, that he would be there without first ringing up? Did they count him as he had counted them? Yes, that's how it was. They had his number.

"Mr. Preminger, how do you do?" a man hidden behind the others in the corridor said. "We have not yet had the pleasure. I am Mr. Salmi, first president of H.T.R.A., the Harris Towers Residents Association."

My God, Preminger thought, the Father of my Condominium!

"These good people—may we come in?—are associated with me on the Committee of Committees." Preminger stood aside. "They are chairmen of the various committees that exist in our condominium to enrich the social and cultural life of the residents, make our bylaws, establish liaison between residents and management, and adjudicate complaints."

"I found the wristbands," Preminger said.

"Forgive if you will our vigilante aspect. We are here to welcome and invite. Normally, of course, Miriam—Mrs. Julius Schreiber—would have been by to do this, but your father died while Mrs. Schreiber was abroad."

"She's still there," someone said.

"So this extraordinary convocation has no purpose other than to bid you welcome and to officially acknowledge the Towers' sadness at Phil's—your father's—passing."

"Hear hear."

"You know," Salmi said, "we don't normally jump all over a new resident like this. Harris Towers is first of all our home; only secondly is it our community. I'm not going to talk a lot of Mickey Mouse to you. We don't, for example, even have our own flag like a lot of the condominiums do. The management had one designed, but we voted not to fly it. The Stars and Stripes is good enough for us. Still, for many of the residents—I don't except myself—Harris Towers has provided the first opportunity we've ever had to participate on a pragmatic, viable level in the shaping of the quality of the community life. I want to underscore that word 'participate.' I'll be coming back to it, if you'll bear with me, more than once tonight. May I sit down, Mr. Preminger—Marshall?"

Preminger waved him to a seat.

"Listen," Salmi said, leaning forward, "we've got a piece of Chicago here that belongs to us. Do you gather my meaning? What we do with it isn't anybody's business but our own. I'm talking about the principle of anything between consenting adults —not on the smut level, you understand. This is a great principle, a *great* principle. One of the great ideas of Western Man. We can use this place as an ordinary bedroom complex—a home first, I said, you'll remember—or we can reach out and touch our environment, shape it for good or ill. The choice is each individual's to make, and the choice is *ours*. Boy oh boy, I must sure sound corny to you. I must sure sound like a fanatic. But wait, you'll see. But what am I doing monopolizing? I said 'participate,' and I *meant* participate. Mr. Ed Eisner has the floor."

"All I have to say," said Mr. Eisner, "is I've been living here since the place opened. That was January of seventy, and I told my wife a new decade, a new tomorrow. I spoke better than I knew. I never had any desire to lead men. I've got an I.G.A. Big deal, it's a small franchise supermarket, I'm a grocer. I still go to business, but I'm here to tell you that I'm more interested in this place than I ever was in my store. That's my livelihood, but I'm telling the truth. I should have made this move years ago. I live to come home every night. Weekends are like a vacation for me. I don't even want to go away anymore. If you ask me, Miriam Schreiber was nuts to go abroad. Not me. I've got a community. I don't mean *I* have, I don't mean *me*. I'm chairman of the Buildings and Grounds Committee. We serve for eighteen months, and my term was up this past June. Let me tell you something, I fought like hell to retain my chairmanship— promises, deals, even a little mudslinging, if you want to know. I said my opponent who happens to live in Center House wanted to use the fountain out front as a private lake. 'A private lake'— what the hell does that mean? I sweated the election, I ate my heart out. My wife said, 'Ed, what do you need it, it's a headache." You think I want power? I don't give a *goddamn* for power! You think I care about being a big shot? Some big shot. No, what I care about is the buildings and grounds. That the fountain works and the lights are lit in the halls and no one is stuck in the elevator and the crab grass should drop dead. What I care about is that there ain't no litter and when a rose is planted a rose comes up. I'm on the janitors' asses like a top sergeant. They hate my guts, but I get things done."

The speech was crazily moving. Preminger felt a swell of sympathy for Mr. Eisner, for all of them, though he did not know what to make of their strange call. They spoke to him like evangelists; their eyes shone. He brought chairs from the kitchen for those who were still standing, and found himself nodding at what they said, listening as carefully as he ever had to anything in his life. One by one each had his say. Never had people spoken this way to him, so clearly seeking his approval— more, his conversion, as if without it they would not be able to go on themselves. He felt wooed, bid for at some odd auction, standing by as his value rose and rose, fetching sums undreamed of.

"I think," a man said, "he needs a clearer picture of the overall setup."

"This is Mr. Morris Barney," Salmi said. "He edits the house organ, *The House Organ,* and writes the highly readable column 'A Story Within a Storey.' "

"Three buildings," Barney said briskly, naming them on his fingers, "North, South and Center. Two of them, North and South, high-rises, sixteen stories, each accommodating one hundred twenty-eight apartments, two hundred fifty-six for the pair. Center House, though only eleven stories high, has twenty-two apartments to the floor or two hundred and forty-two in all. This gives you a total of four hundred and ninety-eight units, a figure carefully thought out by the owners—"

"We're the owners," a woman said.

"We're the owners. We *are* the owners," Barney told her, "but let's not kid ourselves, this place didn't go up by itself and it didn't go up because of *us*. Harris is the brains."

"A brilliant man," President Salmi said.

"—carefully thought out by the owners beforehand, the total falling just two units shy of the number officially designated by the U.S. Government as a project. This eliminates a considerable amount of red tape and static from the FHA should an owner find it necessary to sell. All right, four nine eight units, three zero five of them occupied by married couples—six hundred ten marrieds. Plus a hundred eighteen solitaries—the single, widowed, widowered and divorced, a handful. In addition, seventy-three apartments owned by brothers, brothers and sisters, mother/child or father/child relationships—two or more people living together as a family with a designation other than married. Two hundred and three of these in all. In only two apartments in Harris Towers are there married couples with children—seven people. All right, here are your figures: six hundred ten man-and-wife; one hundred eighteen solitaries"—I'm a solitary, Preminger thought—"two hundred and three in mixed families and two couples with three children. A total population of nine hundred and thirty-eight people. The median age is sixty-one."

"Thank you," Salmi said, "for a brilliant breakdown." He turned to Preminger. "Almost a thousand people," he said. "Many small towns aren't as large. We're practically a government," he said breathlessly. "We're a microcosm. If we can make it work here, why can't they make it work on the outside? Do you follow me? The answer is simple. Where are your blacks? Where are your PR's? The answer is simple, my dear Marshall. There aren't any. We're not only a community, we're a *ghetto! You* know things, you're a scholar. Athens was a ghetto. Rome was. For slaves read custodians, read carpenters, gardeners and the three lads in the underground garage. Read lifeguards and the girls in the office and the executives of the corporation and you have the new Athens on the North Side. Twenty-five people, outsiders, twenty-five on the nose to support the life of nine hundred and thirty-eight, one to thirty-seven. Not a good ratio, Preminger. Count police, fire, civil service and spoils appointments in Chicago as a whole and you have one to less than nineteen. How do we catch up? What's the economics, Mrs. Ornfeld of Budget?"

Mrs. Ornfeld of Budget looked like all the clubwomen who had ever introduced Preminger to his audiences on the lecture circuit. When she spoke, however, she sounded tougher than any of them ever had, biting off her words like a lady Communist. "Bleak," she said. "Four nine eight apartments. A maintenance that varies with the size and location of the unit but averages two hundred and fifty dollars a month." (Were they dunning him, then? Was that what this was all about?) "Times four hundred ninety-eight makes a nut of one hundred and twenty-four thousand, five hundred dollars. That's the sum we turn over to Harris each month and which he disburses as expenses and payroll. One hundred and twenty-four thousand five hundred dollars—and its *pea*nuts." She pronounced the word as if she were shelling them in her mouth.

"Shall we raise the maintenance?" It was President Salmi. "Shall we, Marshall? What happens when they strike? When the staff strikes? Shall we raise the maintenance? What do you say we each put in an additional fifty a month? The median age here is sixty-one, Barney tells us. We're approaching fixed incomes. Because we're a new Athens on the North Side will the foundations help us out, do you think? Shall we nickel-and-dime ourselves and raise the monthly maintenance gradually until the five extra dollars becomes ten and the ten fifteen and the fifteen thirty and the thirty the original fifty we were so afraid of, and the fifty some outrageous figure we can't even conceive of now? One day it will come to that. It *will*. It will have to. But wait. I see an alternative. We cut down services. We drain the pool, fire a janitor or two. Run the heat and air conditioning only at peak times. Watch the flowers die. Learn skills, basic mechanics and carpentry and the electrician's wisdom. Do for ourselves. But! But don't ask *me* to be your president! I'll not preside over such an organization!"

"Don't ask me to oversee that sort of budget," Mrs. Ornfeld moaned.

"I wouldn't print such news," Barney said.

"So you see, Marsh?" Salmi said. "Are you looking at this picture? Paradise. A paradise these houses and towers. Open not yet two years, a one hundred percent occupancy since barely March. Do you see? Are you watching? Here too is the decline of the Roman Empire, the dissolution of the city-states. How does it feel to be in history?"

Preminger nodded.

"So when I *say* participate, I *mean* participate," Salmi said. "It ain't all sweetness and it ain't all light, and all worlds go broke and every hope wears a thin tread and punctures like a tire. The forecast is not terrific and the times they are a-changing. What happened to Dad, my dear young orphan, happens also on a scale so massive as to be incomprehensible to finite minds like ours. Death is built into the universe like windows in walls."

Moved, Preminger sat silently on the rug. He was not embarrassed by the speech. None of them were; he heard them breathing, sighing, felt the calm induced by truth. No one hurried to break the silence Salmi had shaped. Here, at last, was his father's eulogy, the *shivah* perfected. If he hadn't thought they would take it as a stunt he would have crawled to the mourner's bench and sat on it.

"But cheer up," Salmi said quietly, "take heart, my friends. Land maybe ho, my good Marshall. If all is losing, all's not yet lost. We're organized. We gamble against the house—do you like the joke?—but we're informed of the odds. Most of them"— he indicated the residents throughout the buildings—"think we're too self-important, 'Squeak squeak,' they say for Mickey Mouse. 'Neigh,' they go for horseshit, our neighbors and neighsayers. But perhaps we haven't explained ourselves properly. We may not have made ourselves clear."

"Trust the people," Mrs. Ornfeld said.

Salmi turned fiercely to Morris Barney. "You could write an editorial. I've told you this a hundred times. Lay it on the line, let them know. Wake them up!"

"My press is free," Barney said.

"Yeah, yeah, sure."

"They don't want to read that stuff, Herb."

Salmi turned back to Preminger. "Well, I'm an old war-horse," he said apologetically. "I make these speeches. Look, there are committees—Entertainment, Activities, the newspaper. A few like Buildings and Grounds and Units and Budget are largely watchdog to see that the management keeps up its share of the bargain. But there are others—the Good Neighbors, Emergency, Security, Education. New Residents I foresee will soon be absorbed, since we're one hundred percent occupied. My colleagues have mimeographed sheets which explain the function of these committees. They'll leave them with you. You'll look them over. Sixty-one," he said wearily. "The median age in this room is that. It feels like ninety. Oh, boy. Oh, well. Read the stuff. Think and study. See where your talents lead you."

"I will."

"How old are you?"

"Thirty-seven."

"Thirty-seven," Salmi said. "You're the youngest resident, you know that? Younger even than the children of the two couples whose children still live with them."

"I am?"

"Yeah," President Salmi said, "you're the hope of the future, the new generation."

"Was my father on a committee? Is that why there's an opening?" Preminger asked. "Do you want me to carry on his work?"

"Your father was here for the ride. He rode us piggyback."

"I'd like to do some special pleading," Morris Barney said. "My understanding is that Marshall is studying for his doctorate. He probably has a flair for writing. I could use a guy like that on the paper."

"Not so fast," Mrs. Ehrlmann said, "a college man's natural place would be on my Education committee."

"Thirty-seven and built like a horse," someone else said, "a shoe-in for Security."

"I have a heart condition," Preminger told the husky man who had spoken.

"I hoped this wouldn't happen," Salmi said. "Let's not bum's-rush this man. It's enough right now to get a commitment of interest from him. *Are* you interested?"

"I *am*," Preminger said earnestly. "It's a question of where I'll be able to do the most good."

"Sleep on it, Marshall," Salmi, rising, said.

"I will, but I think I can give you assurances now." It sounded grand. Such words had never been in his mouth before. He could taste them. He could give assurances, pledges, wheeling and dealing in the stocks and bonds of the civil. He spoke from the highest plateau of the civic and formal. Men in groups, he'd noticed—till now he'd never been one—no matter their private status or lack of it, regardless of their ordinary one-on-one style, often spoke with a fluency that surfaced like submarines in the middles of seas. Where did they come from, these facts at the blunt fingertips, these figures sitting on the tongue like names and primary colors, all the law-court style like foreign language converted in dreams? Were we political then, our causes and positions mysterious and concealed and only waiting on us to be revealed at rallies and assemblies, or even in mobs? He'd thrilled to the articulate accounts of eyewitnesses breathed into microphones offered like cigarettes, to all the passionate summations of the rank and file and spiels of the momentarily possessed, fearing in their charmed patter only the failure of his own. How had he, thrity-seven, a Ph.D. candidate and heart patient—yes, you'd think that would count for something, add at least to his vocabulary of pain and fear—waiting on his next attack (and an ex-seventeen-thousand-dollar-a-year lecturer at that, though the lectures had all carefully been worked out in private and delivering them had involved no more than simply reading aloud), managed to avoid his share of public speaking? Why had there been no issues in his life? "I think I can give you assurances now," he repeated, trying to stand. He loved whoever loved him. If there was fury in him, vengeance and retaliation like the wound springs and coils in bombs, there was also gratitude—what they offered was rebuff's sweet opposite—and eye-for-an-eye obligation like a perfect bookkeeping. He stood before them and held his hands like pans in a scale. "It isn't a question of sleeping on it. All that's at issue is which committee can make the most of me, of whatever minimal talents I possess. Later this evening I intend to put through a long-distance call to a colleague in Montana. I shall ask him to forward my belongings to my Chicago address—this as an earnest of my commitment to make a life here.

"You may not, however, be aware of the exact status of my proprietorship in Harris Towers, and I feel under a certain obligation to apprise you of it. In all fairness, I am not yet technically an owner—nor shall I be until my father's will has been probated. Shirley Fanon has apprised *me*, however, that my prospects are positive, and that so long as I occupy these premises and fulfill my financial obligations to the condominium, I enjoy the full rights of surrogacy." They looked a little restless. He tried again. "Before you go," he said, "I'd take it as a kindness if you'd let me try to thank you. You've shown your kindness by coming here tonight. I haven't given you coffeecake or offered you drinks or any of the hospitality I'm certain I would have received at your hands in your homes. The cupboard is bare. Whatever I had your Emergency Fund Committee provided and it's all gone. I plead lassitude."

Now they seemed not only restless but uneasy. He couldn't help himself; he couldn't stop. "I've lived provisionally here," he said. "Like someone under military government, martial law, an occupied life. This isn't going as I meant it to. I'm a stranger— that's something of what I'm driving at. My life is a little like being in a foreign country. There's displaced person in me. I feel—listen—I feel . . . *Jewish.* I mean even here, among Jews, where everyone's Jewish, I feel Jewish. Does that make sense? Something in me was left out. Damn. I mean, why is it that the only place I can think to be, to live, is *here?* I mean, you just told me: I'm the youngest of nine hundred thirty-eight people. It isn't as if I *earned* this place the way the rest of you did. Or even had it in my mind as a goal. I saw it once with my father when it was still a hole in the ground. To tell you the truth, I didn't trust it. I thought it was like buying property in a swamp, that my dad was being taken and the buildings would never go up. I thought it was a scheme. I didn't like the looks of the coat of arms sewn on the salesmen's jackets. I have no *good* imagination," he said. "Nobody cheats me, but I feel it coming. But what Dr. Salmi said about the possibilities here, that was very meaningful to me. I want to do my share. I *will* do my share." He looked around to see if they had understood him. No one seemed to know what to say.

Dr. Salmi did. "It ain't the All-Star Game," he said. "It ain't church. We see to it there are no fire hazards, that people, they throw a party in the party room, are responsible for cleaning the place up afterwards."

"Yes," Preminger said, "that's what I want."

"That the grandkids come for a visit they don't scream in the halls and run the elevator all day up and down so you can't get it when you need it."

"Of course."

"That the bricks don't come down on our heads when we walk by outside."

"Yes."

"That people park only in the space assigned them and the guy who plays accordion for our dances takes a ten-minute break, ten minutes, no more, every hour on the hour. That the newsprint for the paper comes wholesale from a friend's cousin and a good chlorine level is maintained in the pool at all times."

"Sure," Preminger said.

"That we got a community here and an investment to protect," President Salmi said, his eyes fixed narrowly on Preminger, "and that when someone sells he sells to the right sort—no Chinks, no PR's, no spades."

When they left he put their mimeographed sheets aside, wanting neither to throw them away nor to find a place for them— like his father's, the dead man's mail, which continued to come.

For a week or more he gave himself over to the chores involved in setting up a household. He wrote letters to his bank in Montana and closed down his account, arranging for a cashier's check to be sent him. He consulted with Shirley Fanon about the steps he'd initiated to probate his father's will. He called the phone and electric companies and had everything put in his name. He stocked up at the supermarket and bought some clothes. He packed his father's things away and put up a notice on the bulletin board in the game room saying that whoever wanted anything of his father's could come up, look through the stuff and take away what he needed. (First he'd checked with Fanon to see if it was legal. "Sure," the lawyer told him, "none of that's in the inventory. Give it all away if you want.") No one came for three days. Then an old man showed up who did not even live in the building. He had ridden buses, he said—an hour and a half from the Southwest Side. How had the notice come to his attention? Preminger never understood. He had brought shopping bags, and Preminger helped him to fold his father's expensive clothing, the nifty bellbottoms and wallpaper prints, the psychedelic ties and turtlenecks and wide belts and leather vests, into them. He had to give the old man carfare to go home.

He rode buses himself, down to the near North Side or out to Lake Shore Drive or up to Evanston, occasionally drifting even further, to Chicago's gilt-edged northern suburbs, Winnetka and Wilmette and Kenilworth, all those expensive citadels which simply to see triggered wonder at the immense wealth in America, at the vast depth on its bench. Who *were* these people? How could they have gotten so much money? How could there be so many of them? Their homes made his mouth water. They looked like fraternity houses, country clubs, embassies. Tudorial, stately, with high green hedges and curving driveways like painterly exercises in perspective. Blue Lake Michigan sucking up to their backyards. Attached to their carriage houses and wide garages were basketball hoops, gleaming cat's cradles of white net, taut and tapered as hourglasses. He imagined lean, expert girls in blue jeans, home from Radcliffe, Holyoke, Smith, setting them up, pushing them in, playing Horse and 21, with their tan, continent boyfriends who had once been pages in the Senate. The cropped lawns, green as felt on gaming tables, made him gulp, and an occasional sound from the swimming pool of splashing water like polite applause made his heart turn over. Lake Michigan *and* a pool. Twice, when he saw strings of Chinese lanterns set out for parties, he had to shut his eyes.

He came to shop, it being simply good sense, he told himself, as immutable as that rule of the highway that one eats where the trucks are standing, that one should buy where the rich do, go to their bakers and butchers, find out how they come by their vegetables and which fruits they are eating. (And it could be justified economically. Weren't things more expensive in the slums? Wouldn't a single Rolls-Royce, properly cared for, last all one's life, mellowing, blooming with use, ever perfecting itself, cheaper in the long run than the three Fords, two Chevies, pair of Dodges, one Pontiac, two Buicks and trio of Oldsmobiles that was the average man's portion?) But the fiction that he had come merely to shop wore thin, though to preserve it he always brought something back with him—a Black Forest chocolate cake, a Spanish melon, tins of Dutch herring, Russian caviar, pickled rinds. Now, when he went on these excursions, he went obsessively, growing angry and genuinely dangerous.

He had been safer in Missoula. Even if it had its better neighborhoods and occasional mansion, Missoula was still the West, where wealth was expressed in land no man could walk in a day, and which, for all its vastness, looked no different square yard for square yard—perhaps poorer, actually—than the place where one lay down one's picnic, and where the stores were franchises one had grown up with: Penney's, Woolworth's, Rexall's and Howard Johnson's, a two-bit Hanseatic democracy of the ordinary. Chicago was different in kind. In the neighborhoods filled with their Village and Paoli and Chelsea chic that he tramped through, Chicago grieved him, tore at his spirit and opened old wounds he was helpless to stanch. He roamed Rush Street, Old Town, Lake Shore Drive and Michigan Avenue like someone seeking pornography, desire and need clobbering his spirit, drooling before the lush goods in the shop windows, eyeing the young housewives and fashionable women like a soiled madman. He was jealous of the well-dressed children, envying them their door-manned prerogatives and elevator buildings and begrudging them what he imagined would be their French and their quick minds, their nannies and good manners. A sycophant, whenever one bumped into him *he* apologized, diseased at the figure he cut in front of them. He walked lasciviously past brownstones, studio apartments, tall high-rises beehived with bachelor pads, the shared flats of stewardesses, young lawyers, radio announcers, journalists and photographers, sketching in their perfect taste and lovely freedom, their ease as they idly drummed a steering wheel, double-parked in small, open convertibles, persuaded of their ability with wine, their stereophonics and terrific records. (*Tapes*; they would be tapes now.) In a leathercraft shop he was annoyed with himself because, unlike the slim owner in the jeans and turtleneck, he was not a homosexual. He watched the young man greet a woman just returned from Europe, looked on as, laughing and talking, the faggot embraced her. Why, he likes her, he thought, he really *likes* her. Yet she doesn't mean a thing to him. See how his eyes were open when he kissed her. Mine would have been shut tight and my cock would have been out to here. He hated himself because he was not artistic, light, healthy, easy. If such a girl kissed me I would ask her to marry me.

For more than a week he went to such sections of the city, hunting them like a ghost, restless, yet coveting tweed rather than flesh, wools and leathers more than body and form. Perhaps he yearned for an encounter, but in their bars and cocktail lounges he was silent. Nothing happened, he had no adventure, and after the first strong flush of sexuality he was as before— as he had been all his life—calmly admiring, sedately appreciative, his very hopelessness satisfying his lust by quenching it, by stripping him of illusions and granting him a sort of amnesty. All his life he had disposed of his sexuality this way. His tastes and greeds kept him single, fashion's narrow bigot.

In despair he turned back to the condominium, hopeful of a ride with Mrs. Riker to the High-Low, the Stop-'n-Shop, the I.G.A., washed up on the condominium as on some shabby strand of the average. Never letting on and nursing his grudge like a gent, but for all that some wild and even noble revolutionary instinct smoldering in him. It *wasn't* fair, it *wasn't* right. Why *couldn't* he have the things he wanted to have instead of the things—and those in probate—he had? Secretly he was niggered, chinkified, PR'd. If President Salmi knew his thoughts he'd find a way to break the will.

While the cupboard filled and he waited for his possessions from Missoula, he occupied his time by examining libraries— Northwestern's was not far—purchasing stocks of paper, ballpoint pens, pencils, a new dictionary, a thesaurus. He priced electric typewriters. He even began to work up some ideas for a new lecture—on condominiums—and though he actually wrote about a dozen pages (perhaps twenty or so minutes of platform time), he worked desultorily and with no conviction that he would ever finish it. Indeed, he was more conscious of himself than ever. He knew he was lonely and began to miss his father, fantasizing a dignified life for the two of them in the apartment together. Actually he knew more people here than in Missoula. What *had* his life been like there? The same, he decided, certainly the same, yet somehow he hadn't noticed. Maybe this was a good sign. Perhaps unhappiness wakes you up, a signal to the spirit like a chronic cough. All right, he was up.

He wondered how he'd managed to pass time since his heart attack. If he really was awake at last, then didn't that make him a sort of Rip Van Winkle? Had he slept twenty years? Who'd robbed him in the night, then, of the beard he'd earned in his long sleep? How did he recognize the cars? Why was he not astonished by the jets circling his head in their holding patterns above O'Hare? Why weren't the styles strange to him, the length of women's skirts and the cut of men's pants? How did he know the name of the President, and why didn't television frighten him? In aspects other than the impersonal he was a true amnesiac, the public life realer to him than his own. Here he was, a thirty-seven-year-old graduate student—how did he know his age? who'd been keeping track of it for him?—lacking only his thesis for his Ph.D. in . . . what? (He knew, but could not remember why he'd gone into the field. He had no interest in it. He was no scholar. The collapse of the job market had been the one fortunate aspect of his academic career. Why impose him as a teacher on students who probably had more interest in his subject than he had?) He was certain only that he had been no better off in Missoula than he was in Chicago. It was solely this which kept him from returning there at once.

Concomitantly he understood something which could yet prove to be valuable. He understood how unhappy he was—understood, that is, that it was no mood. He did not discount other people's unhappiness. There were those who lost limbs, whose health failed, who couldn't make it at today's prices, those whose loved ones died, who would never get what they wanted and who wanted it more for exactly that reason, those whose reputations were stripped away, those who had done great crimes and knew they'd slipped up, that even now the net was tightening. There were those whose expectations, so nearly realized, were disappointed by technicalities, those who were habituated to subtle poisons, those who were condemned. Even now, he supposed, there were children lost in the forest, and there were those whose plane was going down in the mountains and those whose bodies were being humiliated by sadists. People were drowning who had simply meant to go for a sail in the lake. There were cars overturning, burning, their drivers still alive but trapped by steering wheels and stove-in doors. He *didn't* discount other people's unhappiness. More power to them. All he knew was that he was as unhappy as any of them, as unhappy as anyone who had ever lived in the world. And this was a fact, as true of himself as his right-handedness.

Something else was true. For the first time in his life this man, this in-his-best-moments hypochondriac who feared illness and saw mortality in the headache and the common cold, who prized experience and blessed whatever of geography he had seen for its mystery and disparateness, who honored the accomplishments of others and waited in suspense for their new inventions and next books, who melted at all kindnesses to himself as involuntarily as he grew stiff-necked at slurs—this same fellow sat on his mourner's bench (even now taking a certain—yes—pleasure at the juxtaposition) and quite seriously, and for the first time in his life, considered suicide. At last a quick and even violent death was preferable to what he now understood he had always, if often unwittingly, endured. *He had been left out.* Jesus, it was the complaint of a kid in a schoolyard, a thing fat boys confessed to their pillows. Only that. Wallflowered by life. Left out. Not through conspiracy, as little through fault, luck of the draw in an unlucky world. Left out. Many are called but few are chosen. And some, like himself, weren't even called. Left out. How do you goddamnit like that?

In the books he'd read and films he'd seen the characters found a parade and joined it. They bought loud clothes and a bunch of balloons. And the triumph of pure trying was satisfying, even thrilling, as all existential assertions are thrilling, as all little motions are—the cripple's faltering step and the mute's first word, garbled, ripped from a torn cone of throat and lovelier than an aria. Energy admirable at long range, other people's wills and small defiances a beautiful metaphor. How he'd wept when men climbed the moon, the more impressive for its pointlessness. How impressed he'd been at apothecary measures of all strangers' bravery, little guys' puny resistances, Denmark's treatment of its Jews, his father's sideburns—all that judo of the spirit. But what did any of that come to? A life of stumble, of maimed conversation, effort a lousy substitute for results—and in the end just another compromise. Why *should* he settle; why *should* he make deals with his needs? Why *should* certain men live? There was nothing for it but to cut throats and slice wrists. To be or not to be, you schmuck. Why couldn't he do it, then? Fear? A little, but nah. Scruples? The notion that as a suicide he would end up with even less than all those compromised cripples and mitigated heroes with their qualified lives? No, no. Why then? Because by now he had lived too long with a sense of justice, with the conviction that if you pay and pay eventually they must give you something for your money, that otherwise they would be shut down. Christ, he thought, his blood still in his veins, his brains and liver and other organs where they were supposed to be, his internals stashed away in the drawers and cupboards of his belly like things in a well-ordered household, I am religious, I am a religious man. I believe in God.

About a month after coming to Chicago he received the shipment from Missoula. When the Railway Express man came to his door, Preminger, forgetting it was he who was responsible, was very excited. Packages, boxes and cartons addressed in an unfamiliar hand still had the power to give him hope. When he saw that they contained only his own things—his books and typewriter, his small, cheap assortment of dishes, cutlery and glasses, his everyday clothes (he'd brought with him all his grand stuff, dressing for his father's death as for a cruise)—he was disappointed and didn't even bother to unpack it all. What had he expected? Toys? Rich gifts from mysterious admirers? There wasn't even a letter to give him the gossip about the few people he knew in Montana, and he guessed that the sender, a graduate student who lived in the same rooming house and with whom he'd gotten drunk once or twice and gone to a few movies, must have been pretty pissed off for all the trouble he'd caused him. He had known it was an imposition and had made his request with a greater urgency than he'd felt, pleading his altered life, hinting that windfall kept him in Chicago, not so much to boast as to get his acquaintance off the dime. "Oh, and listen," he'd said on the telephone, "don't bother about the liquor." (A half-bottle of Scotch, a fifth of Beefeaters still in its cellophane truss.) And told the student to keep his Activities book. (A not inconsiderable gift—about a hundred dollars' worth of tickets for plays, concerts and football games.) But the booze and tickets had been sent as well, a sign from the West—that new life or no, he was a pain in the ass. He moved the stuff onto the bed in the second bedroom where, along with the deflated basketball and the odd game or photograph that had survived his father's compulsive redecorating, they already seemed further vestigial artifacts of a prior life.

It was a year that the summer had its teeth in the city, the weather like a tricky currency. One watched it like the stock market. Highs in the hundreds were not uncommon. The sky was white and cloudless. There was a drought. The leaves on the trees were a golden green and rattled like gourds in the softest wind. Preminger, who'd lived in the West, sometimes looked alertly behind him when he heard this sound in the street, as if expecting snakes in the trees. People moved outside on their balconies, not because it was cooler there but to be closer to the phenomenon. It was odd to see them suspended there, on the sides of the buildings, like balloonists in baskets or a hundred teams of window washers.

One day, the first since the occasion of his public drowning, when people were sunning themselves in the chaise longues and deck chairs, Preminger went down to the pool and discovered that it was being drained. The lifeguard explained that it was always closed after Labor Day. As he stood there, the phone rang; the lifeguard excused himself, listened for a few moments and nodded. When he hung up he clapped his hands for their attention.

"That was the office," he told them. "It seems that because of the heat a lot of the residents have been complaining about shutting down the pool. I've been instructed to fill her up again. They're going to close down the other two but will keep this one open until the weather breaks." Several people applauded. The lifeguard gestured that he had more to tell them. "Only," he said over their enthusiasm, "only there won't be an official Red Cross lifeguard after today, and the management says that, like always, swimming will be at your own risk, only more so. I'm supposed to fill the pool and turn my chemicals over to the Activities Committee who'll police the pool and provide its own lifeguards." A cheer went up, and Preminger, who'd never before been in on an eleventh-hour stay of execution, joined in.

A woman raised her hand.

"Yes, Mrs. Krozer?" the lifeguard said.

"This is the only pool that will be open?"

"That's right. This one will service all three buildings."

"Won't that make it awfully crowded? What about guests?"

"Sunday rules." On Sunday the pool was closed to guests.

Preminger raised his hand. Would they be able to swim that afternoon?

"It's going to take a few hours to fill it up," the lifeguard said. "Anyway, I think they mean for the committee to get squared away first. They said there's a special session of Activities going on right now."

When Preminger left his deck chair a couple of hours later he saw that a stack of a special mimeographed edition of *The House Organ* had been placed on one of the marble tables in the lobby. Taking one from the pile, he looked it over as he rode up in the elevator and saw that his name had been put down as one of the volunteer lifeguards.

His phone was ringing when he opened the door to his apartment.

"Hey, Montana, hot enough for you?"

"Who is this?"

"Wa'al, pardner, some folks roun' these parts call me Harris. It's the management his own self, stranger."

"I was going to call you."

"Ain't that sumfin? Ain't that a how-de-do?"

"I'm listed in the paper as a volunteer lifeguard."

"Thass right, deppity."

"Nobody asked me anything about it."

"Mister, this yere condominium needs a lifeguard."

"It'll have to get someone else."

"Rein up a sec, son. If you read that notice proper, you'd a seed that your name's only been put in nomination. You ain't been elected yet."

"Elected? You *elect* the lifeguards?"

"Shoot, boy, it's a *de*mocracy, ain't it? Ain't President Salmi told you?"

"This is ridiculous. No one had the right to nominate me."

"Looks to me like a clear draft choice. Will of the pee-pul."

"Will of the people."

"Well, not *all* the pee-pul. Salmi dragged his feet some when he saw your name on the list Activities come up with. He's still a mite uneasy about you since you made that speech to the Committee of Committees assembled."

Preminger recalled his queer emotion that evening and winced. "I was very vulnerable," he said. Then, "How did you know about that?"

"I read the minutes."

"The minutes? There were minutes?"

"It was a duly constituted meeting. Sure there were minutes, of course there were minutes. I take an interest. I always read them. I swan, it purely tickles me what these folks are capable of." Harris chuckled. "That last is off the record, friend."

"Sure."

"What's that you say? Cain't rightly hear you."

"It's off the record. I swan."

"Much obleeged."

"Why'd you call me?" Preminger asked.

"I told you. I take an interest."

"I purely tickle you, too."

"As the driven snow, buddy," Harris said.

Preminger got the name of the Activities chairman from the lists they had left with him and dialed the number. "Dr. Luskin?"

"The dentist is with a patient. This is Dr. Luskin's nurse, Judy. Did you want an appointment."

"No. This is Marshall Preminger."

"Marshall, how are you? It's Judy Luskin. Congratulations."

"What for?"

"I heard about your nomination for lifeguard. My sincere good wishes to you."

"Have we met?"

"Formally not, as it turns out. But I saw you at the pool. I knew you wasn't drownding." The fatso. "As a matter of fact it was me who told Howard what a good swimmer you are."

"Would you give Dr. Luskin a message for me? Would you please tell him that I don't want the nomination and that my name should be taken off the list?"

"Have you found a job, Marshall?"

"Just tell your husband, will you please, Nurse?"

Within the hour there was another call. It was Salmi and he was very angry. "You said, 'All that's at issue is which committee can make the most of me.' 'I want to do my share,' you said. It's in the minutes. Well, now we know which committee can make the most of you. Activities. And you balk. Is that how you do your share?"

"I wasn't even asked."

"You weren't even asked. Did you ever? He's standing on ceremonies, a born lifeguard and he stands on ceremonies. If you saw someone drowning would you wait to be asked before you jumped in?"

"That's not the point."

"Would you?"

"Of course not, but—"

"I told you. A born lifeguard. The instincts of a natural life-saver."

"You're crazy," Preminger said. He was unable to restrain himself. "Do you know my condition? Do you know that I've been contemplating suicide? That I ride buses to strange neighborhoods and eat my heart out when I see the way other people live? How do you expect me to—?"

"The buses stopped."

"What?"

"The buses stopped. Almost two weeks now and you ain't been on a bus. You get what you need in this neighborhood and you come home."

"Is that in the minutes?"

"It's a community, Preminger, we told you that. It made your eyes water when I described it. You had a hard-on from it. What do you think, in a community you're invisible?"

"Listen, I don't—"

"Preminger, I ain't got time for all this. It's a heat wave, a record-buster. Scorchers and corkers. Every day an old record falls and a new one is made. Air conditioning ain't to be trusted. There's a drain on the power. Brown-outs are coming. The weather people have seen nothing like it in their experience. My people need that swimming pool. They're getting up there. Swimming's their exercise. Dr. Paul Dudley White wants old people to go swimming, the Surgeon General does. But there's danger. It needs supervision. The regular lifeguards go back to college. They got to come out of the pool, their lips are blue. This is a job for a young man. You're thirty-seven. Who else is thirty-seven here? Most of us won't see *fifty*-seven again. 'All that's at issue is which committee can make the most of me,' you said. You thanked us. You wanted to put cheesecake in our mouths for coming to you. We left you our literature.

"Listen," Salmi went on softly, "you think this can last forever? It's a natural phenomenon. Such heat is an act of God. God gave us jungles for the heat that lasts forever, He gave us deserts for it. He didn't put it in Chicago. It'll break—it has to. I give it three weeks, four at the outside." He was speaking very softly now, almost conspiratorially. "On Halloween it'll be so cold you won't even be able to remember it, and you can go back to your—

back to your thoughts. What you were talking about. But I'll tell you something. You won't. You'll have different thoughts. Better thoughts."

"Forget that stuff about my thoughts," Preminger said. "Sure it's hot and we need the pool, but you don't understand something. I'm working on my thesis."

"You passed your prelims?"

"Yes, I—"

"Your orals? You've taken your orals?"

"Yes."

"Your thesis proposal has been approved and you've got someone to work with?"

"That's right."

"Are you writing? Have you done all your reading yet?"

"Most of it."

"Have you blocked out your first chapter?"

It was astonishing to him how well they knew the jargon. He would have thought they would have no notion of all the stages involved in earning a doctorate, but almost every one of them had a precise understanding of his graduate status. Their children had familiarized them with it, their married sons and daughters off in universities. Learning was old hat to them, the crises and obstacles as familiar as a fever chart. They'd broken the code. "Yes," he said wearily, "my first two chapters are written. I'm on my third."

"Then you're sitting pretty," Salmi said, "it sounds to me like you can work at home. You can do your footnotes later at a library. You can work up your bibliography afterwards."

"That's right."

"You've got to get out of that apartment. It was better when you rode the buses. As it is, you're around more than the vegetables. Get a clipboard and write at the pool. You got a clipboard?"

"No."

"We'll get you one. We'll get you a pith helmet and suntan lotion."

"I haven't been elected yet."

"A formality. Tomorrow morning you'll be up on the high chair with a whistle on your neck."

He agreed to stand for lifeguard.

One thing puzzled him: Harris had said Salmi was reluctant to have him. That afternoon when he went down to the office to sign some papers Fanon had left for him he ran into Harris and mentioned what was on his mind.

"Salmi," Harris said lightly, "Salmi's a figurehead. It's a puppet regime."

In fact he was elected, but not before the threat of a runoff between himself and Skippy Fisher, an old vaudevillian who was very popular with the residents. In the twenties Skippy had been a feature performer in *The Ziegfeld Follies*. It was said that he'd introduced "Melancholy Baby." When Preminger heard about the tie he refused to run against the old-timer and withdrew his candidacy. There wasn't anything Salmi could say to get him to change his mind. But Preminger reluctantly agreed when the President asked for a few hours to try to work out a deal.

Two hours later Salmi appeared, smiling. "Congratulations," he said, "all the precincts have been heard from. It's you."

"What about Skippy Fisher?"

"Skippy's pulled out. He's withdrawn his name from nomination."

"Why?"

"He pulled out. He sees it isn't for him."

"What happened? What did you do?"

Salmi smiled. "I said there'd be a whispering campaign. I told him I'd tell people that what he really introduced was 'She's Only a Bird in a Gilded Cage'—*real* golden oldies. I said I'd let everyone know he's incontinent, that he makes weewee in the swimming pool. That even if he managed to save you he'd pee all over you."

"Jesus," said Preminger. "The Making of the Lifeguard, 1971."

"Don't worry about it. They didn't really want him. He was the sentimental favorite. When you get to be our age, sonny, you can't always bring yourself to violate your feelings."

So Preminger, newly orphaned Montana scholar, the faint smell of smoke from the back room still lingering in his nostrils, through bald power plays released a college boy to return to active duty and at thirty-seven years of age and for the duration of a capricious heat spell, became the duly elected lifeguard pro tem of the Harris Towers Condominium on the North Side of Chicago. It was the first elected position he had ever held, his single incumbency and, he had to admit, his best prospect, the only game in town.

What was astonishing to him was how quickly and completely he assumed the badges of his office, how comfortable they made him feel and how powerful. He'd had hints of something like it before: several summers back, on his one trip to Europe, he'd left his hotel and been wandering the streets of Rome when, turning a corner, he'd come suddenly upon the Colosseum. He'd seen pictures of it, but always before he'd merely glossed its reality, the Colosseum as a possibility not actually registering; yet there it *really* was in the street, as anything might have been in the street; it wasn't—this struck him as odd—even guarded; he might have pulled off a piece of one of its shaggy stones and slipped it in his pocket and gone off with it, a piece of the actual, honest-to-God Colosseum in his pocket. Important things actually existed and they had the effect on you they were supposed to have, a Lourdes efficacy in nature and history that was astonishing; yet one rarely took the fabulous enough for granted. He discovered afresh how vulnerable, like all men, he was to play, to signs and the simple power of images, what tremendous realities adumbrated in a toy. Strap a holster about your waist and the body automatically adjusts, the center of gravity shifts, the pelvis boasts and you sway, lope, bowleggedness in the centers of the brain. Sing sea chanteys in a canoe and feel love's moods in parks.

There really was a whistle. There really was a high wooden platform chair with a beach umbrella blooming from it. There were sun lotions and mysterious silver pastes for the cheekbone beneath each eye, like the warpaint of Indians. There were quires of Turkish towels, neatly folded and giving off from their stacks a sort of glowing energy like that which came from place settings in restaurants before anyone has eaten. There were sunglasses for the King of the State Troopers. There was a first-aid kit. In it were bandages, adhesive, Atabrine tablets, salt tablets, smelling salts, Mercurochrome, iodine, salves seasoned with antibiotics. There was a syringe and, God help him, a hypodermic already fitted with a single ampoule of morphine. There was digitalis.

He sat on his high platform and surveyed the pool, his eyes sharp, his concentration immense. He might have been riding shotgun in a helicopter over the Pacific hunting astronauts, or in a small plane above the Alaskan tundra looking for survivors. Or he strode along the pool's concrete apron—his feet wet, slapping down smart footprints as he went along—or occasionally stooped, hunkered down, lowering his hand into the seemingly blue water to palm a handful and draw it toward his mouth, licking his tongue into it like a dog to taste the chlorine level. (Though they had an agreement. A janitor saw to the actual maintenance of the pool, while Preminger reserved the right to spray down its concrete deck with the hose.) His great pleasure made him guarded, suspicious of himself, wary lest he abuse the authority to which he had so quickly and luxuriously adapted. Not only religious, he thought, not only God-fearing, but at rock bottom an incipient Fascist as well! What a rogue! I must vow to use my power for good.

And he actually made some such vow, determining to play ball with the residents, to look the other way when they brought drinking glasses down to the pool, things to nosh—strictly forbidden—or when they went in without first using the footbath. On his own initiative he even suspended Sunday rules from time to time and told oldsters whose grandchildren had come to visit them that he would admit them to the pool. He was a stickler for water safety only—something which, with these old-timers, was not a problem anyway. Bridge and kalooky players, mahjongg enthusiasts (there was something curiously Oriental in the way they silently passed the tiles back and forth to each other, studiously picking over the ivory like children examining pieces of Lego) did not chase each other around the outside of the pool or push one another into the water. They did not leap two and three and four from the diving board or play Cannonball, jumping up and clasping their knees to their stomachs to pounce upon the heads of the other swimmers. In fact, they did not even go into the water much—once in the morning, perhaps, to wade in the shallow end and maybe again in the afternoon to tread water for a while and get their suits wet. A few of the more ambitious women and some of the men would occasionally dog-paddle or sidestroke a length or two of the pool, but except for these times when Preminger was all business it was pretty much a sinecure. With their cooperation, born of age and of that in them which was inflexibly sedentary, he managed to run a pretty tight swimming pool.

Only the grandchildren, infrequent visitors now that school had begun, gave him any trouble, and on these he unleashed all the authority he could muster, in fact all that with their grandparents he had kept stifled out of a deference not so much to their age as to his own character. With these children, however, awed as he was by his responsibility for their safety, he was ruthless, discovering in his shouted instructions and commands, and in the pitch of the whistle he blew at them, a barely controlled hysteria. "Out of the pool. Sit in that lounge chair for ten minutes!" "No running, no *running*. I've already warned you." "*Shallow end, shallow end!*" The mothers and grandparents beamed at the disciplinary figure he projected, a manifestation at last of something they had threatened the children with for years, the man who would do things to them if they did not behave in restaurants or went too close to the cages in zoos. Yet when he saw what the score was, how he was being used as a bogyman, he rebelled by determining to settle an old score: the ancient saw about how long one must wait before going into the water after eating. His mother's generation held that at least an hour had to pass before one could safely swim without cramping. Nothing had changed. Forgetting that it was they who had installed him in the first place and that his expertise, like his helmet and lotions, came from the office itself, they turned to him as their lifeguard, to arbitrate when the children's nagging became too much for them. The boldest thing he did during his tenure was to assert, once and for all, *ex cathedra*, that there was nothing in it, that the incidence of cramp during digestion was no greater than afterwards, that time wasn't in it at all, that being wet wasn't. To his astonishment they abandoned at once a position they had held all their lives.

But at last even the presence of the children grew familiar, and he became indifferent to all but the most flagrant violations of safety, indifferent to everything save his own still surviving image of himself as their lifeguard. Though it was just here that he hedged. Harris had had Fanon draw up a disclaimer of responsibility for the safety of the residents during this special session of the pool. This each resident had been made to read and sign before being permitted to enter the pool area. Seeing in the document a loophole which might have left him holding the bag should anything happen, as if responsibility traveled a circuit and had if it were not at one point along the line to be at another, Preminger wrote in above Harris's a disclaimer of his own: "And while Marshall Preminger, acting lifeguard, will do everything in his power to maintain order in the pool and save the life of anyone who through carelessness or accident finds him- or herself in difficulty, it is nevertheless understood that the said Marshall Preminger is not *legally* responsible for the safety of the swimmers." (And did they see, he wondered, what a guy he was, how his lifeguard's italics saved him, how while exempting himself from legal responsibility—just good common sense, just good business practice, just wise stewardship— he did nothing to repudiate the more important guilts?)

But no one drowned. It never came up. Only once did he find it necessary to leave his platform to help someone. Lena Jacobson, standing in perhaps four feet of water, had suddenly begun to dance and moan. "I'm cramping," she cried. "I'm cramping." She looked toward the platform.

"Are you in trouble?" Preminger called.

"It's nothing to write home about," she said, "but I've got this terrific cramp in my right leg. It pinches. If you'd be so kind?"

"Hold on," Preminger said, "I'll get you." He climbed down from the platform and entered the pool at the shallow end, wading heavily toward the center rope near which Mrs. Jacobson stood. "Take the rope," he said. "Hold on to that."

"You know I didn't even see it," she said, "in the excitement I didn't even see it."

Meanwhile he continued to wade toward her, the resistance of the water forcing him into a sort of odd swagger.

"Just in time," she said when he had come up to her. "That was a narrow squeak." He took her arm and they strolled toward the steps. It was exactly as if he were taking her in to dinner. Meanwhile she chatted amiably to him. "I've been walking in swimming pools all my life and nothing like this ever happened before. I can't get over it. One minute I'm having a good time and the next I'm not. It's just like, you know, life."

"I'm glad you didn't panic."

"No. I kept my head. I got a cool head on my shoulders."

"How's the cramp now?" He helped her up the steps.

"I can't even feel it. It's like it fell out of my foot. There's just a little tingle like pins and needles."

"That can be worked out with massage," Preminger said.

"Would you do that?" she asked. "If you don't want to touch my varicose veins I could put on my slacks."

"Don't be silly." Preminger moved her to a chaise longue where he had her stretch out her legs. He pulled a chair up beside her and began to knead the right calf. Two or three people had gathered to watch. "Step back, please," Preminger said, "give this woman some air, will you? Show's over, folks." They didn't budge, and he returned to Mrs. Jacobson's right leg, extemporizing massaging leverages as he went along. First he pulled two fingers down the back of her calf, then pinched in a lateral line, then jabbed in a vertical. He plucked at her varicose veins.

"If it hadn't been for this one here," Mrs. Jacobson told the bystanders, "I might not be alive to tell the tale. It was like crabs got me. It was terrible. All I wanted was to sit down in the water. I tell you, my entire life passed before my eyes. Oh yeah. There. That got it good. That's right. I saw my childhood home in Poland. I relived my courtship and how we came to America and the place where we lived in Philadelphia. I saw the look on the mover's face who broke my mama's furniture when we came to Chicago, he should be moved himself in a truck a thousand miles. I saw our wedding."

"You married the mover, Lena?" a woman asked.

"I married Jack. I saw our wedding."

"Hey, Lena," a man said, "did you see your wedding night?"

"Shh. He's only a boy," she said, indicating Preminger, bent over her right leg. She laughed and touched Preminger's shoulder. "He wants to know did I see my wedding night."

"What else did you see?"

"I saw my mother's recipe for *lokshin kugel*. I saw the good times and I saw the bad."

"It's better than a picture book."

She maneuvered her left leg into Preminger's hands. "She says it's better than a picture book. I saw all the good kalooky hands I ever got and Paulie grow up and move to California." She swung her legs over the side of the chaise longue and sat up. "Listen, this is some lifeguard we elected. Darling—I can call you that because I'm an old woman and you're a young pipsqueak—I'm telephoning Jack what you did, and if he don't say whenever you're downtown you can park for free in the garage I don't know my old man."

"Lena, you tell Jack what he did, he may come and do the boy an injury."

"You hush. She says Jack will do you an injury."

In fact he was invited to dinner. What he found surprising was how much he looked forward to it, and how disappointed he was when it was postponed. Jack Jacobson called him from the office. "Listen," he said, "we talked it over. We invited you to come over for supper. What does it mean for a snappy young man to eat supper with a couple of old fogies? You'd be bored stiff. Give us a few more days on this. We'll get some people together. My daughter Sylvia flies back from Cincinnati the middle of the week. She should be there. Let's make it Friday night. That way no one has to go in on Saturday. You got something planned Friday night?"

"No," Preminger said, "not Friday."

"Then we're in like Flynn. Friday it is. I called you first because it's in your honor," Jacobson said. "Leave everything to me. I got some people I especially want you to meet."

Friday he closed the pool early and went upstairs to prepare for the dinner party. He showered carefully. Two weeks in the outdoors had given him an excellent tan. The swimming had done him good. A lot of his pot had disappeared and he could see his major ribs. Dressing scrupulously in a blue summer suit he'd had cleaned for the occasion, he carefully removed the lollipop headed pins from a crisp new shirt and placed them in a glass ashtray. He was amused by the cunning ways new shirts were folded, he was very cheerful.

But the party was a letdown. Sylvia, a pretty woman about his own age whom Preminger assumed to be divorced, had a date that evening and had to be downtown by eight-thirty. Preminger resented that no one had thought to fix him up. He'd assumed that people like these, family people, were always on the lookout for eligibility like his own. Yet no one had approached him with the names of likely girls or pressed for his attendance at their tables. Willing to serve as the bait in their legendary machinations, this was the first time he had been to any of their homes. The other guests were all from the condominium, and he couldn't imagine who it was Jacobson had wanted him to meet.

"How about you, Preminger?" Jacobson asked, "you good for another bourbon and ginger ale?"

"Is there club soda?"

"*Club* soda. Ho ho. We got a real *shikker* in this one. He drinks like a goy. Lena, we got any seltzer for Buster Crabbe?" Buster Crabbe was only one of the names of swimmers he was to go by that evening. Johnny Weissmuller was another. And once Esther Williams.

"Ask him if he'll take Seven-Up."

"Water, I think."

"Water he thinks," Jacobson said.

"A busman's holiday," Lena said.

Jacobson brought his drink. "Want a piece of candy? Make it less sour?"

The décor in the Jacobson's apartment was nothing like that in his father's. They had moved from a large apartment on the South Side and brought all their things with them. Seven rooms of furniture crammed into five. Preminger was certain the heavy pieces were absorbing all the air conditioning in the hot apartment. In a while Jacobson, sweating, told Lena to open a window.

"Won't that work against the air conditioning?"

"It ain't on," Lena said. "Air conditioning gives Jack a cold."

Preminger hated people who got colds from air conditioning.

"Only place I don't catch cold from air conditioning is in Chinese restaurants in California," Jacobson said.

"I see."

"Don't ask me why."

The conversation was pretty much what he heard at the pool, from the women names he was not familiar with, and from the men dark, illiberal talk of stores broken into and advancing hordes of blacks. He was astonished to learn that many of the men carried guns. Jacobson showed him one he wore inside his jacket. Someone else moved his hair with his fingers and showed him a scar. He kept silent, but even without his saying anything they seemed to know his position and sought constantly to provoke him.

"You're a college man," one said. "I suppose the talk up in the ivory tower is that the *shvartzers* are abused, that we been robbing them blind for years, that we're slumlords and get them to sign paper they don't understand. Am I right?"

"They try to see both sides," Preminger said mildly.

"Both sides. Hah. You hear that? Both sides. I work with these people. I worked with them all my life. Yeah, yeah, and in the old days I lived next-door to them. They're shiftless. On one side they're shiftless and on the other side they're worthless. There's your both sides."

"What's the matter," someone else said angrily, "the Jews weren't oppressed for years? They were oppressed plenty, believe me. But they didn't go crying to the NAACP."

"They went crying to the B'nai B'rith," Preminger said.

"You compare the B'nai B'rith to the NAACP? The Jews are the best friends the Negro ever had."

"We vote Democratic. We got a name for ourselves all over the world as nigger-lovers."

"Just more anti-Semitism," someone said sadly.

"I'm not going to change your minds," Preminger said. "Why don't we just stop talking about it?"

"That's the ticket," Lena Jacobson said. "He's young, he's an idealist. Leave him to heaven."

During dinner they wanted his opinions on Vietnam, on welfare and minimum hourly wage laws. What concerned them most, however, was the campus situation—SDS, the Weathermen. Why were they so angry? They saw him, he realized at last, as a representative of the younger generation. He was there to be baited.

"For God's sake," he cried, "look at my hair. Is it longer than yours? Am I wearing bellbottoms? Is anything tie-dyed? I swear to you, I washed my hands before I came to the table."

"Drugs. What about drugs?"

"I take ten milligrams of Coumadin."

"You hear? He admits it."

"It's a blood-thinner. I had a heart attack."

"Do you smoke Mary Jane? Have you ever smoked horse?"

"You don't smoke horse. You inject it."

"You know an awful lot about it."

"Oh, for Christ's sake."

"Do you drop acid?"

"I'm thirty-seven years old."

"This boy saved my life," Lena pleaded.

"It's true," Jack said. "No more."

They ate the rest of the meal in silence.

Afterwards they went back into the living room. Marshall poured himself a very large bourbon. Two of the women went into the kitchen to help Lena with the dishes. A third walked around the apartment and studied the photographs—there might have been a hundred of them—on the Jacobsons' walls. "Lena, this one of Laurie, it's very nice. I never saw it."

"The one with Milton's grandson?" Lena called.

"The blond?"

"Sherman. Milton's grandson."

"Who's Milton?" a man asked.

"Wait, I can't hear you, the disposal's on."

"I said, *who's Milton?*"

"Milton," Lena called from the kitchen, "Sherman's grampa. Paul's partner's father-in-law." She came into the living room, drying her hands on a dish towel. "A brilliant man. And what a gentleman! You remember, Jack, when we were to California and he had us to supper in his home? Brilliant. A brilliant man."

"What's so brilliant about him?" Preminger asked.

"He's eighty-four years old if he's a day."

"But what's so brilliant about him?"

"He's brilliant. A genius."

"How?" asked Preminger.

"How? How what?"

"How is he brilliant? How's he a genius?"

"That's right. He's very brilliant."

"How?"

"He's eighty-four years old if he's a day."

"That doesn't make him brilliant," Preminger said.

"I didn't say that made him brilliant."

"I saved your life," Preminger told her, "I think that entitles me to an explanation of how Milton, Sherman's grampa, Paul's partner's father-in-law, is a genius."

"Hey, you," Jack Jacobson said.

"No, Jack, he's right. You want to know why he's brilliant? I'll tell you why he's brilliant. He's brilliant because he's got brains."

"What sort of brains? What does he think about?"

"He's retired. He's eighty-four years old. He's retired."

"I see. He's retired," Preminger said, "does that mean he isn't brilliant anymore?"

"He's just as brilliant as he ever was."

"How?"

"He's got a house."

"He's got a house? That makes him brilliant? That he's got a house?"

"He's got fifteen rooms."

"So?"

"It's on a hill. In the Hollywood Hills. On a steep hill. On the top of a steep hill in the Hollywood Hills. They call it a hill. It's a mountain."

"Then why do they call it a hill?"

"With a private road that winds up the mountain. And when you get to the top there's his house. With a patio. Beautiful. With a beautiful patio."

"How is he brilliant?"

"I'm telling you. In the patio there are marble slabs. Slabs of marble. Like from the most beautiful statues. And the truck that brought them to set them in the patio broke down on the hill. On the mountain. And the old gentleman was so impatient he couldn't wait. The driver went back down the hill to get help, but Milton couldn't wait. Eighty-four years old and he picked up the slab from the back of the truck and put it on his shoulder and carried it by himself up the mountain. It weighed ninety pounds."

"Oh," Preminger said, "you mean he's strong. You don't mean he's brilliant. You mean he's strong."

"I mean he's brilliant."

"*How? How is he brilliant?*"

"When his wife saw what he was doing she nearly died. 'Milton,' she yelled, 'you must be crazy. Carrying such weight up a mountain. Wait till the truck is fixed.' But he wouldn't listen and went down for another slab. And for another and another. He must have carried eight slabs up the hill. A thousand pounds."

"That makes him brilliant? An eighty-four-year-old man carrying that kind of weight up a mountain because he wasn't patient enough to wait for the truck to be repaired?"

"Ah," Lena said, "it was an *open* truck. He thought people

would steal the marble before the driver came back. He worked five hours, six."

"What makes him brilliant? How's he a genius?"

"Wise guy," Lena screamed, "when the driver finally got back with the part for the truck Milton couldn't straighten up. His neck was turned around from where the weight of the slabs of marble had rested on it and he couldn't move it. He was like a cripple. He couldn't straighten up. He couldn't turn his head. They had to put him to bed!"

"*What makes him brilliant?*" Preminger was shouting.

"What makes him *brilliant?* I'll *tell* you what makes him brilliant. He was in bed five months. Paralyzed. The best doctors came to him. They couldn't do a thing. It strained him so much what he'd done he couldn't even talk it hurt his neck so. He had a television brought into his bedroom. He watched it all day. Everything he watched. If his family came to him he waved them away. He watched the television all day and late into the night. And his favorite program was Johnny Carson. He stayed up for that. And one night Johnny had on a—what do you call it—a therapist, and the therapist was talking about how arthritics could be helped by exercise and she had this gadget it was like a steel tree. It was set up on the stage and there were bars and like rings hanging from it, and the therapist showed how a person could straighten out a crooked limb or a bad joint by hanging from a ring here and a bar there and stretching like a monkey."

"So?"

"So? So he ordered one and had it set up in his living room. Jack, you remember, you saw it. In the middle of his living room like it was a piece of furniture, and every day he'd practice a little. Then a little more. He'd pull this way and he'd pull that way. And even though it hurt him this brilliant man didn't give up. He practiced pulling and hanging—eighty-four years old—and finally it began to work. And Milton can turn his head today. He can nod and shake it as good as a person half his age. He can even straighten up a little. So now you know. *Wise guy!* Now you know why he's such a brilliant genius. There, *are you satisfied?*"

. . .

The dinner party changed nothing. He still reported for duty at the pool every morning, and though he rarely climbed the high platform any more, he was able to survey the pool from where he sat beside them gossiping.

Harris went in for a dip one day. He swam five or six strong laps and took a large bath towel from Preminger's stack.

"Mr. Harris," Preminger said.

"That felt good. You got it made here, you know that? This is the life."

"Can I ask you something?"

"Gee, I've got to get back to the office. Talk to me in the shower."

In the men's shower room Harris turned on the cold tap and stood under it.

"What I wanted to know," Preminger said, "was why you wanted me as lifeguard? Salmi was against me, you said, yet he practically rammed the job down my throat."

"Ain't you having a good time? You want to quit? You're looking better every day. Terrific tan. I put a tan like that at a thousand bucks, *low* season. Some muscle coming out in the shoulders, too. You were sick, this sort of exercise must be opening up your arteries like the Lincoln Tunnel. What's the matter, can't you stand prosperity?"

"No, no, I enjoy it. Until I get going on my thesis again when the weather breaks. It's good for me. I just want to know why you picked me."

"Why you winklepicker, ain't you figured that one out? Who else *was* there? Peckerhead, seventy-two percent of these guys still go to business. It's in the minutes. What have *you* got to do? Who else *was* there? How'd it look if I left a vegetable in charge of my pool? If something happened you think that 'Swimming at Your Own Risk' shit would be worth boo? You at least *look* like a man. Dunderbone! What's wrong with your *kopf*, my dear young *putz*?"

He wants me out, Preminger thought. He wants my apartment for a few cents on the dollar and that's why he speaks to me like this. I'll smile. I'll thank him for his information. I'll be polite. He wants to get my goat. He wants to get my goat for a few cents on the dollar.

There was a personal letter for him, the first he'd had since coming to the condominium. As there was no return address, the envelope told him little more than that it had been mailed from Chicago. He waited until he got upstairs to open it.

It was from Evelyn Riker.

Dear Marshall (I knew your father so well. We were such friends. I can hardly call his son *Mr.* Preminger),

Perhaps you're wondering why I've been so remiss in not writing sooner. Since that day of your father's funeral I've hardly seen you. At the pool, of course, the few times I've been there (I've been reluctant to be seen at the pool for reasons you will be quick to understand without my going into them here), you've seemed so busy that I hesitated to interfere with your duties, or to do more than nod pleasantly, as acquaintances will. I had nevertheless determined to speak to you at the earliest occasion, but each time something has held me back. My bourgeois modesty, you will say, or, less kindly, my petty bourgeois regard for even the faintest blush of scandal. It may be, as anyone who takes the trouble to keep up must know, a permissive society, but not at Harris Towers. For all its underground garages and Olympic size pools and master antennae, Harris Towers has not yet entered the twentieth century. But I digress. I had started to say that I had determined to speak with you at the earliest opportunity, first to clear up any misunderstandings that may have developed between us, and secondly to go on from there to form a firmer relationship based on mutual trust, common interest and, I confess it, the fact that I feel a wide gulf between myself and many of the people here.

After my husband left me—you did not know that we are separated, and thought that perhaps I was a widow, or even that I went behind my husband's back, that otherwise I could not possibly have "taken up," to the *limited* extent that I did "take up" with your father, but there, I think, you underrate your father, or underrate me—I found Dad's sympathy and understanding immensely important, whatever that sympathy and understanding may on his part have been inspired by. (I do not impute his motives. If Harris Towers is suspicious, I at least am not. Let that much be said for me.) There *are* no dirty old men, only lonely and frightened ones. As there are lonely women. (And lonely sons?) But I had not meant to impose my thoughts on you so abruptly and formidably. My pen, I fear, carries me away.

I had meant to talk to you. But your position, as lifeguard, intimidated me. What *would* it have looked like? A woman. A young lifeguard? I'd have been better off, if that was in my mind, at the Oak Street Beach, though I would, let's face it, have had stiffer competition at the Oak Street Beach than at Harris Towers. All the *more* reason to avoid you here. For these arguments would have been the first ones made by my—our—good neighbors. That's why I think it a good thing that this Indian Summer of ours must soon end. (Despite the fact that I personally enjoy hot weather and always have. I am one of those who would rather burn than freeze.) You will be able to return to your studies, and I will be able to be your friend on a more ladylike scale— befitting our ages. (I know I'm older, forty-four to your thirty-seven, but there is, when you come right down to it, a less telling difference in our ages—yours and mine—than there was in mine and Dad's.) So I am glad, as I say, that the season must end, that even now cold air is moving down from Canada, that there's snow in the Rockies, that passes in the western mountains are already closed. It will be our turn soon—I mean Chicago's—and when this heat is broken, then perhaps . . .

Though that's selfish. When I think of the many old people here and realize that for some of them it may be the last warmth they will ever know—save for fevers, save for deceptive flushes—I must, in all frankness, pull in my own desires somewhat, abate my wishes. Yet one cannot live with such premises, can one? One must neither gloat over one's food nor pretend an abstract sorrow that it is not in someone else's mouth. I have never forced dinners down my child's mouth by telling her that the starving children of Europe would be grateful to have such food. In that respect, at least, I am no "Jewish Mother." Which, incidentally, brings me around to a question I have been meaning to ask you since we first met. Have you read *Portnoy's Complaint* by Philip Roth? If not, it is highly readable and I strongly recommend it to you. The chances are, however, that you have already read it. My feeling is that while it is very funny, Sophie really rather spoils the book. I do not deny for a moment that such persons exist, though in all probability they exist in no greater numbers than stingy Scotchmen or stupid Polacks. Yet even if they existed *en masse* their thinking is *so* superficial that surely no work in which they play so central a role can be really important. Characters should be profound. At least that's my feeling. I don't recall seeing this point made in any of the reviews I read, though perhaps in the more learned journals some critics have already said the same thing. If you know of such viewpoints I wish you would let me know about them as it is always a pleasure to see one's own ideas confirmed and expressed more articulately than one can quite manage oneself. Still, I may be all wet about this. A film I enjoyed and can heartily recommend is Mike Nichols' Jules Feiffer's "Carnal Knowledge." There the characters are all Portnoys —though without their Sophies—who seem hung up in the same way that Alexander was, yet I laughed and laughed it rang so true. Men are sometimes *such* babies. (How odd it is that "Babe" should be exactly the term used by certain kinds of men when referring to their women!) I was in any event very pleased to see such a strong film from Nichols after his disappointing "Catch-22."

Do let me know what you think of some of my opinions as I am anxious to have your views on these matters.

Very truly yours,

Evelyn

P.S. I have been looking high and low for the key to Dad's —your—apartment. So far I have not had much luck, but something has just occurred to me about where I may have left it, and I am pretty certain I will soon be able to lay my hands on it.

She has it, Preminger thought; *she has the key*. She's only waiting to see how I respond to her letter. He would have called her up at once or gone down the hall and knocked on her door, but slow and easy does it, he cautioned himself. He didn't want to frighten her. He'd play it her way. He would say that he quite understood, that he had guessed her feelings and for just such reasons as she had elucidated in her letter he had held back and not made any overtures to her at the swimming pool, that he had the same reservations she had about *Portnoy's Complaint* by Philip Roth and that while he too had enjoyed "Carnal Knowledge," she made a mistake if she thought that all men were like that. Some were capable of quite mature relationships. He liked to think that he was one. If she did happen to find the key she must be in no hurry to get it back to him. There was no reason for her to try to send it through the mails. She could, if she liked, bring it over at her convenience. She knew his hours at the pool. Otherwise he was always in, rarely out. He had *not* known her husband had left her. That was a shock. He couldn't understand a man who could be that thoughtless with a woman as obviously thoughtful and superior as herself.

He wrote all this out very carefully, making several drafts before he was satisfied, then went to the phone and dictated it to Western Union.

In the summer's last days the heat lost its nerve and the temperature, like a failed expedition, began a hasty retreat down the slopes, but the South Tower pool was more crowded than ever, thick with people who had not been in it all summer and who now, in the last week it would be open, found themselves rummaging its waters and equipment, the Styrofoam kickboards, striped polo balls and outlandish toys. Last-flingers—some of them actually on vacation—who out of some deep sentimental instinct, like people who crowd aboard a train they have never ridden but which is about to be taken out of service, they squeezed their feet into rubber flippers, scurried to do one last memorable milestone lap, one final dive, kissed the snorkel, cruised on ribbed, rubber air mattresses. Yet despite this element of the frantic, their overall mood was mellow with reconciliation and detail.

Beside them at poolside, his distinguishing characteristics as their lifeguard worn thin (as on ocean voyages the initial mysteries of ship and crew diminish with custom and ultimately accommodate themselves to that democracy of voyagers, passenger and sailor both drawing near land, and it suddenly occurs to you that the deck steward also has an address and the captain hand luggage), easy now because here it is autumn and no one has drowned or been seriously in trouble (so he'd saved them after all, standing by like a peacetime army), his pith helmet and whistle nothing more now than bits of eccentric jewelry, Preminger melded into their midst, listening, hearing them, never so comfortable (unless it was driving in that limousine to his father's funeral), nothing on his mind save their voices, monitoring their babble like a ham of the domestic, listening so hard that he was able to pick out individual conversations.

He heard how each had got his condominium, from the initial examination of the site through the decision to join and the payment of the deposit to the moving in, stations of the legend, infinitely the same, infinitely different and, for him, as compelling as an account of lost virginity. He was moved to offer his own variation. "I'm in probate," he said with his eyes closed.

"Taylor was in probate," someone said.

"It was different," said another. "Irene died almost a year before Rose moved in, right after she put down the deposit. Irene never lived here."

"Probate's a technicality. It's as good as yours."

"Possession is nine-tenths of the law."

They spoke of individual courtesies shown them by Harris, of cocktail parties given for them when all that had existed of Harris Towers was the architect's model, of a dance at the Standard Club five years earlier, some of the women in gowns they had bought for the occasion, their husbands in black tie for the only time in their lives save for getting married or for their children's weddings. "It was beautiful. Freda, wasn't it beautiful?"

"Harris had the mayor's caterer for the evening."

Those were the days, they said, when the condominium was just a dream. And Harris the dreamer. A young Aeneas in the myth. Themselves cast as skeptics, historical obstacle, stunned only retroactively by the cutting edge of his bold imagination, like self-confessed victims in anecdote, all admiration now for the force of his enterprise, his vision which had seen the three buildings already standing when all that had existed was an abandoned warehouse surrounded by vacant lot and prairie. They told of his struggles with the bankers and recounted his wheedling, piecemeal favor by piecemeal favor, his concessions from politicos and zoning big shots and, once, how he'd gotten an actual law through the Chicago City Council, the future condominium's very own legal and bona fide ordinance, signed by Mayor Daley himself. The legend of how Harris had built the condominium, Preminger saw, was only a universalizing of their individual stories about how they'd come to be a part of it. Yet why couldn't they speak of *him* that way? And why had they written off his probate, dismissed it as natural order, ordinary sequence? A life had been lost, death was in it. (And at such moments why did he loathe his swim trunks and wish to put by his whistle and scatter his lotions?) And they spoke of how Harris had recruited his prospects, many of the future residents of the place, a laborious, close-order piece of patient scholarship, choosing and rejecting like some Noah of real estate, a brave man hand-picking his crew, sieving the South Side, as if what he proposed were an expeditionary force or a crusade or a mission in history. (Ah, Preminger saw, because he'd inherited it, because it had fallen in his lap.)

"In nineteen fifty-five he saw that the South Side was going," said a woman with white hair, "that the colored were making a mockery of the neighborhoods. He understood what was happening to my husband's business before my husband did."

"What, are you kidding? During the *war* he saw it coming, as far back as that."

"He told me that at the I.C. station at sixty-third and Engelwood he saw a family of hillbillies get off the train, *shkutzim*, low-class whites from the cottonfields, and he knew what was going to happen. This was in nineteen forty-seven."

"This was before he had money. This was before the banks would even look at him."

"Now they ask *him*."

How comfortable Preminger is nevertheless, how close to sleep. If someone were to call for help now he could not move, his lassitude locking him up in warm baths of the intimate. He lies back on the chaise longue and watches them, sees their heavy busts in profile, the huge passive breasts of other listeners rising and falling, the deep unconscious percussion of their breath. The fat thighs of the speaker, the muddle of hair at her crotch, her legs wide, stately, an abandon that is at once rigid and relaxed like the lines of upholstered furniture. He hopes the heat will last forever. He hopes his bladder will never fill. He wishes never to move, simply to be there always, their talk climbing the white, hairless insides of his arms like flies. Blood moves in his penis as he listens. His clipboard and his scant notes lay abandoned across his knees. He nudges it aside and it falls to the concrete, a heavy weight gone. He loves their voices cracked by age and child bearing, by lullabies and screaming their children out of streets and the paths of cars.

"Julie never wanted to come here. Julie wanted Florida. He wanted the excitement of the dog track and the jai alai. You know what I got against Florida? I got nothing against Florida. It's the way they dress. The loud shirts and Bermudas and the cockamamy sailfish on the men's caps. And the slacks on the women. People our age look foolish dressed like that. You'd think they'd have better sense."

"The kids don't come to Florida."

"They come. Christmas they come. They come and they leave the children with you, and then off they go, off like a shot to the Doral and the Fontainebleau, and you're the baby sitter. You see them at three in the morning when the night clubs close."

"All my friends are in Chicago. I'd be a stranger in Florida."

Individual hairs of his head stand stirred by their collective breath. He has never been this relaxed, even in barbershops under warm towels. He knows now how much he wants to lie in rooms where others are talking, to graze in orbit round their monologues. If they noticed him something would be lost, his euphoria bruised by their attention. He's held by these matrons, by their legends of founding, the condominium an Athens, feeding him the only history he has ever cared for. Condominium. He thinks the word. It hums. Mmn. Mmn. Mom is in it. Om is.

It's Saturday. It's Sunday. (Has he eaten? Has he been upstairs at all?) Those who are not widows have been joined by their husbands. (And how pale these are compared to the women, how marked for probate.) He listens, listens. He loves their voices too, the hoarse voices of the men, this one a printer forty years, his lungs damp, mildewed with ink, scratched and scorched by metal filings, enough case in them by now to set a short sentence, loves the guttural bark of the wholesaler in fruits and vegetables, the rumble of the one who has spent his life in underground parking garages, the screech of the man who has supervised kitchens in hotels. The men's voices fertilize the women's. Their sounds fuck. The lifeguard merged with the group beside the pool, neither raised above them on the platform nor cruising beneath them in the water doing the lifesaver's imposing laps, leading his body through a narrow wake like the long welts of allergy, incognito in boxer trunks, in his tanned son-in-law's body, his arm along one of the heavy metal tables cut to hold a pole that blooms a sunshade. His ass in a cat's cradle of plastic sling, the tightly wound strips like huge lanyards from summer camp engraving his calves. Many such impressions here—the backs of men's legs, women's backs and arms taking the mold, their skins a sort of stationery, raised letter invitations—Preminger wanly concupiscent at these stains of flesh and contact, the pink stripes of blood like foot and fingerprint, like the red hemi-oval bite of a toilet seat or elastic's pucker on the skin. Shoe-less as a *shivah* and sockless too, his naked heels crossed on the hot concrete.

He sees the others. (Sunday rules: the people here all from the single tribe.) The men shirtless, in bathing trunks. Some in a pelt of body stubble the shape of a man's undershirt, others smoother than women and with incipient, undifferentiated breasts like the uncloven tits of eleven-year-old girls. He sees the lightning strokes of old operations, the zippers and fossils of healed scars. He sees long testicles winking dully in great nests of jockstrap and the multiple vaccinations on the arms of the women, like the seals and stamps of official documents. Much care has gone into selecting their bathing suits. There are no bikinis, no ban-danna prints. The women's suits are one piece, black or the oxy-dized red of deep rust, only a little white piping running around the suits like a national border. Their feet are squeezed into pumps, the broad heels a sort of clear, frozen aspic with flecks of gold and silver foil floating in them like stars. They do not actually sit together. They sit in small groups, constellations of between three and seven, but arranged as they are, it is as if they are one group, people ringing a campfire, perhaps.

Preminger's ears are grown enormous, like deep-dish radio tele-scopes. He hears everything as he sits, neutrally naked as the rest. Their voices flow into his brain like bathwater filling a tub.

"I'm telling you, Dave, you think this is an operation? It's home sweet home and I ain't knocking it, but I got a kid brother in California who lives in a condominium that would put your eyes out. Half the apartments out there have their own swimming pools."

"I'm happy with this one."

"Of course. I'm just giving you a comparison."

"I don't want the responsibility of a pool."

"I'm not selling you one. I'm just trying to give you an idea of the scope."

"I read there's one going up in New York City—Onassis has one—that's being built with two sets of corridors."

"Two? What for? What's that supposed to mean?"

"Two sets of corridors. One for the residents, one for the servants and delivery people."

"Jesus. Wouldn't you hear them? I mean they'd be moving around like mice in the wall. You'd hear them."

"They'd be trained. They'd take their shoes off. You might hear John-John. He'd be running up and down the second corridor with his friends all day. You'd only hear John-John."

"Two sets of corridors. That'd mean two sets of elevators too. Christ, the maintenance on a place like that'd have to be twenty-five hundred a month."

"Grace, tell me, you still looking for a girl?"

"Bernadine's going to give me Fridays."

"I thought she goes to Dorothy on Fridays."

"We worked it out. Howard's divorce came through. The judge gave him visitation on weekends. He brings the kids over and leaves them with Dorothy so she needs someone to straighten up on Monday. Bernadine goes to Olive on Mondays and Flo doesn't need Helen now that Frank isn't working so she comes to Dorothy on Mondays and I said I'd take Bernadine on Fridays."

"Ex-cons I use, retards, wounded vets, all the handicapped."

"Me too. That's what the schmucks who work for me are like."

"No, I mean it. It's good business. They live by the skin of their teeth, those fellas. You never have no labor trouble from them. They don't ask for raises or fringe benefits. The big fringe benefit is that they're working at all."

"You feel that sun? It's like a vacation. I tell you it eats my heart out. This is the life. This is the life and I'm going to be sixty-four years old."

"You're as old as you feel."

"You know something?"

"What's that?"

"If I was ten years younger I'd be *fifty*-four. If I was thirteen years younger I'd still be over fifty."

"Sunrise, sunset."

"Yeah. I think I'll go in the water. How's the water?"

"Terrific."

"Cold?"

"Not once you get used to it. The air is colder than the water."

"I'm going in. I got to take a leak."

"You got Blissner's place when he lost his job."

"That's right."

"May I ask a personal question?"

"What I had to give for it?"

"If you don't mind."

"Thirty-two hundred fifty above cost."

"That isn't bad. It's the eighth floor."

"He asked four thousand with the carpets and drapes. I told him to take them."

"So he did?"

"The drapes. He had to eat the carpets."

"All my life I've been busy. Now the kids are grown and Lewis sold the store, what do I do with myself? Sure, it's wonderful to relax and sit by the pool, but that's five months a year and I've got an active mind. What do you do the rest of the time? I thought about this very carefully and for me the answer is volunteer work. There's plenty of trouble in the world that those who have the time can do something about. We don't just have to stand idly by. If I can lend a helping hand to those less fortunate I've got no right to sit back. Beginning Tuesday I'm recording the weights for my Weight Watchers Club."

"My manager's landlord's a Pakistani. So Steve, that's my manager, and Milly are going to Peewaukee for the weekend and they want to leave the baby with the landlord. His wife had made this standing offer when they moved in. So they go down to Mr. Pahdichter and they ask if it'll be all right and the Pak says—I can't do his accent like Steve—'Oh yes. Very good. But does the baby eat, does the baby eat, curry?' "

"They gave him to eat curry? A baby?"

"They're very modern people."

"Feldman?"

"I'm sunbathing. I'm getting a tan."

"You're beautiful. If they had a beauty contest it'd be you hands down. The rest of us wouldn't stand a chance."

"Yeah. Right."

"So?"

"Sew buttons. So? So what?"

"So when are you going to let me get you on the Johnny Carson show?"

"That again."

"I can do it. I got connections with the higher-ups. When's it going to be, Feldman? When does America look you over?"

"A week from Thursday."

"What a wit. You really have to let me do it. You could show him how you take a sunbath. They'd introduce you as this big sunbathing expert from the North Side. Johnny'd take his shirt off and everything. It'd be a sensation. You and Johnny with your shirts off. The people wouldn't know where to look first. You'd tell him when to turn over and he'd do these funny takes. Come on, Feldman. I'll call up right now if you give me the word."

"Why don't you go on the Johnny Carson show?"

"Me? What do I know about sunbathing? It's got to be you."

"I still say you should have gone out. You had no right to stay in with two pair."

"Queens and jacks?"

"Gert was also showing a pair of queens. You should have gone out."

"It's my money."

"You ruin it for other people, Lenore. You draw their cards. That's why nobody wants to sit to your left. You asked and I told you. I always say what I think to a person's face. I can't be a hypocrite."

"Excuse me for living."

"Should I call Johnny, or should we wait till he takes the show out to Hollywood where we can get you real sunshine?"

"We'll wait."

"No, it's no good. In California sunbathers are a dime a dozen. It's got to be you and it's got to be New York."

"Never buy a typewriter till there's ads in *Fortune* magazine showing some new breakthrough, some terrific advance. Then wait a month and a half and call around the various companies. Chances are they'll be putting in new equipment and letting their old machines go. This tip works for other industrial equipment as well. Don't waste your time with the mass-circulation magazines. The breakthrough campaigns are aimed at the big corporations before they try to reach the individual. You can look at *Fortune* in any good branch library for nothing."

"Where do you get this stuff? I don't need a typewriter."

"Never mind. Just file it away in your mind so you can remember. Another good buy is Christmas cards. February and March are the best months for that. The new lines ain't out yet and the prices are even lower than in the January clearance sales. Christmas is still fresh in people's minds in January and though the prices have come down the markup is still terrific. Find out *exactly* when fruits are in season. The Department of Agriculture puts out a pamphlet. It's free. Write away for it on a post card. It's like a timetable. It tells when strawberries are ripe in stores in exactly your section of the country. When Temple oranges. Nectarines, grapes. When melons. Everything. The thing is when they're ripest they're cheapest. People don't know that. Everything is supply and demand. And tubes. Use tubes, never aerosol cans. You can squeeze tubes dry, get all the paste or shaving cream out of a tube. With an aerosol can the gas may go flat or the mechanism break, something can always go wrong. Also it's a lot more expensive to make an aerosol can than a tube. Why pay for the package?"

"Where do you get all this stuff?"

"*Changing Times, Kiplinger's Newsletter, Consumer Reports.* They've paid for themselves I couldn't tell you how many times over. I figure in the last nine years I've saved thirty-seven thousand dollars."

"On *toothpaste?*"

"I don't make a move without those books. Also it's fascinating reading. With me it fills a, I don't know, need. What other people get from astrology."

How account for so much skin? Is something violated here? So much flesh. Preminger sees it through half-shut lids. Their pale meat at odds with their beautiful voices, their bad glands spilling over banks of throat in goiter. He sees humps, coronets of kyphosis, sees mottled, purplish necks given the last of the summer's sun, sees psoriasis like bubbled, flaking paint, sees flab like broken bones clumsily set by quacks. He shuts his eyes.

"Zionism. Don't make me laugh. When they say they made the deserts bloom they mean they got engineers who found a way to build on sand. They mean Levittown, cellars in the Sinai. It's the same everywhere."

"I'm gonna go in. Is it cold?"

"Just at first. Not after you get used to it."

"To hell with it. I need a coronary from icy water?"

"My sentiments exactly. Want to play cards? A couple hands of gin?"

"You?"

"Why not?"

"You got cards?"

"Upstairs."

"I don't know."

"Come on."

"All right."

"If I could find a buyer I'd sell."

"Where would you go?"

"That's the thing."

"Did you hear about Ruth-Ann?"

"What about him?"

"Packed it in. Sold out to Tom-Ted."

"Her? I don't believe it. Where'd you hear?"

"Mary-Sue."

"The auto battery manufacturer?"

"Yeah."

"Rob-Roy told me the business was doing so well."

"Rob-Roy's giving up the restaurant."

"What'll she do?"

"She's going with Chuck-Burger."

"Well, listen," he heard someone next to him say, "this is costing you money." It was the excuse people made when they wanted to get off the long-distance telephone.

"So your problems are solved. You'll have Bernadine on Fridays."

"Do I need her? What's the matter, the place is so big I can't do it myself? Twenty minutes in the morning and it's straightened out. It's good enough."

"Then why bother?"

"Because," the woman said, "because I miss her. I miss the company." She was crying.

"Harris. At the Standard Club. A tartan cummerbund. A powder-blue dinner jacket. The orchestra was playing 'My Fair Lady.' "

"The summer's over."

"I know."

"October, November—they can shove it. The Chicago winter. It's not a heated garage. All night you're up wondering will it start, won't it start? Scraping the goddamn frost off the goddamn windshield with the little goddamn piece of plastic like a tiny red goddamn comb. Cold weather."

"At least in Miami that's one worry you don't have."

"If it ain't one thing it's another. In Miami if it don't hit seventy one day it breaks your heart."

"That's if you're on vacation. When you live there all year round you don't worry about it so much."

"In the summer you step out the door you get cancer from the sunshine."

"Everything's air-conditioned. In the gas stations the toilets are air-conditioned."

"There's Portuguese man-of-war in the ocean."

"Who goes in the ocean? You have a pool. In the winter it's heated."

"Who you kidding? If it ain't one thing it's another."

The speaker sighed. "They're we're agreed," he said.

"Did I tell you," someone said, "they want me to go into the hospital for tests?"

There was no talk of their children or grandchildren. As if

they did not exist. Where were the photographs that should have been passed around? The color snaps, indistinguishable one from another, of four- and five-year-olds, scowling on lounges in pine-paneled dens, their pale skins bluely cosmetized by inexpert photography? Why did no one speak of these children? Why didn't they speak of their sons and daughters, those scattered accountants and lawyers and professors and journalists? Why did they deny them? (He'd met Audrey of Audrey-Art Underwear, a woman now, old as himself. They existed.) Where was their famous doting, that far-fetched fanclub love? And who talked of recipes, who spoke up for food? Who limned soup and catalogued vegetables? Who advised on meats, the secret special places of the beasts where the sweetness lingered and the juices splashed? Where was one who would describe dessert, who would convey custard and teach sponge cake and the special creams, who dealt in celery as if it were currency? (And where, for that matter, did Wall Street figure, over-the-counter, the American Exchange?) How was business? But most of all, what about the *children?* Who'd blacklisted them? Why? We exist.

"*Whose rule,*" Preminger spoke up, "*whose rule was it that there are no guests? Who made that up?*" He spoke louder than he'd intended, for he heard his question make a hole in their conversation, his voice overriding theirs like a bulletin. "*Who made that rule? Who agreed to such an arrangement? I demand an answer!*" he shouted. "*Who decided that Sunday rules shall apply all week long? Who banned the children? Who decreed that flesh and blood shall be snubbed? Who's responsible?*"

"That's just management policy, son," a man said quietly. "It makes good sense when you consider that this one pool has to service all three buildings."

"*Crap,*" Preminger yelled back. "*Until the last day or so it's been practically empty. Why would you agree to such a disgraceful idea? Unless you really wanted it that way. Am I right?*"

"Easy, there, fella."

"*My father would never have agreed to the setup. And he'd have had pictures of us. He'd have passed 'em around. He'd tell you about my days on the circuit.*"

"That's right," Ed Eisner said, "he was very proud of you."

"*Shit*," Preminger shouted, "*he never said a word. Like the rest of you. You should see the place. A swinger. He had hair like a pop star.*"

"Come on," someone said, "Why don't you take it easy? Are you feeling okay? You want a glass of water?"

"I feel terrible," Preminger said quietly. He was very calm now. His outburst had shocked him, and he was deeply embarrassed. "Look," he said gently, "I am deeply embarrassed." He stood up. "I wish you'd try, if not to forget, then at least to forgive my outburst. If you no longer wish me to serve as your lifeguard I understand and will, of course, step down. Indeed, in the light of my exhibition just now I seriously question my capacity to supervise this pool. Indeed, rather than charge you for imposing Sunday rules I suppose I ought to thank you. It was probably one of the more fortunate aspects of my position that the rule was imposed. I am, as some of you may know, a terribly unhappy man. I'm thirty-seven, ripe for conventional, even classical, introspection, a cliché of a man. What I would have you understand, however, is that if my case seems overwhelmingly typical, it is nevertheless unrelentingly true. Like all clichés. Perhaps a lot of what's troubling me has something to do with my virginity. It may seem odd that someone my age should be a virgin. I didn't want to be one, *don't* want to be one. I assure you I have all the normal drives. Yet somehow it never really fell my way, just never came up. I don't even think about it now.

"By moving here, I had thought to change my life, to alter its conditions by manipulating its geography, but I see now that this has little to do with it. As I overheard many of you saying yourselves. One's mental health is like one's height. Trauma isn't in it. You're happy or you're not. And of course the details of my existence have done little to promote even the aura of tranquility. Though I've had my opportunities. I was, for example, a minor figure on the lecture circuit at one time, but my career was manufactured, almost an accident. I was trading on an extremely limited inventory. The fault was largely mine, though not exclusively. Economic factors and the general climate of taste probably contributed at least a little to my undoing, as well as the political circumstances of our serious times. I have no clear ability to judge. Nevertheless I once had a small reputation. Now of course my name is faded. I'm very lonely, and not in the best of health. A few years ago I suffered a heart attack. The doctors all assured me that an attack that comes so prematurely can be a kind of blessing in disguise, for it warns its victims that something is radically wrong with his life. Shit, I knew that.

"Now I'm having a nervous breakdown. It's as real as sore throat. A nervous breakdown. Though you know, it's very odd, I can truthfully say that I feel no different than I did before. I'm as unhappy as I was before, but no unhappier. Nor have I misrepresented myself in any way. Except, of course, for that wild talk about my father a few moments ago. These are all things I would tell you privately did we but know each other better. If it weren't for my nervous breakdown I wouldn't be talking to you like this. So I guess the essence of a nervous breakdown is that it makes you go public, like floating an issue of stock.

"Now you must excuse me. Stay well. If you haven't got your health, what have you got? . . . Your good name?"

He went upstairs, politely smiling his refusal to those who tried to help him.

Evelyn Riker's second letter was waiting for him, slipped under the door. He opened it calmly, astonished that madness was so rational. He could read. He remembered everything. He could turn the key in the lock, change his things, hang them up. He could empty his bladder. Remember to lift the seat, flush the toilet. How was he mad, then? In what did it subsist? Unhappiness. Unhappiness was his only trauma, his single symptom. Misery as fixed and settled as his overbite, as incapable of being altered as of making parallel lines meet in a painting by staring at them. He was weeping. Even as he read Evelyn's letter—the hope it gave him suffusing him like an injection—he could not stop crying.

Dear Marshall,

It was sweet of you to answer, but my goodness, a wire! It must have cost you a fortune. Or are you one of those big spenders for whom money is just a convenience, there to enjoy when you have it but not much missed when it's gone? I rather wish my husband had been more like that. To tell you the truth, money was one of the biggest bones of contention that arose between us. I don't mean that Jerry was stingy or I profligate. Indeed, if anything he was more than generous. It's just that having made a big cash outlay—the condominium, for example—he could never stop worrying about where he would get the wherewithal to justify his expenditures. He was the only man I've ever known who worried about what inflation would do to his pension when he had to retire in twenty years! Naturally enough, this quality in him led to bickering between us. I know he didn't mean them, but sometimes the man would say awful things to me, dangerous things for a man to say to a woman, or for a man to say to anyone, for that matter.

Yes. He could follow. The words made sense. Then how was he mad?

One of the biggest blow-ups of all was after he bought a new car one time, a car that was far too big for us, incidentally, and which as a matter of fact I had counseled him against purchasing. I took it out one day, and while I was shopping someone skinned our rear fender and put a nasty dent and scratch in it, about a half inch deep and as long as your arm. A brand new expensive car. Can you imagine how this would make you feel?

Yes, he could. Then how was he mad?

When I discovered this after I came back out to the parking lot I naturally hoped that the driver might have left a card with his or her name and telephone number on it. If it had been me—after all, one is insured for this sort of thing— I would certainly have done so. I looked everywhere, but there was nothing. You can't imagine how sorry I was that there were retractable windshield wipers on this particular model, for otherwise the culprit might have left a message under the wiper blades. Of course I had shut the windows and locked the doors when I went in to do my shopping, so he couldn't have left it on the seat even if he had wanted to. To make a long story short, I looked everywhere, in the grillwork, even in the gas cap, the crease where the trunk joins the body—everywhere one could conceivably leave a notice. I know what you're thinking, that I was naive to expect someone to offer information against himself, but that's the way I am, willing to think the best of others till I'm proved wrong. Well, I was certainly proved wrong that time.

At any rate, when I told Jerry what had happened he didn't blow up at me. He was very understanding about the accident and said that such a thing could have happened to anyone. Where the fight started was when I suggested we put in an insurance claim anyway. We had fifty dollar deductible and a scratch like that would cost a lot more to repair. They probably would have had to put on a whole new fender. It wasn't even the fifty dollars we'd have had to lay out that bothered Jerry. We have a vandalism clause in our policy, and I think the insurance adjuster would have gone along with the idea the the gash may have been inflicted by vandals, but Jerry was afraid that after paying the claim they would drop us. He said it was just this sort of nickel and diming that upset insurance people the most. And he stood pat. I couldn't budge him. I thought it was ridiculous to drive around in a beautiful new car with an imperfection like that, and I told him so, but all he was worried about was that the insurance company would abandon us and that he'd have to pay a higher premium to get reinsured with a high risk company. We had words—hard, bitter words—but Jerry was stubborn. After that, cuts and dents grew on the car like a disease—and I wasn't the one who put them there—but Jerry would never put in a single claim. I saw that it was a neurotic behavior pattern and—what can I tell you? —the marriage went to pieces. Ultimately he left me. That's when I became friendly with your father.

Anyway, I didn't mean to burden you with all this detail. The point is that I don't want you to spend your money on telegrams. We're neighbors. As you say in your telegram, we live a few doors down the hall from each other. Actually, it made me very upset to see that wire. My hands shook so when it was delivered that I couldn't even open it. I thought something had happened to Jerry. We're estranged, but the man is still my husband. When you've lived with someone for almost twenty years you don't forget him just like that. Also—I'll be very candid—there was something too *importunate* about sending me that wire. What would have been perfectly acceptable in a letter seemed, frankly, "overzealous" —this is the best word I can think of—set down in a telegram. (Perhaps this is what McLuhan means when he says that "the medium is the message.") Maybe I share some of the responsibility for this. I think I've left you with certain faulty impressions, and I really believe I ought to undo these if we are to become friends. We simply have to set out on a footing of mutual understanding and respect. It's no accident that my first reaction, my *instinctive* reaction, to your wire (after I saw that it was not bad news about Jerry), had to do with the importunity I have already spoken of.

If you will forgive my opening up a subject which I know must be a very sore one with you—if you will permit me, this is, to probe areas which your normal filial affections and recent harrowing loss must certainly have left tender—I will be even franker. Perhaps you are wondering why I say my "instinctive" reaction . . .

Yes. He *was* wondering that. That's what he was wondering. Then it was normal to so wonder. Then how was he mad? He wiped the tears from his eyes. When would they stop? He has lost a pound of tears so far. When would he begin to weep blood, when vision itself, weeping light till none was left to weep, then weeping dimness, then darkness? Then what? Calcium, marrow, all the chemicals of his body, all the juices of his glands. Then how was one mad who could parse sequence like a scholar at the blackboard? Weeping hair, skin, bone, gut, shit, nails and all, weeping his life and, when there was no more left, weeping death and even time.

... and here I will have to make certain "confessions" which I have not offered earlier—out of fear and jealousy and my own sense, however misguided, of protecting you, I suppose.

Yes. Protect me, he thought, weeping.

I never lost your father's key, and it is not altogether true that I never used it. I did use it—*once*—the night of Dad's death. Phil had begun to call me on the telephone at all hours. Sometimes my daughter would answer. She knew his voice, though he was so nervous about what he considered our "relationship" that if I wasn't home he would try to disguise it or pretend that he'd gotten a wrong number, representing himself to her as a merchant or salesman or some such nonsense. But Sheila is no dummy. She knew his voice and began to suspect things between us that simply weren't true, a relationship as fictitious as Phil's voices. He made her very uncomfortable, and I warned him that if this continued I would have to seek other outlets. It wasn't the neighbors I cared about—I had weathered their gossip and scorn when Jerry left me—but my daughter's opinions did matter. That was *all*. The mother of a child from a broken home taking up with a man almost old enough to be her grandfather! That wasn't the case, it was never the case, but from the peculiar ways Phil behaved she had, I suppose, every reason to suspect it was. I told him in letters that his behavior must change. (Letters I did not read to you that day.) But despite my entreaties it didn't. He tried openly to hold my hand at the swimming pool. If I went into the water Phil went in too, cavorting, swimming between my legs, coming up behind me and diving down and raising me to his shoulders, touching me beneath the water where he thought it would not be noticed, challenging me to races and giving me headstarts so that he could catch up to me and make rough body contact, dunking me, pulling off my bathing cap and teasing—all masquerading as play but clearly the sublimated physical activity of a youth a third his age. It got so bad that I couldn't go into the water, or I'd use my red guest band to swim at other pools. I couldn't elude him. He followed me.

I liked Phil. All this was only toward the end. Even then, when he was calm we got along beautifully. He was a fabulous conversationalist. But he became less and less calm. I decided that I had to return his key. (Which, thank God, Sheila never knew I had.) To return it in a letter, however, seemed too cold and cruel. After all, we would still be neighbors and have to live on the same floor. To pass it to him at the pool was out of the question. I thought someone would see me, or that he might make a scene. I knew that the only way was to bring it to him, and that's what I did that night—the night he died.

Sheila was watching TV in her room, and I told her I was going out for a while. I made up some excuse—I don't even remember what it was. I came down the hall and rang Dad's bell. There was no answer, though I could hear music playing inside the apartment from Phil's new stereo, the Beatles, I think. I pressed the doorbell twice more, and when there was still no answer I let myself in with the key.

Your father was in his shorts on the couch. They were these skimpy silky bikini things and I would have left at once, but not after I saw his face. He looked awful. I asked what was the matter and he said he was a little uncomfortable. Naturally I forgot about the key; I must have slipped it back into my purse. I went over to him and he asked me if I would turn off the phonograph. He said he was very tired. I did what he asked and returned to him. He was sweating terribly, his face was pale, and it was clear to me that he was very ill. But even *then* he misunderstood why I was there. He tried to smile. "Evelyn," he said, "this wasn't how I expected it would be. I'm sorry it turned out like this, kid." I told him I thought we'd better call a doctor, but he said no, he thought it might be only a little indigestion and that he was already beginning to feel a little better.

Marshall, he was—hard. I told him he'd better just lie still and that I'd try to get some help, and that's when he became aroused. I was very frightened, but to tell you the truth I was more afraid of what could happen to him if I struggled with him than of anything that might happen to me. I held him up, and all the time he was kissing and touching me, and to calm him I said we'd better go into the bedroom. I wanted to get him to lie down, you see. I helped him into the bedroom and that's when he asked to make love to me. I told him it was crazy, that we had to wait until he was better. I didn't want to upset him. I promised that if he let me call the doctor I'd wait with him in bed until the doctor came. He agreed, and I called the number he gave me and got the answering service. I told the girl it was an emergency, and she said she'd get the doctor at once.

Then your father made me keep my promise to lie down next to him. Marshall, he had taken off his *shorts*. He was very excited because he didn't understand why I had come to his apartment, and he just kept—well, thanking me. I let him undress me, and because he was so ill and moved so slowly I actually helped him. I threw my clothes off as if they were on fire, and I suppose this excited him even more. I got him into position and all I could think was, I don't know, that this was better than that he should he hard, that that would be a terrible strain on his heart, and I wriggled like a mad woman because all I wanted was to bring him off. He came almost at once, and he died on top of me.

I got out. I couldn't wait for the doctor. I cleaned his penis. I looked around for any evidence, and destroyed it. I ran away.

That's the story. Now you understand why I couldn't come to the chapel or the funeral. That's the story. Please don't answer this letter.

There was a postscript: "I'll get the key back to you."

Then how was he mad? Didn't he see the inconsistencies in her letter? "I don't want you to spend your money on telegrams. We're neighbors. As you say in your telegram, we live a few doors down the hall from each other." And all that stuff about "if we are to become friends." If she'd looked for evidence, why hadn't she taken the letters with her? And after telling him the whole story about that night why hadn't she simply enclosed the key? He could drive a truck through her ambivalences. Then how was he *mad*? And what about his reactions to what he'd been told? Were *they* mad? Was it mad to be stirred by that part where his father went swimming through her legs? He was hard as the mourner's bench he sat on when he read that. Was *that* mad? Or his own ambivalences, his disgust and jealousy at her final revelations, were they mad? Was the awful pity he felt? Then how had his nerves broken down? His inkling that the key might still turn in his lock—was that nuts? Or, modifying inkling to simple bald hope that it would, was *that*? If only he could stop this damn weeping.

No longer were the tears coursing down his cheeks like anguish in a prizewinning photograph; now he was sobbing, bellowing, howling. He stuffed a handkerchief into his mouth. Choking on it, he pulled it out. (Was that, self-preservation normal as apple pie, was *that*?) He was astonished to be insane yet see so clearly, every reaction fitted immaculately to its cause like a Newtonian law.

He huddled on the mourner's bench and had an idea. He phoned Evelyn. She answered on the second ring. (Was it nuts to suspect that having slipped the letter under his door she would be waiting for his call?)

"It's Marshall," he sobbed. "I got your letter."

"Oh."

"Yes. I got it. I read it. I understand."

"Oh."

"I agree about the telegrams." He was squalling into the phone, He made a stutterer's effort to speak plainly and said goodbye clear as a bell.

He waited on the mourner's bench for three hours but she

never came. He'd shown every patience, giving her time to do the supper dishes, to think up something to tell Sheila, to wait until Sheila was asleep, to prepare herself. He didn't even leave the bench to urinate, fearing that he wouldn't hear her timid knock in the toilet. All hope left him. He understood her reluctance; he understood everything. And he stopped crying.

He stepped out onto the balcony. He saw the skyline, the lighted windows that ran across the horizon like a message, like signal fires of the abandoned on those desert isles of his hypotheses, like bonfires on moutain tops for the search plancs to see. He saw all the warehouses, office buildings, hotels and apartments. He saw the houses and condominiums, service flats, bed-sitters, kips and billets. He saw barracks and bunkers and chambers in university and wards in hospitals, saw all places where being lodged, those visible and those invisible—rooms underground, basements, shelters, code and map rooms, vast silos beneath the desert and under the badlands, Sweden's civil defenses, the booths in tunnels where officers stood watching the traffic, the cars in those tunnels, the passengers snug in their moving envelopes of space, subway trains and staterooms beneath the water line— saw the cabins of jets and two-seaters and the berths in trains, their club cars and coaches, the locked toilets on buses and the vans of trucks, the wide ledge behind the driver where the helper snuggles. There were palaces and theaters, arenas in the open air, auditoriums where people sat listening to orchestras, stalls and dress circles and private boxes and the gods. There were pits where technicians recorded those performances and prompter's boxes in theaters where a man, crouching, followed what the actors were saying, his fingers moving along the lines of the script as if it was in Braille. There were caves. There were mud huts and huts of straw and the hogans of Navahos, all the earth's vulgate architecture, its mounds and warrens, Rio's high *favellas* and Hong Kong's sea-level houseboats. There were cellblocks in prisons and the tiger cages of solitary. The world was mitered, walls and floors and ceilings, angled as the universe and astronomy, jointed as men.

There were balconies like this one he stood on, with railings like this one. He raised one leg over and now the other. Intestate, sitting there for a moment perfectly balanced, he pushed off gently and began his fall.

As he plunged he addressed the condominium, quoting from the lecture he had been preparing. "From what incipit, funda- mental gene of nakedness," he gasped, "came, laboring like a lung, insistent as the logical sequences of a heartbeat, the body's syllo- gisms, this demand for rind and integument and pelt?" But it was too difficult. His velocity shoveled the words back into his mouth, the air that forced itself into his lungs canceling his breath. All he could manage at last, with great effort, the greatest he had ever made, were individual words.

"Cage," he shouted. "Net," he screamed. "Pit, sheath, vesicle, trap," he roared above gravity. "Cell, cubicle, crib and creel." He tried to expel the air that suffused him, billowing his body like a flag. "Nest," he yelled, "carton, can." His descent pulled the wind, igniting it like a fire storm. "Jakes," he squealed, "maw!" But it was too much. He could open his mouth but couldn't close it. So in the split seconds he had left he had to think the last. *And the hole*, he thought, *the hole I'm going to make when I hit that ground!*

About the Author

STANLEY ELKIN was born in New York City in 1930, raised in Chicago and earned his Ph.D. from the University of Illinois. He is the recipient of the Longview Foundation Award, the *Paris Review* Humor Prize and Guggenheim and Rockefeller Fellowships, as well as a grant from the National Endowment for the Arts and Humanities. He is the author of a collection of short stories, *Criers and Kibitzers, Kibitzers and Criers,* which have been widely anthologized, and of three novels, *Boswell, A Bad Man,* and *The Dick Gibson Show.* Having lived and written abroad, primarily in Rome and London, Mr. Elkin now teaches at Washington University in St. Louis, where he lives with his wife Joan and their three children. Currently he is at work on a new novel.